CRITICAL ACCLAIM FOR
MARCELLE BERNSTEIN

Sacred & Profane

'The menace builds throughout this psychological
thriller . . . Gripping'
Sunday Times

'Passionate and memorable'
Daily Express

'Mesmerizing, brilliant . . . A riveting read'
Manchester Evening News

Body & Soul

'This amazing novel will widen your eyes and tug
at your heartstrings . . . Read it and love it.
A beautiful story'
New Woman

'Memorably erotic'
Daily Mail

D0528357

Also by Marcelle Bernstein

NON-FICTION

NUNS

FICTION

SADIE

SALKA

LILI

BODY & SOUL

SACRED & PROFANE

SAINTS & SINNERS

Marcelle Bernstein

BANTAM BOOKS

LONDON · NEW YORK · TORONTO · SYDNEY · AUCKLAND

ECL 08455754

SAINTS & SINNERS
A BANTAM BOOK : 0 553 50469 X

First publication in Great Britain

PRINTING HISTORY
Bantam edition published 1998

Copyright © 1998 by Marcelle Bernstein

The right of Marcelle Bernstein to be identified as the author of
this work has been asserted in accordance with sections 77 and 78
of the Copyright Designs and Patents Act 1988.

All the characters in this book are fictitious,
and any resemblance to actual persons, living or dead,
is purely coincidental.

Condition of Sale
This book is sold subject to the condition that it shall not,
by way of trade or otherwise, be lent, re-sold, hired out or
otherwise circulated in any form of binding or cover other than that
in which it is published and without a similar condition including
this condition being imposed on the subsequent purchaser.

Set in 11/12pt Plantin by
County Typesetters, Margate, Kent

Bantam Books are published by Transworld Publishers Ltd,
61–63 Uxbridge Road, London W5 5SA,
in Australia by Transworld Publishers (Australia) Pty Ltd,
15–25 Helles Avenue, Moorebank, NSW 2170,
and in New Zealand by Transworld Publishers (NZ) Ltd,
3 William Pickering Drive, Albany, Auckland.

Reproduced, printed and bound in Great Britain by
Cox & Wyman Ltd, Reading, Berks.

For Eric, and that sea walk. For Lesley.
And for Helena.

Acknowledgements

I would like to express my thanks to:

The National Childbirth Trust. Watts & Co. Ltd, Ecclesiastical Furnishers. Maria da Graças Fish of the Cultural Department, Brazilian Embassy. Richard Lazynska. Mary Craig, for her insights into miracles.

And – as ever – to Jo Goldsworthy and Caradoc King. And to Francesca Liversidge.

Chapter One

Believers said, these things happened and they were signs of the endless mystery. Her detractors said, this woman beguiled the people. Not so long ago, she would have been accused of witchcraft.

Here is the way it was.

At precisely twenty past three on the afternoon of 17 March 1946, a tiny white puff of cloud appeared in clear skies over the pulsing, chaotic sprawl of São Paulo. It was poised directly above the valley of the Anghangabaú River, almost hidden now by the newly constructed viaducts and bridges. Here in the city's heart, the air was pungent with eucalyptus leaves and gasoline. Dilapidated buses idled through a swarm of people and animals. Gypsy women with black braided hair, babies strapped to their backs in shawls, sold cigarettes and candy. Sitting before buildings of pale peeling stucco, flower vendors watched over fragrant buckets. Sombre men with soft brown eyes drove half-starved, burdened donkeys through dusty cobbled squares.

It was a humid day. In the warm corridor created by the intense heat of the baking land below, parcels of hot damp air rose quickly to great heights through the cooler, drier atmosphere like bubbles in boiling water. Within fifteen minutes, fed with moisture by a sultry wind from the jungles of the Mato Grosso, the cotton ball of cloud built rapidly to billowing, monstrous cumulus, a churning mass dazzling as a glacier against the brilliant blue. A lone pilot, who fought to retain control of his bucking biplane among the turbulent, formless currents of hot air, reported later that the clouds pushed their anvil-shaped heads to 60,000 feet above the surface of the earth.

The dense clouds seemed literally to boil as eddies of air spiralled and spun. Huge wavelike curves were suspended, apparently unmoving, within the swirling mass. At first white as foam, they swiftly darkened to dull gold, flushed with red. That gave way to a luminous grey streaked with weird colours – blue, pink, yellow – fluorescent in their intensity. The eastern half of the sky was filled with these violent storm clouds while the western half was still bright with sunlight. But within minutes, the heavens turned an eerie green and then an ominous purple. The clouds swelled in size until the whole sky became so heavily overcast it was as if dusk had fallen. Streetlights were hastily lit in wealthy parts of the city, and schoolchildren ordered not to attempt to leave for home.

The din of São Paulo – the insistent throb of music and factory machinery, the clatter of building sites – seemed to fall silent in the face of this sinister phenomenon. The magnificent horses of the Paulista cavalry faltered, tossing their heads and breaking step. In the Zoological Park on Avenida Miguel Estefano, Amazon parrots and jungle jaguars, red cranes and tiny monkeys the colour of ripe limes did not seek shelter as normal before a storm, but crouched or perched stock-still, all hoots and howls suppressed. Even the cattle lowing frantically in the abattoirs were briefly mute. Even ragged children, foraging for rotted food among the *favelas* of planks and tin that fringe the city, stopped their squabbling.

In the hush, a new sound commenced. Faint at first, distant, it grew louder and louder until it resolved itself into a giant humming like the swarming of a million bees. People – singly, in couples, in great groups – stared upwards. A gloved and hatted woman shopping on the Rua Augusta, a tail-coated diplomat leaving the Canadian Consulate and a twelve-year-old Italian immigrant dragging his club foot as he hunted for discarded vegetables at the Carlos de Campos Street market, all shared the same shiver of apprehension. But there was nothing to see, even when the sound was directly overhead. Nothing but the enveloping clouds. These had a biblical quality, majestic and awe-inspiring. The blackness beneath them now was total and complete. Day into night. Armageddon.

Everyone hurried to find lights and hold back the darkness. But there was no one to light a lamp in the desolate room at the far end of the Rua Santa Rita where a young Polish woman lay dying.

There had been no wind like it in living memory. A scorching blast howled through São Paulo, tearing off roofs and doors. In the stately tree-lined Avenida Paulista, even newly built mansions lost balconies, while older buildings in the city centre were left askew on their foundations. Wire fencing was twisted into rope or wound into crude balls. Sheets of corrugated iron were wrapped around electricity poles. An imported Mercedes open tourer was lifted bodily from the road in Bela Vista, its goggled driver still clutching the steering wheel, and dropped like a toy from a height of ten feet. A dozen chickens in Pacaembú were plucked clean of all their feathers as if the wind had prepared them for the pot. The havoc lasted only a few seconds in any place before the wind whirled on.

Then the lightning came. Spectacular bolts, originating in the bank of thunderclouds, were peculiar in their intensity, even here where weather conditions were often violent.

The woman on the bed opposite the open window of the rooming house stirred, shifting her weight on the mattress. The first spear of lightning threw the room into dramatic shapes of black and silver, showing for an instant the painfully angular body beneath the scant coverings. The flash of light disturbed her, and slowly the heavy eyes opened. She turned her head to find a cool place on the pillow.

In the age-speckled mirror on the door of the wardrobe beside her bed, the reflection turned too. Lightning-lit, the eyes were set deep in shadowed hollows. The skin was stretched taut over the planes of the face, the wide, tender-lipped mouth was dry. The astonishing, flaming hair was flattened and darkened by sweat until it clung tight to the skull beneath. She looked like a woman of sixty. But even in extremity, a harsh

12

beauty touched the angle of the jaw, the straight nose, the broad, calm forehead.

The lightning flashed again, piercing the half-pulled blinds at the window, and this time the woman saw herself in the glass. She stared at her ruined face until she could no longer hold up her head. Tears glistened. Her thin hands fluttered on the blanket.

Livid flashes every second provided almost constant illumination. They lit up the green-painted walls of the dilapidated room, the two sagging basketwork chairs, the scarred table-top. The woman's few belongings were pinpointed again and again by the lightning: a comb, brown metal hairpins in a pot of flowered china, powder compact of imitation tortoiseshell, an almost empty packet of cheap cigarettes.

The table bore a jug of water and a used glass, an untouched plate of black bean stew. Beside it, a cup was full of cold *verde maté*, herb tea. There was a labelled bottle of medicine with a sticky spoon beside it, a tube of medicated cream. On the black and pink tiled floor at the end of the bed, a bunch of wild flowers, clearly picked by a child, stood in a jar next to a worn shoulderbag. This was the single item in the room which had obviously once been costly: good leather, heavily creased now and darkened from use, strap discreetly gold-buckled.

The Polaca had lain here for many days. She had moved into the room only two months before and few people in the building even knew her name. A fortnight ago, she became sick. She had had no visitors, but her dying brought some to her. Old Senhora Sayão would come to help her reach the communal lavatory. The senhora had little to do, she was very deaf and her sight was failing, but she had time in plenty. Besides, she was basically kind, and pragmatic. If the Polaca survived, she would be grateful. And if she died, the senhora would maybe help herself to a trinket for her trouble.

Cuci Santos lived on the other side with her young son, Tomas. Barely twenty-two, with wild black hair and a raucous laugh, she worked at home on an ancient Singer sewing shirts for a local wholesaler. Two or three times a month, when the rent was due or Tomas needed shoes or medicine, she would pick up a man for pleasure and to earn five cruzeiros.

Six weeks before, she had caught the base of her thumb beneath the swift foot of her sewing machine so the needle had darned through the web of her flesh. The Polish woman had come swiftly in answer to her screams, withdrawn the needle, and cleaned the wound. She had been cool, reserved to the point of rudeness. But Cuci did not notice. The thumb healed with astonishing speed – overnight, in fact – and an odd friendship had taken root in the unlikely soil of Cuci's garrulous gossip and the assenting silence of the European. So Magda Lachowska heard all Cuci's troubles, about the terrifying fits from which Tomas suffered, when he fell down and she had to prevent him from swallowing his own tongue. In return, Cuci received only the bleakest details from the Polish woman: her former employer would no longer have her in the house with his family, fearing the skin infection from which she

14

suffered. She missed the children. She had no men friends, indeed no friends at all. It was Cuci who had brought in the food, though she knew the Polaca could no longer eat: it was all she could think of to offer.

Now Cuci ran along the metal walkway which girdled the outside of the building, holding down her billowing skirt. Iron stairs spiralled downwards, narrow as a fire escape. These open spaces were used as extra rooms by the families living in the cramped interiors. As she passed, women were grabbing up babies, snatching damp clothes from the railings, slamming shut the flaps of pigeon coops.

Cuci knocked on the peeling door of Magda's room, entered without waiting for an answer.

'You all ri'? The storm don' bother you?'

She could hardly catch the faint 'Please . . .'

'You maybe wanna drink?'

Cuci turned on the room's single tablelamp. By its weak light she filled the glass from the jug of water. Supporting Magda's head with one hand, she waited while the Polaca tried to sip the water. But the woman, too weak to swallow, gagged so it dribbled from her lips.

'Try,' urged Cuci. 'You've had no eat or drink for three days now, you mus' try.'

When Magda could not, Cuci poured a little water onto a towel and wiped the sick woman's face and throat to cool her. Her movements were gentle, protective of the patches of itching, scaly skin which had grown noticeably worse in the last few days. The Polish woman's hands, she observed, were so affected now they were clawed and rigid, as though the sore skin had shrunk on the flesh. She said, 'I better close the window,' and felt the sick woman stiffen as if in protest. She thought perhaps the head shook as if to say, No. But long afterwards, when she was asked about it, Cuci could never be sure whether the Polaca had merely trembled.

Cuci hesitated, then left the window open to the storm. What difference would it make now? The end could be only a matter of hours. She said, 'The old lady goin' come sit wit' you, later on.' Better not be too much later, she added to herself.

Magda's lips moved but she was beyond words.

Gilberto Freire earned his living photographing near-naked girls for magazines. For the son of a porter at the Carlos de Campos Street market he was doing very nicely, renting an apartment in one of the first skyscrapers built on Avenida Ipiranga, high over the city. At around twenty to four, he was treating a massive hangover with a glass of rum when he became aware of the commotion beyond the dimmed living room. He opened the blinds.

It took him a moment to realize what was happening. He forgot his headache as he ran for camera and tripod. It was not the right equipment, but he set it up on the balcony, focused and shot as much film as he could lay his hands on. He photographed the black cloudbanks and the city beneath, stark and surreal in the lightning flashes.

For a long time before the freak wind came – two hours, perhaps, or three – the only sound in the bleak room had been the woman's uneven breathing, shallow and laboured. Now, as the wind passed into the distance, it faltered. Something in her throat caught and rattled. Her body twitched in spasm, a bubble formed between her lips as her soul budded there. She became still.

There was the briefest silence. Inside the room and beyond it, over the stretch of wasteland where a couple of mules stood with lowered heads, it was as if the earth held its breath. For one second, two, three, the world was frozen.

Only one person witnessed all that happened next, and he was not yet seven years old. The boy Tomas Santos, who had been sick and off school again, pushed open the door and peered in.

The wind had woken him from a restless sleep on the floor. He had had a fit the previous day, and the bromide he had been given still fuzzed his head. His mother's murmur, low and lazy, came from the curtained alcove and the bed he shared with her at night. Then a man spoke, a voice Tomas didn't know. The child was used to this; his mother always gave him a coin afterwards.

Tomas supposed from the darkness it must be very late, but he didn't feel sleepy any more, just a bit hazy and slow. He thought about the Polish woman next door. He had been forbidden to visit her, but curiosity was stronger than fear: his mother had said the Polaca was dying, and he wanted to see. He got quietly to his feet.

He pulled the Polish woman's door almost closed behind him and stood against the dark green wall, making himself mouselike and invisible, on tiptoe with apprehension.

When he was sure nothing moved in the dimly lit room, he took a giant, slow step towards the bed with its curly metal bars at head and foot. He waited a long moment, then took another. Grandmother's footsteps. When he could have reached out and touched the woman who lay there so still and flat beneath the coverings, he stopped. He listened for almost two minutes and knew, with absolute certainty, no one else breathed here. He had no sense of another person's presence. The figure on the bed was rigid, but there was no tension, no flicker of life.

Still keeping his eyes on the dead woman, Tomas took another giant step, to the table. With covetous fingers he pushed aside the metal hairpins in the china pot and lifted out his quarry. It was a string of glass beads threaded on silk. He squinted so the light made the beads iridescent. He fastened them around his throat.

Just then, from somewhere outside, the humming of many bees came into the room. It grew in intensity, until the air seemed to thrum with it. He pressed his hands against his ears to stop them hurting. He was concentrating so hard on the noise that at first he didn't notice the other sound. With a shiver of fear he recognized the demonic hissing made at carnival time by the men who dance in devil masks. But there was no one here but him and the Polaca. He was now badly frightened, his fingers tingling. The Polish woman's room, still lit intermittently by the brilliant lightning flashes, seemed to be going in and out of focus.

He shut his eyes tight. When he opened them

again, it was just in time to see the most astonishing sight of his life.

A huge ball of orange-red light came in through the open window. It floated through the air, zigzagging from side to side. It was alive, he was sure: he could see it – sense it – pulsing. Afterwards, Tomas was adamant that it actually entered the building, it was inside the room. He explained that it seemed to be looking for something: he got the impression it wanted the Polish woman. Later on, he changed his description – it wasn't really a ball, it was shaped more like a fat tyre with a rippled edge.

But that was much later. At the moment it was happening, he was aware of a screaming note in the hissing, like rockets going off for the feast day of São João. His legs gave way and he slid down until he was huddled, shivering, his back to the wall. Even in his panic, his eyes were still riveted by the ball of orange fire.

Lightning flashed again, throwing the room into exaggerated focus. In the glaucous depths of the wardrobe mirror, something moved. Tomas uttered a shrill howl of terror. He remembered copal candles flickering in the cemetery on the Day of the Dead, dancing death masks among the gleaming tombstones, silver ghosts lured by cinnamon cakes . . .

'Tomas!'

A moment later, Cuci Santos threw open the door of Magda's room. Her flowered dress gaped to the waist, her breasts hung bare, nipples dark as garnets. The man was behind her, hands at his crotch as he fumbled with the buttons

19

of his trousers. Both stopped stock-still. Tomas scrambled to his feet and rushed towards his mother, knocking over the flowers he himself had picked for the Polish woman, trampling them in his haste. He flung himself against Cuci, locking his arms tight around her, burying his face against her thighs. When she instinctively put her hand on the nape of his neck, her fingers caught on the frail necklace of glass beads. It broke and scattered on the tiled floor.

When Cuci said nothing, Tomas moved his head and looked up at her wide eyes, her mouth slack with astonishment. The man's face bore the identical expression. Tomas turned and saw what they saw.

The ball of orange fire seemed to collapse violently inwards, becoming a diminishing fountain of light. Where it had been, beside the bed of the Polish woman, there was mist in the air. No, fog, a greenish fog trailing thick, gaseous wreaths. It smelled bad, like when he struck sulphur matches, only this was stronger. It sent fingers curling down his throat so he began to cough until tears came into his eyes and his mother clutched him tighter. She was coughing herself, so was the man. Later, they said they had thought they would all suffocate.

It was suggested to them long afterwards that perhaps, coughing so badly, maybe blinded by the smoke, they could not clearly see what they claimed. But even the passage of time did not alter their conviction: they never doubted their own eyes.

They all saw the body of the Polish woman,

lying on the bed, move in the midst of the green gas. It jerked briefly, unreal as a puppet. Then, still prostrate, it appeared to rise from the mattress, as if lifted by unseen hands, the thin blanket trailing behind.

Describing what had occurred, Cuci Santos could not confirm the smoke, only a lingering odour which she described as sulphurous. Much later she changed her testimony. Yes, she said, as the body hovered above the bed, there had been smoke. The man who followed her into the room, one Rico Gomez, said he had seen the mist, and could identify the smell. It was exactly the same as the oxides of nitrogen produced by electrical discharges from the machinery at the electrical plant where he worked.

None of them noticed the bird fly in through the open window. But with the next flash of lightning it was there, a mottled white pigeon, exhausted from its battering in the wind, flapping clumsily over their heads. Half dazed, it landed heavily on the metal rail at the foot of the Polish woman's bed, balancing itself with outstretched, ruffled wings, a piece of straw caught in its beak. Tomas thought he recognized it as one of Jorge's, but he was never certain so later, when this too was endlessly discussed and disputed, he kept quiet.

The dead woman gave a harsh, shapeless cry.

Tomas Santos peed his pants.

At the new geophysical observatory seven miles from São Paulo, a number of disturbances were recorded. There were abrupt fluctuations in the electrical currents flowing through the earth. In addition, there was a change in the intensity of the earth's magnetic field. Such changes normally indicate the sudden flow of a strong electrical current. In this case, it seemed to show that a current of over a hundred amperes was flowing for a period of more than fifteen minutes.

When at last the wind subsided and the darkness lifted, after more than an hour, people emerged cautiously into the streets. There was an extraordinary feeling of relief. Strangers grinned at each other, grasped hands, hugged, laughed aloud. It was as if they had all escaped some dreadful, nameless calamity.

Not all had escaped, of course. Amazingly, only fourteen people had died in the city, in ways no one could ever have imagined. A man working on a ladder painting a hallway slipped as the gale smashed down the long windows. He fell awkwardly, so his head was trapped between two of the ladder struts. The ferocity of the wind swept his body across the room, neatly decapitating him. Another man was found dying, a long splinter of wood driven through his stomach with the force of a nail. Neighbours hunted frantically in the ruins of her house for a woman who had been ironing in her kitchen. Eventually they saw something pale high up in a tree in an adjoining garden: the naked body of the woman, wedged tightly into the fork of a eucalyptus tree.

Another forty were injured and maimed – fractured skulls, broken jawbones, severed limbs. Three children were crippled for life. Several people were struck by flying objects – half a tin roof, timber, a table, in one case a large, clawing cat.

On the positive side, a number of long-standing family feuds were patched up in the hours immediately following the darkness and the storm. And more than a thousand babies were conceived, many out of wedlock.

Gilberto Freire went into his darkroom. Checking the developing negatives from the series of sky pictures, he picked one up with his forceps from the metal tray to discard, marred as it was by light. But then he saw that what seemed to be fogging on the negative was in fact two blurred vertical bands of brightness that did not extend past the picture area, as they would on a fogged negative. There were several others with similar flaws. He turned them this way and that. Something wrong with the camera. Or the film, maybe. He scratched his scalp to help him think. Then he printed the negatives with the others.

When he examined these particular photographs a little later, he knew he must still be very drunk. His camera had recorded two gigantic luminous pillars. They hung in the dark sky, great columns of light like giant neon tubes.

He sat at his dining table, the just-dry photographs spread out before him in a space cleared of dirty cups and plates, holding his curly head in his hands. These pillars were like nothing he had ever seen, or ever dreamed of. He was certain they had not been in the sky he photographed that afternoon. Maybe no human eye could see them, only a camera lens. He could roughly estimate their size from the way they dwarfed the many-storeyed buildings beneath them, and the knowledge made him faint with fear. And excitement.

He brewed himself a cup of black coffee and stared out of the kitchen window. Everything was almost normal again. Sunlight was already breaking up the cloud, the air smelt fresh, though there had been no rain. In the street below his window he could see smashed red tiles and the glitter of broken glass. Watermelons, honeycombs encrusted with dead bees, mangoes, black sapodillas, all still lay where they had fallen on the cobbles, spilled from their stalls by the wind. A bicycle had been hurled through a baker's window to come to rest among the display of pastries. The front door had been wrenched from the samba school opposite and the needle of the gramophone they played day and night had stuck in a groove. Somewhere out of sight a megaphoned voice was still exhorting people to buy tacos. A woman was screaming, children crying.

Gilberto Freire looked again at his work. There was no mistake. The gigantic tubes of light were on half a dozen separate prints. Freire noticed they were in a slightly different position on each one. Against the buildings beneath, it was possible to measure how far they had moved. He calculated that in sixty seconds they had travelled the length of two football pitches. But what, in God's name, were they?

He was not a religious man, but his mother, though she never learned to read, used to recite bible stories she knew by heart to her son.

Including the one about the pillars of fire. Could that be what his camera had filmed? A sign from God? Or were they beings from another world? He dismissed both possibilities. Far more likely, the military were trying out some kind of new weapon. Whatever it was, he knew one thing: there was money for him here. These pictures would make the front pages across the country – across the world!

He carried his coffee into the living room, turned on the radio and listened to a news bulletin about the electrical storm and the way the city had shut down. No mention of any pillars of light.

Closing his front door behind him, he went down in the elevator to the telephone booths in the lobby and asked for the number of the picture desk at the local office of the *Latin America Daily Post*. The switchboard was jammed. Never mind. It would be better to go in person. He put the photographs carefully into a folder with the negatives. He listened to the radio as he combed his thick hair and splashed his chest liberally with cologne. He put on a fresh shirt, arranged his leather jacket with studied negligence round his shoulders.

Another news item about the storm, the lightning flashes, the astonishingly sudden fall of darkness. Nothing else. The lack of corroboration of what he knew did not bother him, merely fuelled his excitement. He alone, it seemed, had witnessed the true phenomenon of the afternoon. And he had the pictures to prove it.

Gilberto Freire went out in such a hurry he left his radio set full on.

(It was to play nonstop for two days, until the

caretaker finally turned it off when he came back from identifying Freire's body in the city morgue. The elderly man glanced at a framed photograph of the former tenant, wearing white tie and evening dress with a barely clad girl on his arm. He reflected that Freire had not looked like that on the mortuary slab. Victims of road accidents were often the worst to identify, they'd told him. Freire had apparently been out celebrating all night long, and must have been very drunk.

In a rare gesture of respect, the caretaker took the picture from the wall and placed it face down on the table. Beside it, he put the sealed plastic bag the hospital had given him, containing some small change, cheque book, the gold watch with the smashed face and the papers the police had not kept. There must certainly have been more money, but the police did not give it to him, and he knew better than to ask. There was also a carrier bag holding Freire's shoes and belt. The parents might like to have them.

The black leather jacket he gave to his son-in-law.)

The woman who had been dead fell back on her pillow.

She opened her eyes – everyone in the room could see the feverish glitter in the light from the open door. Tears shone on her cheeks.

She spoke. She said something in a voice deep and hoarse as a man's, not like her real voice at all. It must have been in Polish, they decided later, for no one could understand her. Her dry lips scarcely moved, her throat was parched. But the urgency in her few words was electrifying.

The man and the woman and the child watched her in stunned silence until Tomas quavered, 'But she's *dead*.' Behind them, old Senhora Sayão gave a hoarse sob of fear. She stood in the doorway, one hand grasping the doorpost for support, the other clamped over her heart.

'Look at her face! Her hands!'

The skin of the Polaca's face and throat, her bare arms in the cotton nightdress, was scorched and scarlet in irregular patches, as if she had been badly burned. As they stared, she pressed the heels of her clenched hands against her eyes, as though they pained her, and straightened her legs in a convulsive movement. The pigeon, alarmed, flapped into the air and circled the bed before settling again, this time on the railings at its head. As it did so, the straw fell from its beak upon the crumpled sheet.

Seeing this, old Senhora Sayão gave another sob and crossed herself. She dropped heavily to her knees and started to mumble, for she had not stopped to put in her teeth:

'*Minha mãe . . . Madre de Deus . . .*'

They said, these things happened:

There were wonders in heaven above, and signs on the earth beneath. At the ordained hour, a cloud came over the earth. The city of São Paulo was bathed in supernatural light, then plunged into the heart of darkness. *In the darkness, know that I am with you.*

There came a rushing mighty wind from heaven such as had never been known. *When the wind*

27

blows, know that I am with you. The wind is my sign. In the midst of this great wind, Magda Lachowska died.

After the last breath had departed her body, her room was filled with the heavenly fragrance of lilies, and glowed with a radiant light. For at that moment she was found by angels, enveloped in great feathered wings of eternity and caught up into paradise. *Angels of God ascending.*

There was no doubting this, since witnesses attested to watching her lifeless body lifted from her bed within a great cloud of vapour.

She afterwards described this remarkable religious experience. It was, she said, as if God were drawing up not only her soul but her body to himself. She looked upon his face. In that instant, her heart was pierced by his love. Amid the excruciating pain she felt great joy. She spoke of mystical marriage, unutterable ecstasy, love beyond measure.

She had seen the torments of the damned in the valley of weeping. Yet she was certain of life eternal, an awakening to a new world.

For she herself was brought back to life. *And I will give thee a crown of life.*

She shed miraculous tears of crystal. *And he shewed me a pure river of water of life, clear as crystal, proceeding out of the throne of God and of the Lamb.*

Her afflicted skin was healed perfectly by cloven tongues of fire which lay upon her, and which many saw. *And ye were as a firebrand plucked out of the burning.*

She caused the boy Tomas Santos to be instantaneously cured of his fits.

A white dove came to her bed bringing, from a church five miles distant, a fragment of the Blessed Sacrament to sustain her, for she had taken neither food nor drink for ninety days.

At the same time, many strange signs occurred which were beyond nature. First there came the humid chaos of the skies, the darkness which is beyond light. A monstrous humming was heard, like the whirring of a million great insects. And most terrible of all, twin pillars of light flamed in the blackness above the city. These pillars were the tokens of a heavenly covenant, for they were visible only to the righteous. (And, of course, to the readers of the *Latin America Daily Post*.) *Then the Spirit of God moved upon the face of the earth. And God said, Let there be light, and there was light.*

Four main witnesses gave testament to Magda Lachowska's encounter with the divine. A neighbour and her seven-year-old son, believers said, a man in his forties and an elderly lady.

An amateur whore, sceptics sneered, and her illegitimate brat, who suffered fits. A fornicator and an old woman, deaf and almost blind. *Those* were her witnesses.

Chapter Two

Janie Paxton hummed under her breath. She could remember only the refrain: *If you can't be with the one you love.* Then something about loving the one you were with.

The man lying with his head between her breasts stirred. She pinched his shoulder and said, 'I must get up.'

He groaned and squeezed her waist more tightly. 'No.'

'Yes.' But it was good to lie in their shared warmth, the sheet still damp beneath her. The room smelled lazily of coffee and perfume and sex. The prospect of the long drive back to Derbyshire did not appeal.

'Stay,' he muttered. 'Go t' sleep.'

'Can't. I've a ton of work to finish and Adam's coming home the day after tomorrow. Darling, I told you. Half term.' But of course he had forgotten. Kids and their needs meant nothing to those who did not have them. She put the thought away for the moment. 'You could always try tempting me.'

'God, no. I couldn't manage it again.'

She giggled. 'You young things have no stamina.'

'I'm not one of your macho figures.' He nuzzled her breast, licking the soft nipple until it stiffened under his circling tongue.

'Down in the jungle,' she whispered, 'something stirs . . .' She reached for him.

He resisted, half laughing, half irritated. 'Don't. I mean it, I'm knackered. Didn't reach Heathrow till two in the morning. It's my jet-lag day.' He yawned and rolled over, pulling from somewhere under the covers the hat she had bought as a love token on her way here, from a pavement trader in Oxford Street, and put it on.

She watched. It was ridiculous, the worst kind of tourist tat. But the old-fashioned bobby's helmet in black and silver had been irresistible in her happy mood. She stretched. 'You can't expect me to take you seriously when you're wearing that.'

He removed it, positioned it over his soft penis instead, and said in the hoarse voice of a street-hawker, ''Allo 'allo 'allo. What 'ave we 'ere? Our latest sex aid, straight from the mysterious Orient via the sweatshops of Taiwan.'

She patted the long silver spike which crowned the helmet. 'Just look,' she drawled, 'who's boasting.'

'I don't recall any criticisms twenty minutes ago.' He balanced the helmet on her head with a perfunctory kiss. 'Trollop,' he said, affectionately, and gave her a light smack on the bottom. While she was still wondering whether it was worth the trouble to take offence, he sat up. Seeing his open suitcase on the floor, he kicked the duvet back abruptly. 'Sod it – I meant to go to the laundrette. It closes at eight.'

'You need a washing machine.'

'Like hell I do.' He rubbed his hands over his chest. When he spoke again, his mood had darkened. 'What I need is someone to look after stuff like that for me.'

'You need the love of a good woman.'

Sarcasm certainly wasn't wasted on him. 'I'll have to look out for one,' he said, his voice hard, no joking.

'Just don't ask me.' It was out before she knew it, the automatic rebuttal of any hint she should play that part.

He didn't even smile. 'Madam, I wouldn't dream of it.'

'For this small mercy, much thanks.' She smiled, but she meant it to sting.

'I remember you telling me you don't do that kind of thing any more, for any man.'

She said slowly, 'So I did.' The trouble was, she reflected, the two of them saw each other in isolation. Because their relationship was private, because they met occasionally and alone, each presented only what they wished the other to know. So after more than six months, he was still the dynamic young television producer with a freelance news team, flying in and out of trouble spots, based in a prestige block in the City, single, no worries. And she was one of London's best-known feature writers, hard, successful and married. Though in her case, she added wryly to herself, with all the emphasis on the 'was'.

Janie Paxton had specialized in bitterly ascerbic interviews with the successful and infamous. She had ridden – more, had helped create – the media passion for exposing personal pain. Agonizing childhoods, desperate marriages, neglected re-sponsibilities were all, in her hands, woven skilfully to provide motivation, explanation and justification for the driven lives of men and women at the top of their professions. She could apparently ask the simplest question and glean from the response the most penetrating personal insights. It was said that being interviewed by her was like being on the psychiatrist's electric couch. (The fact that she had said it first was now lost in the mists of newsprint time.) What marked her out from the general run was that she managed to combine it with a wry and redeeming humour. Despite the cruel truths she uncovered, interviewees regarded being one of Paxton's People as a matter of pride, proof they had arrived. Occasionally, one of them would whinge afterwards, but most wrote thank you letters and framed the interview.

As is often the way, Janie herself could not explain how she achieved her results. She researched her subjects exhaustively and then put it all out of her mind. Deliberately, she never had a plan of campaign, a list of questions or a preconceived idea in her head. Like a potholer descending into the dark unknown, she went into each interview full of anticipation and nerves. Beforehand she was invariably sick with apprehension, afterwards desperate for a drink. In the days after handing in her copy and before publication, she was so high on adrenalin she could not stop moving.

It seemed the bubble would never burst. She took her column from the *Daily Mail* to the *Evening Standard*, finally going to the highest bidder and *The Times*. Her husband, Paul Land, whom she had met at the *Mail*, became night editor on the *Guardian* where he remained throughhout her rise. No doubt partly as a result, their relationship suffered. Both of them were permanently tired, every discussion became an argument. She thought now that this stemmed from the stress of the pace she set herself, and her growing inability to handle it.

Whatever. The result was that her concentration and confidence wavered. The interviews lost their edge and bite – and she lost her readers. She had left the paper one jump ahead of being invited to do so, after overhearing the features editor say to the chief sub, as they discussed the layout of her page: '. . . on the wane. Pity.' She had slammed into her office and written her resignation there and then.

Paul did his best, understanding her fury and despair. He watched sadly as she began drinking earlier and earlier each day. (She always had an answer: she needed it to wake up. To slow herself down.) He urged her to move on, try television. He pointed out, with a great deal of truth, that it was a pity she could not bring the genuine wit of her column home with her. There was another row, their worst yet.

The following week she went to bed with a man they both knew. It was not her first infidelity, and she scarcely troubled to hide it. Not long after that, she moved into the house in Derbyshire which they always rented for summer holidays.

Her reputation was sufficient to bring in a good deal of work. She had ghosted a couple of big-selling kiss 'n' tell books by soap stars, and was working on a third. It was not arduous. Two weeks in a hotel room with the actress concerned talking into a tape recorder, then three months at the word processor for her, was well-paid labour. True, it afforded scant satisfaction and little recognition. On the other hand, her time was now her own. And she took another lover.

While he showered, she sat on the bed wearing his pyjama jacket, finishing her cigarette and putting on her make-up, a mirror propped against her knees. He came into the room with a glass of orange juice, a towel round his waist and stood facing the dressing table with its tilted pier glass. She glanced at him appreciatively, at the compact body, skin sleek on the muscular back.

Without turning round he said, in a conversational tone, 'Stop singing that fucking line, will you?'

She hadn't even been aware she was doing so. *If you can't be with the one you love. If you can't be with the one you love . . .*

'Soooorry, darling,' she drawled, teasing him. 'Don't take it personally.'

'It's never personal with you, is it?'

'What on earth are you talking about?' She smoothed off the foundation under her jawline.

He shrugged. 'I just get the feeling I'm less important than the sensations I provide you with.'

She smiled at his reflection in the glass, raising her eyebrows. 'Don't be so sure of that.' She put on spectacles, positioning them on the end of her nose so she could see to make up her eyes. 'You'll be telling me in a minute I'm just using you.' She started smudging on shadow with her middle finger.

He stared at himself, leaned forward and pulled out a white hair from his parting.

She said absently, 'You'll make it worse. Now two will grow.'

'You're not listening.' His voice was cold. 'And that's an old wives' tale.'

She thought he was going to add something else, but he didn't. What he had not said sounded a warning somewhere in the back of her mind, but she ignored it, searching for the dark brown pencil in her make-up bag.

'Darling, you've just got home, you've been working without a break for two weeks. You're tired.' She started drawing a thin line over the lashes on her left eye, her tongue poking into her cheek with concentration.

'Face facts.' He spoke to the pier glass. 'This isn't getting either of us anywhere.' He stared moodily into his tumbler of orange juice. 'Do you realize you never even call me by my name?'

She laughed. 'So it was something I *didn't* say.'

He ignored that. Why hadn't she noticed until now that he had no sense of humour?

'This is ridiculous.' She kept her tone light. 'I thought we just had a lovely fuck.' She reached for her drink and in the mirror his eyes followed her hand. He never touched alcohol. She gave him a coquettish smile, tipped back her head and drank defiantly. His face was set and hard. Remote. As if he was looking at a stranger he didn't much care for, not a woman he'd just made love with.

He shrugged and moved to the window so his

back no longer blocked her view. Janie saw her own reflection again, saw herself as he had just seen her. A woman in her mid-thirties who'd had a long day, her normally carefully tended hair rumpled unflatteringly from her recent exertions and topped, ridiculously, with the black and silver helmet. With glasses perched on the end of her nose, one eye made up with smoky lid, the other absurdly bare, like a panda. Or, she thought coldly, a clown.

Janie took pride in having few illusions, about herself or anyone else. She knew that her appeal lay in her quick mind, her elegance, her grooming. She was not a tall woman so she dressed cleverly to give the impression of long legs. Her face was wide at the cheekbones, narrowing almost too suddenly to a pointed chin. Though her features were not particularly distinctive, her expression was so vividly alert that no one noticed. Under strongly marked brows her eyes were a curious speckled greenish-brown, the colour emphasized by a smattering of freckles beneath them. She had a straight, narrow nose, a determined mouth and expensively cropped dark, almost black hair, sleek to the shape of her head. A fashionable cut but chosen for other, more practical reasons. A frequent traveller, she needed to be able to take care of it wherever she was with the minimum of time and effort.

She knew she was also sharp, amusing, incisive. But these assets were not apparent at the moment, and he had obviously forgotten she possessed them. Instead, she saw with his eyes the first tentative lines of ageing, the almost imperceptible puckering of skin on her throat. And beneath the unbuttoned pyjama top, her bare breasts, drooping a little, faintly veined with blue, were defenceless and somehow sad. She looked tired. She looked old. She looked, not to put too fine a point on it, like hell.

Janie suddenly felt vulnerable, diminished. That her body was calmed and sated made it difficult to connect with what was happening. She pulled the jacket together. Tearing off the stupid helmet, she threw it on the floor with such force it hit the bedside table and rolled under the bed. She yanked a comb through her hair.

'I thought the whole point of our relationship was we both wanted it this way.' It came out in a smaller voice than she had expected. Blast.

'I admit that's how it started. But time's going on. No one gets any younger. I need . . .' he took a swallow of juice, 'more than you can give me.'

With her eye make-up completed, she recovered some self-assurance. 'And to think,' she spoke deliberately, wanting to annoy – wanting to hurt – 'only a few minutes ago I thought *I* needed more than you could give *me*.'

He said wearily, 'I'm not talking about sex and you know it. I'm talking about making a life with someone. Christ, I'm almost thirty-two.' He swung back to face himself in the pier glass, pulling at the skin beneath his eyes, examining himself critically. 'I can't go on indefinitely living out of a suitcase and screwing other men's wives.'

'Include me out. I don't come into that category, if you don't mind.' Anger had finally taken her over. 'How dare you talk to me like that, you . . . you . . .' She couldn't think of a name bad enough for him. 'You stinking *creep*!'

The adolescent insult made him laugh out loud. She gave a shout of fury and jumped off the bed. She caught up her clothes and vanished into the bathroom.

When she emerged she was dressed in her black interview suit, sheer black tights, white silk shirt. She had painted her lips a deep, untouchable red. It was a signal – to herself and to him – that whatever happened, she would never kiss him again. She was putting on her shoes when he came in from the kitchen barefoot, wearing jeans. His smile was abashed. 'I made some coffee.'

'No time now. But thank you.' She was very cool and calm, her social self. She moved about briskly, fitting her hairdryer into her overnight bag, checking the bedside table for her flask of Estée Lauder, the black velvet mask she wore to sleep if he woke in the night and decided to read. She very much wanted to take the three-quarter-full bottle of whisky: she had after all provided it herself. But that was the kind of snippet he could mention to someone afterwards, it might prove irresistible – she knew it would to her. She clicked shut her briefcase. 'I think that's it.' Turning towards the door she added, 'Be seeing you, then.' Her dismissive tone gave the words the lie.

'Look, Janie . . .'

She waited, the set of her shoulders defensive.

'. . . I really don't want it to end like this.'

She turned, eyebrows arched with theatrical surprise. 'You could have fooled me.'

'I didn't mean it the way it sounded.'

She said, musing, 'I wonder what brought on this sudden obsession with your age and your grey hairs.' Something flickered behind his eyes and she pounced. 'There's someone else. That's it, isn't it?' She didn't need his look of annoyance and complacency to tell her she was right. Someone else. Someone younger. 'You smug bastard,' she said, evenly.

'Hold on. So you can have an almost ex and numerous former lovers and nothing sticks. But if I see another woman, I'm a bastard. Haven't you heard, we men have equality now?'

'There's been no one since I've been with you, and you know it. I may have had a life, but I've also got standards.'

Offended, he said sharply, 'You and me both. Mine also include taking care of my responsibilities.'

Janie stared. He just didn't talk like this.

'My God,' she said finally. 'She's pregnant.'

He opened his mouth. Closed it again. A succession of emotions flickered across his face: self-congratulation, a tinge of guilt, excitement, uncertainty.

She wanted to hit out, scream. But it was too late. She remembered her reflection in that bloody helmet and added to herself, with the painful honesty she used to bring to her work, *and it always was.* She kept her voice under control. 'You should have told me when I phoned you.'

'I know. I'm sorry. Only you were so happy I just . . .'

On her way here from Bedford Square she'd

gone to Fenwicks, and the incredible amount of money she had just been discussing made the Cerruti jacket appear affordable. She was pretty sure she would turn down the proposed project, it just wasn't the kind of thing she did. But at least it was an offer on the table. She thought of that overheard 'on the wane' in the office, so casual, so cruel – and defiantly added a von Etsdorf velvet printed scarf and a Givenchy lipstick. She'd put the last two on straight away. She knew she'd sounded absurdly cheerful when they spoke. She'd joked about it, how spending money before she'd earned it always cheered her up.

'And you couldn't bear to spoil my mood. How kind. Or maybe you just fancied one last bang for old times' sake.' The words were bitter, but what did he expect? She pulled on black kid gloves, to hide the fact that her hands were shaking. He remained silent, stirring his coffee. She added, tartly, 'You don't take sugar, remember? Or is that an act too, you poser?'

Stung, he said, 'Look, I've never been with one woman so long. It's been over a year, you know.' He sounded sulky, aggrieved. Childish. The jut of his lower lip like a little boy. 'I didn't plan for this to happen. But now it has . . . I can't explain. It's altered everything. I never even thought about kids, not even when this thing with Chrissie started. But to hold my own child . . .' Now it was out, he was bursting to talk about this new wonder in his life. Not the woman but the expected child had done this.

She said, spiteful, 'You don't know the half of it.

In a few months you'll be buying toy bunnies and changing nappies and putting its name down for nursery school.'

He looked stunned, but not in the way she had intended. 'God, I never even . . .' He smiled to himself, clearly delighted with this image of fatherhood. 'You could be right, at that.' He walked across and put an arm around her shoulders. She recognized it as affectionate - and totally without any sexual feeling. She couldn't believe how fast their relationship had changed. He said, coaxing, 'Don't walk out on me like this, I didn't do it to hurt you. We were friends first, remember? Have a cup of coffee, you look as if you could do with it.'

She was stiff at first, within his embrace, and then let her shoulders drop. He was right. It would have come to this sooner or later, she owed it to herself to behave elegantly. If true love was a mutual giving, then what they'd had was a mutual taking: they had liked and satisfied each other, and themselves. He hadn't broken her heart, after all. Make sure he knows that. Her pride was her own business.

'All right.' She sat, crossing her legs deliberately high, drawing off her gloves. He went into the kitchen for the coffee pot and biscuits, his voice reaching her indistinctly. Relief made him garrulous. It was a minute or two before she took in what he was actually saying.

'. . . her parents this weekend . . . end of lease . . . wedding in . . .' He came back into the room. 'Or else I won't be the only bastard around here.' He smiled broadly as he handed her the cup. 'I knew you'd understand. And I'm sorry, Janie, I handled it badly, I shouldn't've told you like this. You deserve better.'

'Thanks,' she said drily. 'So you're getting married.' She lifted the coffee cup in an exaggerated salutation, as if drinking a toast.

He was genuinely concerned. 'Didn't I say that first? My brain must be addled, it's all been such a rush . . .'

She simply turned him off. He went on talking, gesticulating, relaxed now, and pleased with himself. She watched him without seeing him: just another man who loved the sound of his own voice. His face was good, the bone structure strong, well-marked eyebrows. If she'd been meeting him for the first time, she'd have believed him to be thoughtful, intelligent, caring. Everything she now knew he was not.

Janie drank her coffee and planned her route back – Hatton Garden, Holloway, Highgate, then the M1 – no, maybe Highgate was a mistake, the rush hour started early these dark nights. The thought of the car running silent in the darkness, tape playing, taking her away from London, back to the isolated house waiting among the high Derbyshire hills, brought her suddenly to her feet: she could be home in four hours.

There was nothing here for her any more. *If you can't be with the one you love.* She put her gloves on again, picked up her handbag and overnight case. He went ahead to the front door, still talking over his shoulder, and held it open for her. His manners were excellent: she could almost see his mother standing behind him.

He said politely, 'Let me take your bag down for you.'

She summoned a smile and tapped his bare chest with a kid-covered finger. 'You'd give a whole new meaning to room service.'

He caught her hand, pulled back the cuff of her glove and kissed the inside of her wrist. 'If anyone ever doubts you've got style, refer them to me.'

Her walk to the lift, knowing he was watching, was jaunty. At least until the doors closed behind her, she was her old self. Whoever the hell that was.

Chapter Three

The camera lingered on the exceptional face. Seen in close-up so they filled the small screen, the often-photographed features seemed more than mortal. Janie focused on the remarkable woman who had long ago entered her subconscious. Half the world, she thought, must instantly recognize her.

Under the broad forehead, shadowed eyes were eloquent with experience. The wide, tender-lipped mouth, still shapely as a girl's, spoke of compassion. It was a face of infinite resignation, as if no act, however terrible, was beyond comprehension and forgiveness.

It was the face of an ageing but still beautiful woman – and according to the clear tones of the voiceover, it could be that of a living saint. Mama. The peacemaker. She was revered by half the modern world, and the other half was aware of her name and reputation. The film used photographs and film footage to recount the first astounding occurrences, the inexplicable happenings which so early in her religious career had given Mama her legendary status.

Janie watched as the voiceover described the dying vision, so well known it had assumed an almost mythical quality: the glowing figure visible only in the glass, the all-encompassing wings, the raising up. The twin images of heaven and hell, her description of the first as pure clear light, the second grotesque as a Goya painting. Then Mama's resurrection and the piercing of her heart – *transverberatio*, a phenomenon familiar to the Church from the lives of early saints. The tears of crystal, the healing of her skin and of the epileptic boy. The vanishing. And then, years later, her emergence, from the remote mountain retreat, to the *favelas* of São Paulo that stank of mud and excrement. Here, among the poorest, the discarded people who lived on black beans and bones from the slaughterhouse, she was already surrounded by a small band of dedicated followers.

There were interviews. Not with the four original witnesses, all now either dead or untraceable, but with people who had been in São Paulo that March day in 1946 when it all began. Some were on old film, made many years ago, but others were contemporary, with people who had been young at the time. Remarkably, their descriptions of the terrifying storm, the lightning and the ferocity of the wind, the strange whirring sound of many invisible insects – all these things tallied. But no witness could corroborate the twin pillars of light reproduced on the front page of the *Latin America Daily Post*. The photograph thrown up on the screen clearly showed the huge size of them, glowing like great neon tubes in the dark sky above the lighted buildings of the city. The photographer had apparently died in mysterious circumstances the very night he took the pictures, but a couple of photographic technicians were brought on to argue briefly over whether such an effect could be faked. The result was inconclusive.

Then the programme returned to Mama, and the evidence of her ability to rescue the helpless and transform lives. This was said to have begun when local women discovered she could grant them painless childbirth. Among the *favelados* her fame spread and believers began to flock to her in great numbers. It was then that the universal 'Mama' was first used for Magda Lachowska.

The programme went on to detail the early, tentative miracles; the way her shadow made arid paths green as she passed, and lavender plants bloom where she had stepped; the clear spring water that was said to bubble up in the filthy sewers of the *favelas* at her bidding. There were the first healings: the afflicted baby, the lamed girl, the young man in a year-long coma.

Mama's name became linked with the fight against injustice. Wherever there were people imprisoned by corrupt regimes, wherever there was torture, mass murder, she was there also. She spoke out against the treatment of Buddhist monks in Tibet, the deaths of street children in Brazil at the hands of the police.

On the screen appeared the old black and white photograph the world knew so well, that provided the first big and unforgettable image of Mama. Taken by a Magnum photographer in Hungary, it showed Russian tanks lumbering down a wide street. Mama stood alone in their path, dressed in her long-sleeved pale robe, coatless even in the snow, a frail and indomitable figure with arms held wide.

After this, her role as world peacemaker

burgeoned. She exerted an extraordinary degree of influence with world leaders. She became a mediator, bringing together the heads of warring states, rival politicians. She conducted open discussions, public meetings where people of all faiths and political colours met together. These frequently ended in spontaneous prayer.

The publicity engendered by these preceded the curious story of the way the old and frail Pope John XXIII had overruled dissent within the Vatican and insisted that Mama and her group be swiftly awarded the status of a recognized religious order. It had been decades since a new order was born, and by 1965 Mama was at the head of one containing both men and women. There were the years of consolidation, as houses were established wherever the needs of the people took her, and the arduous duties she undertook as head of an organization spanning five continents. Money poured in to her cause, for the middle classes everywhere found in her someone doing exactly what they would do – if only they had the time. In view of her heroic virtues, said the voiceover, her eventual canonization was assured . . .

'Bollocks. Total bollocks.'

Abruptly, Janie pressed the button to pause the video on the woman's face. Weird, weird. No way was she going to get involved. She would tell Bob Dennison in the morning that it was impossible: if they wanted a book about this woman, they'd have to find another writer. She had no patience with this kind of thing, with visions and mysterious happenings, with inexplicable healings and tears of glass. They had obviously worked well enough for Mama. But the people who believed in her were simple, unsophisticated, largely uneducated. These were her congregations, her followers. They needed these powerful images to impress them, for the stories would be carried from place to place by word of mouth.

And gain in the telling, she thought grimly, clicking the video stop button. Mama was no saint, but a palpable magician.

The image of the woman's face vanished from the television screen. In its place, a man in a grubby raincoat emerged from behind a tree, grimaced obscenely, pulled open the coat. A second ungainly figure, clearly a man in a red cloak, shrieked and started running away.

'Und here ve see Heinz,' a silly voice said, 'der Stuttgart rapist, out for his afternoon stroll . . .'

She sighed and switched off. Reruns of old *Monty Python* programmes were the last thing she wanted. She moved her feet off the brass fender and heard the rustle of paper. She could tell they were bills just by their sound. Telephone, council tax, electricity, gas. All the usual, going back two months: she'd almost forgotten about them. She reached for the redirected envelope. An 's' added to the Mr before Paul Land. Flat 2, 28 North Hill, Highgate, London N6 crossed out and The Little Barn, Redesdale, Derbyshire written in Paul's precise blue handwriting. Envelope and postmark told her it was the bill for Adam's school fees. It had been opened and neatly resealed with Sellotape. He'd stuck a little yellow Post-it note inside ('Your turn, I think,') with an arrow pointing down at the total. That was all. The curt wording was typical of him. He loved words, he spent his days editing them, writing headlines and crossheads; he prided himself that a story on which he had worked was improved tenfold, and he was right. He loved words, and so he wasn't going to waste any more of them on her. She reflected that he used to be generous, once. How he had changed. Then honesty made her add, I changed him.

She sighed again without noticing. The bills were the reason she had watched the video about Mama. Money – or rather, the lack of it.

She tipped the reluctant cat off her lap and heaved herself out of the chair. She checked the dying log fire and bolted the back door. She filled her hot-water bottle from the kettle, turned out the lights and went up the narrow stairs.

A minute later she clattered down again. In the light from the upstairs landing she found her empty glass and poured another whisky. She considered adding water but decided against it. The house creaked comfortably, settling around her. Beyond the garden, on the bleak Derbyshire hills, a dog fox barked, the sharp fierce coughing unmistakable.

In the darkness, she noticed the fading glow of the television screen. She hesitated. On the floor lay the discarded file of interviews with Mama which had arrived with the video. On an impulse, she took it up with her.

The moment she woke, Janie knew something was different. The light streaming in from the two skylights above her was pale and promising. There were no blinds, she loved to be woken by the growing light. Yawning, she pushed aside the file of cuttings she had been reading until 2 a.m., leaned across and drew the curtain.

From this tiny window she could just see the triangular ploughed field which lay between her home and the open land which swept up to the horizon. Yesterday, the earth had been a nondescript grey-brown. This morning, it was silver, glistening white in the early autumn sun. She thought it had snowed in the night, until she noticed the untouched hills beyond, the dark trees.

Downstairs, she pulled on her wellingtons and a tweed coat of Paul's over a pair of his pyjamas, drew back the bolts on the kitchen door and went outside. Across the cobbles, she climbed onto the step of the stile and wrapped her arms across her chest for warmth as she contemplated the spectacle before her.

It was more lovely, more rare than snow: a field of gossamer. She had only heard of this incredible exodus before, but she recognized it immediately. A myriad tiny black spiders had turned the field into a huge single cobweb, a glittering net laced with waterdrops. Each insect had shot out a thread from its tail, making itself buoyant and lighter than air.

She watched in fascination as, hauled by its little silken sail, each one floated to an unknown destination. Some of them would end up just over the hedge. But others would be lifted high by the wind and carried hundreds of miles, to land on the tops of mountains, on remote islands, even on ships at sea. And no one knew what made them leave the relative safety of the long grasses and give themselves over to this dangerous enterprise. Maybe they couldn't pay their bills either.

Janie stared out over the silvered acres. There was a theory that overcrowding drove them to seek new food sources, as if they knew by instinct what fate held for them if they stayed still. A huge risk, but at least they were making a bid to survive.

Later, working at her desk upstairs, she got to her feet and looked down the narrow dormer window at the field again. The sun was high now, and the field was its usual brown: all the spiders must have dispersed on their odyssey.

By a strange coincidence, on the wooden desk-top beside her AppleMac lay a letter from Robert Dennison, publishing director of Odyssey Books, suggesting the meeting they had had two days before. She had been intrigued by his proposal for the book on Mama, flattered and grateful that he had thought of her. They went back a long way and he was aware she was having problems. Gerald Dennison, the journalist and Bob's twin brother, was one of Janie's oldest friends: the three of them had shared a flat in Westminster until Janie married. Gerald had been her features editor on the *Mail* for a time, and she and Bob had kept in touch. They lunched each other on expenses, she interviewed several of his authors.

Now she stared at the letterhead. Odyssey. Idly, almost for distraction, she turned to the word in her Penguin dictionary. *Prolonged adventurous journey*, it read; *account of this*.

A prolonged adventurous journey would be an understatement for such a massive undertaking. To write the only authorized biography of Mama was a challenge and a hazard: if she got it right she would retrieve her lost status and more, and make a great deal of money. If she did it badly, she would have wasted at least eighteen months of her life and probably made herself even more unemployable.

On the other hand, if she didn't sign the contract with Odyssey, then she would be staying still, and that would be unbearable right now: she must at all costs keep busy. And whatever she felt about Mama, the truth was that the woman had intrigued her for a very long time.

The decision, she realized, was easy after all.

She was lying in bed when an anxiety that had not entered her head in years was suddenly there, fully formed, insistent, frightful. Panic-stricken, she pushed back the duvet and ran to her desk, scrabbling for her diary. She checked the date, squinting fiercely at the page. Then she checked the red-circled days on the preceding month. And the month before that. She found her glasses and stared at the pages again, and for a long time. She couldn't believe what she saw. No matter how long she looked, the dates remained the same. Apprehension gave way to cold certainty. She hurled the diary on the floor and went downstairs. The whisky was downstairs.

She would regret it later. But she needed it too much right now to care.

As soon as the shops were open, she'd drive to

the chemist and get a pregnancy test. It would be something to do, though she knew it was a pointless exercise. It was true, of course it was true. How could she have been such a fool? Alerted now, she acknowledged changes in her body that had been noticeable for a couple of weeks at least, possibly longer: the tingling in her breasts, the increased sensitivity of her skin as if she had a temperature, a faint feeling of nausea when she cooked. Even when Adam had begged for fried bacon, she'd had to refuse.

Oh God. She swallowed a mouthful of whisky so fast she couldn't taste it.

There was no doubt in her mind, no tiny corner left for self-deception. The irony of it was painful: when she'd been desperate to get pregnant again, with Paul, nothing had ever happened. For a minute or two she let herself believe she could keep it. She would have again those wonderful early weeks, when a baby is like a little scented god, infinitely precious, infinitely demanding . . . Adam would love a brother . . .

And then she had a thought that made her teeth clatter on the cold rim of the glass. He'd got her pregnant – and bloody Chrissie as well. What stinking luck. You *fucker*. She found she had said the words aloud, savagely, and then heard herself laugh. God, she must be losing her mind. Her eyes filled with tears and she wiped her nose with the back of her hand.

Common sense kicked in. Have the baby and then what? The father was a write-off. She would not dream even of telling him. She probably would not have done so even before he announced his

marriage plans. And he would not change them for her. But he was a generous man, and she could just see him handing over some cash along with pitying looks. No thank you. No handouts. She alone would have the years of worry, of commitment, of curtailed freedom, of money problems. She was already a financial and emotional mess. She could scarcely handle the responsibilities she already had, so how did she think she could operate at all if there was a baby? A baby meant equipment and clothes and tiny jars of food. Bottles and nappies and toys. Babysitters and au pairs, nannies if she was very lucky and worked very hard.

There was the Odyssey book, that would pay for help.

Yes, but how could she work, how could she do her research, and travel, when she was pregnant? They didn't even let you on planes after a certain date.

She felt a mist gathering in her head. What a mess. What lousy timing. She and Paul had longed for another child, had even spoken of adoption. But they had waited, at first out of hope then later, she thought now, out of the slow-growing realization that their moment had passed. And then she had had a brief affair. When she was being kind to herself, she thought it happened because of disappointment with their marriage, which felt increasingly sterile both emotionally and physically. When she was being self-abusive, she thought she was a tramp. (Where had that word come from? It was her mother's word, not her own.)

There had been other men before Paul. She was young, affluent, educated, she used birth control: responsible sexuality was her right. Everyone did it. There were several affairs, of varying intensity. The real truth, Janie thought now, was that she was in revolt against her cool upbringing. She proudly declared herself amoral, at least in the amatory sense. Her choice.

She did not, however, always choose wisely, and had left her job as a researcher at the London bureau of *Time* magazine when her latest beau, the chief feature writer, turned out to be just embarked on his second marriage.

At the *Mail* she met Paul. He was charmingly, candidly, openly available and as if astonished by this, she married him. And for a long time, it had been good. He was fun, sensitive, intelligent. Too good to be true. They fitted together, they understood each other's work, they even wanted to buy a flat in the same part of London. Love, the real thing, for the first time in her life. She didn't have to think where that led her, she just went.

They had started a baby almost immediately. The time of her pregnancy was wonderful, followed by the hideous reality when Adam actually arrived and her days and nights became an endless exhausting round of feeds, nappies, baths. She lost all sense of her own identity, totally absorbed by this tiny, needy creature in a way she could never have imagined. Those years took for ever to pass – and yet it seemed almost no time before Adam had been three and then five. He was at school, becoming a separate person. She was already working part-time and then inevitably it became

full-time, increasingly absorbing and demanding. It was impossible to tell whether it was that which caused their marriage to become the background to her life, and no longer the focus. But when she was being honest, she knew her own nature: work was an acceptable excuse to get out of the house and away from damnable domesticity.

Success changed her in many ways. She had always been busy, but now she was preoccupied. Even Adam's birthdays took her by surprise, so she had to rush around at the last minute buying presents and organizing parties, ringing up instead of sending cute invitations as other mothers did. She forgot Paul's entirely one year, remembering it only in the middle of an interview in Bahrain. When, finally returned, she apologized and gave him a suede jacket from Liberty and a bottle of Dior Eau Sauvage, his smiling shrug as he opened the airport bags had shown her just how far apart they had grown.

And she forgot other things, as well.

She forgot to wake in the night at the slightest sound, as she had through Adam's baby years. She forgot just how desperately she had yearned to hold someone small and new in her arms.

Most completely of all, she forgot how much she had loved Paul, once. Sex with him had undeniably been the supreme experience of her life – the mutual tenderness and consideration, the wonderful conversations afterwards, the jokes – the Michelin stars they awarded each other for performance, certain that they would be together for ever. She forgot the way she had stayed in bed for hours after making love, not to leak any of his

creamy seed that this time might somehow make the hazardous journey to fertilization. It had all seemed so strong, so sure. Sometimes she could hardly believe it was all coming to an end in dry legal phrases about property, money, visiting rights.

She should have had more sense. Only at the time she hadn't cared about sense, or caution. The sensation of freedom, of new beginnings, of her own self, which her infidelity had given her had been heady after the years tied to Adam and the house. Heady and addictive. It was the forbidden she sought, the mystery of the man she did not know. Inevitably another experiment – which was how she thought of them – followed. She had not told Paul about either man. There had been no need: he said he could smell them on her skin. It had seemed almost a tribute.

What he had not known, and what she had not told him, was how brief they had been: one-night stands, just about, except they happened to be with men she knew and quite liked. Liked enough, anyway. But when Paul accused her, when they rowed, she was damned if she'd give him the satisfaction of learning they had meant so little to her. She allowed him – no, she led him – to think they had been passionate encounters, though in truth the sex had been less important than the delicious secrecy. Her pride was more important to her than his.

For two years now, or longer, she had not even imagined falling pregnant. The need for a baby grew out of love, desire, contentment, and she didn't feel any of those things any more.

Until this last year. She had certainly desired, she thought she had possibly loved. But while she definitely had not wanted a child, she was accustomed to not conceiving, convinced that now she never would, so contraception did not really seem important. Not that she had been careless. The pill had given her high blood pressure, so with Paul she'd used a diaphragm when she had used anything. With other men, she insisted on condoms. Now, with a man she enjoyed and had now left, a baby had happened anyway. All the time she had been grieving over the end of an affair like an adolescent, she'd been ignorant of her real problem.

God, oh God.

She bought the pregnancy test kit, droppered urine onto the white pad, and waited. She did not even need to look to know the blue stripe for positive had appeared. She felt the loss of hope without knowing what it was she had been hoping for.

She had a hot shower and washed her hair. She had already done both that morning, at 5 a.m., but the process satisfied her desperate need for something to do. Wrapped in a towel she sat down on the edge of the bath. Her head hurt and she massaged her scalp, rubbing her fingers through damp hair. There was no doubt about what awaited her. It had all been resolved when he told her about his baby. His *other* baby. Janie believed in instinct, and she believed in facing up to reality. The very fact that she had reacted as she did, had pulled on her gloves and walked away, showed what her decision must be.

She would go further. Even if their day together had been perfect, even if they had parted in total affection till the next time, even if there had been no pregnant Chrissie, it would have made no difference. This was not the time. He was not the man.

Not only had he enjoyed two women for the last few months, going unsuspected from one to the other, but he had managed to impregnate both of them. And they said modern men were producing fewer sperm. It was funny, even she could see that. But still, she felt like a locker-room joke.

She hoped Chrissie had found the silk night-dress left forgotten in a drawer, and given him shit over it. She hated him. And she needed to go on hating him. Right now, anger was all that held her together.

She pressed hard on her waist as if to squeeze out the unwanted growth in her body. But all she could picture was a tiny, waxen bud of life. She could almost see it, luminously pale, floating softly in a warm sea. It wasn't a growth, no matter what she told herself. It was a new little life she had so carelessly allowed to start. That she was going to have to end.

Her reaction amazed her. Until Adam was born, she'd not thought of herself as maternal, and her emotional response to her son had always surprised her. She hated sending him away to boarding school, losing his presence, his puppy kisses, the ridiculous drawings he scrawled on every piece of paper he could lay hands on, the way he proudly got his own breakfast at weekends, leaving a crunchy trail of Coco Pops from the kitchen cupboard to the sofa in front of the television.

How she missed him, the smell of his hair. For a second she could almost catch that milky, talcumed scent of a new baby . . . Don't. She blew her nose, pulled on pants and loose jeans, found a big soft comforting sweatshirt.

In her office she checked the number – one she hardly ever needed these days – and dialled. Waiting for Dr Simon's receptionist to answer, listening to what sounded suspiciously like the soundtrack to *The Magnificent Seven*, she picked up the file of cuttings and looked for the twentieth time at the Jane Bown photograph illustrating the *Observer* piece. Mama had posed in sunshine, looking directly into the camera's gentle gaze, the penetrating eyes glowing with hope and spirit. It was a face of great wisdom, yet it seemed almost transparent with innocence. Unaccountably, her spirits rose.

And then she noticed something else, and forgot her phone call. She stared at the photograph, absorbed and intent. Bown had so contrived her shot that the woman stood between camera lens and the dying sun, her complex, contradictory features topped with the upswept knot of fine pale hair, emphatic against the sky. The sun's rays, fanning out behind Magda Lachowska's head, created the impression of a glowing halo, solid as the aureole round a medieval icon.

Chapter Four

At 6.45 a.m. Josef Karms walked down the double avenue of limes which stretched two hundred yards from his front door. He savoured the limpid light and the liquid birdsong: the simple pleasures conferred by ownership of an English country house (William and Mary, small at twenty rooms, but elegant) were sweeter to him than he could have believed. The tricks life played were strange indeed.

He had flown in from his Caribbean island the previous week, and gone straight to the Herefordshire estate. It never ceased to sadden him that at his age he could not withstand the long harsh winters there. Or, for that matter, the short wet summers.

On the oval lawn, the helicopter was ready. In just over two hours he was looking down at the private landing pad on top of the City offices.

After his breakfast meeting in the boardroom and a half hour's rest before he showered again, he had a luncheon appointment in Knightsbridge with his youngest daughter by his third wife. They had eaten in the good room at Daphne's, where Nuala was much greeted by young men and women who toyed with their food and appeared to spend at least half their time ignoring their companions and conducting urgent telephone conversations.

Josef Karms observed the hair-flicking girls with pleasure. For the men, with their immoderate laughter and soft hands, he had only contempt. It was not as a European magnate he sat among them, but a gaunt youth, collar of the oversized grey Polish Army uniform loose around his throat, with cropped hair and tired, experienced eyes, a survivor, by a hairsbreadth, of bitter fighting. The memory of long ago deprivation lent a special savour to the goat's cheese and anchovies, the brill and Chablis, so that he consumed them with more than his habitual speed and concentration. Nuala's mother, twenty-five years his junior and of the same type and class as the women here, always complained he ate like a starving Armenian. It was a phrase Josef had heard her father use; she was only parroting him, it meant nothing. But it never failed to wound.

Afterwards, Nuala had insisted on driving him to Piccadilly herself. He was delighted to be seen with her, although it cost him a considerable effort to lower himself elegantly into her Alfa Romeo.

Nuala had not noticed, bless her. She was young enough to assume her father was ageless and self-obsessed enough to be unaware of anything that might suggest otherwise. It was true she had teased him about the bags under his eyes being packed, and even suggested plastic surgery. 'Why not?' she had demanded. 'Everyone does it in the States, men and women both. Nothing else about you looks old at all. And you're in really good shape.' She'd glanced across at him, mischievous as she used to be when she was little. 'Maybe you're at it already?' she said.

He said something – anything – to cover the moment. It unnerved him, to hear her articulate what he had once secretly contemplated. But that had been long ago, when every time he went through passport control at an airport or the borders of any Eastern European country, he had done so with the old familiar chill. No one had ever recognized him, no finger had ever pointed, and then such drastic action had ceased to seem necessary, or desirable. To anyone of his age and background, plastic surgery suggested guilt, the need to hide something. And he was no criminal.

To occupy his hands, he lit a cigarette, and deflected Nuala easily enough with talk of clothes – three wives taught one something useful, after all – and by the time they finished discussing the merits of Donna Karan and Joseph, they were almost in Piccadilly. She was telling him about some couture clothes auction her mother was planning and for which she was modelling, chattering excitedly about the chance actually to meet Jean-Paul Gaultier.

When Nuala pulled up outside Number 56, he got out of his seat with only an involuntary grunt or two as she sprang out and came round in front of the little red car. She flung her arms about his neck and he sniffed her smooth skin. 'Delicious smell,' he said, 'what is it?'

'Angel. Nice, huh? Costs an arm and a leg. Only about two places stock it.'

He made a mental note to have a large bottle

delivered to her flat. The porter already had the side door open for him – he never used revolving doors, you were too easy a target, imprisoned within the slowly turning glass – and he paused to look back at her. She blew extravagant kisses, using both hands in that theatrical way of hers, and climbed into the driving seat.

He was gratified to see Oliver Jodrell coming in immediately behind him in time to witness this little cameo. As he greeted the Englishman, he contrived to look a shade embarrassed but with just a touch of complacency, as befitted an older man surprised in the company of a lovely young woman. He did not refer to her while they crossed the lobby together. The two travelled up in the lift to the top floor. Oliver Jodrell talked about cricket. Josef Karms did not listen.

Nuala Karms edged the Alfa Romeo back into the traffic, calculating just how long it would be before her father's surprise bottle of perfume arrived.

Robert Dennison travelled by cab from the offices of Odyssey Books in Bedford Square. He thought he might be late, which annoyed him: a meeting with an editor, a newly acquired author and his fiercely protective agent had gone on longer than Dennison, at any rate, had intended. An opinion-ated little author, too, who had brought with him to the company a number of books linked to lucrative television series, and as a result believed the sun shone out of his bum. Which Robert Dennison had to admit, in publishing terms, it did.

56 Piccadilly stood back just behind the Lis Frink sculpture of a horseman, incongruous amid the traffic and tall buildings, a graceful interloper from another world. Robert Dennison paid off the taxi, glanced at the brass nameplates on the wall – there it was, *Krzysztof Foundation* – and pushed his way through the doors. The hallway was pleasant enough but impersonal – palms and mirrors, neutral carpeting. He had been there only a moment when Janie joined him. He thought she looked very smart, very strained and far too pale. Must be nerves.

'You look delectable, dear heart. Gorgeous scarf. Perfectly matches the lipstick.'

'You can have some, then.' She was incredibly fond of Bob, whose curling hair and slightly slanted eyes reminded her of a faun. Or a satyr. She kissed him firmly on both cheeks. 'Thank you, Roberto. Such rare praise from you makes the hour choosing them in Fenwicks time well spent.'

He giggled. 'Don't you dare go all girly on me. I like it when you're stern. Ready for the lions' den?'

'As I'll ever be.' He thought she still sounded doubtful.

'Had time to go through the cuttings and videos I sent?'

'Yep. Interesting.' Her tone was non-committal but he wasn't concerned. That was the way she operated: very cool, unruffled, permitting no excitement to show. He remembered his brother's story of how, in the old *Mail* days, they had set up an interview with the Duchess of Windsor. The whole office had been abuzz at the coup, but Janie had drifted off to Paris in well-worn Levis, a man's white shirt and a leather jacket. Afterwards, their Paris bureau man had commented on how great she looked. Apparently she had turned up at the vast house in the Bois de Boulogne in a Valentino suit and hat with an eye-veil: the Duchess had greeted her as a soulmate. So now Robert Dennison felt pretty sure this flat approach was the green light.

In the lift, the operator pressed an unmarked button. The doors finally opened inside the penthouse suite. There was the carpeted hush of money, the scent of lilies from an arrangement standing on what appeared to be a considerable portion of a pillar from the Parthenon: Janie and Robert exchanged amused glances.

'Miss Paxton. Mr Dennison. Good afternoon.' A woman rose smiling from an empty desk. She could have been almost any age, all Elizabeth Arden complexion and careful vowels. She gestured to closed double doors on the far wall. 'The committee will be ready for you in just a few minutes.' She took their coats, brought coffee and a plate of Fortnum's chocolate biscuits. Robert eyed them and whispered to Janie, 'I see they use that nice little shop on the corner.'

'D'you know any of these people?' Janie kept her voice equally low, gesturing with her head towards the closed door.

'Some. One or two are interesting, one at least is . . .' his voice dropped lower, 'notorious. Lady de Lisle – once Zazi Castellòn.'

'Oh, right. The *grande horizontale*. Spanish, isn't she?'

'Possibly. Others say Austrian.' Bob Dennison raised a knowing eyebrow. 'An understandable error. In a manner of speaking. Or should I say, of technique.'

Janie giggled. 'Don't tantalize.'

'The lady is said to be known admiringly by former lovers as the Viennese Oyster. Hence the confusion.'

'What *is* a Viennese Oyster?'

'Physically impossible, one would have thought.' His expression became positively satyric. 'Discretion forbids further elucidation. Though I think we can safely assume it's not her catering they are recalling in tranquillity.'

'Naughty you.'

'Naughty *her*.'

Just then a tall man came out of the conference room and introduced himself as Oliver Jodrell. He fairly glowed with self-confidence and a sunbed tan. Janie mistrusted him on sight.

'Good to see you again,' he said warmly to Dennison, shaking hands, leaning forward in boyish eagerness. 'And Miss Paxton, such a pleasure.' He had the unmistakable quick voice of a born salesman. She stiffened as he moved too close, but he was oblivious to subtle body language and took her hand firmly in his own, his left cupping her elbow in the new Cerruti jacket. It was a manoeuvre she intensely disliked: the old smoothie. And was that a Guards tie he was wearing? Surely no one bought striped ties from choice any more.

'I'm delighted we'll soon be working together,' he said. She murmured something polite. 'Now,' he went on, 'I'm about to introduce you to some members of the Krzysztof Foundation. As I'm sure you know, the foundation was formed by a number of international philanthropists together with some of Europe's leading businessmen. They're a very varied group, drawn together by their support of Mama and her work. I think you'll probably recognize some of them. They're all big in their fields, of course. Demanding schedules and so forth. So we're only able to assemble six or seven at any one time in London.' He ushered them before him through the open doorway.

Venetian blinds were closed and, in the lamplit room, seven people sat at irregular intervals along the length of a huge glass table. To Janie's eyes it all had the appearance of a stage set: the pictures on the walls – country scenes – the furniture, even the receptionist, were impersonal, as if they'd been put in place by an agency for the afternoon. Also, the air of studied formality gave the impression that everyone there was elderly, though later she realized at least two of the men and one of the three women were actually only in their late forties.

Oliver Jodrell introduced the newcomers in words which, though accurate, were somehow embarrassingly PR-ish ('Mr Robert Dennison the distinguished publisher, Miss Jane Paxton the award-winning journalist') and then went up and down the table giving names. Some of the faces were familiar to her – and, she could see, to Robert. Already she had glimpsed Edward Pelling-ham, a one-time cabinet minister and now something impressive in the City. He was leaning across to Monica Ziegler, widow of the Swiss herbal medicine millionaire. She was the most robust-looking woman Janie had ever seen: she looked as though she ought to be wearing national dress and holding a large cheese.

'Mr Josef Karms you know of course, of Karms Pharmaceuticals . . .' Janie inclined her head to the oddly exaggerated, actorish face she had seen a thousand times in business pages and gossip columns. He was sitting beside a red-headed woman dressed in a harsh emerald green. Oliver Jodrell had moved on to stand beside a tiny woman, dangerously thin and elegant, reminiscent of Wallis Windsor. 'Lady de Lisle . . .'

Janie was riveted. She remembered now: South American. Probably. As her charms faded and demand flagged, Zazi Castellòn had married an elderly English baronet, Crispin de Lisle, to the loudly expressed astonishment of his remarkably varied circle of intimates. It was a first marriage for both, and childless. Zazi successfully reinvented herself as a socialite and became a fund-raiser for the most deserving charities.

Oliver Jodrell was now beside a tall man whose bald head and polished spectacles gleamed equally under the lights. 'Professor Whitely has kindly travelled up from the University of Surrey . . .'

When Robert and Janie were settled in their chairs, and the murmur of conversation had died, Jodrell stood at the head of the table. He was clearly a professional manager, very much in his element running the meeting.

'Now we come to the last item on today's agenda and by far . . .' he gestured expansively towards the newcomers, 'by far the most important. We all share the long-held desire of the

Krzysztof Foundation that Mama should put down on paper the details of her life, define for us her beliefs and her hopes. This, as you know, she has repeatedly refused to undertake. She is so busy, there is so much to be done, the calls on her time are so numerous. A couple of years ago, we suggested to her that instead, an authorized biography should be written during her lifetime. And you also know how fiercely the lady hath protested.' He waited for the polite laughter. 'We believe this can no longer be delayed. There have recently been three books written about her by outsiders. These were pathetic efforts from our point of view, but they sold in appreciable numbers. Mama's reputation sold them, and other people benefited.' He looked round at them all. 'Those profits should have gone towards the work. And now Mama is approaching her mid-seventies,' he went on. 'We're all well aware that if, God forbid, anything should . . .'

Janie lost the thread momentarily, her professional ear alerted by the incongruity of that remark – *God forbid* – from so unlikely a source.

'But that will be after her death,' Jodrell was now saying. 'And we trust that is a long way off, and it does not concern us at this moment.' He paused, and looked towards Robert Dennison. 'So we approached Odyssey Books. They are a small, independent publisher with whom we have negotiated a contract that gives us a measure of control. We have proposed, and Mr Dennison has in essence accepted, that the Krzysztof Foundation place a very considerable sum of money at the disposal of Odyssey Books. Now this is not

71

normal publishing procedure – but as I said, Odyssey is not a large firm. The Krzysztof money will go a long way towards the costs of producing the book – writing and research, editing, printing and distribution.'

He looked questioningly at Robert Dennison, who added, 'There'll also be a very big spend on publicity and promotion. We are certain you will see a handsome return on your investment.'

Down the table, Josef Karms stirred. It was the almost imperceptible but deliberate movement of an experienced bidder in an auction house and equally effective to the trained eye: Oliver Jodrell nodded and paused politely for the older man to speak.

Josef Karms remained seated and his voice was low. Even so, he dominated the room effortlessly. Janie realized that although he was not a very tall man he had the bulk of one, his heavy shoulders minimized by expensive tailoring. She thought of the American president who'd said, *Speak softly and carry a big stick*. She wondered what Karms's stick was.

'Publicity makes me nervous,' Karms was saying. 'We must retain control, at whatever cost. We cannot take any risks with the reputation of a woman who, when all is said and done, is an inspiration in today's world, a moral leader. We are well aware there is a movement afoot already to make her officially the saint so many of us know her to be.' He looked round at them all, drawing them in, confidential. 'There must be no whiff of scandal or impropriety. I do not for a moment suggest there are grounds for believing this could happen. But we must be realistic. And sadly, it is precisely these things which sell newspapers and persuade people to buy books. We all know they do not have to be true to be damaging. Indeed, the last few years have shown clearly that unfounded rumour may all too readily be accepted as fact.' He shook his great, theatrical head slowly and rumbled, 'The world is a sewer.'

Oliver Jodrell waited a respectful moment while everyone in the room considered the sad implications of this statement.

Robert Dennison nodded. 'Be assured that we intend to be most careful. We are not interested in sleaze.' He smiled. 'I think I can claim we're the one publishing house in London which has never been involved in a libel case. And we have agreed to make joint decisions with you over foreign rights and newspaper serialization. The same applies, of course, to film or television – all the imponderables where things could, from the point of view of the foundation, slide into questionable areas.'

'Now . . .' Oliver Jodrell turned to Janie and his voice brightened. 'Miss Paxton, who as you all know has a considerable reputation for incisive writing, has accepted a joint invitation from Odyssey Books and ourselves to set the record straight once and for all. She has kindly agreed to write the authorized biography.'

Janie cleared her throat to interrupt him. 'I'm sorry,' she said firmly, 'I'm afraid I haven't got quite to that point just yet.' She glanced at Robert Dennison beside her and added, 'I understood we were here to discuss details, and that my answer was conditional upon what was said.'

For a moment – no longer – Oliver Jodrell appeared disconcerted. 'I should perhaps have told you both that Mama has decided she will indeed co-operate completely and wholeheartedly with this book.'

'Really co-operate?' Janie had promised herself to say very little at this meeting. She was there to listen, to learn. She had intended to give nothing away, and certainly not to get excited. But she simply couldn't help herself. She and Robert had been through it again and again: all the interviews Mama had given over the years would be available to her, many members of the order had guaranteed their assistance. Even Mama's brother had agreed to talk freely to her. She would be given copies of films made by television companies and by the Krzysztof Foundation for fund-raising purposes. She would be allowed to observe Mama at work in different locations around the world. And then, when the material was collected, Mama would, probably through an intermediary, comment on observations and correct any errors before the book was finally finished. 'At that point,' Robert had said, hopefully, 'with any luck you'll get a chance to sit down and talk face to face.'

'But you can't guarantee it?' she had asked.

Robert had shrugged. 'That's why the foundation's putting up so much money – they can't force her to do anything. And she absolutely refuses to make any promises.'

Both of them had accepted this: it had always

been part of Mama's mystique that she was so aloof, so chary of the media. That was precisely why they continued to be fascinated. All her time and energy went to the people who needed her so desperately, and to them she denied neither access, nor time, nor love. But now Janie was being told that she, too, would be granted some of that time.

'Are you saying Mama will really co-operate?' She repeated her question. Despite herself, she found she was perched on the edge of her seat with eagerness, like a little girl. 'She'll actually give me interviews? Talk on tape, answer detailed questions? Answer *any* questions?'

'Certainly. You will have whatever you need,' said Oliver Jodrell. His expression was bland. Under Janie's steady scrutiny, it faded slightly. 'Within reason,' he added. She thought she caught the suspicion of a sideways darting glance at Josef Karms.

'Do we have your assurance on that?' Robert Dennison was clearly equally taken aback.

'Oh, absolutely.' Jodrell glanced down the table. 'Could I perhaps ask Lady de Lisle to explain?' He half-bowed towards her as he spoke. She looked at him coolly, head erect. Janie noticed how black her hair still was, the coarse-textured curls cut by an expert hand to taper into the nape of her neck.

'I had a meeting with Mama a week ago, when I accompanied her to visit orphanages in Slovenia.' Her voice was as distinctive as her appearance, heavily accented, deep. Her head and features seemed almost too large for the narrow shoulders, giving her an oddly masculine look. 'I took the opportunity to persuade Mama that she really owed it to all of us – and indeed to herself – to speak freely to you. It took a little time, but eventually she concurred.' On her lips, the precisely chosen word was long drawn out. The woman had a delivery like Eartha Kitt.

Janie sat back. 'I see.' She thought for a moment, her usual scepticism returning. 'But why? I mean, this is a contradiction of what she has always said about no personal publicity. How did you do it?'

Even Zazi de Lisle's shrug was an elegant understatement. 'I simply told her as an old friend . . .' the voice dropped even lower, the *rrr*'s rumbling soft as a purr '. . . that she must realize it was time to let the world truly comprehend what a treasure it possesses in her.'

A well-bred murmur of agreement rippled down the table. As it faded, Robert Dennison said thoughtfully, 'I take it she will not change her mind.' He doodled something on a small pad. 'It could be very embarrassing – and costly – if she talked at length and then retracted what she had said.'

Zazi de Lisle lifted a dismissive hand, and her words held a most definite rebuke.

'Once her assurance has been given,' she said firmly, 'Mama does not revoke it.'

Janie took the train home that night, so she could write up the meeting. She had not made notes – that would have suggested a firm commitment – but she did so now. She did not intend to forget what had been said, in what tones, and by whom.

She sat staring out into the darkness beyond the speeding carriage. She didn't see her own reflection in the glass, or the papers spread out in front of her. She was high on excitement, in that marvellous early stage of a project when the whole thing promised to come together and the hard slog had not yet begun. The book would be wonderful, she knew it. At this moment, anything was possible and attainable. Perfection. Dazzling reviews.

In her mind's eye she went the length of that long table in the office in Piccadilly, saw those faces again, recalled gestures, snatches of conversation. She focused on the jewels of the women, whether anyone had on a waistcoat. Someone – who? – had the tiny red badge of the Légion d'Honneur in his lapel. As she had moved to her seat, she had caught the scent of old malt, although only coffee and bottled water were in evidence. More than anything, she tried to recapture the feelings they had each aroused in her, the vibrations she had received from them. It was hard to do with such a large and mixed group, far easier with individuals. Even so . . .

Oliver Jodrell was a type: he could as easily be selling used Mercedes. A man whose scruples were lodged in his wallet. Josef Karms was something else. She couldn't be sure how she knew it, she certainly didn't know what it was, but that superb façade did not conceal the threat he carried with him, the sense of menace he brought into that neutral room. She shut her eyes and focused on him. The groomed hair, worn overlong and curling onto his collar at the back, the aquiline nose on the face which age and indulgence had rendered fleshy. The immaculate clothes, the watch as discreet as only platinum could be, the white double cuff of his shirt – and then she had it. Everything about Josef Karms shouted moneyed ease. But his hands said something else. Not in condition – the nails were manicured and polished. But the shape, broad palm and stubby fingers, the way he held them before him, wide apart, balled into loose fists, ready for action. She saw them again, resting on the long table, wide thumbs uppermost and wrapped round the first fingers, the backs darkly pelted. It was as if he had long ago altered everything he could about himself. Only his hands remembered the reality of him.

The other men – the token banker, the token lawyer, the academic whose features she vaguely recognized – were just the sort she had expected. Not memorable, or out of place. Solid figures in their fifties and early sixties who knew their way around, whose secretaries probably had the home phone numbers of a couple of junior government ministers and a newspaper managing editor or two.

It was the women she had found unlikely members of the board of the Krzysztof Foundation. What on earth was Monica Ziegler doing away from a racecourse? The coffee-skinned woman in emerald green – wasn't she sister to someone rich and slightly sinister? An oil magnate? An international fixer? Something like that.

And Lady de Lisle. There were more stories about her than she could have had hot dinners:

apart from the Viennese version Janie had also heard she was a belly-dancer from Tunisia and the illegitimate daughter of a Brazilian cardinal – it depended whether you chose Taki or Dempster for gossip about the glitterati. Yet from what she had said, she was clearly a long-standing friend of Mama. More even than that: she looked to be a real influence on her.

What a weirdly disparate bunch. Janie stuck her chin in her hands and stared out at the blackness beyond the window. Not what she'd expected at all. Shady, that was the word for them. An old-fashioned word, but perfect. A group of people who appeared substantial and impressive. And yet she was willing to bet each and every one of them had something to hide.

Like many journalists, Janie was an odd mixture of cool professional cynicism and the naivety that comes from a kind of laziness: simpler and quicker to accept the facts presented than to question too much and ruin a good story. She had been hired to do a job, to write a sympathetic biography of a remarkable woman, and that was what she intended to do.

So now, when somewhere in the depths of her mind the faintest, unnameable, dark little doubt stirred for the first time, she pushed it firmly aside.

Chapter Five

Janie woke in the night totally alert, senses sharp, full of anxiety and a deep dread, the sound of her own blood in her ears.

She played back in her mind the voices she had heard again in her sleep.

You will have whatever you need. Within reason.

We must always retain control. At whatever cost.

She shivered, as much from the words as the cold. It had been over a month since the Krzysztof Foundation meeting. Strange that they had come back to her only now. There must be a significance her dreaming mind had grasped, but her consciousness could not.

She had been making her plans, writing to ask for interviews, laying the groundwork for the book, and forgetting how firmly her hands were tied. *We must always retain control.* Of one thing she was sure. The foundation would watch every word she wrote.

Obstinacy had always stood her in good stead. Maybe she could find a way round this. She would have a damn good try, anyway.

She lay for a long time while worries wheeled in her brain, first one glimpsed, then another. The weather was proving fierce and she was unaccustomed to the bleakness of hills she had previously known only in summer. The rain must have woken her, drumming loud on the slate roof and the dark glass of the skylights. Slates already needed replacing and, after tonight, probably more would have slipped. And roofers were expensive; it could mean a rent increase.

Money. The book. She was getting to the stage where she felt she was losing control of the material, there was so much on the files. Maybe she needed tranquillizers, Prozac or something. Had she paid Amex for air tickets yet? A lot of bills this month, and Adam needed sports kit, a new coat. Adam was getting so big . . . They were almost over, the childish years, and she had scarcely savoured them, choosing instead the greater excitements, the more dramatic rewards, of her work.

Another thought flitted past, familiar and so sharp she always blocked it. Only like this, by herself in the night, it would catch her unawares. Because she had been given another chance, another opportunity. And what had she done? She had rejected it, savagely and legally, with cold steel and a suction tube, in an abortion clinic in Marylebone.

Her despair was so acute it felt physical, punishing her with the dull hollow ache of a bad period, throbbing deep and desperate. Loneliness emptied her out. She couldn't go on like this. Her need for someone's touch, for tenderness, for the simple consolation of a warm body beside her own, was overwhelming.

Properly awake now, eyes burning, she stared into the blackness. She decided to get up and make some hot milk. She would add whisky, of course, but she was still at the stage of refusing to admit this was what she really wanted. She needed it, to get through, that was all. Maybe she was drinking a bit more than she should, but she was no alcoholic. She never ever had a hangover. Once she'd had that first drink of the day, she was just fine.

She got out of bed and pulled on Paul's dressing gown, felt her way to the door. Six narrow stairs led down to the landing below. Two doors led off this, the bathroom and Adam's room.

Until she and Paul separated, they had used the barn for long weekends. During the summer holidays one or other of them would be there with Adam, and they always spent a week at Christmas. They had never bothered Len Smedley about the primitive electricity, not least because he insisted that, as they were supplied from the generator on the farm, further demands would endanger the entire system. They were used to flickering lights, the occasional loss of power.

So it was no surprise when she flicked the switch beside her door and nothing happened. She took her little torch from the dressing-gown pocket. The tiny light beamed for a second, then died.

'Damn, *damn*.' Her voice sounded very loud. It was her own fault, she should have checked the batteries. She put a hand on the wall to steady herself and started to descend. On the fourth step she paused. In the black space of the empty landing she felt, rather than saw, a heavier shadowing. There was no furniture on the landing, nothing. And yet something inhabited that space. She could not see, she could only sense the solidity, the bulk of it. Tiny hairs prickled along her arms. She stood rigid and wide-eyed on the stair. Maybe she was ill, or hallucinating. All her senses were heightened. The weave of the carpet was almost painful beneath her bare feet. She could feel where the label on Paul's pyjamas scratched against the back of her neck. The drumming of the rain seemed louder on the roof, the soft banging of wind on the glass in the room behind her was now an urgent rapping.

She held her breath. The Little Barn, where she had lived alone for months now without a trace of anxiety, seemed somehow full, occupied by something she did not recognize. She was aware of it around her, tangible, powerful: a sense of visitation unlike anything she had ever experienced.

She ran back up the stairs, tripping over the trailing belt of her robe, slamming the door shut. It was made of three broad pine planks, with a black metal latch like a country gate, which lifted and dropped into a holder. There was no lock but Paul had fixed a bolt high up: there had been a time, when Adam was small, when they would make love in the afternoons while he napped, and they did not want him to walk in on them naked. She shot the bolt.

Back in bed, she wished she had let the cat come up with her, but there was no way she was going down for it now. It occurred to her to turn on the radio, but she was reluctant to make any noise. This was all completely idiotic, of course. Even if she had believed in such fancies, nothing had ever been said about the barn being haunted.

Joan Smedley at the farm was a garrulous and lonely woman who gossiped endlessly given an opportunity: she would have surely discussed such a thing with enthusiasm. And the handyman, who had renewed some floorboards when they first moved in, had worked on and around the farm for thirty years. ('Man and boy,' he always recited proudly, as if the first had preceded the second.) She recalled him telling them with relish about a young farmer who had once owned the land: they'd found him dead against a wall, crushed by his own bull. Paul had covered Adam's ears when he got to the gorier details and they declined his offer to point out the wall in question. Al Cotter, she decided, was not a man to spare their feelings. If he knew about hauntings in the barn, he would have made sure they did too.

The wind had not abated – had grown stronger, if anything, with a wild note she had not registered before. She was struck by the ridiculous idea that she must not look up at the skylight, in case some-one – some thing – was there.

In darkness she started to dial Claudia's number, but stopped herself. Claudia would not object. But Lewis was not the sort of man you dared disturb in the middle of the night. The only other possibility was her sister. She hesitated, her hand on the receiver. Sisters they might be, but they were old protagonists. Louise, the younger by four years, had given up work with open relief before her first child was born, declaring that now her family was her first priority: Janie had missed neither the implied criticism, nor the success of the marriage. Harold was a wine merchant, a

Dickensian man with a tongue as dry as his best sherries. He was a head shorter than Louise, but neither seemed to notice.

Last weekend Janie had driven Adam to Northamptonshire. The seventeenth-century farmhouse was a showpiece surrounded by fields, a swimming pool set into the cobbled courtyard, a couple of glossy ponies in the looseboxes. The three older children and Adam immediately disappeared to play. The baby, George, started to grumble and Janie fed him spoonfuls of puréed chicken while Louise finished cooking. The smells of roast potatoes, the huge brass pots of dried rose leaves and waxed floorboards, induced an uneasy mixture of envy and irritation: to live like this, Louise must work twelve hours a day on the house. She had always been middle-aged, even at twelve.

Janie teased her younger sister for being so houseproud, for her seemingly constant pregnancies. This had become ritualized between them, a joke. ('Nice pram. Get it with your regular user's coupons from Mothercare?') Janie pitied Louise for being so tied, so confined. Louise considered Janie had sacrificed a happy private life to professional success. And yet both were conscious that they might be masking other, more ambivalent feelings; little girls still, secretly wanting whatever toys the other had. So Janie had been astonished to find herself admitting, without preamble, 'I was pregnant, Lou.'

Louise kept very busy over her saucepans. Without looking up she asked, 'Was?'

George was warm on Janie's lap, with that

special heaviness of sleepy contentment. She wanted to lift her head and howl. It must have been in her voice when she said, 'Three weeks ago.' She swallowed. 'It's gone. All over.'

'Oh, you poor girl.' Lou turned then, frowning, the wooden spoon dripping gravy still in her hand. 'You lost it?'

'Not lost. More deliberately mislaid.' Making jokes to mask the hurt.

'Janie!' The shock open on her face now.

Janie shrugged. 'No choice, really.'

'The man wasn't . . . ?'

'He wasn't someone I wanted to marry. Or even live with, to be honest.'

'I'm so sorry.' Lou sounded as if she meant it.

'It would've been single mum stuff. Not very stylish.'

'Children aren't,' Louise observed. 'No matter what the magazines tell you.' She came over and put her arm round Janie's shoulders. 'How awful, to go through that. You should've told me, I would have come.'

It was her touch, more than the words. Janie bent her head over George. She only realized she was crying when she saw the dark patches among the blond down on his almost bald head, and wiped them hastily away. And all the time, genuine as Lou's concern was, underneath it she could sense a faint triumph. Louise had achieved her children, had chosen to devote herself to them. They were the only thing she had ever done better than her elder sister.

Then Harold had come in, started to chat, opened a wine he was particularly fond of. The moment had passed, and they had not returned to the subject. A couple of times, she caught Lou shooting her furtive, worried looks. By then, Janie had got herself together, and she made sure they were never alone before she left, so she would not fall victim again to sympathy.

Now she let her hand drop from the phone. She did not want Lou apprised of any more weakness.

Somewhere outside a door banged in the wind – she must have forgotten to bolt the coalhouse – and she shivered. She needed to talk to someone, and there was only one person she could call at this hour.

Paul's voice was muffled, grumpy. 'Uh . . . yeah.'

'It's me.' Hearing him, so familiar, she longed to tell him about the abortion: he suddenly seemed the natural person to share it with. But common sense, thank God, prevented her. 'Look, I had to call you, sorry. Only I'm going mad here alone. I just need to talk.'

There was a long pause. She could hear rustling as he shifted in the bed. 'What the . . . God, it's the middle of . . .' Then he said, 'Janie? 's that you?' and she recognized the pain in his voice. Then a note of alarm as he forced himself fully awake. 'What's wrong? Something happened?'

'No. I mean, yes. Paul . . .' she was whispering, 'there's something on the landing.'

'Burglar?'

'No. I don't think it's a person. It's a . . . feeling.'

He was alert now, his voice sharp. 'Sounds like the whisky talking.'

'No it's not.' He hated her drinking. 'Something

woke me and I was going downstairs and then I felt this *thing* in the way.'

He asked, resigned, 'Where are you?'

'Bedroom. I ran back. The whole house feels – malign. Hostile. The sodding generator's acting up again.'

'For Chrissake, Janie, just call Len Smedley, he'd be there in two ticks. Or phone the police if you think there's someone in the house. Though there's certainly nothing in it worth stealing. How long ago was this?'

'About fifteen minutes.'

'Have you heard any noises since?'

'No. Just wind and rain.'

'So describe what happened.' He listened intently while she went over it. Then he said, carefully, 'I don't honestly think a prospective attacker would stand around on the landing in total silence for a quarter of an hour. Think about it.'

'No. I'm being stupid.'

He said, 'You're certainly behaving right out of character. You're the least spookable person I know.' He always used to say she had no imagination, a charge which never failed to infuriate, probably because it was true.

'It's just that I felt so . . .'

'Yeah. Well. There are times when being alone isn't much fun.' He said this with some bitterness. Now he had the picture, now he had assured himself nothing dramatic had occurred, the cool, withdrawn persona he had constructed to deal with her infidelities was back.

'Are you alone? Now, I mean.' She had a sudden picture of a woman slumbering secure beside him.

Until this moment, it had never occurred to her that Paul might have someone else. Now it somehow seemed obvious. The flare of jealousy astonished her. Did he hold the other woman as she slept, his leg over hers? Did he tuck his hand into the warm secret space at the top of her thighs so she woke wet for him?

'Look,' Paul said tersely, 'don't, OK? Don't start.' Warning her off.

She said hastily, 'I'm not. Just talk to me for a bit, could you? How was Adam on Saturday?'

'Good. Happy.' He paused. When she said nothing he went on, with obvious reluctance, 'He's joining the film club, they're going to learn how to be Quentin Tarantino. At ten years old.'

'I thought Quentin Tarantino *was* ten years old.'

'You always were prone to exaggeration.'

'Go on talking.'

He was brusque. 'Not now.'

'Please, Paul. I need you to.'

He sighed. 'We haven't spoken for months and now you ring me up demanding conversation at two fifteen in the morning.' She thought he said it without too much rancour. The storm of feeling she had provoked in him seemed to have faded with time. Was that good or bad? Did that mean he'd forgiven her, or just stopped caring? Perhaps she would never find out: in the last months, it was as if Paul had constructed a fortress around his emotions.

'Go on. Tell me about the office.' They used to have wonderful conversations in bed, picking over gossip, stories, assignments, feuds.

'Rife with rumour and riddled with intrigue, as

usual. Word is, David's to be booted out to make way for a bright lady from the *Mirror*. She drinks at the Groucho and her self-esteem is sufficiently honed to shatter the glass ceiling. You don't have to rack your brains, do you?' She could hear him starting almost to enjoy this. 'They sent Alan Chase to Washington and his wife loathed it and said, we go back to London or I leave you. Ken brought them home but he was furious and stuck Alan on Obits. He poured out his heart to one of the librarians. And more than his heart: she got pregnant and now his wife wants a divorce anyway. Colin's on the wagon and Jeremy Fields is writing his third thriller. He's moved into a bloody great mansion in Brent or somewhere and he's asked for a raise. Business as usual, in other words. Oh, and Howard Pearson died.'

'God, I thought he died years ago.'

'He only looked as if he did.'

'Did you write to Mrs P.?'

'Of course. And before you ask, I didn't add your name. Write your own letters.' He yawned. 'Look, I can't talk any more. Now be sensible. Decide if you really think there's anyone there, or whether your imagination's working overtime. Then either ring the police or, better still, the farm – they're nearer. Don't hesitate if you're really worried. And call me in the morning, tell me what happened. Now I'm going back to sleep. If I can.'

'Yes. Thanks, Paul.' She meant it. His concern reached over the telephone to her. He was not indifferent, despite the curt notes. She had hurt him, perhaps she still did not appreciate how much, and he was protecting himself. But Paul had always responded to an appeal for help: it was one of the first things she had loved about him. For a fraction of a second, she was tempted again to confide in him. But of course that was impossible. Instead she said quietly, 'I feel better just for talking.' She put the phone back on its cradle. She would not sleep. But now she could get through the night.

Chapter Six

Driving out through the shabby London fringe of the Commercial Road two days later, Janie thought the buildings could hardly have changed from the Forties. Only these days the low depressing skyline was dwarfed by distant tower-block homes and offices where Docklands had transformed the Thames. But if the buildings of the East End of London had not changed, their occupants had. The furriers and tailors were long gone.

Now another, more exotic lifestyle brought new vigour to these grey streets. Outside food shops, great trays of unfamiliar vegetables flourished, their fleshy opulence incongruous on the grubby pavements. Metal trees supported plastic bags of candyfloss, giant blossoms of pink and blue. Dress shops that had once sold black cocktail gowns and carried European names – Venners, Edelstein, Zweim – were now Warris Sundram, K. L. Shukla, Asha House of Fashion, their windows alight with a myriad bright fabrics. Swathes of shocking pink organza shot with purple and gold, acid yellow raw silk combined with lime green, braids of silver and flamboyant chiffons, embroidered wool shawls, silk damasks woven with strands of peacock feathers.

Janie – suddenly conscious of the drab figure she cut in her discreet stone-coloured mac –

passed the White Swan public house and Cable Street, then turned into a short street where a piece of wasteland that had clearly once been a row of back-to-back houses and then a bombsite, was now a parking lot, and almost full. The surviving side of the street was a forbidding wall of red brick.

As instructed, she found a wooden door three-quarters of the way along. It opened onto a perfect period country garden, where in spring magnolia trees would flower, and roses begin to twine around trellised arches. Beyond these, the long Georgian façade of Chalice House, the hospice that was Mama's first English foundation, looked into the sun.

In the big reception hall cream plastic chairs clashed with the formal beauty of old wood floors and a magnificent curving staircase. In the U of the staircase, suspended from a long chain stretching up to the third floor and which must once have carried a chandelier, hung a single bulb in a round paper shade. There was no one there, but she could hear a chanted prayer from behind double doors.

The chanting stopped, and a hymn began. No wavering old-lady falsettos here, but zest and vigour, deep male voices holding it steady, in a way that made her almost want to join in.

As she stood irresolute, wondering where she should go, a young woman dashed past carrying a tin tray with a linen napkin spread upon it. On this sat a cup and saucer of white china, a packet of camomile tea bags and a steel pot for hot water. She knocked on the door beside Janie, which opened to reveal a large desk in a small office. The young woman handed in the tray.

'For Mama,' she said reverently.

The hospice director had a broad, ruddy, outdoor face. His baggy black trousers were held up with an overlong, stylish belt, his shoes were heavy-soled. He fairly bubbled with enthusiasm.

'Mama doesn't always give us notice when she's travelling. On the other hand, I can think of times when we've expected her hourly and she's finally turned up five days late.' He shook his head admiringly. 'What a woman. D'you know how old she is? She arrived at seven, she's been over the whole place and then she'll talk with the patients – that's really why she's here, of course. Have you seen her with people yet? It's quite something.'

'The idea was for me to visit the order's houses in various countries, to see the work. Then when I'd gathered my material, I would hopefully have a number of interviews with her. There's a lot of ground to cover.'

Jim Harley drummed his fingers on his desk. Behind him, a large framed poster carried the violet-blue logo and a single line of print: THE CHALICE OF THE GRAPES OF GOD.

'I'll show you over the building. I'm sure there'll be a couple of minutes for you to meet her.' He said it casually. She started to thank him but he wouldn't have it. 'No big deal.' Janie smiled at him. She liked him more and more. Everyone else had made Mama seem utterly inaccessible.

He handed her a collection of pamphlets from piles on his desk, decorated with the familiar deep violet-blue logo of Mama's order: the two open curved hands joined at the wrist, fingertips bent back to form a cup overflowing with grapes. The logo was executed in a flowing Art Deco style so it could have been either a flower or the celebratory vessel.

'Mama faced some opposition when she first brought the Chalice to this country. You can imagine. Until then she'd been very much associated with desperate poverty . . .' All this Janie knew. The Chalice was in South America of course, where her work so famously began in the *favelas*, the slums; then countries where wars had brought havoc and suffering – Bosnia, the camps of the Palestinians on the West Bank. She was in Hungary for the uprising, in Romania when Ceaucescu ruled, in Cuba, Haiti . . . 'Well, anyway,' Harley was saying, 'there was a fair old stink when the Chalice wanted to open up here. People took it as a slight, assumed it meant the home of the welfare state was falling.' He cocked a quizzical eyebrow. 'Interestingly, the same people were not prepared to take the homeless and give them the care Mama does. You will not, I think, hear criticism from our patients.'

'Where do they come from?'

'Some through other charities who've found them on soup rounds. Most come direct from the streets. From the arches around the South Bank, or the doorways of the Strand. Some have medical problems, we've a few alcoholics, several need psychiatric care. You'll see.'

He showed her round the house: the simple surgery, the various offices. There was no hint of the impersonal bustle Janie associated with such places. The door of each room bore a different name – Standfast, Welcome, Hope. All their doctors, he explained, gave their time for minimal payment. The rest of the staff, members of the Chalice, wore the order's robe in the distinctive deep violet-blue rough weave. Men and women alike wore this: the Chalice was a double order, Jim Harley pointed out, like some of the great religious foundations of the past.

He led her into a room with a polished wooden floor and a single bright painting clearly done by an amateur, where a group were drinking coffee.

Jim Harley poured some for Janie and chatted to those near him as he did so. A couple of them – a dark woman with pink earrings, an older man in a brown shirt and baggy cardigan – talked shyly about whether Mama would come in to see them. Opposite Janie, a woman in a pink flowered miniskirt showed fat dimpled knees and stared at her with fixed and obvious aggression. Standing in the corner of the room a slender, tousle-haired man, his thighs narrow in pale blue jeans, shouted to himself, in desperate, shrill cries.

A nurse stopped by Janie's chair and offered her a biscuit. She started to say, no thanks, but the youth hurried from his corner and grabbed a chocolate bar from the plate. The nurse caught his wrist, not hard.

'Say "thank you", David.'

David jerked his hand from hers and dropped the biscuit. He went back to his corner. The nurse said in a low voice, 'There's nothing wrong physically – you heard him shouting – but he

96

doesn't speak. Some sort of trauma. He'd been on the streets since he was fifteen. Anything could have happened to him.'

'But he will be able to talk again?'

'Maybe. It could be years, though. Nothing we've been able to do has had any effect.'

Jim Harley walked over to Janie, tapping into a computer diary. He consulted his watch and led the way at top speed to a room with *Faith* printed on the door. He slid back a panel, peeped in. 'This way.' They entered a doorless office, where a window overlooked a narrow ward containing six beds.

A group of three people – a couple of nurses, a man who looked like a doctor – waited by the door. Just beyond them a woman stood beside the nearest bed.

The occupant of the bed, could have been either man or woman, had reached that final stage of life where subtleties like sexual identity, or race, or status, or language, had ceased to matter. Skin so faded could once have been brown or white. Eyes so heavy no longer held colour. Nothing was important but that last tattered vestige of life.

The woman standing was Mama. Even had Janie not known, it could have been no one else: the intensity of her presence was tangible in that quiet room. Even before Janie saw her face, it was apparent in the way she held herself, with a mixture of supreme arrogance and supreme humility: this was a woman who knew what she was doing. It was evident in the way her staff watched her, confident, observant, without anxiety.

She wore the famous creamy robe, the hood

now pushed back. The long garment emphasized her extreme thinness, her height. The bound hair was the colour and texture of silver-gilt wire. Her skin was pale, taut over the high cheekbones, the line of the jaw. She was looking down at the patient, and only a softening round the throat, at the temples, a spray of fine lines round the eyes, hinted at her age. That and the narrow, practical hands, folded now below her waist. The skin there was creased from hard work and exposure to weather. They alone placed her in her seventies.

Mama took in at a glance the paraphernalia around the bed: tubes and pumps, an oxygen cylinder, a plastic pouch of saline solution. All had now been disconnected. Nothing more to be done. Beneath the covers the patient's bony body was visibly tense, fighting to die.

No one spoke. Mama now was looking at the patient – or rather, her gaze was fixed at a place just above the recumbent shape. At last she bent over the bed, felt for the pulse at the wrist.

For ten minutes, fifteen, she received the dying hand in both of hers. She was utterly still, her slender height curved over the bed like a great, pale-plumaged bird. Her eyes were closed as she concentrated. She seemed to be listening intently to the pulse; more, to the beat of the heart making it, to the sounds of the body holding it.

Mama was not a doctor. There was no hint of a medical examination here, of procedure or inter-vention. There was instead a simplicity, an energy, a feeling of holiness, that was felt and transmitted. And the person in the bed, held in this quiet grasp, appeared somehow to alter. Janie could not define it; watching from behind the window, she could only sense the change.

A quarter of an hour passed. Longer. Still this ritual continued, the two people involved in it separated from the others in the room by more than the space which lay between them. The medical team did not stir, they must be accustomed to this. At one point the patient in the bed – a woman, Janie saw now – lifted her head to look at the creamy figure beside her, before sinking back against her pillows.

Finally, Mama laid the thin hand softly back on the sheet. Still, nothing was said.

At Janie's side, Jim Harley whispered, 'That woman's had a bad time. She's dying in terrible anger. We see that a lot. She has no religious faith to help her through it – not many of the people here have. But look.'

The patient opened her eyes. Even through the glass, the expression on her face was clear: serene, accepting. The rigid strain had gone out of her. She and Mama regarded each other. Still neither of them had uttered a word.

The woman in the bed moved a hand as if to wave.

Mama turned away, came towards the window, to the little group gathered there. Janie saw that her expression too had altered. She looked strained and drawn, as she had not done before. Her forehead was puckered. She seemed older, the skin loose on the bone, testament to what she had endured. She moved with difficulty. It was as if, Janie thought, she had lifted from the dying woman – what?

99

Janie turned to Jim Harley with raised eyebrows. He answered as they went back into the corridor.

'Don't ask me. I don't know. It isn't a miracle, the woman can't possibly live. But it sure as hell is something.'

'Mmmmm.' Janie felt less certain than he did. 'You've seen it before?'

'Everyone who works with her sees it. No emotional fireworks, no spectacular cures. Though there *are* cures, occasionally. But it's more the feeling that someone holy has touched you. I can't really be more precise than that. I'm not a doctor, I'm not a priest. I just run this place and find the money and the staff.'

He chose seats for them both at one of the two long tables in the big room where they had drunk their coffee. Most of the people she had met earlier were still there, and a few more had joined them. Mama came in when everyone was seated, gracefully refusing the offered seat at the head of the table. Instead, she paused beside the elderly man in the baggy cardigan and murmured something. He got to his feet, went with evident pleasure to the head of the table, and she took his vacated chair. She was now seated beside the young man David who had been shouting to himself earlier. At no point did he acknowledge her presence, or even glance at her.

Jim Harley said a short prayer and the frugal meal began. Mama did not speak. She shared the meal with them as an act of community, but kept her head bent, as if she were deep in thought. It was almost as if she were alone. She managed this without being distant or rude; obviously this was the way she normally behaved. She ate sparingly: a small bowl of soup, bread, an orange. Everyone drank water. The others, seeing how tired she was, talked quietly among themselves.

How tired and, Janie thought, observing her in profile from the other table, how beautiful. For it *was* beauty. She made no concessions, no effort to please. Her body was angular, ageing, the bones tight against the skin. Her hair was pulled harshly back, she was a stranger to cosmetics, to fashion. And this was her strength: she was unique, an original, starkly elegant in her simplicity. Even her movements, her gestures, were slow, pared down, as if she was conserving her energy, and this gave her an almost balletic grace.

Just once, towards the end of the meal, did she pay attention to anyone else. She turned her head towards the young man who sat beside her, apparently oblivious to her gaze or anyone at the table. Her look was calm, nonjudgemental, without expression.

When they finished eating, everyone stood again and murmured another short prayer. Only David remained seated as the others dispersed. The angle of the sun had altered since the meal began, and he seemed absorbed by the way its rays sparkled on the glass water jug.

Janie, waiting for Jim Harley to finish speaking to a man in the order's violet robe, was the only one who saw Mama stop behind David's chair, saw the sun catch her silver hair. She put a hand briefly on David's shoulder. It was a casual gesture, comradely almost. She said nothing. David turned to her.

It was the first time Janie had seen him respond to anyone. Watching his profile, his head tipped back as he looked up at the figure standing behind him, outlined against the sun's rays, Janie saw his eyes widen, his mouth open slightly. They were caught in a moment of absolute stillness, the woman in white and the young man gazing up at her, linked by her hand on his shoulder, the two of them timeless as figures in a Fra Angelico fresco. Then Mama lifted her hand, moved on.

On her way out of the room, her head inclined as she listened to one of the male nurses, Janie noticed her lift a corner of her robe and touch it to the fine skin beneath the outer corners of her eyes with the gesture of a woman blotting tears.

The two women spoke together, finally, in the hallway at four o'clock that afternoon. Mama was sitting on a hard-backed chair, waiting for her car and talking to Jim Harley and the head nurse. Extraordinarily, indoors, she had on sunglasses, expensive-looking dull silver with exaggeratedly long wrap-around lenses. The sort, Janie noticed with some amusement, worn by teenage boys with money to burn. They were incongruous on her and at the same time oddly mysterious; she could have been wearing a veil. Her already pale skin – the creamy matt skin that goes sometimes with red hair – was almost transparent with tiredness and she had a worn look despite her height, her straight back.

When Jim Harley introduced them, Mama said,

'I am happy to meet you,' and sounded as though she meant it. 'But you must forgive me,' she added. 'It has been a long day.' A deep, almost hypnotically slow voice. The hint of an accent giving a caressing quality to mundane words.

It was the first time Janie had heard her speak. For a second she was taken aback by the perfect English. But of course Mama knew many languages. Or perhaps needed none. So much television footage showed her communicating with equal ease with a small boy in Ethiopia or an old man on the streets of Cairo.

'Mama is addressing a dinner in Oxford tonight,' Jim Harley was saying. 'She needs to rest first.'

Janie did a rapid calculation. Mama had been here at Chalice House from 7 a.m., so must have risen around five. A dinner in Oxford could not be over until ten at the earliest. And she had been on her feet much of the day. It had not occurred to her what phenomenal physical stamina the older woman must possess, and she wondered what it was that compelled her to make such efforts. She looked at her with new admiration and just then, as if she had intercepted the thought, Mama smiled at her.

'You are the journalist? Oliver Jodrell, I think, told me about you.'

'That's right. I'm writing the book suggested by the foundation.' She paused. 'I wonder if we could talk soon when you're not so busy. There are so many questions.' She waited. Mama's expression, behind the dark glasses, was impossible to read. She answered politely without answering.

'I hope everyone is helping you.'

Janie recognized the sheer professionalism of the often accosted celebrity. 'To be honest, I haven't asked for help yet. I wanted to get the early research done myself. There's a lot of material to go through.'

'Much of it is history – and much more is nonsense. I trust you can discern the difference.' Janie looked at her sharply to see if this was a joke, but there was no hint of it. So she treated it seriously herself.

'There *is* a lot of nonsense written about you. Why is that?' She spoke directly, almost offensively, accusing. It was part of her technique, the way she worked. It would, she knew, provoke a strong response. She was curious to learn what it would be.

Mama took off her sunglasses. Like this, close to her for the first time, Janie could see her eyes clearly and she almost gasped at the radiance of them. They were extraordinary, like jewels in her head, the stunning unearthly blue of lapis lazuli. Like the jewels, they could have been formed of mineral, so intense was the clarity of colour. Cynical as Janie was, she felt instinctively that to be the recipient of such a gaze was to receive a benediction.

Mama looked at her steadily. The amazing eyes, the mouth still wide and generous, the look of experience survived written on those drawn features, made a lasting impression on Janie: an image of sensuality transmuted by the spirit.

'That I cannot tell you,' she said, regretfully.

Janie had intended to ask another question but

there was something about this woman, some power of spirit, that made her eager to please her. She found herself saying instead, 'Thank you for letting me see you with your patients today. It was an experience for me. You show great pity for them.'

The minute she had spoken, Janie regretted it. The blazing warmth left Mama's eyes. It was as if she was disappointed that Janie had failed to understand. Her interest in the younger woman seemed to evaporate and she glanced around. A short, barrelly man in a violet-blue robe immediately crossed the hallway to her side. His skull was shaved smooth and this gave him an ageless look, anywhere from thirty to fifty. His eyes were quick and dark under black brows. His robe was sleeveless, his arms muscular, hands clasped loosely and held below his waist. He could, Janie thought, have been a bodyguard, or a Tibetan monk. He inclined his head to Mama in a way that managed to combine respect and familiarity: someone to be reckoned with. Behind her Jim Harley said, very low, 'You will always see Tomas with Mama.'

As if he had heard, the man looked towards them. Janie was acutely conscious of those intelligent eyes on her face, steady, without embarrassment. It was not in any sense a sexual look. He was considering her, calmly, making up his mind about her, committing her to memory. She wondered, for an uncomfortable moment, if he knew she drank too much.

He bent slightly at the knees and offered Mama his arm. She seemed scarcely to touch it, but used his solidity to rise smoothly from the chair. She said goodbye to Jim Harley, adding a few quiet words to the head nurse, touching her arm with a gesture which held respect, affection and long familiarity. She turned to Janie and said, as though nothing had happened between Janie's remark and this moment:

'They do not need pity. They need to be treated as human beings.'

She continued to look at Janie, and the younger woman was conscious of her subtle mixture of softness and strength. Then she put on the sunglasses again. An orderly sprang forward to open the front door and the dark man in the sleeveless robe led her out.

Janie went slowly through the Chalice garden. It could belong to a country convent, she thought, as she passed a hedged herb garden with gravel paths. As she walked away, her head was ringing with Jim Harley's praises of Mama. She saw again the hospital staff, waiting patiently as Mama watched over the dying woman.

In their hands, Magda Lachowska was a deity in the shaping.

Chapter Seven

The boy Patrice Akonda cared for his brother while his mother worked, for she went out every morning in the dark to clean for Madame Bivigou. Patrice was not yet eight years old and small for his age, so he liked to feel important, which he did as he pulled his older brother to school on the low wheeled trolley the sisters had made for him. They were a nursing order with long service here in the Republic of Gabon, and had cared for Jean Akonda since the accident which had crippled him. Jean was a beautiful boy with golden brown eyes and happy despite his circumstances. These were not good: six months ago, when he was fifteen, he had been knocked down by a motorcycle and suffered a severe fracture of his left leg. It was set in plaster, but something was wrong inside. It never healed.

After this, Patrice had caught the whispers and murmurs of a terrible anxiety about Jean among the adults. He heard the nursing sisters tell his mother, there is no life in the bone, the bone is dead. They used new, ugly words. Necrosis. Suppuration. Ulcer. They said, eventually they must take Jean's leg off. He imagined them chopping the slim brown limb on the edge of a board, the way his mother did the chickens' legs when she was cooking. It made him hurt just to think of it.

It got so he could think of nothing else but Jean's leg. His brother was proud and he used to run, and now the leg was shorter than the other, because of the dead bone. Also, it pained him constantly: Patrice had seen him crash his fist down hard on it to punish it. And he hated the trolley. Although it gave him a measure of mobility, it left him down by people's knees like a dog. He never said it, but he believed no girl would go with him now. He made jokes about that. Patrice did not understand the jokes, but he understood the anguish behind them. And sometimes, at night in the room they shared, he heard the harsh, grown-up sound of Jean's grief.

Patrice asked in class if people could grow new legs, and Mademoiselle N'Goua shouted at the others for laughing, and smiled at him, and rubbed his hair. After school, she gave him dragées and said, some for Jean, mind. He saw the sadness in her face. She must have listened behind the door too, when the sisters and the doctor talked about the leg.

Though he loved dragées, he put most of them in his pencil case for his brother, anticipating his grin when he saw them. He couldn't tell Jean about the chickens' legs. He realized it was up to him to get the leg mended, then they would not need to take it away.

Chapter Eight

Janie made a telephone call, to Rome 69884244. A woman answered so rapidly she could make out only a single word. '. . . *Vaticano*.'

On a bitter November afternoon, she arrived at Vatican Hill and made her way to the Arco della Campana, one of the three entrances to the walled, gated and guarded city. St Peter's Basilica rose grey and corpulent just beyond.

Beneath the stone archway two Swiss Guards, caped in black against the cold, grasped medieval pikes in white-gloved hands as they barred her way. The older man clicked to attention and the plume in his steel helmet shivered. Janie started to speak and without any facial or verbal expression the guard said, 'Permissions Office. First left. *Buon giorno*.' He must repeat it a thousand times a day.

The office proved to be just inside the archway, a long room full of people clutching forms and waiting for passes to be distributed by two harassed clerks who first had to confirm each appointment by telephone. Vatican City is a foreign state on Italian soil, with its own laws: no one is allowed in without a reason. Janie sat at a table to fill in her details, the name and title of the man she was to see, and eventually received a pink form stamped and signed by the counter clerk.

Outside the office, she hesitated, trying to align the rapid directions she had just been given with the baroque buildings around her. A City of Rome policeman pointed the way through another archway to a square where a central garden surrounded a fountain. She was struck by the silence, the absence of traffic noise and passers-by. Within this private state, all the paintwork was immaculate, the roads swept.

A group of nuns in formal dress, clearly residents here, billowed past with bulging shopping bags, long loaves tucked under their arms. Each had a dark red heart embroidered on the breast of her habit: Janie wondered if their order looked after the Pope's personal household and apartments.

Beyond the wide oval arms of St Peter's Square she reached the Piazza di Pio XII. She crossed to the east side, to the Palace of Congregations, a modern L-shaped building of brick and pale stone. Beside the entrance, about four feet apart, stood two men in dark blue uniforms. They faced the many windows of the Apostolic Palace. They appeared to be unarmed, but held themselves with the alert stance – feet planted slightly apart, bodies tilted a little forward as if ready to move in any direction – of men carrying weapons. There was a Vatican Central Office of Vigilance: these, then, must be the Vigilance guards. Beneath peaked caps, their heads were close cropped. Their necks were broad, shoulders heavily muscled. Suddenly she felt less inclined to joke about the security here.

The Sacred Congregation for the Causes of Saints was on the third floor. She found the reception desk where no receptionist waited. Beyond were upright chairs, a palm in a terracotta pot, fronds tipped with brown. On a low table there was a copy of the Vatican newspaper *Osservatore Romano*, the station magazine *Radio Vaticana* and a neat pile of photostatted pages. She picked one up. It was an article in Italian, evidently from a magazine. Stapled to it were translations in half a dozen languages including Japanese. She read: '. . . *concept of martyrdom has been widened. It is possible to be a martyr of charity . . . give their life so that others might live, to die for peace and for justice is martyrdom for the sake of the kingdom.*' She tucked it into her briefcase for later.

Corridors led away from the reception area, cream-painted, empty and echoing. She heard a distant door click open, the polite murmur of receding voices. It felt remote, a donnish backwater, cut off from worldly matters. It was a surprise to hear quick, feminine footsteps, to see a middle-aged woman with perfectly cut grey hair, a silk shirt under a grey business suit. 'Miss Paxton? Paola Zegna. The cardinal is expecting you.'

Janie was stunned. She had thought she was seeing a subsecretary, a Signor Calli, who would explain the processes of the Congregation. Even after years interviewing important people, she quailed at the thought of facing a cardinal without her usual careful preparation. Her nervousness must have shown in her face, because Paola Zegna gave her a reassuring smile.

'I think you will find the cardinal is . . .' she hesitated, 'not what you expect. Not a traditionalist.' She led the way along one of the many cream corridors, walking so swiftly Janie had to half-run to keep up. The odd phrase floated back to her. '. . . wonderful man . . . worked here all his . . . writes his own . . . no bureaucratic . . .'

The pile of thick white linen-weave cards lay on the secretary's desk.

Cardinal Norberto Uguccioni Cardinal Prefect
The Sacred Congregation for the Causes of Saints

Janie slipped one into her pocket. The crowded outer room of the cardinal's suite had the antiquated air of a busy solicitor's office a quarter of a century ago. Old black telephones, a heavy electric typewriter. Behind the door, a man's formal black suit and white shirt hung in a plastic bag, cufflinks in place.

In the cardinal's large corner office, Janie put down her briefcase, her eyes drawn by the huge painting which covered most of the wall behind the desk.

It looked as if it had been executed in the Twenties. A white-haired man in a cream robe was standing, hands bound, encircled by fire. The flames swelled around him like the sails of a ship. A spear had been thrust into his side and out of his blood rose a white dove, wings flecked with scarlet.

The juxtaposition of violence and peace held her transfixed. At first she hardly registered the deep, musical voice just behind her. After a moment it repeated, 'The Martyrdom of Polycarp.'

Still staring at the picture she said, 'I don't think I ever . . .'

'Early bishop of Smyrna,' the voice continued. 'Suffered his martyrdom at two o'clock in the afternoon on the twenty-third of February about the year one fifty-five. Or so they say. One does rather wonder how they could be so precise.'

Janie turned. The man behind her was short and broad, his almost bald head tanned beneath the round zucchetto of scarlet watered silk. He wore a cassock in fine wool of deep pink-purple – a colour she had only ever seen in Rome – piped in scarlet with many scarlet buttons. Round his wide waist ran a heavy cummerbund, again in scarlet watered silk, with two long falls down the front ending in thick fringes. A gold cross swung low on his chest. He was still looking up at the picture.

'They say his flesh smelled of baking bread and the fragrance of incense.' He turned to her, held out a hand: for a moment, she wondered whether she was supposed to kiss it. 'Miss Paxton, good afternoon.' His grip was warm, he inclined his head slightly, a courtly movement.

'Good afternoon, Your . . .' She hesitated, at a loss, conscious she should have asked his secretary. '. . . do I say, Eminence?'

He closed his eyes in assent. The effect was oddly demure. She looked back at the picture.

'I wonder why the artist chose to paint him looking so happy? No man could have been burned alive with that expression on his face.'

'I wouldn't be too sure about that. Pavlov showed conclusively in his later lectures that if one area of the brain is in a state of great excitement, the effect is to inhibit other areas. So if St Polycarp's nervous system had been sufficiently aroused by ecstatic visions – and we know that at a certain point of physical and emotional collapse, a mystical trance was commonly experienced by saints under martyrdom, or in cramped cells – then pain stimuli could be blocked. He'd scarcely have felt the fire.' He glanced up once more at the painting. 'I do hope that is the way it was for him. Certainly we now think this might be the explanation for the tranquil deaths of many martyrs. Please.'

The cardinal gestured her into a seat opposite his desk, settled himself in his own heavy leather chair. 'OK. Shoot at me.'

She gave a start. 'I'm sorry?'

'Is that not the correct term? Begin.'

'Oh. Yes. Right.' She put her tape recorder on the very edge of his desk. 'May I?' She clicked the button. 'It's really good of you to find time to see me yourself.'

'I have . . .' he glanced around at the piles of manuscripts heaped on the floor, the tables, the windowsills, 'plenty to do, as you may observe. But there is no great rush. No *panic*. I may be working on files started by my predecessor – and, I might add, I have been occupying this chair myself for nearly thirty years. Or I might be working on something begun more than two centuries ago. So you see, I do have the odd half-hour available.'

'You are the official saintmaker, then?'

He shook his head, reproving. 'The Church doesn't make saints: God alone provides the grace for that. We merely conduct the business of identifying them, putting them before the people. It's a continuous process and highly formalized. We used to do it in a courtroom setting – defence lawyers, the Promoter of the Faith appearing for the saint, and the Devil's Advocate for the . . .' he lifted an eyebrow and said delicately, 'other side. We would even open up graves and examine the corpse.' His bright eyes noted her expression. 'For centuries, it was believed the bodies of true saints smelled sweet. Anyway, we abolished the old adversarial system in 1983 and now it's done on academic lines – research, writing, a dissertation.'

He picked up a small round tin from his desk and struggled to open the lid. 'This is the darnedest . . .' He finally levered it off and leaned across the desk to offer it to her. It contained boiled sweets dusted with icing sugar. 'Candy? The lemon's OK.'

She took one, already charmed despite herself. She was intrigued by the magnificent clothes and the informal manner, the odd mixture of excellent but stilted English and Americanisms he must surely have gleaned from films. 'We can concentrate on pursuing the truth here,' he went on. 'It's like detective work, I suppose. I'm a professional investigator.' The cardinal smiled for the first time. 'The Philip Marlow of the Vatican.'

Janie said nothing, halted in her tracks by this unlikely private eye in ecclesiastical purple. He picked up a letter from his desk, a second sheet stapled to it: she recognized it as the one she had sent to his subsecretary. 'And you are researching a book, I see, on Magda Lachowska. How can we be of service to you?'

'They say she is a living saint and that after her death she will surely be canonized. I thought I should find out something about that process.'

He repeated her words meditatively. 'A living saint.' He made it almost – not quite – a question. He folded the letter neatly back into its creases, smoothing each crease between his fingers. 'A living saint,' he said finally, 'is a contradiction in terms. Canonically speaking. Sainthood is something that grows over time.'

'But surely with Mama, it would happen almost automatically? Thousands of people owe their lives to her intervention and help. She has devoted herself to the innocent victims of violence. She gives hope – and she gives bread. And it's not only the poor who revere her. She's a world figure, received by heads of state wherever she goes.' Janie shook her head. 'I'm very ignorant, but if people are already claiming she is a saint, can even the Vatican ignore strong public feeling?'

He tapped the edges of the letter on his desk as he considered her. Then he said calmly, 'These things take many years, and so they should. Whatever the feelings of the people, she must await the considered judgement of the Church. We do not create media saints to order. There really is no such thing as fast-track canonization.' He held up a hand against her unspoken protest. 'Yes, I am well aware of the demands that the Holy Father speed up the process for Mother Teresa. But how this would work, how soon we may expect results – nothing is clear as yet.' His expression gave nothing away. 'What *is* clear is that we must be guided by the Holy Spirit, not by campaigners.

And the road to canonization is long – fifty years is average, many take a century or more – and complicated.'

Her initial impression had been mistaken. At first glance, encased in the rich robes of office, he had appeared plump, soft. Now she saw he was built like a boxer, solid and hard. His tone, too, had hardened.

'It is not for me to comment at this time. Nor, with respect, is it for you to conjecture. *If* – and I stress the if – Magda Lachowska were put forward for canonization, first we would investigate her thoroughly, how she conducted herself before her claimed visions began, the way she treated her workers. Her writings would be examined for the most subtle nuance. We would interview witnesses and read testimonies. Then, in addition, the Church would establish tribunals in each country where she operated so that witnesses could testify about her life and works. That testimony alone could take a decade. And then it would be years more to prepare the documents for the judges assigned to evaluate the tribunals.'

Janie asked, genuinely puzzled, 'Why subject her to all that, when she has so clearly done so much good? I don't understand. Surely there can be no question that she deserves the title? She has already earned it.'

'In the early days, you know, martyrs were swiftly declared saints. Who could doubt that a Christian stoned to death would be admitted without further ado straight through the gates of heaven? But things are not so simple now.' He stared into space, just above her head. His eyes were half-closed. He was obviously thinking deeply.

Finally, without warning, he leaned towards her, picked up the tape recorder, clicked the *off* button and said, 'We will speak off the record. Yes?'

'I should prefer to quote you.'

The cardinal appraised her. She could read nothing in his dark brown eyes. 'You may if you wish, of course. But in that event I fear you will have to make do with history and platitudes. This is a Vatican matter, you understand . . .' He let his voice slide down into regret, let her absorb the implications for a minute.

'However,' he spread his arms, 'I would not like you to receive false facts, to be given misinformation, perhaps by omission. If I could guide you, Miss Paxton. Deep background, I believe our American friends call it.'

This time it was Janie who deliberated. She did not doubt that the cardinal was, in a very real sense, a man of God. But she understood he was far more than that. Behind his benevolent exterior and predilection for lemon sweets was a sharply honed and determined intelligence, a deep subtlety of mind. Anything less would not have brought him to the position he occupied. He was a prince in this private city-state, this closed world of political conflict and theological dispute.

She nodded agreement. She really had no choice.

The cardinal, with unexpected deftness, took the tape from her machine before placing it back on the desk.

'There is a problem with Magda Lachowska.' He leaned back, hands once more folded across his stomach. 'And if you consider, you will appreciate it. It may be that she is truly a mouthpiece of God. Certainly she does appear at times to be taken over by some higher force, to become the instrument of some greater power. But regard her with a more cynical eye. She is undoubtedly clever. Perhaps she is more manipulative than she appears.'

Janie opened her mouth to argue: I have watched this woman console the dying. I have felt the room hum with the force of her presence. But she did not say these things. She was not here to put forward her own opinions.

'It is not impossible,' the cardinal continued, 'that she is actually undermining the power of the Church. Not deliberately, but because people do not quite comprehend her. I understand she urges the use of birth control. If the church endorses her too strongly too soon, we may find we are actually encouraging the devil's work.' *The devil's work.* The phrase sat oddly with so sophisticated a man. She noticed he was twiddling his thumbs. 'So here is our dilemma. Magda Lachowska may be calculating most precisely the effect she wishes to produce. Or she may be doing, unaware, the very things which set her at the centre of a popular craze. A cult, in fact.' The thumbs were still now. 'Is it the Church her followers worship – or Mama herself? It is in the light of such concerns that we would urge caution.'

'I suppose she *has* inspired a personality cult.' Janie conceded it with reluctance. 'And I can see the Vatican would dislike that. But surely Christianity itself began as a cult, as a movement worshipping a crucified man.'

'Saints were always the object of cults, not inquiry, that is true. It was thought heaven and earth met in the bodies of martyrs: no wonder they were the sites of miraculous events. Their blood and bones, their hearts and toes and finger-joints, even the instruments with which they were tortured, their rosaries and clothes – all were considered to have magical properties, to cure illness and ward off evil spirits. And it is no different today: the bloodstained white mittens of Padre Pio fulfil much the same function.' He sighed, and Janie repressed a shudder. 'It is created by the demands of the people,' he added. 'And it would seem that Mama is highly sensitive to these demands.'

The cardinal contemplated his wide view of the Apostolic Palace and she followed his gaze. What went on behind the many small windows? Other conversations like this one?

'Unfortunately,' he continued, reflectively, 'the word cult has now been debased. We see the object of a cult as some kind of mad guru with hypnotic ability. But if a cult is what people want, they do not seek official approval first. You have only to think of the United States, where there are many hundreds of different religious organizations. Most are local and usually small. But many are huge – and rich. You can watch their television programmes put out by their own stations, get yourself healed, take part in the singing, join them electronically, send them your credit card number by e-mail.'

To her surprise, Janie felt almost defensive. 'But those people are charlatans. Performers. Mama does not do such things. And she is indifferent to material possessions. She eats virtually nothing, she always wears the same clothes. I'm told the rooms for her use in the various Chalice Houses are almost bare.'

'I don't doubt that. But I think you will find she does not reject the credit cards. Everyone needs money, Miss Paxton. Even Mama cannot run her vast organization on faith alone.' Again, he paused with that same deep concentration she had seen earlier. Another decision? When he spoke, his words were slow, measured. 'You should ask yourself too who supports Mama with large sums of money. The little people, of course. Thousands of hands giving thousands of coins . . . It mounts up.'

Janie nodded slowly. Of course much of Mama's money must come exactly as he said, as tiny sums from all over the world. But if a local American preacher could be rich enough to run his own television station, then the amounts sent in to Mama and the Chalice must be vast indeed.

'Such a woman,' the cardinal was saying, 'does attract very strange people, who attach themselves to her for all sorts of reasons. In the case of Magda Lachowska, there are also powerful individuals, international corporations. The influence she wields is astonishing.' He paused. 'Perhaps they wish to expiate their own sins. Or perhaps they are using her in some way, for motives which might be open to, let us say, misinterpretation.'

Janie stared at his twirling thumbs, fully alert now.

Was he telling her the Krzysztof Foundation was suspect? She had been dubious enough herself about some of the board members after that first meeting: she remembered her musings on the train home. But her doubts had been stilled when Robert Dennison forwarded their first handsome cheque. Had she been taken for a fool, blinded by the gloss and glamour? She thought of the invitation to the gala fund-raising evening at the Waldorf-Astoria in New York, the card even now pinned on her noticeboard. She had been delighted when it arrived with a note confirming that her flight would be paid for by the foundation.

'Now *I* am not saying these things are so,' the cardinal went on. 'The Church is not saying this. But . . .' he gestured towards the window, the buildings beyond, 'here, we are the protectors of two thousand years of faith.'

He watched her carefully, as if he wanted to be assured of her comprehension. His dark Italian eyes gave no clue as to his own thoughts on what he had just said. It was the shrewd, worldly gaze of a lawyer or a banker.

A banker. Calvi. Now she remembered – the collapse of the Banco Ambrosiano a few years back, the supposed suicide of Roberto Calvi in London. It was widely understood that the Vatican Bank had played some part, had done business with Calvi after he had been jailed for fraud. And she had read of other, vaguer theories, never proved, involving the Mafia and the Masons.

It was the stuff of fiction but nonetheless she was furious with her own naïvety. The Vatican was no different from any other organization. These clerics spoke the language of commerce in order to fund and preserve the institution which kept them. It was an open secret that the Vatican was always desperate for financial aid. And how much money must Mama bring in each year? Enough, Janie wondered cynically, for her to be made a saint?

She said none of this to the cardinal. Instead, she asked, 'What else is needed for Mama to be canonized?'

He held up a hand. 'You argue that Magda Lachowska is a people's saint already. They have acclaimed her, she belongs to them. I'm not at all sure about the effect the *process* of canonization would have. The financial cost is incalculable – expert advice, the gathering of material, even the price of the party if there is a canonization. That alone is like a huge wedding. And one must admit the process is intrusive and bureaucratic. Would Mama herself want that? Maybe she would prefer that we used the money and energy that canonization would take, to help the people who need it, whom she loves so much.' He paused, and his eyes were quizzical. 'Or maybe she would rather have an account of her life that accords with what her followers already believe and causes no disturbance.'

'Like my book?'

'Tell me. Did you initiate the idea of writing about Mama? Or did she come to you?'

'The foundation . . .' she began. Then she

added, 'Yes, I see. All right. Suppose the process does go ahead. What happens?'

'If all goes well, the person is appointed a Servant of God. They become the Blessed So-and-So. Not all go on to be canonized, of course. That process may take a further ten years. Or maybe four hundred.' Her expression clearly afforded him considerable amusement. 'And then, ever since the Middle Ages, we have demanded that candidates for sainthood must have at least two miracles credited to them, and one must take place after death.'

Janie must have shown her surprise because the cardinal smiled faintly. 'Even if we knew Mama walked on water every day to work, that would have no bearing on her case. We get a lot of criticism, they call us the miracle factory, but let me tell you, that is an area of real debate amongst us here in this office.'

'Why? What is a miracle?'

He repeated, 'What is a miracle?' He gazed up at St Polycarp as if seeking inspiration. 'How long have you got, Miss Paxton? A miracle is man close to the divine. A miracle can come direct from God. Or it may come after the death of a saint, in the form of those many thousands of answered prayers. Some people believe you cannot separate God and miracle. Either way it is a gift. On the other hand, the sceptic says it is a violation of the laws of nature, and that alone is proof against a miracle, since we know the laws of nature are firm and unalterable.'

'And what do you say, Your Eminence?'

He was still looking at the painting of the white-haired man, the flames, the blood, the dove. 'Of course the Church believes in miracles. The Pope accepts that God has performed them, that he has done so in the past and will probably continue to do so.' He rubbed his fingers together as if the tips were dry; a scholar's gesture belied by the strong, practical hands. 'The Holy Father has declared that humanity needs scientifically demonstrable proof that God intervenes in history. The Consulta Medica is made up of leading specialists who consider all potential miracles, using the most up-to-date methods. They cover all possible specialities. In the old days we would simply have accepted that someone like Magda Lachowska had miraculous powers. But now we demand that a cure can be proved scientifically, we want guarantees supplied by the science of medicine. And once a cure is accepted as miraculous, it cannot be overturned no matter what evidence is later uncovered. So you see how careful we have to be.'

'Are all miracles medical cures?'

'Virtually all those we accept. And we have now this conundrum: without miracles, we can have no saints. And without modern science we cannot have proof of miracles. The day will undoubtedly dawn when we renounce this requirement as a confirmation we can do without. But it has not arrived yet.' He turned a heavy ring of gold upon his finger, not aware that he did so. 'It seems to me that science has ripped meaning from the very word "miracle". I fear to see faith retreat before the inevitable advance of science. Because if science explains the miracles, it will leave the Church without its mysteries.'

'But do you think Mama performed miracles, then?'

He turned back to the window. The light had changed while she had been in his office, mauve shadows stretched across the grey stones of the square and a few lights had started to appear in the buildings around them. The cardinal clasped his hands behind his back, the broad fingers interlacing.

'I think, this is a woman with a strong glamour, she exerts a kind of bewitchment. Or should I say bedevilment? She is a wish-fulfiller, maybe a sorcerer. There are those who call her a miracle-monger.'

'That sounds derogatory. And obviously people *want* miracles.'

'Of course. They always have, and I imagine they always will. They crave the supernatural and the inexplicable and this puts us in a difficult position. We clergy tend to be most reluctant to recognize this very simple human capacity to accept the extraordinary, to wonder and revel in the incredible. For its part, the Church both loves them – we too need these strong moments of belief to light candles in people's hearts – but it also dislikes them intensely.' He examined the tin of sweets, shaking them to check the colours, finally picked one out. 'Perhaps we know too much.' He popped the sweet into his mouth and offered the tin to Janie. 'Or perhaps we do not know enough.'

'So you're saying, unless after death Mama provided an approved miracle, she wouldn't be canonized anyway? But you know as well as I do,

Mama does these things very quietly. None of her followers makes a fuss when . . .' Janie glanced at the cardinal and added cautiously, '*if* she cures someone. It's just accepted as a matter of course: it's what she does. Sometimes the cures are gradual, she hears about them perhaps months later. Maybe the same low-key approach will be taken after her death. In which case, there may be miracles but they would not necessarily be in the public domain.'

'That may always have been true. There have been virtually no miracles from communist countries – but that does not mean they have not occurred. Now the climate is changing, I predict a flood of claims from such places as Poland.' He gestured up at St Polycarp. 'Though I daresay he would still have a rough time of it if he turned up in Smyrna these days.'

'What about the people who have seen Mama healing others? Not all of them are believers or even sympathetic. They were witnesses, why not question them?'

'Ah yes, Mama's witnesses.' The cardinal was still looking at St Polycarp, she couldn't read his expression. 'One has heard about the four who saw her in that room in São Paulo when it all began. An unlikely collection, as I recall.' He folded his arms. 'Are any of them still alive, d'you know?'

'I do, as it happens. A journalist in São Paulo did some research for me. It turns out the old lady – Senhora Sayão – became very confused and senile. But she still apparently remembered exactly what had occurred at Mama's deathbed, which seems remarkable. Never varied from her original statement. She lived for another ten years, anyway. The man they called the adulterer, Rico Gomez, seems to have had the worst time. He was divorced soon afterwards and began drinking heavily. Sounds as if he never stopped. He became very reclusive and refused to discuss Mama with anyone. He died in the mid-Fifties. Liver failure. Cuci Santos, the woman he was with, looks to have been very different – delighted to tell it all to the press and anyone else who'd listen. Presumably she made money out of it. She was one of the first people to follow Mama to her mountain retreat. She and her young son seem to have stayed for years, until the poor of the *favelas* brought Mama back to the city. Then some time in the late Fifties Cuci and the boy vanished.' Janie frowned. 'I thought that odd. I mean, the whole business brought her a lot of attention. You'd have thought she would have loved that.'

'Perhaps,' the cardinal observed, 'she moved on to more profitable areas.'

'Yes. I wonder what they could have been? But it's a pity. The son, Tomas, would be in his fifties now. I'd love a chance to talk to him.'

The cardinal glanced at his watch. 'And I too should love to continue talking, Miss Paxton, but I fear . . .'

It was smoothly done. Janie got up, saying ruefully, 'You've given me a very great deal to think about. I'd no idea it was all so complicated.'

'Complicated? I think not.' He came round his desk. 'I believe saints should surprise us. Saints are men and women like you and me, they have the same experiences. But it is their insights into these experiences that are remarkable. That is what they all have in common – and that is what makes them unique.' He smiled as he walked her towards the door. 'Do you read Mrs Browning? A delightful woman, so fond of Italy. She it was, I think, who observed:

> *Earth's crammed with heaven.*
> *And every common bush afire with God.*

So simple. We forget such simplicity at our peril, Miss Paxton. I hope you won't forget it in your researches.'

Cardinal Norberto Uguccioni shook her hand once more. As she turned away, he added, 'I think you forgot something else, though.' He was holding out the tape he had taken earlier from her machine. As she closed his door, she saw him turn back to his desk and his papers.

It had grown so late, all the adjoining offices were deserted. Paola Zegna had started to lead the way down the wide corridor when the telephone rang back in her office. It continued to ring as they walked on, and she hesitated, half-turned.

Janie said, 'I'll be fine. You go on and get it.'

Clearly relieved, the secretary said, 'You'll surely need directions. Would you wait for me at the entrance? Down those two flights . . .' She gestured towards the wide, curving staircase. 'I'll be right with you.' As Janie left the room, she heard the secretary's voice crisp on the telephone.

She waited a good ten minutes in the hallway,

watching through open doors the life of this silent and secretive city. A post office van shot past bearing the Vatican insignia. The Vatican Bank, the telephone exchange staffed by nuns, the private mint, even the electricity generating station, were exclusively its own. Somewhere, she knew, there was a Vatican railway station. As a separate country, it even issued its own passports, had its own duty-free shop.

Eventually she grew restless. There was still no sign of the secretary. She scribbled a note on her pad: *Ms Zegna. Had to leave for another appointment. Very many thanks.* This she signed and left propped against the potted palm.

The short day was drawing to a close and the great iron lanterns set into the walls cast long shadows as she crossed the tiled square. She must have taken a wrong turning then, because after another two hundred yards nothing looked familiar. She had no idea where she was, and there was no one visible she could ask. At this rate, she would still be here at midnight: she remembered that all the gates of the Vatican were locked at twelve, and no one could leave or enter without permission. No other state in the free world sealed its boundaries each night.

Just as she reached a flight of shallow steps, a contingent of nine Swiss Guards and their officer swept down, heels ringing on marble. She stood aside as they passed in their sixteenth-century uniform of blue and orange.

Turning right through a gateway set in the middle of a narrow street, she reached a cobbled courtyard surrounded by three-storey buildings. It must be a tradesman's area: there were plastic boxes designed to hold dozens of bottles, several metal trolleys stacked neatly against a wall. She could hear music somewhere near – not the sound she would have expected here, of bells or organ or choir, but techno music, the hard repetitive modern beat alien in these surroundings. She glanced up a dim alleyway between buildings, saw someone in a dark doorway, black caped and capped against the cold, shoulders moving with the beat. Beneath the cape she glimpsed again the orange and blue of the Swiss Guard. Conscious of scrutiny, the man turned towards her. In his billowing Renaissance costume, in the half-light, he might have been regarding her from another century. He was young, dark-eyed, smooth-shaven. A narrow white ruff encircled his throat, a cigarette dangled from his lips and he held a steaming mug in his left hand: she could smell hot chocolate.

Ten minutes later, with the guard's directions, she was again on Vatican Hill. St Peter's Basilica was lit now, gleaming with many lights. In gloomy catacombs beneath the high altar the saint's bones lay in their casket. And beyond, in shrine and grotto, in chapel and mausoleum, tomb and sarcophagus, were those of past popes: it was sacred, a place of pilgrimage.

Perhaps one day another pope would lead solemn ceremonies here, ordaining that Mama herself be venerated as a saint throughout the universal church. Maybe decades or even centuries would pass before it happened. And maybe it never would: the more likely outcome, she thought, if the present Vatican hierarchy had its way.

That, surely, had been the clear message. The Vatican could not attack Mama, could not disown her. She was an embarrassment they would prefer to do without. But her power base was strong, and growing. The papers were full of the story that when she arrived recently in Argentina, people queued in a line stretching fifteen city blocks to see her. Many had waited eighteen hours through a freezing night. If the Vatican attempted to marginalize Mama, how much money, how many influential sponsors, might not be lost?

A light rain was falling. Busy with her thoughts, Janie somehow lost her footing on the slippery pavement and saved herself from falling only by stepping down into the road.

EEEEEEEEeeeeeeeeee!

The car horn was so close it made her jump out of her skin. A scarlet Lamborghini on the right side of the road, she had no excuse for failing to see it. The headlights blinded her as the car swerved to avoid her, tyres screeching. Someone close behind her stumbled as she leapt backwards, a hand grasped her arm. The driver yelled '*Cretino!*' through the window as he passed.

Dizzy with shock, Janie tried to thank her rescuer, a middle-aged man, with what dignity she could muster. He shook his head, clicked his tongue reprovingly.

'You must be more careful, signora. It's a miracle you weren't killed. *È un miracolo!*'

Chapter Nine

The day after Janie got back from Rome, she went to see Adam. It was just midday as she drove up to the handsome Edwardian house. A small, solitary figure sat at the top of a flight of steps, sturdy in grey flannel trousers and strident fuchsia-red blazer. He waved at her approach and disappeared inside to tell the school secretary his mother had arrived.

When he got in the car, he gave her a quick kiss on the cheek and she drove off.

'You've done it again,' she said, laughing. 'You've grown.' He grinned uneasily. She stopped herself: mothers were so embarrassing. Instead, she talked about the flight back from Italy to get them over the first, always difficult minutes. Even when their separation had been only a fortnight, she never ceased to be startled by the changes in him: already his shoe size was the same as Paul's. The increased confidence in his manner and conversation, his poise, his *neatness*, she always found all this curiously intimidating. It almost made her shy. He was quiet too, perhaps he felt the same. Or perhaps it was something else. Separation was not a new experience, she thought, for them. When he was much younger, when she had been away on a work trip, she would return to find a sullen child who refused to meet her eyes, struggled out of her embrace and moved back behind the shelter of his father. It was as if he was punishing her for deserting him. And people didn't change, she had learned. They simply became more firmly themselves.

In those days Paul had consoled her, had told her how each evening Adam insisted on tracing, on their old globe-lamp, the route her plane had taken, the bit of deep blue or rose-pink or lemon-yellow world she was in at that very moment, whether she was awake or asleep, what she'd be having for breakfast. She had seen Adam's point of view. For a young child, with so short a history, a day is as long as a year. And he was so powerless: he couldn't stop her going, no matter how much he loved her, and so his anger and hurt were his only weapons.

Changing down for a roundabout, Janie glanced at her son's clear profile as he stared ahead, reflected that Paul had always perfectly understood the boy: they were very alike, with their brown-gold eyes, their love of silly jokes. She even thought Adam was developing Paul's high-bridged nose, that made his face all profile. And he already possessed the wide, vulnerable mouth that so quickly turned down in the face of any slight, real or imagined.

Marrying Paul, she had known she was the tougher of the two and the trajectory of her career had seemed to bear that out. But that had evened out now – Paul had the status of his job and a larger income than she, for the first time. The last few months, the divorce proceedings, had shown aspects of Paul she had not suspected. His pain at her brief infidelities had surprised her: did he still love her that much, then? So much that he could never forgive her? It really had not occurred to her until lately that he was still suffering from her actions.

He had been uncompromising, cold, bitter. The nocturnal conversation two weeks before had made no difference to that. She sighed with the thought and Adam broke off the meandering joke he was telling.

'You OK, Mum?'

'I've had a busy few days.'

She pulled into the pub car park on his punch-line which was, incomprehensibly, 'So *he* said, five pee.'

They chose a table in the window overlooking the main street of the village, and giggled about the fact that it was called Main Street. Janie left Adam to order fish and chips for both of them while she bought drinks at the bar, bringing him ginger beer which he hated, but chose because it looked convincingly adult: every sip made him wince.

Happy now, secure in her interest, he talked ceaselessly, pausing only occasionally and briefly to swallow. About Peter Stamford's pet white rat and the new maths teacher. About the boy in his room who'd wet his bed, then enterprisingly poured a jug of water over the rest of it and claimed the roof had leaked. His face was bright with intelligence and humour, he was openly enjoying himself. His shirt had come untucked, brown silky hair flopped over his eyes.

In one of his rare silences, she said, 'You are

lucky, the way you live in the present.'

'Where else could I live?' he asked reasonably.
Without waiting for an answer, he added, 'Dad's
buying my present next weekend.'

They discussed his eleventh birthday and what
he was going to choose when his father took him
to Hamley's toyshop in Regent Street.

Then she said, 'I've been asked to write a book.
A very exciting one, I hope it'll mean I have to
travel quite a bit. I'm going to Poland and I'm off
to America soon. Probably other places as well.'

'Will they pay heaps?'

She smiled at him affectionately. 'That's my
boy. Straight to the important part. Don't you
want to know who it's about?'

'You said America. A basketball player?' His
passion of the moment. She shook her head.
'Winona Ryder?'

'Dream on, Sunshine.' She leaned over and
lightly punched his arm. 'Ever heard of Mama?'

He looked puzzled for a minute, then his face
cleared. 'Oh, yeah, the old lady who wears that
robe thingy. We did her in RE last week when Mr
Patterson was ill and the stand-in didn't have
the syllabus. A whole lesson.' He groaned at the
memory. 'She like, goes round saving people and
seeing things.'

She said drily, 'That's a fairly accurate description, I suppose. Wasn't it interesting?'

'C'mon, Mum! It was all about . . .' She could
hear him quoting the teacher '. . . wonders increasing as the Millennium approaches.' He swallowed
a large forkful of chips. 'Hey, you really meetin'
her?'

'Pretty soon.'

'*Blinder*. Miss said her followers believe she died an' angels brought her back to life. They can't of, can they?'

'A lot of people believe in angels – in the *possibility* of them, anyway. And if you do believe, they can probably do just about anything. Maybe all of them automatically get their first aid badges, which is more than some people managed last term.' She pulled a face at him. 'But she's obviously remarkable, don't you think, if they tell stories like that?'

He chewed thoughtfully. 'She has these visions, she sees things nobody else can. Miss got very excited about them, she said they were . . .' he screwed up his face with the effort of remembering, 'remarkable out-of-body experiences.'

'She's not the only one to get excited. It's really odd. With satellites and spaceships and all the amazing things people can do now, there are hundreds of books about religious apparitions and miraculous happenings and all that kind of stuff, the extreme aspects of religion. It's as if they want magic instead of science. There's a huge appetite for it.'

'Whyzitodd?' he asked, his mouth full. She stopped herself just in time from suggesting he swallowed before he talked. Her mother used to do that.

'Well, because people now are better educated and therefore presumably less gullible. And yet they're getting more and more fascinated.'

'Miss said your lady is a living saint. Except I thought saints had to be dead first.'

137

'I think they do, too. Someone like Mama, someone who has lived a really good and kind life, the Catholic Church declares them a saint a long time after their death. But sometimes people do treat them as if they already were.' She told him briefly about her Vatican meeting. 'Only of course she isn't nearly a saint yet.'

He ate in silence for a minute or two, then changed tack. 'Where are you going next?'

'New York for about three days. Then the week after I'm off to Poland to see where Mama was born.'

'*Wicked!* Can I come too?'

She put on her John Wayne accent. 'Not hardly.'

It was wasted on Adam. 'Oh well. Can we go to Alton Towers when I break up instead?'

'Hope so. I'll do my best. You must remember to be a professional negotiator when you grow up.'

'What?'

'Nothing. Tell me about how well you're doing at football.'

'Huh. Mr James says, it'll take a miracle to get our house a single point this season. He says, we're a load of p—' he eyed his mother and finished lamely, 'poor players.'

She looked suitably sympathetic. 'Goodness. Well, perhaps you'll have one.'

He looked pleased. 'D'you think so? Miss said, because of the Millennium and maybe the end of the world, people will be eager for miracles to give them faith and stuff.' For at least a minute and a half there was silence while he poured more vinegar onto his remaining chips. Then he asked, 'So you don't think the world's coming to an end any minute now? You believe God will look out for us?' He took a sip of ginger beer. 'There is a God, isn't there?'

He was not the only one with questions. Did you tell a ten-year-old that we are but walking tubes of flesh? That we are all Nietzsche's children, shivering in the pointless void? That religion is about fantasy? That the universe was indifferent to him?

She said, choosing her words with care, 'I don't want to influence you. Everyone has to decide for themselves, when they're a bit older.'

'But the Millennium's here, isn't it?' he said, reasonably. 'So I haven't got time to get much older before I decide.'

Oh dear. 'Well, then. You have to think, so very many people do believe in a caring, loving God – and believing makes it true for them. Who is to say if they are right or wrong? I don't know, no one knows.'

'How do I find him then?'

'I suppose you have to search. It's a mysterious quest, like knights and pilgrims. Only a bit different because I'm sure that if God exists, he is somewhere *inside* you. Not an external force but an internal one. So that's where you search. I don't think you can peer around for God and suddenly there he is, like a flag or a tower or something. If there *is* a God, then he's wonderful and inexplicable and . . .' she reached across the table to touch with her fingertips his warm forehead, and his chest above his heart, 'and in here.' She looked down into his intent brown eyes and added helplessly, 'Darling, I can't explain it any better than that. I don't think I believe in God myself. Not right now, anyway.'

He stared at her anxiously for a minute, working something out, then his face cleared. 'But you're all right,' he said. 'You've got no worries. You're *good*.'

She shook her head, overcome. She wondered how long it would last, this lovely, innocent trust. She didn't deserve it, but she could never explain that to her son. She didn't know which was the more important – for him to give it, or for her to receive it. She only knew that both of them were stronger for it.

'Can I tell the others you're doin' a book about old Mrs Angel then? You won't change your mind?'

As always, his rapid change of direction caught her momentarily unawares. 'Oh, you mean Mama.' She grinned at him and pushed the menu across so he could look at puddings. 'I'll have to write it now, won't I, to afford your enormous lunch.'

Afterwards, she gave him a couple of pounds to spend in the village shop, an eccentric place with the original wooden counters and a flypaper hanging above the sliced Mighty White and Mr Kipling tarts. Adam wandered happily around. He bought an airmail letter at the post office booth because he liked the paper, fingered all the packets of biscuits as he tried to decide between Pennysaver Bourbons and Custard Creams, until he discovered half a dozen shelves of videos for rent and insisted on reading the box of each one.

She promised him fifteen minutes, and waited outside. Opposite her, in the churchyard, generations of village families lay one above the other, lifting the level of the earth until the bright grass rose in some places higher than the top of the wall. She crossed the empty road in the sunshine, opened the lych-gate and wandered along the moss-edged path between lichened gravestones. Most were simple, without ornament. One or two had a stone dove or a chunky Celtic cross. Her attention was caught by a fluttering as a blackbird perched on a slanting stone. Behind it, rainwater dripped from the mouth of a gargoyle on the church wall. The bird observed her with a glossy, unfeeling eye, flicked its tail and flew off.

Where the bird had been, the carved lettering was so weathered it had become almost indecipherable. Always curious, without thinking, she made out the words. ... *memory ... infant daughter ...liam ...nd Augusta Old. Born and died ...ember 6 1861.*

That was all. The child had not even lived long enough to be christened. The brief lettering was right at the top of the stone, as if leaving space for other names which had never after all been inscribed. Nothing else – no ornamentation, no loving words, no lines from a psalm, none of the comforting phrases people have always used to soften the bleak impact of death.

The rush of her own pain was unexpected, intense, gripping her in the guts. Oh, God. *Born and died* . . . Her child too, her baby. Born and dead on the same day. She knew, of course she knew, why the poor parents had left the tombstone blank: it was a measure of their speechless grief. She turned, stumbling towards a wooden bench in an alcove of dark conifers.

She wrapped her arms around her body, staring down so hard at the gravel beneath her feet that the tiny stones seemed to move.

She recalled the abortion with horrible clarity. The farce of going through counselling first, the buxom woman in the long skirt and amber beads: 'Just an informal chat . . . if you want to explore your feelings, that's fine. You can say as little or as much as you . . .'

Then – damn and to hell – she'd found she could not, the words would not come. She knew what they needed to hear, that she could not cope emotionally, financially, that she was alone, divorced, already had one child, worked full time . . . but all she could think was that she should get up, get out. The woman was saying quietly, '. . . during the decision process many women see-saw one way, then the other. Part of the difficulty is hormonal and part stress. It's a matter of balancing the practical and the emotional . . .'

Janie knew she had already done her balancing, and the practical had won. There had scarcely been a contest. Until now. Until she sat in the clinic's carefully neutral room with its discreetly placed boxes of tissues and the table marked by many plastic cups of coffee, and felt her nostrils flaring at the faint whiff of antiseptic that meant danger.

The woman was holding out a box of tissues towards her. '. . . let go,' she was saying. 'Don't you worry, just let it all out.'

Janie longed to lay her head on the table and

sob out how much she wanted this baby. What she actually did was sit bolt upright, using every ounce of self-control. The counselling session was superfluous, her decision already made.

But on the day of the abortion she was assailed by a hundred indignities she had not envisaged. The fact that she was older, by maybe ten years, than the majority of the clinic's patients. Old enough to know better. Old enough to have her life in order. She lay in a small ward with three other women and realized that none of the staff, passing the door, so much as glanced in. The patients were invisible, part of the furniture, bodies, not personalities. It was oddly humiliating.

She had imagined this would be far more upsetting than any physical humiliations: she was strong as a horse. Here, too, she was wrong. The enema embarrassed her. The white paper nightgown gaping open at the back was surely designed by a sadist.

She had woken with a raging headache, vomit rising in her throat so she gagged. A nurse brought her a steel bowl and placed it on her knees, tastefully covered it with a paper towel. Barely an hour before they had put her baby, or what remained of it, in a similar bowl and covered it with another paper towel, left it on a trolley while they finished with her.

Janie looked across at the gravestone of the nameless baby. Perhaps hers would have been a girl. She had not asked, to keep hurt at a distance. It had worked for a time. Now she understood: she had rejected her baby's death as she had rejected its life.

For it *had* been life. It may have been no more than the yolk of an egg, but it enclosed the earliest stuff of dream and memory. It was the blueprint of a human being. Even then, it had carried the map of its own destiny. Sex, idiosyncrasies, hair colour, eyes . . . Already these things had been determined. What had she done?

Still staring down at the gravel, she became aware of the blackbird from the tombstone – or one just like it – hopping along the path in her direction, watching with head cocked on one side. Now the glossy eye seemed cold and reptilian. She gave a violent shudder and straightened up. Jesus, she was going out of her mind. With shaking fingers she opened her bag and fished around for the tiny bottle of vodka she had started carrying. She didn't much like the taste, but at least no one could detect it on her breath.

By the time Adam came out to look for her, having worked his way from Danny de Vito via Steve Martin to *Thunderbirds Three*, she had blotted away the mascara under her eyes and brought out a smile from somewhere. But in the car park, before they opened the doors, she hugged Adam close for a long time, her face against his hair, his head somewhere under her chin and his arms tight round her waist. They had long ago got into the habit of saying their real goodbyes by themselves. Then, when she dropped him at the school steps twenty minutes later, he'd give her the quick peck on the cheek that was the public farewell of all the boys.

Only this time, after he turned away, he called

her as she got into the car. As if he'd intuited the depth of her need, he careened back into her arms, nearly knocking her over, clumsy in his uncomprehending desire to console. 'Take care, Mum. Send us a card from Poland . . . lots of stamps . . . Love you.'

'Love *you*.' She tugged his ear gently. 'Fwog.'

He grinned, endearingly gap-toothed. A small fortune, that lopsided smile had cost her in tooth-fairy money. 'Loggit,' he said, and both of them giggled again.

'Don't forget now,' she added. 'Cut out anything you see in the papers about Mama and start a file for me in case I miss it, OK? You're my official researcher as of now. Payment guaranteed.'

The last she saw of him, in the rearview mirror, he was running backwards up the school steps with both his thumbs triumphantly raised.

Driving home in the fading light along a dual carriageway, she came to a place where half a dozen bunches of flowers were piled beside the road. Someone must have been killed here.

She could have died herself on Vatican Hill, under the wheels of a scarlet Lamborghini.

As if the sight of those flowers released recollections she did not even know she had, she suddenly remembered, just before she stumbled, being jostled violently from behind. She had not slipped from the pavement after all: she had been pushed. She tried to recall the man who had 'rescued' her, who had been so close behind her as she fell. His fingers had been tight on her arm but she could not see his features. Try as she might, he remained anonymous, a businessman in a belted mackintosh, his eyes masked by horn-rimmed glasses. Why had she assumed he was a businessman? He must have carried a briefcase.

But would such a man want to push her under a car? What possible reason did anyone have to harm her?

She was desperate for a drink. When she saw a Little Chef sign ahead, she turned in and stopped the car with relief. A cup of coffee was better than nothing. She went to the washroom and splashed her face with cold water. Staring at herself in the glass as she combed her hair, she thought, *just because you're paranoid doesn't mean they're not out to get you.*

Chapter Ten

The train for Swinoujście belonged to the Fifties: painted in vivid orange and green, bright as a child's toy. On the platform, she had bought a tiny bunch of purple flowers, their velvety texture irresistible as rich fabric. The flowergirl attached them to her lapel with a long dressmaker's pin. From a kiosk she got a warm *kielbasa*, a sausage wrapped in bread, and a warmer can of *piwo*. It was the first beer she'd had in Poland: it was cheap and unpleasant, but she was glad of it by lunchtime.

As she ate, they passed through undistinguished towns. People lived in stained grey concrete housing blocks that must once have promised progress, and were now despairingly shabby, balconies strung with washing lines in defiance of the ever-present black soot, the result of boilers burning brown Polish coal. Once they reached the countryside there was almost no traffic, and little activity in the villages. Occasional groups of women toiled among rows of cabbages, tall poplars marked the running of many rivers and the roofs of ancient towns made red-tiled patterns on the land. Ploughs toiled, mostly pulled by horses but sometimes by broad-backed oxen. Once she even saw a solitary man pushing a small plough himself. Traditional farmhouses built entirely of wood, or more modern ones of red brick, were surrounded by barns and outhouses. Often the wide chimney-stack was bedecked with an enormous, unruly nest of sticks beside which a stork patiently waited, one-legged and utterly still. Later, they passed an industrial wasteland where no birds flew, no animals grazed. Nothing flourished here but towering metal chimneys, smouldering beneath an ominous slate-grey cloud of pollution.

Briefly, the train ran beside the Baltic. Between spruce and conifers bent and curved by the strong wind, she glimpsed narrow beaches of fine white sand blown into rounded dunes, and beyond them the flat metallic sea. They passed shipyards. She could see a couple of looming grey hulls, hear the striking of metal, the sound of drills. But most of the area looked deserted. Gates were padlocked, there were few cars or lorries.

Outside the station at Swinoujście she noticed an encampment of Gypsies on a piece of grassy land facing the building. Barefoot and beaded, their skin grubby, hair hidden beneath headscarves and bodies plumped by layers of cardigans and skirts, the women stood, almost all with a baby on their hip or swaddled on their backs as they begged, mainly from tourists. Their eyes were soft, their faces hardened before their time by poverty. Behind them the men lolled watchfully, talking among themselves, handing round bottles, conferring. They wore hats and shoes and exuded a spivvy skimped stylishness.

There were only two taxis, of unfamiliar make and uncertain age. The one she took smelled faintly of sweat overlaid with a strong cologne, and onion. The driver extended a hand, shook hers in his warm grasp and said, 'Jerzy Pozomiek.'

He said a lot more as they started off, driving fast with one hand on the wheel, through hooting queues of the tin baby Fiats that were once the national car and the gleaming new Mercedes and Peugeots now replacing them. Girls of astonishing beauty, with tangled blonde hair and fake leopard coats, strode through the traffic.

They passed expensive clothes shops, packed cafés, boutiques where plate-glass windows, brilliantly lit, glowed with jewellery of gold and amber. They drove through streets of solid, middle-class, nineteenth-century houses, peeling and dilapidated now, divided into dozens of flats. Finally, they reached Magda Lachowska's childhood home.

It was one of a row of cramped dwelling houses in a narrow street, overlooked by more ugly highrise apartments. At one time, the whole area must have been full of such homes, built probably eighty or ninety years ago. They had clearly been overtaken and then left behind by progress. Or maybe the money just ran out.

But when Janie saw that the street name had been changed to *Ulica Magda Lachowska* another reason occurred to her: perhaps this little area had been left untouched because of this woman, the town's most important export, their single claim to fame?

As they neared the house, the driver became excited. '*Mamusia!*' he enthused. 'Yes. Yes! *Mama!*' The house itself was trim and clean in a way it could surely never have been when the Lachowska family lived there. In contrast to the neglected buildings in the centre the paintwork here was fresh, the guttering new, the roof cared for. Tubs flowered in the square of garden. The front door stood invitingly open. She was about to go in when she realized that all the other houses looked remarkably similar. She took a few steps along the cobbled area, looked in at the windows of the house next to Mama's, then the two beyond. All were empty. There was no furniture, no sign of life. But curtains hung at the windows, the walls were painted. The whole street was just like a stage set. Or a museum.

She went back to Mama's house. In the dark hallway a table with a fawn crochet cloth did duty as a desk. It was covered with booklets and leaflets and photographs of Mama, and in the middle a cut glass vase displayed a bunch of artificial tulips. On the wall above them hung a huge gilt-framed oil painting of Mama, as she must have been in her thirties. It was done without any great skill, almost certainly painted from a photograph. She was rigidly posed with her head at an angle, wearing her customary robe. The colours were too bright, the whole thing more real than reality. Below it, a small brass plaque engraved in Polish carried an incomprehensible message and the printed words: *Krzysztof Foundation*. On either side of the picture hung short red velvet curtains, and the whole thing was spotlit. It reminded Janie of the copy of *The Last Supper* reverentially revealed behind swishing drapes at Forest Lawn Cemetery in Los Angeles.

Janie said, 'Good morning,' and the woman behind the desk greeted her pleasantly. '*Dzien dobry.*' She pointed above her head to a hand-painted sign requesting 7,000 zlotys. Janie handed over her money – less than fifty pence – and received in return a blue ticket and a thin printed booklet. For another 8,000 zlotys she bought from a glass case a tiny plaster figure of Mama in her pale robe, the face sweet and unrecognizable. It could have been an image of the Virgin Mary. The woman finally smiled thinly, and gestured for Janie to go in. A group was just leaving, and she stood aside for three women and an elderly man to leave. It took her a few moments to recognize that they were speaking German, but it was a dialect which sounded Dutch. Then she remembered, this place was almost on the German–Polish border. The travel agent had suggested she fly to Hamburg, but she had wanted to see something of Poland.

The leaflet in her hand, written in various languages including English, claimed that the house today looked just as it had when the young Magda Lachowska lived there. Janie doubted it, though the structure had clearly not been changed. No walls had been knocked down, the kitchen was still basic – a stone sink, a small oven built into the wall and heated by coals, a wooden cupboard against the whitewashed wall. There was no fridge but a larder with narrow shelves. A zinc bathtub hung on a nail beside it.

She turned back to the interior of the house. The staircase climbed steeply up the side of one wall but it had no banisters on the outer side. Instead, a thick rope ran from top to bottom.

There was a single room on each floor. One bedroom held two small beds covered with unashamedly new nylon satin quilted spreads, and two utilitarian wooden chairs. There was no space for any other furniture apart from wardrobes of cheap wood veneer.

The largest bedroom had been turned into a viewing room, with a heavy blind on the window and three rows of chairs facing a white screen. A short black and white documentary was showing: it clearly ran over and over again throughout the day. It opened with a picture of the house and a voice told her in English that here Magda Lachowska had been born in 1924 to a simple, close-knit family. Pictures now of a couple on their wedding day. Her father Miro worked at the port, her mother Maria was a housewife. She had two older brothers – two little boys appeared on the screen – who later acquitted themselves with bravery in the Polish Army – there were two young men in uniform. There was a drawing of the school she had attended, bombed during the war, and then the film showed a number of people, in their sixties and seventies, who spoke of the young Magda in glowing terms.

'She was marked out, even then,' one woman claimed. 'She was kind to everyone, and beautiful as an angel.'

'We all knew she was remarkable,' said a gnarled man. 'She used to visit the sick daily. We all remember her here with thanks and with pride.'

'That child was a saint,' according to another woman. 'Such humility. Such grace.'

The other interviews were in the same vein. A

woman in a wheelchair declared, 'She was the person who held her whole family together. She nursed her mother for years, it was wonderful to see.'

'When Magda was little, we used to watch her playing with her brothers. They took such care of her, they were so proud, you wouldn't believe.' The speaker was a man who spoke with a flat, rapid delivery that made her suspect he was reading off a card.

Janie watched the rest without much interest. They all sounded as if their lines had come from the *Lives of the Saints*. She was not surprised to see that the final credit was for the Krzysztof Foundation. As she went downstairs, she could hear the looped film beginning again, this time in Polish. 'Magda Lachowska was born in this very room on 12 April 1924 . . .'

The living room on the first floor had clearly been the focus of a good deal of well-meaning attention. The wooden floorboards had been renewed and scoured, while the ornate iron fireplace was far too large for the area it had to heat, and too obviously expensive for such simple surroundings.

The walls were painted dull cream at the top while the lower half was a shiny khaki. There were light bulbs in etched glass holders on the walls. All round were blown-up photographs of Mama: praying alone, addressing her followers, holding a child in her arms. Many showed her on formal occasions – shaking hands with politicians, meeting heads of state. Here she was with the stout German Chancellor Willi Brandt, there on a balcony in Cuba, the ageing Fidel Castro behind her in his combat jacket. She was pictured in a group of world leaders at the UN, in the front row between Maggie Thatcher and President Mitterrand. Other, earlier photographs showed her younger, even more slender, but the hair still the same moon-silver blonde. In one she was talking with Indira Gandhi, the two women in their long robes close together, Mama's forehead, like the Indian leader's, formally adorned with the vermilion caste mark. In another, she was with the Israeli Prime Minister Golda Meir inside the Knesset, among a group of politicians in open-necked shirts and *kippahs*. There was even a photograph where President Kennedy stood on one side of her, and Jackie, smiling in her crisp little suit and pillbox hat, on the other. Janie stared at that one for a very long time: this was the stuff of which myths were made.

And there were other pictures. Not the studied poses but snatched news shots: Mama hurrying across a deserted street among battle-scarred buildings, the hem of her pale robe mudstained. Mama talking to a group of dishevelled men cradling rifles, their dark faces tired but intent. In another she crouched beside a distraught African woman, steadying her with both hands on her shoulders. At their feet lay the sheeted corpse of a child. Behind them, the makeshift tents of a refugee camp stretched into the distance.

Janie found it difficult to relate these images to this house. It was trim enough now, painted and empty. Full of the Lachowski family – the parents, three children, and she'd read somewhere that the sick grandfather had lived with them for years – it must have been unbearable. Where did they all sleep? And although it was well known that Mama came from simple people, Janie had not appreciated until now that they must have been desperately poor. And yet today Mama moved among the world's elite with confidence and grace. She talked to politicians and heads of state, and they listened with respect. How had she done it? What drive and determination had taken her such an incredible distance from her roots?

Janie went back into the kitchen and opened the back door. Outside, she lit a cigarette and stared around. The little yard was empty apart from a low cage of wire netting with a wooden hutch at one end, where the family must have kept a hen or two. It occurred to her that there was no bathroom in the house, so where had the lavatory been? A low surrounding wall gave an easy view of the backs of the other houses and she could see that each had a small outhouse with a sharply sloping roof built beside the kitchen door. She went over to the wall and looked at the adjoining outhouse. Below the half door was a glimpse of what looked like the base of a water closet, the sort that had to be emptied by hand. Someone must have had the Lachowski outhouse demolished as unsuitable for the home of a national heroine.

It was very quiet. A baby cried somewhere high in one of the apartment blocks, and the sound carried clearly. Presumably, before those were built, other rows of little dwellings adjoined this one, and more beyond them. It was a depressing thought. She dropped her cigarette and ground it out. The whole trip had been an expensive mistake: there was nothing here for her after all, no insights, no revelations. The house had been sanitized. She couldn't get any feeling of the life of its former inhabitants, no intimation of any vitality it must once have held. She'd just check out the family photographs and leave.

These were ranged on a shelf covered with a long, fringed, maroon velvet runner. There were no candles, no incense, but it breathed the atmosphere of a shrine. They were all in elaborate, highly polished frames and those of the children, in particular, exuded the faint perfume of melancholy; expressions of hope and promise not yet touched by life's troubles, by wars or illness, by failure or discontent.

Some of the photographs were tiny, the edges of the paper cut and frilled, others were bigger formal portraits. There were adults and children and even a picture of what, the printed notice beside it informed her, was the grandparents' grave. This was framed in carved ebony and showed a double headstone, with a photograph on each of the deceased and their names beneath.

The central photograph was by far the largest, its position and the elaborate swoops and curlicues of the silver frame confirming the subject's importance. The hand-printed notice beneath identified it for anyone left uncertain.

Janie examined it carefully. The beautiful wide eyes solemnly considering the camera, the smooth fat ringlets, the dark dress covering her knees, white stockings, black leather boots to the ankle with many-buttoned sides, told her nothing.

Nothing except that this child was well loved, indulged. The slight heaviness of the cheeks suggested plenty of good meals, the confident, too-aware gaze reminded her of old Hollywood photographs, of the young Elizabeth Taylor: another little girl who knew her own worth and, with that knowledge, lost something precious. She was posed with one hand on the arm of a delicate chair in what was evidently a photographer's studio. The huge Egyptian vase behind her, and the draped curtain behind that, provided no clues. There was a tiny, scrawled signature in the bottom right-hand corner.

On either side of it and tiny in comparison, were photographs of the parents, clearly taken around the time of their marriage. They were faded sepia in their oval pewter frames, the mother long faced and plain but with merry dark eyes, the father managing to appear sombre and shifty at the same time. They looked an ill-matched couple, though perhaps this impression was reinforced by the fact that their likenesses had been done separately, not together. Neither looked anything like the little girl Magda – nor even, come to think of it, like the photographs she had seen of Magda today. But traces of both parents could be seen in the faces of their sons, in the shape of the head, the look in the eyes.

There were two photographs of the brothers. One showed young boys, playing cowboys and Indians – western hats, Indian feather headdresses and bare chests – standing among fruit canes in a summer garden. It was a moment caught in time. Janie could even make out the grazes on the knees of the smaller boy, the Indian.

The second was of one of the boys, a little older, maybe ten or eleven, his hair brushed smooth for the special occasion. He wore a pale suit and beneath short trousers his legs were thin in ankle-length white socks and sandals. He had an adult-sized tie with large, dark dots. The boy was posed on a kneeler before a pedestal draped with lace. With white-gloved hands he held a prayer-book. He looked wan and rather sad.

For a long time, Janie looked from the photograph of the boy – Romuald, said the hand-printed note below it – to the main picture of the child Magda. They were no more alike or dis-similar than a million other siblings: she just could not put her finger on what bothered her.

Finally she went back to the front door, where the elderly woman was now staring disconsolately out at the street. She thought about asking for permission to examine the photographs more closely, but realized there was no way she could make the woman understand what she wanted.

In the front room, a couple had come down the stairs during her brief absence, and were now looking at the pictures, talking to each other in the hushed tones of people in church. When they had left, she reached up for the frame holding Magda's picture, and took it to the clear light near the window. Now she could see that what had looked like a crease in the plump flesh of the wrist was in fact a slender gold bracelet.

Replacing it, she noticed that the back of the picture was of thin wood, with a long piece hinged on to make a stand. The backing was held to the frame with four pieces of bent metal, one in the middle of each edge. On an impulse, she pushed her thumbnail under the lowest piece of metal. It was soft, and moved easily. She glanced round the room: she was still alone. Quickly, she straightened the other three pieces of metal, and picked the back off. Underneath was a piece of black matt paper, beneath that again the creamy card of the photograph's surround. She'd been afraid she might have to take out the photograph itself which, she thought, could have stuck to the glass after all these years. But there was no need: the name of the studio was printed on the back of the photograph itself and visible just above the edge of the surround. It was in curling art nouveau script designed to impress, and though faded to a dull purplish brown it was still legible.

Studio Zygmunt 60 Nowy Swiat Warszawa.

Janie copied the address into her notebook, though she wasn't sure why, slipped back the black paper and the light wooden back and refixed the metal clips. Then she put the photograph back in its place.

The room was still empty, the ticking of the clock loud as a metronome. She picked up the picture of the boy on the kneeler. This, too, she slid out of its frame. It carried no studio name or signature, and it had been made as a postcard, with a line down the back dividing the address and message sections. The printer's details ran along beside this line. It had been printed here in Swinoujście.

She glanced back to the hallway, where the woman still sat immobile, her face upturned to the sun. Janie swiftly checked two or three more.

Several of the portraits were printed on postcards. And of those, most had been done here in the town.

The woman in the hallway was getting ready to close up, ostentatiously straightening her piles of leaflets, removing the stone dog which held the door open. Janie started to leave the room. On an impulse she turned back, unpinning the little bunch of flowers she had bought that morning at Kraków station. The velvety blue petals were soft now but still pretty. She had no idea why she did it, it was entirely out of character for her. But she left them lying, a crumpled offering, in front of the picture of the young Magda on the mantelshelf.

After Janie left Mama's house, she walked to the end of the street. Her taxi waited next to a sign for McDonald's, Jerzy sitting on the edge of his seat smoking a handmade cigarette, the box of papers and another of tobacco beside him. He jumped up when he saw her and threw away the cigarette. He had a photograph in his hand which he showed her, smiling broadly; an elderly woman and a younger man. He wanted to take her to meet his family. For a minute she hesitated. But the train was not until the evening, she had a sleeper booked. She had planned to go to a restaurant, maybe sit in a cinema. She found herself agreeing.

He stopped the taxi outside a concrete apartment block and led the way up endless stairs, clucking his disgust at the graffiti on the walls. Janie thought the bright slogans she couldn't understand, the jaunty cartoon characters, were all that redeemed the place.

The door was opened by a figure remarkably like Jerzy himself: short and muscular with a wide smile and very white teeth. The two men embraced, clapped each other delightedly on the back, roared with laughter. Like Jerzy, Janusz had a salesman's ready charm. He also spoke excellent German, a good deal of English, some French and a variety of other languages, including Hungarian. It turned out he had spent many years as a purser, working first from his home port, then out of Hamburg and Rotterdam.

Now he kissed Janie's hand with gusto, ushered them both into the apartment, explaining as he did so their relationship. 'This my favourite cousin, you understand, what a boy! My mother say, that one will make fortune or go in jail . . .'

While the two men talked she took in the crowded little room. The light was softened by green plants which hung from hooks before the window, flourished in corners, stood behind the sofa and on the table. Four small cages held chirping birds, and she saw at least five big glass bowls, each containing a single large goldfish. Brown leatherette sofa and chairs were covered with hand-crocheted cushions in primary colours, and on the clean tiled floor were several gaudy rugs.

Five minutes later Irena Pozomiek arrived, and Janie saw that it was very much her room. Like her son and nephew she was round and smiling, talking very fast, welcoming her guests, handing out tiny glasses of *wodka* and little biscuits. Everything she had on – blouse, skirt, cardigan, jacket – was strongly patterned in vivid colours, and no item bore any relation to the others. Her hair was a rich artificial brown like her eyebrows, her mouth painted a deep purply red. She said '*Tak, tak,*' a lot, agreeing with everything anyone said.

Janie found they were to eat here, which made her aware she was ravenous. They sat at the round, crochet-clothed table and out of a vast aromatic pot Irina served *bigos*, potatoes and cabbage stewed in red wine flavoured strongly with caraway, heaped over mushrooms and slices of dark Polish sausage.

The talk flowed around and over Janie who, as the meal progressed, stopped feeling hungry and started to feel tired. It had been a long two days. Then Janusz leaned towards her.

'My mother is well-knowing your lady Magda Lachowska,' he said. 'We have a small town.'

Janie stared at Irena. Until that moment, it hadn't even occurred to her that the two women must be very much of an age.

'You knew her yourself?' she asked. 'What was she like?'

Her son translated rapidly. Irena replied, making a rocking hand gesture that meant, a little yes, a little no. It seemed she had been in the same school as Magda for a short time, in a senior class. She had not known her well. Magda had been quiet, dull, she had few friends, the girls didn't like her. Why not, asked Janie. Because she looked strange. Looked strange? When this was translated, Irena crossed her eyes briefly in vivid impersonation. Irena had forgotten about her for years, until about the time Janusz was born, when her name began to appear occasionally in the newspapers.

'In the days when she was coming down from the mountain,' Janusz translated, a biblical phrase Janie rather liked, 'we hear only something. Then in times, much more noise from her. The cures, the savings. And then she make famous.'

'I want to know about her when she was a little girl. Jerzy drove me to her house, I went round it.'

Janusz interrupted at that point, hastily swallowing a large piece of sausage to do so. 'Many people here hate. They say, too many changes, too clean.'

Janie wanted to laugh, but she saw what he meant.

'When they lived there, how would it have been?'

Irena laughed when this was translated for her.

'My God, in those days it was dirty! No running water, the chimneys all smoked. The streets were just earth. The mud!'

Janie was puzzled. 'But the sink had water. And the whole area was cobbled, I noticed that.'

Irena made another of her dismissive gestures.

'They put in water fifteen, sixteen years ago is all. And electric. They make new road all around. But they *pretend* it to be old.' Janusz looked at Janie. 'You understand?'

'Sure.' It seemed slightly ridiculous but not unreasonable, the desire to gentrify their local celebrity.

Janie asked, 'That photograph of Magda, the one where she's a little girl, in the silver frame? Did she look like that when you knew her?'

This time, when Irena got the question, her

bosom shook with laughter. 'No, my darling, *moje kochanie*, no! I remember a girl ten, twelve, fourteen years – too thin, very thin always, skinny. No . . .' Translating, her son traced feminine curves in imitation of his mother's hands. 'The clothes, not good, the hair . . .' Now Irena sketched flat hair hanging round her face, 'Like this, *tak*? No colour.'

Janie absorbed this in silence. Then she said, quietly, 'Were they very poor, her family?'

Irena considered this carefully when it was translated for her. She got up, went over to one of the birdcages and fed the small grey inhabitant some sunflower seeds. '*Tak*,' she said at last. 'I think, yes.' She played with the bird, her back half-turned to the others at the table. 'We are no rich, in Swinoujście, OK? But we live.' Once more, the hand rocked: a little bit yes, a little bit no. 'Then sometimes bad things happen. When Magda Lachowska very young, the father run away.'

'Where did he go?'

Irena's shrug was a masterpiece. Who knew? Who cared? Janusz lifted his hand to his lips as though emptying a glass.

Janie asked sharply, 'You're saying he drank?'

Janusz nodded, then went on, 'So then the mother is *zrõjnowana* . . . broken? Too many troubles for one person. And for the children, only small money, small food.'

'But how did you know this?'

Irena stared at her, astounded by the question. 'Because people talk. You don't talk in your town?' She started to laugh again. 'When I am a girl we have no radio, no television . . .' she was counting

164

them off on her fingers as her son translated. 'No telephone, no cinema, no records, no milkbars . . . Nothing. Here you can drop dead. So we talk, is all.' She made a chattering mouth of her two first fingers and thumb. 'So we know about poor Maria Lachowska. And I see Magda in school. So sad. So quiet. Old clothes. The eyes . . .' Her own bright brown eyes squinted fiercely for a moment. 'Girls do like this . . .' she mimed whispering behind her hand, 'and I think Magda very lonely.'

'The mother? The brothers?'

'The mother is in house, is keeping old *patus*, he is very ill. Then brothers go.' Her animation fell away. She saw Janie was puzzled. 'Is war,' she said in explanation, her shoulders lifting in a shrug. 'First Russians come take. Then Germans come take.' Janusz translated for Janie's benefit. His mother carried on talking. 'All our young men go to soldiers, to Polish Army.' There was a quaver in her voice, and with quick fingers she wiped her cheek. 'How Poland suffered. I cannot tell you. This poor country.' Despite the rich brown hair, the lipsticked mouth and the assertive colours of her clothes, she was suddenly an old woman. 'Go to soldiers,' she said again. 'The Lachowski boys gone a long time to fight.'

'Did you know them too?'

Irena shook her head. 'The younger boy, Romuald, he goes with Polish Army someplace. The older brother got killed very soon.'

Janie said through Janusz, 'On the film, all the people said, Magda was a wonderful child, a good girl. They said she was remarkable, everyone loved her, she held her family together.'

Irena made a sucking noise, indicating cynicism. She said something rapidly to Janusz and he looked briefly worried.

'My mother says . . .' he glanced at her nervously, 'it's all nonsense. She wasn't like that. She was inside herself, you understand?'

'Selfish,' said Janie and Janusz nodded assent.

Irena said something else.

'She was a nobody. A nothing. A little . . .' he hesitated again, 'a cheap little tart.'

Irena nodded at the expression on Janie's face. Who thought, some phrases are international.

'She went with sailors in the port, from when she was very young. Russian, Chinese, Lascar . . . anything.'

Janie found her voice. 'Does anyone else know this?' The two men looked at each other. Janusz said, 'I think no.' His mother questioned him sharply. When he answered she spoke again, looking towards Janie.

'My mother says, she hear this from my father, he work on the docks. She liked Maria Lachowska, she don't want to hurt her. Is better to be quiet.'

Janie nodded. 'How old was Magda when she . . .'

Irena made a sucking noise, showing how hard it was to remember. 'Is after Maria get ill. Maybe she did it for money.'

'Were you both still in school then?'

Irena was emphatic. 'No!' She was herself again, with peals of laughter. 'Only Magda. Fifteen, maybe sixteen. I was too big for school. Looking for man to marry. So I marry my soldier.

166

Later is time for babies.' She leaned across and rubbed Janusz's crewcut hair. 'Always time for babies.'

He grinned and extricated himself. He brought in a coffee pot and poured with professional deftness, proffering each cup on a small tray with cream and sugar. Janie stared at her pad, at the notes she had written earlier in the narrow house on the other side of town. She stirred her coffee. The room was briefly quiet but for the chirruping of the birds. She watched Janusz, who was chatting quietly to Jerzy.

She thought of the photograph of the little Magda. So shiny and curled and confident. So plump and gold-braceleted. That was the picture of a cherished bourgeois child, not a thin little scrap from a poor home where a drunken father disappeared, leaving a desperate woman to struggle alone.

Studio Zygmunt, Warszawa.

Out of her thoughts Janie asked, 'Did you ever go to Warsaw, when you were a child?'

Janusz translated and Irena went off into one of her peals of laughter.

'Warsaw? *Warsaw?* Never was I to Warsaw.' She laughed so hard she had to wipe her eyes with the edge of her cardigan. 'Gdansk, yes,' she went on when she recovered her composure. 'Even Kraków one time. But Warsaw . . .' She shook her head in amazement at the very idea. 'People from Swinoujście do not see capital city. Only Janusz know Warsaw.' She looked at her son with pride.

Janusz translated and added, 'Now some

peoples visit, but in old days no. Big journey. Very expensive.'

Janie was certain now that the photograph was not of the young Magda. That was why she got nothing from it at all, no sense of the person she was looking for: it was a different person. But why would anyone take the trouble to find this picture and present it as Magda Lachowska?

There must be a reason. Perhaps the town simply couldn't find one of her. But there were pictures of everyone else, surely there would have been one or two of the young Magda. Maybe if she had looked as Irena described, then perhaps the Krzysztof Foundation decided this beautiful child was what people wanted to see, not a thin little wisp with unkempt hair.

All right, she could accept that.

Janie let Janusz pour another cup of his excellent coffee. She smiled her thanks and enjoyed this odd encounter and the comfortable room, and was grateful for what she had discovered. Then she thought, wait a minute.

'Janusz,' she said, leaning towards him, putting a hand on his arm. 'You and your mother have been incredibly kind already but . . .'

Jerzy drove with Irena Pozomiek in the front seat, directing him, talking non-stop, pointing out the biggest buildings in the town, the concrete Russian military base and the hospital that served its staff. It was evening now, most people were home. Irena guided them to five apartments. Of the four people they eventually talked to, all were around her age. The three women and one man were happy to reminisce about Mama, and Janusz became adept at asking the same questions without Janie's prompting. He received, and passed on, virtually the same replies from all four. But they were replies very different from those Irena had given her earlier.

Tak, Magda Lachowska had been a wonderful girl. Yes, so happy, so full of joy, of love. Such a smile, such radiance. Everyone was drawn to her. The family were close, loving, those boys adored their sister. The father? Yes, a good man, worked hard, did his best . . . The mother? A saint, poor soul, sacrificed herself for the children, scrubbing and cleaning. Of course, she knew what a treasure she had in Magda. Most certainly, even then the child was touched by the finger of God . . . When, prompted by Janie, Janusz asked what had happened to Magda when she left Swinoujście, they were unable to supply even an idea. She had gone, that was all they could remember, after the death of her dear mother. Much later she had reappeared in South America. By then, of course, the miracles had begun.

The last person they took her to see was a farmer. The car swung past the port and drove out of Swinoujście. Passing what looked like a warehouse standing alone, a cluster of cars around it, they heard the repetitive beat of music and caught the flash of lights inside. 'DiscoPolo,' Janusz told her. Jerzy asked him something and he laughed, and obligingly sang the English lyric to a melody which might have been composed by a three-year-old. *Polka-dotted knickers, polka-dotted knickers.*

The farmer was gentle and soft-spoken, with

the uncomplicated face and blue eyes of a man for whom the truth is a simple thing. He told them just what they had heard before. Driving away, Jerzy spoke swiftly and seriously. His aunt and cousin nodded, then Janusz translated for her.

'He thinks, we could talk to twenty more people, and they will say the same words. They are not making you a lie: they only want to tell you something good to hear.' He patted Janie's hand. 'Perhaps is no big deal. Mama is good woman, great. Does many big things. So if there is a little bit of story-making by people in the town, what matters?'

He was right, of course. These people were guilty only of the same deception as the black and white documentary made by the Krzysztof Foundation. The foundation might have a hidden agenda but Irena's friends clearly did not. It had all been long ago, and the past was a better place.

The Magda they remembered in Swinoujście was no more real than the plaster figure in her bag, no more real than the painted likeness behind its curtains in the drab hallway.

But Irena had pulled back those red velvet curtains just a little to reveal something disturbing. Magda had had troubles. She had not been a loving, friendly child, not a little saint in the making. She had been thin and lonely and selfish. She squinted. And screwed sailors before she was sixteen.

The long day and the strain of the unaccustomed language had tired Janie. The car was warm, the others spoke softly in Polish, she felt her mind drifting. In those slipping seconds she released, somewhere deep in her unconscious, the dark doubt about Mama which she had felt before. Just for a moment, it stirred again, and stretched, more strongly now. There was no time for comprehension: it was gone, and she slept.

Chapter Eleven

On the Internet, the entry for the Chalice of the Grapes of God ran to many pages. It began by welcoming the visitor to the web site, and suggested, 'Make your visit count, load this image.' It gave the address of the motherhouse in Rome, then Mama's birthdate: b. 12 April 1924. A photograph started to feed into the screen: as the sun's rays appeared at the top she recognized Jane Bown's portrait, the one that had been adopted and used so widely it had almost become Mama's symbol. Janie had even seen it badly reproduced on T-shirts. Then came a brief description of Mama: mystic, healer, a conduit of grace. The next line said:

Learn More about Mama:
* An introduction to Mama
* Mama Prayer Groups
* How You Can Help. Addresses of Chalice Houses
  around the world.

There was a long article detailing all the familiar early happenings, naming the first four witnesses to Mama's death and rebirth: Cuci Santos, Tomas Santos, Rico Gomez, Manuela Sayão . . . Janie reeled through it all at top speed. She slowed down when she reached a leader reproduced from *The Times*:

The media has itself helped create this superstar saint. Perhaps this explains how she has been able to transcend religious barriers. It is remarkable that a Christian should be accepted by followers of all other great faiths – Moslem, Hindu and Jewish – and universally regarded as a deeply holy woman. They all walk in candlelit procession to honour her, all take part in twenty-four hours of prayer, with priests of all denominations holding different parts of the service.

Janie stared at the words on her blue Apple screen, scratching her fingers impatiently through her hair. Maybe she was too cynical to be writing this book. Religion for her belonged firmly in childhood. It was all tied up with Sunday morning services followed by a big family meal. She and Paul had not wanted a church wedding, had been married in a register office from her grandmother's home in Lincolnshire. Later, back in London, she had dutifully taken Adam to their local church when he was at junior school in Putney. She had received little bunches of daffodils on Mothering Sunday happily enough, had even managed to make him silver-foil-covered crowns with jewels of Rowntree's fruit gums so he could be one of the Three Kings at Christmas. That was the extent of her religious conviction. And yet now, here she was struggling with questions she was unfitted to tackle.

She got up from her machine, yawning. She had been unable to sleep last night – and so many others before it – and when she did, the sad ferocity of her dreams was so disturbing she woke in a panic. She dreamed of a sea of tiny, naked babies and surfaced through them to find her face wet, her throat tight, choked by pangs of bitter regret. At any rate, she told herself grimly, she did not need an analyst to interpret those images.

Today – last night – she had made tea and started work at three o'clock. Work was the only resource she felt would not fail her. It was Sunday morning, and she'd seen no one since Thursday. Saturday had been Paul's day to take out Adam. She had wanted desperately to ask Paul, could she go instead? She had not done so. He would have agreed, but in that way of his she knew so well, not commenting but making it clear he was aware she had nothing else to do with the day, no one else to see.

Face it, girl, she said to herself, you're in a state. The operation – no, face that too, the abortion – was only eight weeks behind her. Her body had healed, her mind had not. She was bad-tempered, had no appetite. Her answering machine was full of messages she couldn't be bothered to answer. Not even the work ones: Bob Dennison at Odyssey had phoned at least three times. Her nice GP had said, look, it's hormonal, your body was getting ready for a baby. She had listened, made some sensible comments, had altogether been as sympathetic as a waiting room of patients outside would allow. She had let Janie run over her appointment time, told her to come back next week if she needed to. Then she wrote out a pre-scription for a week's supply of sleeping pills: not enough, as she jokingly said, to do any damage.

Janie leaned over to flick up a corner of the

blind. It was dark outside, but there was a gleam in the east, it would be light in half an hour or so. An ache of some kind – of deprivation – rose up in her. She went to the deep cupboard in one corner and brought out an old pair of Paul's heavy cords and his favourite thick Irish sweater, the colour of clotted cream. She ran a hand over the ribbed and bumpy fabrics, full of the strong emotion handling his possessions still gave her. He'd asked for those clothes back, along with his dressing gown, and she had lied. She told him she had already given them to charity shops. It had not been a conscious decision, to lie. It was out before she realized that she wanted those clothes here. Their presence meant something of him remained with her. She rejected the rows and bickering that went inevitably with his physical presence these days. But she understood that, despite the way she had behaved, she still was not ready for the harsh reality of being divorced: she missed him terribly.

In the kitchen, she put the heavy-soled walking boots on the floor for later. The thick socks kept out the cold of the stone-flagged floor while she made herself a cup of coffee and a piece of toast. Then she reached far back in the cupboard, behind the olive oil, for the bottle of Scotch. More had gone than she remembered. She poured some into her mug of tea, sipped it, added a drop more. She left her toast untasted. Casually, almost without watching what she was doing, she found a glass and tipped the bottle of Scotch again.

Breakfast done, she put on her boots, picked up a torch and shrugged into her donkey jacket.

* * *

175

She walked into a long valley she had never come across before, so narrow it was little more than a cleft in the rocks. At the northern end, where she entered, a dark green stream swollen by weeks of rain hurtled over a ledge of rock in a cascade of white spray. Twelve feet below, the stream was broader, swift flowing, so clear she could see pale stones beneath, and a dark flicker of trout. On either side the rocky banks were steep, starred by a few small plants left from autumn, their leaves brittle with frost.

She followed the path of the stream downhill, clambering among the rocks. By the time she realized it was slippery and dangerous she had gone too far to retrace her steps and it was easier to go forward, charmed by the secrecy of the place. She and Paul must have passed it a hundred times and never noticed it was here. But once she had reached more level ground and her effort was less concentrated, she found the beauty of the valley dulled. Her limbs ached with tiredness.

Her exhaustion was mental as well as physical. It was hardly surprising: her life was changing drastically. Her own decision, but the despair was no less for that. She recognized that this was depression, but knew very well the reasons for it. And understanding them, how could she ever hope to come out of it? It was a vicious circle she would never ever break. She was worthless, she had no guts, no strength. She'd lost – no, be honest, she had deliberately chosen to murder – her unborn child.

The truth made her quake. She had shaken her head when Dr Simon joked about the sleeping pills but she could end it all, if she had to. As swiftly, the thought was gone, leaving her full of unfocused anger.

It frightened her, she did not know who it was meant for. It could be for so many people, so many reasons. Perhaps for herself, for her stupidity in letting her body make its own decisions, her callousness in allowing herself, however briefly, to contemplate deserting Adam. Or for Paul, who had let her go without a struggle, who sent her chilly notes without salutation or signature, who had not given her the child she had so much wanted. Or for the man who had fathered the baby, who had casually impregnated her even as he prepared to leave her.

Her mind pounced. She wanted to kill him, to force a knife in deep under his heart. For a moment, for just too long, she actually saw herself doing it. She saw the triangular steel blade of her kitchen knife slipping through the coral-coloured Jaeger sweater she'd just bought him, heard him gasp, experienced his warm blood sticky on her fingers. Then, absurdly, she remembered he hadn't liked the colour and changed the sweater for a dull green one. The bastard.

Janie was not accustomed to physical violence. She yelled a lot, but that was about as bad as it got. And yet she had vividly imagined the knife going in, the initial resistance of his flesh and then the swift glide of the blade . . . She sat down abruptly on a boulder. The violence of her emotions after all this time was alarming.

Growing calmer, she made herself a promise: she would never get involved with another man.

Love was what she didn't want, not again. It brought responsibility, anxiety, dependence and pain. Often it was not love at all, but only lust hiding its demands behind a gentler and less selfish mask. The last time she sought it, she had ended up in an operating theatre with the smell of her own blood in her nostrils. She would manage without love. She would pursue a life for herself that was not based on a sexual relationship.

The rockface at her back rose grey and tall, protecting her from the wind. The sound of the fast-running water was soothing. To leave the narrow valley, she would have to climb back up the way she had come, and she needed a rest first. She pulled up her legs, pressed her forehead against her warm corduroy knees and stayed like that for a long time.

She did not think she could have slept, but the day had changed. The sun had moved so she was no longer warm, but in cool shadow. Even in the enclosed valley she felt cold. Cold and – something else – strange, filled with a painful yearning that belonged to adolescence.

She lifted her head and stared towards the stream. It was running as fast as ever, she could see the white foam where it swirled over rocks, spray glittering in the sun that now shone on the water. The scene had a piercing clarity. Every frond of browning fern, every rounded head of damp green moss, seemed etched as precisely as a pattern on glass. The sharp space around each leaf looked artificial, exaggerated, as if emphasized by a spotlight.

It was then she became aware that the sound of the wild water had faded, receded into the distance. There had been birdsong, a dog somewhere, its sharp distant barks carried on the wind. These had all softened to nothing. It was so quiet, as though she had been struck deaf. Like the moment before you fainted, Janie thought. I hardly slept last night, that's all. And I'm hungry: I was a fool not to have eaten before I left.

Only she was not mistaken: the whole valley was filled with a damp green hush, a vast expectation, a waiting. And then she knew she was no longer alone here, in this quiet place. She turned, almost fearfully, to look downstream.

For a few seconds she believed it was a hallucination. She was hungry, tired, the ideal state for the appearance of a vision, some manifestation. A great animal – a deer – was swimming strongly against the current. It reached a flat sweep of rock, struggled to haul itself from the water. It lowered its head and shook itself violently, the water drops flying, before moving swiftly to an outcrop of rock where it had a view of the valley.

She gazed at the broad backward sweep of many-branched velvet horns, the great heavy head, the length of the magnificent body. It was a male, a stag, powerful in its prime. It stood very still, alert, black silken nostrils twitching, scenting the air. It turned its supple neck and looked towards her. She could have sworn she saw herself reflected, a tiny shape, in the depths of the liquid oval eyes.

In the past, out walking, they had occasionally

179

glimpsed distant does with their young, shying away at the first hint of their presence. This was different. The animal was aware of her but confident in its majesty, and unafraid. It was she who trespassed here.

The light that touched the stag was golden, clear, a healing light. The creamy winter coat gave it a heraldic, mythic quality. If she had seen it at night, by moonlight, she would have believed she was bewitched. But there could be no tricks of the eye here, no mistaken shapes, no blurring or softening of reality. And yet it was mysterious as a white unicorn on a tapestry.

Janie held her breath, filled with a primitive awe. She did not know how long it was before the stag lowered its head and began to move away, taking its time. Gradually, she became aware of the sounds of water again, birds calling. The stag finally reached the more open ground at the valley's southern end. It flung up its great antlered head, broke into a canter and raced out of sight. She had not realized there was another way out, hidden by the curve of rock. It must be an easier route, perhaps even grassland: the boulder on which she sat reverberated to the drumming of the stag's hooves on the hard ground.

It was a long time before she got stiffly to her feet and started down the route the creature had taken. She felt calmer, the anger that had pulsed in her for so long stilled. She walked with a determined step and all the way out of the valley, she thought about the beautiful creature, the wild freedom of it. Once back on the familiar track they had all taken so many times, she found she was planning: she would get back to work. She would write to Adam today . . .

She realized what she was doing and was puzzled. A stag had been in a valley, that was all. So why did she feel such a lifting of the heart? As if something had been given, and received?

Chapter Twelve

They had eaten at the same Covent Garden restaurant before, but that day it seemed a poor choice, half-empty, depressing, a semi-cellar with inadequate lighting. The furniture appeared flimsy, the staff curt. Janie's swordfish was a mistake, lukewarm and tasteless. Perhaps the truth was, normally she would not have noticed these things, or cared. The lunch she shared with Claudia Aubrey every two weeks was not about food, but communication and long affection. They purposely avoided anywhere fashionable where either might meet colleagues, and usually lingered on over coffee, reluctant to part and go back to work.

Claudia had the sharp eyes and sixth sense of all successful theatrical agents for the emotional and physical state of her clients – and by definition in her case, friends – however well disguised.

'You've lost weight.' From her that was almost an accusation. She scanned Janie's face. 'You're looking much better. Over it, are you?'

Janie made a rueful face. 'More or less. I have bad days, still. It's taking longer than I thought.'

'You shouldn't expect too much of yourself for a bit. Everyone makes light of abortions, don't they, so long as they aren't the ones actually having them. Pop in during your lunch hour, we'll have you back at your desk in the afternoon.' She blew out her cheeks in annoyance. 'Bloody doctors. Bloody *clinics*. It's an assault on your body, never mind your feelings. Of course you have bad days, you poor girl. You need a holiday.'

'No time. I'm eating well, though. I shouldn't be thinner.'

'Cutting back on the drink?'

Janie winced. Claudia knew everything about her, but she could never come to terms with this total candour.

'Don't make me sound like an alcoholic. Dorothy Parker drank too much and you're always quoting her.'

'Dorothy Parker also did tranquillizers and barbiturates and was an all-round mess. Come on, get real. You qualify for the title.' Claudia's voice was tough, but her expression was totally sympathetic. 'Don't use booze as a crutch now. It may become more indispensable than it is already.'

Janie reached out to put her hand on Claudia's.

'Sorry to snarl. I know you worry. But as it happens, I stopped. Five days ago. Cutting back doesn't work for me. It's all or nothing. So I'm trying nothing. Anyway, it seemed a good time to make a few changes. And believe it or not, I'm exercising.'

'I'm impressed.' They grinned at each other. Claudia was a big woman who possessed the self-confidence to accept it. She always looked wonderful. She had the lustrous mass of hair, the rich pearly skin of face and neck that can render plump women ravishing. She dressed in brilliant colours, luxurious fabrics, to emphasize her body, not disguise it. 'What brought that on?'

Janie shrugged. 'All that sitting in front of the word processor was giving me an enormous bum and making my shoulders ache. I had to do something.' She added, joking, 'Maybe it's Mama's influence.'

Claudia said, thoughtfully, 'You wouldn't be the first person whose life she's changed. Maybe she really is a sorceress. Isn't that how your cardinal described her?'

'There are plenty of people – men – in the Vatican who believe she is.'

'Well, they would, wouldn't they? I should think she'd drive those old blokes mad. That place is all about male domination.'

Janie stared at her. 'That's it,' she said slowly. 'Of course. It's not what he told me at all. It's not about cults or the fear that she's manipulating everyone. It's much simpler than that. Mama is a woman of influence in a church run by men. She's taken the power they've wielded for centuries. They had it channelled, administered, marked by titles and special clothes. And then this person comes along and she has power too, and they can't believe it.' Janie leaned forward, ticking the points off on her fingers. 'She was a woman, she was young. She was a nobody, she was poor. As far as they're concerned, she should have been mute and helpless, because that's what they're used to. But no, she's just the opposite. She has real influence, she's articulate, people flock to her. And when that influence began to grow, when she started to open hospitals and meet politicians and maybe even influence them, it must all have become totally unacceptable.' She leaned back. 'No wonder she disturbed them in the Vatican. No wonder they hated her.'

Claudia gave her a shrewd look. 'That's quite a speech. I didn't realize you were on the side of the angels here. Thought you were just doing this book for the money, pure and simple.'

'And the prestige, don't forget that. I'm writing about a media saint. She's a phenomenon.' Janie picked up her glass of mineral water and added fervently, 'Don't get me wrong. I don't want to rock the boat. As far as I'm concerned, Mama is just what the Krzysztof Foundation and everyone else says she is – a saint bar the shouting. I go along with it. That's what people want to read about and that's what they'll get.' She held up her glass in a mock toast and drank. Then she added, 'And I need it all to be as quick and as painless as possible. Definitely no headaches or setbacks.'

As the lunch progressed, Janie observed Claudia with growing concern. She was a consummate operator, her own problems were always hidden in public, even from those close to her. But under the professional charm and chatter Janie sensed she was preoccupied; listening, there was something pensive behind her eyes. And she rubbed her forehead repeatedly, a sure sign of stress. Janie leaned forward and caught hold of the anxious fingers.

'Come on, tell me. Tell me how Lucy's getting on.'

Janie and Claudia Aubrey claimed to have met in the labour ward of the Middlesex Hospital. The truth was a little more prosaic. Both had been queuing one afternoon for the pay telephones in the hallway outside the maternity wards, briefly free of the incessant demands of their three-day-old babies for feeding or bathing, burping or soothing.

Janie had at once noticed the big woman reading a script, a briefcase at her feet, glasses jammed among dark curls. What on earth was she doing there, so quiet and preoccupied among these giggling young women chatting to their mums in Willesden? When, after twenty minutes, the queue did not seem any shorter, they had exchanged glances and then grumbled cheerfully, drawn together by the fact that they were the only people not wearing robes and slippers. The script reader was in a long denim skirt, while Janie had brought with her a pair of soft old cords and a matching shirt.

The woman, standing in front of Janie, made her call first. She had an actress's distinctive voice, low and strong.

'Good morning. Claudia Aubrey speaking. David Puttnam's office, please.'

Thoughtfully, Janie rang her features editor, to warn him that her piece on Lauren Bacall was going to be at least a week late due to circumstances beyond her control. As she walked back to the ward, Claudia Aubrey caught up with her.

'I couldn't help overhearing,' she said apologetically. 'I hope it wasn't rude but – *Lauren Bacall*? *Really?* I've always wanted to meet her.'

Janie smiled widely. 'I couldn't help hearing either. David Puttnam? *Really?*'

Janie was right: Claudia had indeed been an actress but had hated the life. 'Too passive, I couldn't stand it. All that sitting around waiting for people to ask you to do stuff in three months' time.' She had worked in her agent's office as a temp and found that her experience in two television comedy series had given her a good grounding. Her father wrote filmscripts, and she seemed to have a feel for the problems of both the acting and production sides. She joined as a junior and ten years later opened her own agency.

After they'd talked for twenty minutes, Janie had said, 'I'll show you mine if you show me yours.' Claudia's baby was a girl, with her mother's dark curls. Adam, by comparison, was so blond he looked bald. They joked that he was the first of a new and hairless race.

The friendship was fuelled by illicit cigarettes and clandestine bottles of wine smuggled in by visitors, sealed by a mutual hatred of the hospital's cod casserole. When they left the Middlesex they kept in touch. Their partners – Claudia lived with a frenetically busy television producer – did not get on particularly well, but that if anything was a bonus, because they were able to talk more freely on their own. And they talked about everything. Men and babies, work and sex. Claudia became closer to Janie than Louise, her own sister. Louise was their mother's daughter. Determinedly unimpressed by Janie's achievements, she yearned only for babies. She did not see marriage as a trap. She saw it as a nursery.

Claudia and Janie, on the other hand, were united by their careers and their ambitions.

Claudia was the first – and for a long time the only – person in whom Janie confided when she and Paul began the slow drift apart. Later, as the bitterness grew, Claudia alone saw the angry tears.

When Janie and Claudia had known each other a year, they shared the first birthday party for their babies. One chocolate cake with two candles, little presents wrapped up in big boxes. It was noticeable then that Lucy was the more physically advanced: while Adam was still contentedly shuffling along on his bottom, Lucy was already pulling herself up against the furniture. Her speech, too, was more developed. She had recognizable words – duck, dog – where Adam was still burbling nonsense. A couple of months later, both children were given the usual measles, mumps and rubella vaccine. Adam grumbled for an hour or two. But Lucy was flushed all that day and refused food. It was a week before she was better.

Four or five weeks after that, Claudia and Lewis began to notice a change in Lucy. She became withdrawn, listless. Where before she had been sweet-natured, slow to tears and full of smiles, now she was fractious and cross. She no longer slept through the night. She stopped talking altogether, she stopped trying to walk. When she started banging her head against hard surfaces – the walls, the tray of her high-chair – they took her to the doctor.

First, a bad case of glue ear was suspected. As time went on, they feared she might be partially deaf, her language development was so poor. At two-and-a-half she began with a special therapist.

After a few visits, the woman warned Claudia and Lewis that Lucy lacked the normal child's ability to read the basic body language of other people.

At three, she was diagnosed autistic. Claudia fought this with total determination, declaring that Lucy did not have the classic symptoms of autism. The head teacher of the school to which she was subsequently sent, which specialized in such children, agreed. Finally a psychiatrist said there had been brain damage. At that point they moved, and changed doctors. The new GP told them he had another child with a strikingly similar problem. The parents were among the four hundred or so families in Britain seeking compensation from the Department of Health, on the grounds that the vaccines for measles, mumps and rubella had caused lasting physical damage to their young children. Some suffered from arthritis or epilepsy, some from conditions which attacked the bowel. But by far the most common complaint was a form of autism.

It touched Claudia's whole life. Where once she had been perpetually light-hearted, she became anxious in her daughter's presence. Janie had seen the change sweep over her as she put her key in her front door. It had taken its toll on her relationship with Lewis.

Lucy was a beautiful girl, but difficult. Years of speech therapy had given her, at eleven, the speech of a six-year-old. Adam did not like to play with her. She was either indifferent to his attempts at friendship or, without meaning to, would behave with a cool violence he did not know how to deflect. She was frequently incontinent. She had almost no social skills: she would clamber over people as casually as if they were part of the furniture.

With great concentration, Claudia sliced her cutlet into tiny pieces and answered Janie's query.

'Nothing new. Just the usual problems. I think when Lucy was younger, I somehow always thought, she's got time, she'll improve, she'll get there one day. And now I have to accept that more than likely, she won't. And the bloody case is still going on, it looms over us. And even if we win compensation, so what? She won't ever be like . . .' she shot Janie a guilty look, 'like other kids. Sorry, sorry. I feel so angry. And guilty. It just never goes away.' She sniffed.

Janie put a hand on hers. Like Adam, Claudia had been going to say. And of course it was true. For years she had veered between heavy sadness at what had happened to Lucy and a kind of sneaky gratitude: thank God it wasn't Adam. Now she said, 'It could as easily have been us. It was just a fluke. There's no reason for you to feel guilty, you know that. And the way you cope – you're fantastic.'

'No, I'm not. I'm so depressed I hate myself. Lewis wants to put Lucy in a full-time special needs school now she's eleven. He says he wants at least the semblance of a normal life again. I'm unhinged at the thought of losing her seven days a week. And God help me, I'm desperate at the prospect of keeping her at home.' Throttled by emotion, Claudia shoved her plate violently away. 'Oh God, why did this have to happen to us?' She reached out a hand. 'I don't want to lay it on you. But what am I going to do, Janie?'

Parting – Claudia was off to a meeting with the head of Drama at the ITV Centre, and Janie left for New York in three days' time – they hugged, hard.

'Take care of yourself, Claud. We'll talk as soon as I get back, OK?'

Claudia smiled, but it was wistful. 'Maybe you could ask your miracle lady to come up with just a little one for us.'

Chapter Thirteen

Romuald Lachowski took a long time to answer his telephone, and his voice seemed very far away. After a pause he admitted yes, he was home, she should visit before dinner time, he got very tired in the afternoons and anyway his daughter might be out then. They agreed eleven o'clock that morning. Janie checked she had her tape recorder and notebook and took the elevator down to breakfast in the pink-neon-lit coffee shop off the main lobby of her hotel.

Nutley, New Jersey was twenty minutes from New York's Penn Station. Standing on Washington Avenue, where weeds grew in the cracks of the sidewalk, she reflected that it could have been two thousand miles away. The place had a deserted, Sunday morning feel. She walked along the wide street with its low buildings, past a delicatessen, a hairdressers where a woman sat alone, draped in black towels, her hair full of the ridged curlers of a perm. Tina Turner sang from a repair yard where an invisible mechanic hammered away among dismantled vehicles.

Janie passed a windowless bar set just beyond a trucker's car park. In daylight, the pulsing light-bulb sign saying GO-GO LOUNGE AMATEUR TOPLESS DANCERS looked sleazy and sad. The apartment block she wanted was right beside a depot of grunting buses. She rang the bell marked 6, speculating what sort of a life could have brought a Polish major to this narrow bleached building. The door was opened by a nondescript fortyish woman neat in a tartan skirt and acrylic sweater. As Janie introduced herself, a man's voice shouted, 'Let her in, Noreen, don't stand there on the sidewalk!'

The woman lifted her eyebrows at Janie. 'He don't like people moving slow,' she said. 'Other people, anyways.' When she got through the door, Janie saw what she meant. An elderly man was standing in the kitchen doorway, a padded leather crutch beneath one armpit, one trouser-leg dangling empty and neatly folded up above the ankle. His face was creased and irascible. Heavy lines from nose to mouth, furrowing his forehead, mapped years of pain. He said to Janie, in only slightly lower tones, 'You're late.'

Janie looked at her watch. It was exactly two minutes past eleven but what the hell, she needed information, not argument.

'Sorry.' She kept her voice neutral. 'Do you still have time to see me?' On an impulse, she held out the orange lilies she had brought to Noreen. She didn't look as if too many people gave her flowers.

'I'll put 'em in water for Da.'

Janie said, 'I meant them for you.' Noreen took them, an odd expression on her face. 'Thank you,' she said in a low voice. 'They're just . . . thank you.'

There was silence behind them. Noreen put a

193

hand on Janie's arm meaning, wait. Then her father cleared his throat.

'Yeah,' he said without much grace. His voice was still loud: he must be deaf. 'I've nothing better to do. Might as well stay. Now you're here.'

Charming. Janie slipped off her coat and Noreen put it on a chair by the door. 'He'll eat outta your hand now,' she said quietly. Janie went across and held out her hand.

'I'm very pleased to meet you at last.' It was her best smile. 'They told me at the Krzysztof Foundation that you were too ill to see me. I hope you didn't mind me phoning anyway. I so much wanted to talk.'

He nodded, mollified but far from won over. 'They phoned me. That guy Oliver Jodrell? He said he thought any more interviews would be too much for me, at my age. He'd heard I'd been ill. I told him, you're right there, I've got enough to do, don't see people no more. Haven't the time for it. Haven't time.' He put emphasis on the last word and Janie remembered he was older than Magda by five or six years, making him nearly eighty. 'That Jodrell, he pulls out all the tricks. Calls me Major Lachowski.' He gave a yelp of amusement. 'Talked about the old days. Speaks perfect Polish.' He gestured to a chair.

She sat, glancing from father to daughter, searching their faces. They resembled each other strongly – heavy features, small bright eyes, tight mouths. No trace there of Mama's aquiline beauty. Noreen took the flowers away and Janie slid her notebook from her bag. 'I'm very serious about this book, I want it to be as good as

194

possible. I need all the background I can get.'

He grunted and moved slowly towards a work-table beside the wall, which Janie hadn't noticed. It held an electric sewing machine, a pair of men's trousers still folded beneath the needled foot. Three or four business suits hung from the top of a cupboard. He angled himself into the chair, propped the crutch beside him and switched on his worklight. Somewhere out of sight Noreen was running a vacuum cleaner over the floor, closing doors.

Romuald Lachowski looked over at Janie from under straggly grey brows. 'Should think there's been enough stuff written about her so you could use the paper to mop up the Baltic. Whyjewanna do any more?' She noticed he did not use his sister's name.

'I was asked,' said Janie. 'And I'll be paid.'

She detected a flicker of amusement in his eyes.

'At least,' he said, 'you're honest. I like that. Most people tell me . . .' he mimicked an earnest, high-pitched voice, 'oh, your sister's so wunnerful, such a good person, we must know every little t'ing you remember about her.'

Janie didn't answer. He put on a pair of black-rimmed glasses and switched on his machine. He was replacing a zip in a pair of cavalry twill trousers.

'Were you close,' Janie asked, 'to your sister?'

Even over the sound of the machine, he seemed to hear her clearly enough.

'About like most kids, I guess. She was younger than we was, we din pay her much mind.' The Polish was still recognizable in his speech.

'It must have been a surprise to you, when you found out what sort of person she had become.'

He kept his head down, deftly manoeuvring the fabric around the foot of the machine. 'I guess. She always was a good little thing. Always doin' stuff for people.'

'Like what?'

He answered smoothly, 'Feedin' people, helpin' them, visitin' them when they was sick.'

Janie nodded.

When Noreen came in to offer a cup of coffee, Janie smiled and thanked her and looked curiously at her left hand: no rings. Romuald Lachowski growled something Janie couldn't understand and the daughter hurried out of the room, to return a moment later with a glass of foaming white liquid, some sort of medication. Janie looked around, at the furniture bought forty years ago and well cared for. Although there were a couple of sports papers opened on the sofa, she could see nothing that might belong to a Mrs Lachowska. Not even a pretty print on the wall, not a women's magazine. And the room had a dry, masculine smell.

On top of the wide-screen television was a photograph in a wooden frame of a thirty-year-old Romuald and a sharp-featured blonde woman holding a little girl. No pictures of any grandchildren. So it looked like just him and Noreen, and maybe she had a home somewhere else. Not much of a life. The old days must be in his mind a lot, he'd as good as said so.

She said, changing tack, 'Have you been back

home? Since the war? You know your house is now a sort of shrine to Magda?'

Nah. He had not been back. What for? When Janie told him about the painting, the film show, he shook his head over his machining and made a dismissive sound.

'There were several photographs of you there,' she added. He looked up at that. 'One of you in the garden with your brother.' He screwed up his eyes.

'Poor Stani. He always had lousy luck. Got killed in the first weeks of the war.'

Perhaps, she reflected, he was too old for regret. There was certainly none in his voice.

'Were you with him when he was killed?'

'Me? No. I was three years younger, not even in the army then.'

'So then it was just you and Magda.'

'I guess.'

'Does she ever visit you here?'

When he didn't answer she tried that one again, a little louder. No response. She said, instead, 'There's another picture of you. Taken in church, in a linen suit and white gloves.'

He said, over his shoulder, 'I got another like it some place.'

'Right. It's nice.' She watched his back. 'Funny that your parents took Magda all the way to Warsaw to be photographed. At Studio Zygmunt, wasn't it? But they didn't take you. Or Stani.' No reaction. 'I suppose,' she went on casually, 'they made more fuss of a pretty little girl than of a couple of scruffy boys.'

The machine went quiet. 'That's what you t'ink.'

'What do you mean?'

His head was still down as he folded the trousers meticulously, smoothing the creases. 'You don' unnerstan' what it was like. We're poor people. Men, boys. They were important. Girls, women – no. They stay in house, marry, go to the husband, stay with the babies. So you have two sons, they bring in wives – you have *something*, you see what I'm saying?'

'Well, I saw the picture of her. The name of the studio was on the back.'

'Sure. An' I'm the king of the Jews.' He lifted his head from his work. 'Anyways, I don't remember no picture like that. I don't remember *any* of her.'

Janie described the plump little girl so carefully dressed, the curled hair, the bracelet. Romuald Lachowski listened without much interest.

'She weren't pretty like you say.' His tone was dismissive. 'She was like a piece a string. An' a little worried face always frownin'.'

Janie said, 'It doesn't matter. I must've got it wrong.'

He seemed angry, suddenly. 'That Oliver Jodrell din' say you'd want all this kinda stuff. I'm supposed to tell you 'bout how happy we was.'

Janie said, softly, 'Were you?'

She couldn't see his eyes behind the black-rimmed glasses, but something in his face altered. He said aggressively, 'What's it to you?'

'I don't know.' She shrugged. 'I just got the impression maybe things at home weren't really quite the way the Krzysztof people want me to think. Not so – pleasant.' She watched him closely. 'You must know how it is,' she went on, her tone sympathetic. 'They do their PR stuff. It's all about money really, isn't it? Mama is a great person, humble beginnings but always loving and caring. Now she needs *your* help to do her work. They don't want any mention of problems. They don't want real life, do they? None of the messy things.' She paused for a second and thought, why not? 'No drunken fathers deserting their families, no mothers struggling to survive. Nothing to spoil the image.' She added, wickedly, sure it would get him, 'She must be rich, now. Magda.' He was still holding the trousers in long-fingered artist's hands. He smoothed the fabric over and over, unaware what he was doing, lost in thought. He didn't speak, and neither did she. She just waited. The silence grew between them until she thought he'd forgotten she was there. Then he sighed heavily.

'So they told you, in Swinoujście, about the Lachowski family?'

What they hadn't told her in Swinoujście, he told her now. He described being woken in the night for beatings from their drunken father, of their mother pulling uselessly at his shoulders, screaming, trying to stop him. His mother with swollen eyes and an arm she couldn't use for months after he had finished with her. Of freezing days when they all had to stay in bed because they had not enough warm clothing. Of the evening they ate the last of their chickens. Of the efforts he and Stani made, as young boys, to do the man's tasks around the house after their father disappeared: chopping wood, mending the leaking roof.

He never once used Magda's name.

When he had finished, Janie said, softly, 'And your sister, a little girl from such a home, managed to do so much for other people. Giving food to them, nursing them. It's remarkable. Isn't it?'

He shrugged. 'If you say so.'

If she had really needed the information he gave her, Romuald Lachowski would have been a grave disappointment. She found it impossible to know how much of what he said was the truth, how much he had been told – and, she thought, most probably paid – to say. She believed his stories about his early childhood. They were too painful to be anything but accurate, and they confirmed her disquiet about the material she had already been fed. But she suspected that Romuald himself, though he clearly did not like his sister, had over the years unconsciously absorbed the idealized, romanticized version of her life. He maybe didn't even realize he had done so. Now it was entrenched in his own mind. And repeated often enough, told to people who knew no different – thus are historical myths created.

At one point Janie said, 'Someone who remembered your sister told me how devotedly she looked after your mother.' She could practically hear the taxi driver's aunt, her magenta mouth full of cake, almost spitting her disgust over the way Maria Lachowska had been neglected.

He nodded. 'A good daughter. She nurse our mother 'til the end. Tuberculosis, no easy. But there was no hospital care like now.' He thought a bit. 'We hadn't got no money anyways.'

Janie said, 'So you say your sister never left home?'

'No, no. Girls no leave. She stay wit' our mother like I say. Took care of everyt'ing.'

Janie said, without any inflection, 'But you were in the army, weren't you, when all that happened. Not anywhere near your home. You wouldn't really have known what went on.'

Again the hesitation, then, 'She tell me much later. Letters reach me and so on.'

'Ah.' Janie was tempted to ask him about the rumours she had heard of Magda's escapades with foreign sailors, but it was the man's sister they were discussing after all. She said, instead, 'And your mother died when?'

He looked at her for a moment with a slightly stunned expression.

'The date? You want the date? I don' – some time aroun' 1943 maybe.'

'Then what happened to your sister?'

The stunned expression was still in place. He said, vaguely, 'Wha'?'

Janie repeated her question. It seemed to annoy him.

'Really,' he said, 'I jus' don' know.'

Noreen came into the room and said, loudly, 'Sure you do, Da. She went to South America. Remember.'

He brightened. 'Yeah, right. To . . .'

'São Paulo,' said Noreen. She sat down and gave her a father a quick, suspicious look.

Janie asked, already knowing the answer, 'What did she do there?'

'She worked for a businessman.' Again, Noreen

supplied the answer. 'A Polish businessman. Very wealthy, I believe. She looked after his children.'

'What sort of business?' This, Janie very much wanted to know. But Noreen just shrugged. Behind her, her father slowly hauled himself to his feet, armed his crutch and shuffled from the room.

When he'd gone, Janie asked, 'Tell me about your aunt. Do you know her well?'

Noreen said quickly, 'I haven't seen her since I was real small. I didn't always live in New Jersey, you know. I was in Toronto for years. She's always busy and all, somehow we never . . .' The sentence ended in a shrug.

'She's in New York right now, as it happens. For a benefit dinner dance. That's why I'm here, too.' She watched the woman's face in vain for a hint of interest. 'Will you be seeing her?' Noreen shook her head. 'So really, you just know about her from what your dad tells you?'

The hesitation was just a fraction too long. 'Guess so.'

No, thought Janie. Someone else gave you all this information. Someone who wanted to make sure people like me got the right story. She remarked, 'He's an interesting man, your father.'

Noreen managed to find an expression that was both pleased and wry. 'He's quite a character. My mum was the only one who really understood him.' She looked worn out, now she stayed still for a minute. 'He can be very difficult sometimes, especially since the stroke.' Janie nodded sympathetically. 'He's more mobile now. But like he forgets stuff, all the time. Then he gets mad at *me*.'

'That must be awful for you both,' Janie said.

'Too right,' Noreen agreed. 'Time seems to have kinda altered for him. He remembers when he was a little kid, that's no problem, it's like those things just happened. But other stuff, it's real weird the way he can't hardly recall things . . .' She suddenly realized who she was talking to. Her eyes widened, and she shut her mouth hard.

'I hear what you're saying,' said Janie softly.

Romuald Lachowski came slowly back into the room. He looked up at Janie from under those straggling eyebrows. He must have been following his own thoughts. 'Sout' America, you say? Long ways from Swinoujście.'

'You're a pretty long way from Swinoujście yourself,' she pointed out.

'An' tha's a fact,' he said, and nodded to himself.

Outside again, waiting for a truck to pass before crossing the street, it occurred to her that she was further than ever from knowing what kind of woman Mama was. Romuald Lachowski had described a cipher, that was all. He had used the same predictable, suitable words she had heard before, words which revealed nothing. Magda Lachowska seemed to have left no impression of herself, no trace. Nor could she reconcile what she had learned from Irina Pozomiek in Poland with any of it. And the photograph of the young Magda was, she was convinced, another child entirely.

It was as if the woman was deliberately eluding her.

Glancing up, she saw a green neon sign above a tarmac yard. JESUS LOVES YOU.

Chapter Fourteen

Janie took a bus down Fifth Avenue to the corner of 42nd Street and her favourite place in the world, the New York Public Library with its massive stone lions, the deep blue banner with the word TREASURES slung today across the high-columned entrance. She trudged up the echoing staircase to the McGraw Rotunda on the third floor. The stone candelabra flanking the marble-edged door to Room 315, the main catalogue room, were already woven with little coloured lights. She went through to the galleried room with its special library sounds: hum of air-conditioning, scrape of chairs, rustle of pages being turned beneath blue-shaded brass lamps. The rows of screens were all labelled. Contemporary Authors, Criminal Justice Abstracts, Social Sciences Catalog Index, Philosophers Index, Bibliography of Native North Americans, Chicano Database . . .

She spent the whole day going through newspaper reports on Mama, working through micro-fiche until her head throbbed. She concentrated on the nationals but went into local papers in the larger cities: Washington, Chicago. At around one o'clock she walked over to a deli and bought a lox and cream cheese bagel, a polystyrene cup of coffee. She had lunch standing on

the library steps – it was too chilly to sit down –
listening to a couple of young black women from
a Schomburg Center group arguing about
genetics, then went back to run through *Time*
magazine from 1960. The first one she looked at
had a specially commissioned painting of Mama
reproduced on the cover over the words WOMAN
OF THE YEAR.

What she found at four fifteen made the eye-
aching hours worthwhile. A tiny reference to
Mama brought up the *New York Review of
Books* for 1986, when Lippincott had published
Church and State by Professor Angus Portmain, a
theologian and academic at the University of
Urbana-Champagne. As it turned out, the book
said little or nothing about Mama: her name had
only been picked up by the reviewer in order to
illustrate the massive power of the cardinals. In
1957 a Commission of Inquiry had been set up in
Brazil by the local bishop to decide whether the
events surrounding Magda Lachowska's alleged
death and return to life, and the successive
miracles claimed for her, could be considered as
divine signs. In 1964, according to Professor Portmain, the commission was dissolved by Cardinal
Cesar Viani before it had reached a decision. It
was an action unprecedented in the entire history
of the Vatican. No reasons were given. No further
commission was ever convened.

Janie read this several times, then literally ran
out to the two telephones in the corridor. Direc-
tory Information gave her the number and she got
through to the theological department on the
Urbana-Champagne Campus. Professor Portmain

listened while she explained herself.

'I haven't actually read your book,' she added apologetically, 'so this is incredibly rude of me.'

He said cheerfully, 'I don't believe I know more than half a dozen people who have read it. I only object when they *pretend* they have. I know just the man you need: a French priest. Faure, Savelle, some name like that. He was a member of the commission and he's still very bitter about the way it was thrown out. Hold on while I find my old address book . . .'

At five thirty she raced back to the hotel through the crowds, showered and washed her hair. She pulled on a short straight black velvet shift, pearl drop earrings and a pearl ring, a black leather coat. She always deliberately underdressed for functions like this: she was an observer, not part of the action.

Many of the people thronging the lobby of the Waldorf-Astoria were familiar from newspapers and magazines: they could have walked out of Fifth Avenue windows. She recognized Donna Karan, Calvin Klein and Bill Blass. Ralph Lauren, John Galliano, Carolina Herrera were all there, in the glossy flesh as well as on the labels. There were socialites and politicians and company chairmen, pop stars and artists, comedians and classical musicians. She recognized several faces she had last seen on book jackets, caught a glimpse of Zazi de Lisle, tiny and dramatic as a humming-bird in electric blue and black with jet jewellery, talking to Liz Tilberis from *Harper's Bazaar*. There were enough Hollywood beauties – male and female –

to make her wonder about the size of the security operation necessary to police all this.

Janie was crossing the lobby, on her way to leave her coat, when the hubbub made her stop and turn. An elderly uniformed bellboy, his round hat on the side of his head, hurried past, his face eager. 'Mama!'

Although there had been no announcement, people seemed to be coming from all directions to converge at the pillared entrance hall. Television lights were switched on, crews were swinging cameras into position, microphones were held high.

All Janie could see at first was a group of men, shaven-headed, clad in the sleeveless violet-blue robes of the Chalice. It occurred to her for the first time that they looked more like Buddhist monks than members of a Christian order. There was a simplicity about them, a serenity, that placed them apart from those around them.

Then the men separated and Mama materialized in their midst. Despite the fuss and noise she seemed cool and unruffled. She turned her head from side to side, acknowledging people she knew, smiling slightly, pleased but clearly not overwhelmed by the welcome accorded her. Janie thought, how does she do it? In anyone else, it would have seemed actressy, the smooth professional patina of showbusiness. But something about Mama, some extra quality, stilled criticism. She had the same serenity as her followers. And there was in addition a clarity, a purity about her. That intensity of presence could not be learned, it was part of her. Classically sculptured features, emphatic without a hint of make-up, she exuded a tangible radiance.

Janie watched the faces of the crowd clustering eagerly around Mama. These were sophisticated city people; whatever generated this enthusiasm, it was not religious fervour. Men in tuxedos craned for a glimpse of her, women waved arms encrusted with jewels as they clamoured for her attention. Someone beside Janie said, as if they were answering her unspoken question, 'All of that stuff she does . . . she's just real *good*.' Janie remembered that someone Russian – Tolstoy? – had said, how complete was the delusion that beauty is goodness. And, she added to herself, how understandable.

For Mama *was* beautiful, with an ageless grace. She was still slender in her customary creamy garments; she seemed untouched by that thickening that comes to almost all ageing bodies, the bulking at jaw and shoulder, hip and thigh which neither exercise nor surgery can halt. Her slight build made her appear tall, but the shoulders of the men around her almost hid her from view. The hair in real life was as striking as in any of her photographs, gleaming sleek and cool, making her easy to follow among the eager press of people around her. Janie noted with fascination the way she held herself, quiet and calm, slow moving, the still centre of the excited crowd.

Watching the woman who had come to dominate her life to such an extraordinary extent, she could understand even in that brief moment just what all the fuss was about.

★ ★ ★

The ballroom of the Waldorf-Astoria shimmered with lights. Janie thought she could actually hear the women in their dresses and jewellery: a faint rustling and jangling just below the music. An orchestra in evening dress played Sondheim and Bernstein as nine hundred diners sat at round tables to enjoy Lobster Thermidor and imported strawberries. Everyone except Mama, who as always would be served a small portion of white fish and vegetables. It was her custom, and long ago accepted.

Janie was at the press table, which meant someone else was paying for the meals eaten here: in her case, the Krzysztof Foundation. It also accounted for its situation at the back of the room near the waiters' door. Somewhere in the room, a bow-tied Oliver Jodrell was in his urbane element as he flattered and flirted, coaxing promises of further donations, of support, of publicity.

She was craning her neck towards the top table where she could just see Mama, when a man's voice beside her said, 'I am aware that everyone in this room is present not for the glamour of the occasion, nor even for the food. They are here, I am convinced, purely to give their support to a worthy cause. They must therefore be kind, caring people. However, the number of furs I can see with one eye closed suggests that neither animal welfare nor the preservation of rare species are of any concern to our fellow diners and dinettes.'

Janie smiled and turned to the man sitting on her left. He had a great voice, deep and difficult to place. Interesting. She looked at him for the first time. He was somewhere in his late thirties, maybe early forties. Around his eyes, lines from the sun, and amusement.

She said, 'I like dinettes. Is it your own?'

'It is now.' He opened the other eye and turned to her. She noticed that the accreditation card above his place setting said simply *David Chester. WWA.* He saw her eyes on it and added, 'Wide World Airlines transport Mama's people all over the world virtually without charge. They invited us tonight by way of acknowledgement. I'm in the legal department. Tonight I seem to be representing the company.'

'I see.' She felt suddenly, absurdly, light-hearted. 'An opportunist. And possibly a plagiarist.'

'Unknowingly.'

'Sadly, that is no defence. My advice to you is, get yourself a good lawyer.'

'Can't. No money.'

She giggled again. 'Then you're very much in the minority tonight.'

'Aren't I, though? I was hoping, if I sat among them all . . .' he indicated the diners at the main tables, 'for long enough, I'd catch rich. Like a cold, or . . .'

'Smallpox,' she suggested.

'Gee, thanks. How perfectly sweet of you.' He looked at her down his nose, which was rather long. 'Still, they do say, stinking rich. Not very nice, so maybe it is a sort of contagion, like a really horrible flu. Only I see it as more like Madura foot or Corrigan's button. You know you've got it, all right, and it really affects your life but without spoiling anything.'

'Madura foot? *Corrigan's button?*'

He shrugged. 'They're in the medical diction-aries, that's all I know. Though come to think of it, they might be cures rather than ailments.'

'Oh, oh,' said Janie darkly. 'A hypochondriac.'

'Don't put me down . . .' He peered at the card above her place setting. 'Don't put me down, Ms Paxton. It's right in there. Hypochondriasis. A chronic mental condition in which the affected person's mind is constantly occupied with the delusion that he is seriously ill.' He started ticking off on his fingers. 'Ailments generally refer to the stomach or the liver. That's me. I used to think it was alcohol, see, now I know it's hypochondriasis. Much better.' He ticked another finger. 'Self-centred and gloomy turn of mind that prevents the patient from doing much of his proper work. I've certainly got that, haven't done a stroke in weeks. And I haven't told you the worst thing.' He gave a melodramatic sigh and attacked his lobster again.

Janie said, 'But you will.'

He gave her the benefit of a wide smile. 'How nice of you to ask. The worst thing is, it will pass gradually.'

She wrestled with her own lobster. 'What's wrong with that?'

'It will probably pass into melancholia.'

'What's the cure?'

'Isn't any,' he said inelegantly with his mouth full. 'Apart from making a strong effort of will and taking up some active work which *may*, I say may, distract my thoughts, the condition is very difficult to treat.'

'So make a strong effort of will.'

He dipped his fingers in his fingerbowl and wiped them on the large linen napkin. 'I lack the will-power to make a strong effort of will,' he said sadly. 'And I actively dislike active work.' He put his napkin down. 'But we've talked enough about me. Let's talk about what's wrong with you.'

'Must there be something?'

'There always is,' he said with mock solemnity, 'when one has lost one's first bloom.'

'Gee, thanks,' she said, smiling, 'how perfectly sweet of you.'

'Nothing wrong with your short-term memory then.'

'Nothing wrong with me at all, really,' she said. 'Or nothing that a month's holiday in some remote and glorious place that has never got round to telephones or fax wouldn't cure. I don't think I even need the holiday, to be honest. Just being able to afford it would cure me.'

He surveyed her with open approval.

'Well,' he said, 'you look great to me. I retract my original diagnosis. I don't think you've lost any of it.'

She picked up her water. 'Ah, kind sir, you should have seen me fifteen years ago. Before marriage and seven kids took their toll.'

'I wish I had,' he said with flattering sincerity. 'My timing always was lousy. But I must say I like the dress. I rather care for that understated severe look.'

'Thank you.' She gestured towards the other diners. 'But among the great and the good and the gaudy, I do think I look a bit too much like the

212

help. I don't dare go to the bathroom in case someone asks me for a safety pin.'

He gave a sudden shout of laughter. The man on her other side decided he was missing something, and started to talk busily to her.

When they had finished the main course Chester asked whether she was with a newspaper or a television station. She explained, briefly, from long habit making it sound as dull as possible. She was writing a short biography of Mama for the Krzysztof Foundation, she was here gathering material, maybe getting an interview.

'She's been going for years, hasn't she? Didn't it all begin during the war?'

'She had the first vision when she's supposed to have died in São Paulo in 1946.'

'Faked?'

Janie considered. 'I don't know yet. Something very strange happened there that day, though. Apparently quite extraordinary weather conditions turned the sky black without warning. Howling winds and people killed. It's all very . . .' she hesitated.

'Apocalyptic,' he offered.

'Exactly. Just that. Apparently there were even pillars of fire.'

He sat up straighter. 'No kidding.'

'Really. There are photos of these huge things looking like giant neon tubes that kind of hung in the sky. It seems that the only person to see them was the photographer.' She laughed. 'And the righteous, of course.'

He was looking really interested now. 'Maybe

you could get hold of the photographer, see if it was a hoax.'

'He was killed that same night. There was an article about it in the *Latin America Daily Post*.' She added, drily, 'And guess what, none of the righteous came forward.'

'Maybe they were killed too.' He paused. 'Still, there's one good thing about being righteous. You do know where you're going.'

'There's more.' She told him how the witnesses at Mama's deathbed saw a ball of fire moving round the room. He listened intently.

'It sounds like ball lightning. Was she living in a tall building?'

'It was an old tenement block,' she said, thinking of the contemporary descriptions, 'and I believe she was quite high up. The witness reports talk about stairs on the outside of the building.'

'They could easily have been metal, like a fire-escape. And there must also have been something metal in the room to attract it. Maybe a chair – or probably a bed. See, it happens occasionally in planes, when there's a lot of electrical activity – storms, lightning. People have described seeing balls of lightning actually rolling along the aisles.'

She was taken aback. 'God.'

He laughed. 'That's just what your witnesses undoubtedly said. Next thing you know, you've got your certified miracle.'

'Have you seen these balls of lightning?'

'No.' He touched the accreditation card. 'But I do fly a good deal, and I assure you it's not that unusual.' He mimicked a rural accent. 'Old air travellers know these things.'

Janie propped her chin in her hand. 'Suppose Mama *was* sleeping in a metal bed. Suppose she died in it. Suppose your ball of lightning really is attracted by the bed.' She screwed up her eyes, trying to imagine it, getting really excited now. 'They give people electric shocks, don't they, to start their hearts again if they've died? They can do it if they're quick. And if the shock's strong enough. Maybe – *maybe* – Mama's just-dead body was given one by the storm.'

'It'd be enough,' he commented drily, 'to wake the dead.'

Janie had anticipated that Mama would make a brief speech. In fact, Oliver Jodrell spoke for her. He stood beside her chair, gracefully thanking everyone for responding with such generosity to the cause of the Chalice of the Grapes of God. When he had finished, there was polite applause.

Then Mama rose to her feet as Jodrell pulled back her chair. She did not address them. Indeed, to Janie, she looked too exhausted to do so. It was as if, amongst these glittering, tanned and toned people, she alone was human, softened by age and effort, worn from her struggles for others.

Standing at the top table, she looked for a long moment over the sea of expectant faces. Then she extended both arms, high, from the shoulder. For a moment it seemed as if she was about to bless them. Like a priest, Janie thought. It seemed a curiously arrogant thing for her to do, this woman who so determinedly refused the trappings of the position she had achieved.

But when Mama completed the movement, she

opened her hands palm upwards, in a generously wide gesture both of giving and of supplication. Held in the spotlight she smiled, her head a little on one side, her remarkable eyes full of such warmth and humour that each person in the ballroom believed themselves the sole recipient of her look.

The place erupted. People rose to their feet, cheering, clapping, calling her name. Despite herself, Janie found she, too, was standing, clapping wildly. And all, she marvelled, without a word spoken.

Mama left the ballroom on that wave of adulation. She never, as Oliver Jodrell explained to her as they danced later, stayed after the main course was served. Her schedule was too punishing to permit late nights. Janie thought, whatever the reason, it enhanced her dignity. Her own was a less certain matter as Jodrell, holding her far too close, his hand planted firmly on her bottom, threaded his way with unnecessary dexterity through the throng: it was like dancing with an ageing gigolo.

'Well, Janie, and what did you do today?'

'Went to see Major Lachowski,' she said laconically. *You patronizing prick.*

She could actually feel the muscles in his arms tighten.

'I thought he was too ill to see anyone. Anyone at all.' Even his voice sounded tight.

'He mentioned your phone call,' she said deliberately.

'Did he indeed?' He was really having to struggle. 'And was he interesting?'

'Not particularly.' She looked away, over his shoulder and added, just to make mischief, 'He's hard to pin down.' She paused. 'He appears to suffer from memory loss. Though I expect you knew that.'

Oliver Jodrell made a non-committal sound. When he spoke again, he sounded almost petulant.

'You're very enterprising, Miss Paxton.' She widened her eyes at the sudden formality.

'Thank you,' she said, though it had clearly not been intended as a compliment.

He continued to guide her round the floor but his mind was elsewhere. He said suddenly, 'I wonder what else you've done on your own initiative.'

'Oh, this and that. Research, a few interviews.'

'I understand you went to Rome.'

She looked up at him. Now how did he know that?

'Yes. I went to the Vatican. It seemed the obvious starting point.'

'You should have told us.' The rebuke was deliberate. 'We could have cut a great deal of red tape for you. Guided you to all the right people.'

Just what I didn't need. She said airily, 'It was very enlightening anyway. And I didn't want to bother you.'

'Nothing is too much trouble for the foundation, Miss Paxton. Please don't forget that.' It was unmistakably a warning.

Quite soon after that, he returned her to her seat. David Chester was still at the table. Waiting for her, she hoped. He asked, 'Are you here alone?'

'In New York, you mean? Yes.' She felt suddenly

217

bleak. She had not had a drink all evening and now she badly wanted one, but the bottles on the table were empty.

'Married?'

'Not exactly. Turned out I wasn't very good at it.'

'Me neither.' He fiddled with the stem of his glass then added, without looking at her, 'I'm in the middle of a divorce, in fact. Feel as if I've been knocked down by a giant truck and I never even saw the fucker coming.'

'Me too. Some days I can't remember what I got up for.'

With some surprise, she accepted his offer to walk her back to her hotel. Going to find her coat, she took a wrong turning, confused by the endless, soundless, softly lit hotel corridors that made her think of the White Rabbit. Passing a door which stood very slightly ajar, she glanced casually in.

Mama stood with her back to the window, arms wrapped round her body. Behind her, lights gleamed in an adjoining building. She spoke, her mouth curving faintly with amusement. As she passed the doorway and the other hidden half of the room came into her view, Janie saw that the person she was addressing was Josef Karms. She halted, intrigued.

The big man sat in Mama's presence while she remained standing. That alone was somehow surprising, though God knew he was arrogant enough. But it was the *way* he sat, his chair canted back, heavy thighs splayed, easing the stiff collar of his dinner shirt with a finger, the other hand hanging open at his side. He looked relaxed and careless, utterly at ease with himself and with Mama. It was a pose which said more clearly than words that there was a relationship here beyond any Janie had imagined. The intimacy, the understanding between them was palpable. It crossed her mind they might be lovers, but she dismissed the idea at once. Absurd. She was forgetting who Mama was.

Still, even Mama had once been young. Who could say how long these two had known each other . . . No. It was ridiculous: she could swear there was no spark of urgency between them, no flicker of anything sexual. Former passions, whether they ended in amity or enmity, left detectable tracks: a residue of tenderness, or faint hostility. A teasing affection, or jealousy. Or bitterness. She sensed none of these; she felt sure Karms and Mama were not lovers, either past or present.

Then Janie was beyond the door and they were out of sight. As she joined the queue and handed over the ticket and the dollars for her coat, her puzzlement grew. Not lovers, then. But what?

As they left the lights of the foyer he paused to pull the collar of her leather coat up high round her throat. 'Don't want you getting a chill now.' It took only ten minutes to reach her hotel: she would have been happy if it had taken longer.

Under the canopied entrance he asked, 'Did you say you had seven?'

She stared at him. 'Seven what?'

'Safety pins.'

She laughed. 'Just the one. I thought you meant kids.'

'You really *do* have seven of those?' His face showed comical disbelief.

'No,' she said, 'ditto.'

'Ditto?'

'Just the one.'

'Great. Hold on to the safety pin, though, I may need it some time.' He turned to hail a cab.

Oh well, Janie thought, it was nice while it lasted. She walked into the lobby and went to get her room key.

Chapter Fifteen

Magda Lachowska, whom the world knew as Mama, closed the door of her room with relief. It had been a long day. She attended so many of these occasions that she no longer questioned what she thought of them. They were necessary, a means to an end: this evening would make $1.2 million for the Chalice. And as much as the money, the order needed the publicity she engendered, in order to continue the work that was so vital to her, that had become her life. The smiling, the speaking, the need of people to touch her – all this she accepted calmly. But more than ever, it exhausted her. For a moment she leaned against the door, too tired to move.

At length, very slowly, she undressed. The room was at the top of the tall, narrow building that was Chalice House in Brooklyn. She could hear traffic far down on the street below, see the flash of neon from an all-night restaurant opposite. Like all the rooms in all the Chalice Houses, it was sparsely furnished. The floor was coir matting – although she would have preferred plain boards – with a single bed, a wooden chair, a cheap built-in wardrobe, a narrow mirror set into its door. Without so much as a glance at her reflection, she took off her robe and hung it up. Then she went into the tiny bathroom to shower and rinse out her under-garments.

She came back in a long-sleeved white night-dress and lay on top of the bed. Thirsty, she drank two glasses of the bottled mineral water she always used. Then she switched out the lamp and closed her eyes. After a while she turned, curled on her side. The neon sign outside lit the room in harsh flashes of lurid colour. She put the backs of her hands over her eyes. Red, green. Red. Green.

He came to her silently, just as he had done all those years ago as she lay dying in the rooming house in the Rua Santa Rita, when he had appeared in the stammering space of her failing heartbeat.

She had been lying as she was now, on her side, head turned to the wall, to another wardrobe with a mirrored door. Her hands had been clasped over her eyes to block out the lightning flashes. Each blaze of white froze the bleak room with its narrow bed and enamel-topped table, her few possessions – cigarettes, handbag, a box of face powder – like random objects in an over-exposed photograph. The flashes grew longer until even through the flesh and bones of her hands she was aware of the livid brilliance of the shabby walls, of the sky out-side the high window.

For days she had felt death stealing towards her, slowing her breathing, stilling movement and mind. She was cold. So cold. Time meant nothing. She had thought it was day, but suddenly it had become black as night. Another lightning flash, and some quality of the harsh, stabbing streak revived memories that made her draw up her knees sharply as if for protection. Fearful images of towers, wires, mud, driving rain . . .

She had never even imagined weather of such ferocity and it filled her with terror and with awe. She thought, this is fire and brimstone. She had deserved it.

After a long time, she had become aware of an uneasy hush. A waiting. She had held her breath, calmer, somehow expectant. She sensed that the storm was no longer directly overhead. She sighed in relief, a sort of peace softening her rigid limbs. She straightened her body in the bed, took her hands warily from her eyes.

The brightness had gone, the thick darkness had become visible.

He was there. She had seen him in the filmed depths of the long mirror. It had been no mere reflection, no glimmer repeated in the dusty speckled glass. It blazed with the ancient light of stars. She had wondered, afterwards, why had she seen him only in the mirror when he had been there in the room with her? It was a long time before she understood: he had permitted himself to be glimpsed without being seen. And even now, knowing beyond all doubt that he was here once more, in this Brooklyn bedroom, she still feared to look on him. Yet she could not bear to turn her gaze away.

He seemed hewn out of the air itself, insubstantial and yet with great weight. Unborn, eternal, everlasting. He was massive, with a translucent magnificence that made her think of ice, of crystal, of a lamp she had seen once, a glowing globe of alabaster lit from within. She believed he had the body of a man. She thought she saw his arms held wide in an eloquent gesture of compassion. She had the impression of mighty thighs beneath a loose garment – but then she could not be sure. Perhaps she only saw these things because that was the limit of her expectation. Perhaps the eyes of her mind furnished him with human limbs, because he had the face of a man.

It was a face of indescribable power, etched with lines of sorrow and acceptance. The beak of the nose was both harsh and gentle, the mouth at once innocent and sensual. The smooth eyelids were heavy, and with a shock of surprise she saw the curved lustre of golden lashes. She had supposed this being to be divine. Now she feared to find it was only her own imagination.

But her imagination could never have given him, behind his shoulders, a great pale mist which lifted and shimmered, flexed and rustled with fierce, independent life. Weak as she was, she gasped aloud at the texture, the opaline colours of this tender pearled plumage: oyster, azure, amethyst. Beautiful, beautiful. She reached out fearful fingers, just as she had done all those years ago. Encountering only cold glass, she drew back with a low sob of distress.

As if in answer he spoke: she felt the deep reverberations of his words surge through her body, echoes of the thunder. She knew the thrill of trumpets, even though she heard no sound louder than the susurration of silk.

Then wings wrapped around her. His whisper was wild in her ears, thrummed against her heart.

It heated her blood so she throbbed with a piercing ecstasy, with a passion beyond anything she had ever experienced. The rhythm that gripped her body was that of the sea. She was consumed by its warm rising, she could not hold back. Faster and faster, until she was caught on the crest. She knew that when it broke, it would finish her. But she could not resist. It was relentless as a sexual embrace, irresistible as music, compelling as a prayer.

On the very brink of her rapture she cried aloud. She had moved and lay now on her back, staring up with unseeing eyes. She was no longer in the shabby rooming house, on the iron bed beside the peeling wall. She was nowhere near the Rua Santa Rita, not in São Paulo at all. She was in a high place she did not recognize, a pure and empty place where the sky gave promise of endless dawns, where distant mountains thrust through coils of cloud and silence sang in her ears.

She was not alone. He was there also. He was neither beside her nor before her, but he filled her eyes and her consciousness.

His presence unlocked in her a ferment of feeling, emotions that seared because they were unaccustomed, as if she were flexing muscles too long untried. Pity. Remorse. Sorrow. Not for herself. For the first time in her life, she comprehended the agony of others, and it was intolerable.

She was beset by foul imaginings rooted in her present and in her past, trapped between memory and history. Appalling images from her own worst dreams crouched on her shoulders. Spectres swarmed the skies, clustered on her back. Now the bruised light was tinged purple-grey, made opaque by clinging webs which veiled her face and coated her hands, caught in her hair and clogged dry as ashes on her lips and eyelids.

Below the place where she was, another landscape emerged from the sinister twilight. She heard cries of lamentation and distress long before she could make out the figures of men and women and children stumbling in terror. Shadows of tragic black swooped on dismembered carcasses. She thought she could discern demons, gobbling grotesques whose near-nakedness was misshapen and muscular as they cursed and clawed at their victims with callous barbarity. The ground was crusted with blood and excrement smeared by the spasms of dying bodies. Twisted figures were crushed by the stony weight of their suffering.

The sobbing and the screams, the abandoned sprawl of the dead, transfixed her heart with pain, turned a knife in her side. There was neither truth nor wisdom: there was nothing. Violence and vice, hysteria and prejudice were all-pervading. Ignorance and superstition ruled. Hope was exterminated.

But for his presence, consoling as a candle in the night, the cruelty would have been beyond bearing. Without the great wings which still encompassed her, she would have collapsed in utter despair. Only her mysterious companion supported and guided her, upheld her in dark space.

Just when she thought she would die if she had to see any more, the haunted landscape began slowly to fall away from her sight. Dense mist rolled in and covered everything, muffled the terrible sounds of tumult until pure silence reigned once more. In the end as at the beginning.

She seemed to waken from a sleep of centuries. When she raised her eyes to the mythical mountains, she found to her horror that they too were becoming more distant. Their brilliance paled, faded, became indistinct, vanished altogether. He was still there, but she could no longer see him, nor hear his voice. She cried out again, loudly this time, desperate: in relief at her salvation, in longing for what she had briefly glimpsed, and lost.

That first time, in São Paulo, there had been people in the room with her. She had not known who they were or why they had looked at her with such alarm and such fear. She was worn out, powerless to move. Some time after that, she was able to hear what was said. A child's voice, shrill with panic, had shouted, but she's *dead*.

She had wanted to tell them: no! Never more alive! But she could not speak for weeping. It was of no importance. The only thing that mattered was to find the place she had seen among the mountains. He would be there. He had promised. He would be with her, and she would know that embrace again.

He had not failed her. Many times since then, unheralded and unlooked for, he had come to her. And always it was the same: he stood in the light, but he cast no shadow.

Chapter Sixteen

Janie was up early next day. After a further two hours in the Public Library she walked across Fifth and then Madison to Grand Central Station. She took her time. It always delighted her, that any conversation on the sidewalk in New York was theatre. She loitered to observe an elderly man, maybe Mexican from his flat dark hair and short stature, in a long dark wool coat with an astrakhan collar and carrying a silver-tipped cane. He was engaged in animated dispute with a young Hispanic wearing black denim and gold jewellery, a long rolled canvas under his arm.

She drank coffee at the station for the sheer pleasure of the building, sitting among the tables at the café high above the concourse where she could read the *New York Times* and look down on the crowded marble hall, now restored to its full Art Deco glory.

For some reason, some association of ideas (stations, journeys, partings), she found herself longing for a brandy. She savoured it in imagination: the look of the liquid in the glass, the welcome of the dark fumes. There was a block of chocolate in her pocket and a couple of pieces stilled the craving, sort of. The craving would always be there. She hadn't had a drink for weeks now. But not drinking never got any easier. One day at a time. Searching for distraction, she looked across the concourse and noticed a woman and a young boy in a denim baseball cap hurrying past. Her heart jumped and for a moment she thought, *Adam*, momentarily deceived by the fall of brown hair under the cap, something buoyant in the walk.

She opened her bag and fumbled for her big wallet where she kept dollars: long ago, as a young journalist, she had been lectured by a photographer for taking out her money in a restaurant. 'I don't want to be mugged in the car park, even if you do.' Unable to see properly, she dislodged the photograph she kept in the back pocket.

The photograph she held had been taken by Claudia: Adam and Lucy in Derbyshire, when they were both eight. A happy picture, children in shorts, holding hands in the sunshine of a field near the Little Barn. Adam had a cut on his foot and one brown leg ended in a white bandage: it had amused Lucy enormously, she thought he'd grown a paw. It was one of those rare moments of harmony, both children brown and joyous: Janie always kept it with her, a sort of talisman.

Just then a voice behind her said, 'Shee-it, Ah'm gonna miss the fuckin' train.' A chair clattered to the floor as the man ran. She realized she was going to be late herself: her appointment with Mama was in an hour's time, in the Sixth Avenue offices of the Krzysztof Foundation. It was a daunting prospect.

As she drew level with St Patrick's Cathedral a man was circling the wide pavement in front of her, a tray slung round his neck. He could have been any age, any nationality. He wore a woollen hat low over his eyes, which were closed. A sign on the tray read: *except for the grace of God I AM BLIND – SO BUY A PENCIL.* The first six words were so tiny, they were virtually invisible. She thought, he's honest at least. On an impulse she fumbled in her bag for change and dropped it into his tray.

As she turned away she glanced up at the steps of the cathedral. There was a flutter of creamy white as a man in a heavy violet-blue robe stood back to allow someone – a woman – to precede him. Janie recognized the shaven head and bare muscular arms, the confident, almost pugnacious stance. She ran up the steps.

Inside the heavy doors, in the foyer, she could see neither of them. She went through another door to her right and was immediately entangled in a group of elderly women in trouser suits, taking pictures of each other. Many of the people thronging the building seemed oblivious to the fact that it was a cathedral. All around her were cheerful voices, the popping of flashbulbs. One woman was even eating a hot dog, the onion sickening against the incense in the air.

In front of her, literally hundreds of candles were banked in three great sections, blazing in their orange cups. She watched a small Japanese woman drop a dollar in the brass box and light another. The heat here was intense, the smell of burning wax overpowering.

She turned to face down the vast length of the cathedral towards the altar. It was so huge, the stone pillars in the distance became a grey mist speared by tiny lights. On either side were dozens of individual shrines, each containing the figure of a saint, each with its own bank of offertory candles.

Janie made her way through the crowd and started to walk down the side aisle, looking in vain for Mama or her dark attendant. By the time she had gone half the length of the massive cathedral, she could have been in a different building. There were no casual visitors here, no voices, no flashbulbs. The organ was playing robust nineteenth-century hymns. A few people sat silent in the pews, each one isolated with their thoughts. And then, about ten yards away, there was a woman wearing the violet-blue robe over her own creamy white one, the hood pulled up to hide her distinctive hair.

It was Mama. She was kneeling before a statue of a woman saint Janie did not know, in the act of lighting a candle. With great care, she placed it among the others which already burned there, watched the flame flare and settle. Then she closed her eyes and bent her head.

Janie slid into a nearby pew. She had no intention of speaking – that would by any standards be an intrusion – but she was conscious it had been a very long time since she had been in any sort of a church. And there was little point in rushing to a meeting on Sixth Avenue when Mama was here.

The mass of tiny flames made the air quiver, the scent of candlewax curled sensuous and heavy around the grey stones. She normally had neither the inclination for prayer nor the habit of it, and she was not even sure that what she was doing was praying. She concentrated hard, thinking about Adam and Paul. Then Claudia came into her mind, and her desperation over Lucy. So that when Mama spoke she jumped, shocked out of reverie.

'I thought it was you,' the woman said, in that faintly accented Middle European voice. 'It is a beautiful place, no?' She sat down beside Janie.

'I have an interview with you in . . .' Janie looked at her watch, 'twenty-five minutes.' She smiled. 'I apologize for being early.'

'Let us talk here instead.'

They sat in companionable silence, listening to the organ playing what sounded like a wedding march, all rounded notes. In the great pillared space Janie saw maybe half a dozen men and women in the distinctive violet-blue robe of the Chalice. Beside her, eyes fixed on the distant altar, Mama was still, very focused, very contained. Janie thought how she had appeared the previous evening, in the midst of her blue-robed followers, surrounded by people clamouring to get near her. How strong she must be, to lead such a life, to bring so many people together and yet remain in control. What skills she must possess, of understanding and of manipulation. She wondered where it all came from.

After a time, Mama turned to her. Her face held a shining, meditative look.

'Tell me about your faith,' Janie said. 'Tell me what you believe.'

Mama said slowly, 'I was born a Catholic, though I knew nothing of it for many years. I never went inside a church until I was in my twenties, and then rarely.'

'But in the end, you found your faith again?'

'You can always find something if you search for it long enough. Even if it isn't there – especially if it isn't there.' Her face was composed, giving nothing away. 'All religions are founded on that.'

After a moment Janie said, 'But you are a Christian.'

'Am I?' She smiled. 'I expect I am. They have claimed me.'

'Many claim you.'

Mama looked at her; those astonishing eyes blazed pale in the still face. 'There is an Arab poem,

> *"Love is the faith I hold; wherever turn*
> *His camels, still the one true faith is mine."*

She was quiet for a moment, as if listening to the words echo in her mind. 'If you want my belief, there it is.'

A man on a pew to their right got to his feet with a clatter as a steel walking-frame banged against the wood.

Janie said, suddenly, 'Why did the Vatican oppose Pope John when he decided to recognize the Chalice as a religious order?'

She had intended to take Mama aback. She did not succeed.

'Very simple. For years I have been urging women to take control of their own lives. In poor countries that must begin with birth control. I want to give them the means to limit pregnancies

233

to two. Three at most. The Church is a male-dominated structure: of course they disapproved of my work. They still disapprove. I still have fierce opponents in the Vatican.'

'Surely one of the reasons for their disapproval is that many people believe you perform miracles.'

Mama looked down at her hands. 'The ability to do what people call miracles is a possession I did not seek.' She looked up at Janie. 'I renounced all possessions long ago. There are times when I wish I could renounce this one, also.'

'When did you first discover you could heal?'

The older woman hesitated and leaned back against the upright wooden pew. Reluctance showed in every line of her body. She said beneath her breath, 'Is this the right thing?'

Janie just waited. Mama went on, musing aloud, 'But the foundation want me to talk to you. Perhaps they are right, perhaps it is time.' She closed her eyes. Without opening them she started speaking again. 'I was very young. Scarcely seventeen. I held a newborn baby. It was dead, strangled by the umbilical cord.' She opened her eyes, but they were fixed, as if she was looking at something a great distance away. There was some undercurrent here which Janie could not catch, something yoked tight to pain. 'I held it for a long time between my hands. Nothing more. Nothing astounding happened.' She drew a deep breath. 'I just saw it yawn. And it lived.' She blinked, at last, and her eyes focused on Janie. 'Then, years later, after I saw the vision that first time, I was shown what I must do. I did not wish it, but the people demanded it of me. There were never any rational explanations.' She smiled suddenly. 'For them or for myself,' she added.

Janie thought of what she knew of this woman: that she was religious, and yet appealed to people of every faith. That she wielded great influence, and yet appeared to be a person of total simplicity. That she was credited with performing miracles, and yet she seemed, with those luminous eyes, to be totally transparent, as if everything about her was there openly to be seen.

'And when you cure someone, what happens?'

Mama's expression went blank, as if she were biting back irritation. 'You are asking impossible questions of me. You must understand, I cannot will it. It is not found by seeking. I am only the instrument, not the power. And you talk as if it all happened immediately. As if, bang—' she clapped her hands together, 'you're well again. Maybe once, twice, I have seen that. More often, months can pass before there is even a slight improvement.' Those eyes were paler than ever in the filmy cathedral light. 'I have said this often. I will tell you again: I cannot comprehend or describe how it is. It is like . . .' her voice dropped an octave, 'a rapture that comes on me, and always in its own time. Nothing I do makes any difference. Sometimes weeks will pass and it does not come. Sometimes months.' She was silent for a while. On the distant altar, the cloth gleamed gold against dark red.

'It is – it must be – a mystical experience. I cannot explain it otherwise. No words can describe it – there is no flash of light, no bells, no music, no incense. Yet I feel it with an intensity that stops the breath in my throat.'

Listening, Janie was overcome by the sensation that she was sitting too close to some incredible source of light. She felt warm and comforted, indescribably happy. For the first time, she could comprehend what the people felt, as they crowded and jostled and reached out to try and touch Mama as she moved among them.

'And still,' Mama was saying, 'I am caught by pure terror each time it enters into me.' She put her left hand over her eyes, as if she wanted to blot something out. Her hand was capable and well used. She wore a cheap watch and the narrow silver wedding band of her order.

It was hard to relate her evident distress with the feelings she communicated to others: the woman was clearly torn in two by this force she was struggling to describe.

'I know after so many years that maybe some good will come of it,' Mama went on. 'But each time, I lose . . . something. Some part of myself. And I will tell you another thing. For many years, I fled from it. I refused absolutely to accept it. I understood that I was able to do . . .' she hesitated, 'certain things. But I would not. I denied it. I could not surrender to something which filled me with such fear.'

Janie said very softly, 'What happened?'

Mama turned to her. 'I died,' she said.

A woman sat down just in front of them. She was carrying a huge bunch of lilies, the pollen-laden heads quivering, scenting the air. Janie sneezed violently. Scrabbling for a tissue, she managed to knock her shoulderbag to the ground. The flap was open, the contents spread across the stone floor. Janie bent to scoop up the clutter of pens, a lipstick, her tiny compact, a timetable, her library cards. Beside her, Mama gathered up her wallet and the photographs that had fallen free. She held them out, then glanced down. On top was the picture of Adam and Lucy in the sunny field.

'Are these your children?'

'Adam is my son. He's older now though, eleven. Lucy is the daughter of a friend.'

Mama went on looking at the photograph. 'Poor child.' Her voice was deep with pity.

'Oh no,' Janie dismissed the bandaged limb casually, 'he just cut his foot, it wasn't . . .'

'Not your son.' She pointed to Lucy. 'The girl.'

Dumbfounded, Janie stared down at the picture she knew so well. There was nothing – *nothing* – in that photograph to hint at Lucy's condition. There were no physical signs of it on her face, her body. She was laughing, beautiful, apparently an ordinary, happy child.

After a moment Mama shrugged almost imperceptibly, a lifting of the shoulders. 'I do not wish to intrude.'

'No. I . . .' What the hell. Mama's instincts were right. 'There is something wrong. But we really don't know for sure even now what it is.' She told, very briefly, the story of the inoculation and its terrible results. Then she added, 'Claudia is going through a bad time right now. Lewis wants to put

Lucy in a special school, a full-time place. It's hard for Claudia to accept.'

Mama listened, still holding the photograph. Very lightly she brushed her thumb across the image of Lucy's smiling little face. After a moment she handed the snapshot back without a word. Janie could sense the sudden exhaustion sweeping over her as with the stiff, uncertain movements of an old woman she fumbled for a pocket. She kept her head turned away, so Janie could not see her face, but the younger woman had the impression she was in tears. Finally, she produced her unlikely silver sunglasses and put them on, hiding her eyes.

As if that were a signal, the dark, muscular Tomas in his violet robe was instantly at her side. Janie, watching as she walked away, thought she had never seen a figure so erect, and so lonely.

Back at the hotel, there was a single flower waiting for her, a deep pink daisy wrapped in brown paper with a raffia bow. Tricky, she thought. There was also a note.

Are you free for dinner tonight? I will come by at eight in hopes. Don't worry if the answer's no – I'll just go away and drown my sorrows. Possibly in the Hudson. David.

The answer – after she had phoned the Matthiesons and cancelled drinks, with fulsome apologies and explanations – was not no.

They went to the Stage on Seventh at Fifty-fourth, walking under an icy, white-ringed moon because he insisted she must see the beauty of New York at night in December, the bare twigs of the city's trees decked for carnival with tiny white fairy lights.

In the noisy restaurant, where the windows were steamed up and conversation was conducted just below a shout, their waiter brought great platters of food. Janie looked up at him. 'I don't think this is what I ordered.'

'Roast beef sandwich on rye, right?'

When he had gone, Janie said, 'It can't be a sandwich. Look at that gravy!'

'Don't panic.' David was deriving considerable amusement from the look on her face. 'They'll give you a doggy bag.'

'They'll need to give me a wolfhound. I'll never get through this.'

'Try it first and see,' he advised. 'If you manage it all, you get to celebrate with the biggest piece of cheesecake you ever saw.'

When they were waiting for Russian tea in long glasses to cool, he pulled a large, card-backed envelope from his shoulderbag and passed it across the table. 'Present.'

She pulled out half a dozen prints. Against a night sky, they showed luminous pillars. Puzzled, she said, 'Aren't these the photos from the *Latin America Daily Post*?'

He shook his head. When she looked more closely, she saw that these pillars seemed to have been photographed through trees. Their shapes were wildly distorted as if blown in the path of a high wind. The ground was whitened in places with what might be snow. David leaned forward and showed her that pasted to the back was a long piece of paper bearing a copyright symbol, the name Archie Weyer and the date 11.4.65. There was also a clipping, cut from a magazine. At the top of the page was the name of the publication:

Scientific American. On the night of Sunday April 11 at his home near Toledo, Weyer obtained these pictures during a thunderstorm as he attempted to photograph large hailstones. Scientific analysis corroborated by reports from Toledo of a tornado experience in the area at that time indicates that he had recorded a pair of genuine luminous pillars. These are possibly tornado funnels, the vortex illuminated by some kind of energetic luminous activity or a strong electrical current.

She said slowly, 'So that's what Mama's pillars of fires were: tornado funnels with energy coursing through them.' She turned to him in sudden anxiety. 'These aren't fakes?'

'I shouldn't think you could have a more reliable source.'

'They look exactly like the South American ones. How on earth did you get hold of them?'

'It was so easy I hate to admit it, but I just rang our meteorological people. They didn't know anything about your pillars of fire in São Paulo, but they came up with these. Do you have copies of the South American pictures?'

'I could probably get hold of them. But I don't think there can be much doubt.' She was still staring at the pillars. 'As far as I can remember, they're identical. I just can't understand why no one worked it out before.'

David Chester stirred his tea. 'Your original photos must be more than fifty years old, I don't suppose many picture libraries have copies now. It'd need someone doing a doctorate or something on Mama to put them together. And you'll have done it before they get there.'

She put her hand on his. 'It's wonderful. Thank you.'

They talked about themselves. She recognized there was a good deal left unsaid, and knew very well why. So it was a surprise when they reached her hotel and he said goodnight formally, arranged to phone her next day and strode off. More than a little disconcerted that she could have been so mistaken about him, she collected her key and walked across to the bank of lifts where the elderly man in a pillbox hat and brown uniform was holding a lift open for her.

As she turned to face the door, David stepped inside.

'Sorry to keep you waiting,' he said to her, for the attendant's benefit. He lifted his eyebrows in unspoken query. Taken aback, she gave a small smile of acquiescence. There seemed no alternative, and she found that suited her. She wanted to feel he had taken charge, taken over.

They travelled up in the lift for seventeen floors in silence, watching the back of the bell-boy's neck. As they walked to her room he remarked, 'It's a long time since I had a chaperone.'

She said drily, 'You certainly appear to need one.'

'Would you rather I went?'

Would she? She didn't know. She only knew that if he stayed, she would not be alone. Was that enough of a reason? To delay the decision, she let her hand drop into his waiting one.

Her room was at the end of a short corridor. She slid the plastic card into the slot on the handle, took it out, waited for the arrow to flash. When nothing happened she tried again. She was very conscious of him there. When her third attempt failed, she straightened up with a hiss of exasperation. He was standing very close behind her, she could feel the warmth of his body.

'Let me.' He reached round, pressed the card in and removed it. Of course it worked for him. She put her hand on the opened door, but before she could move inside, he put his arms around her from the back and unfastened the buttons of her leather coat. He cupped her breasts in his hands. She was wearing a silk and cashmere sweater. Into the nape of her neck he murmured, 'I've been wanting to do this all evening.'

She found herself wondering, had she put it on for just such a reason? To make herself desirable?

He let his hands drop to her waist, move up against her flesh, up under the soft fabric. He touched her nipples through the lace of her brassiere and as she felt them stiffen, she drew a sharp breath. As if at a signal, he eased her into the room and kicked the door shut behind them.

He was almost a stranger, and that was what she wanted. Whatever happened between them would be brief, impermanent. It was fantasy, not reality. It was all she could handle.

She had left her curtains open and the buildings close to the hotel lent their light to the room. She turned so she could see his face, serious and absorbed. He slid her coat from her shoulders, took off his own, let them both drop to the floor. She put her arms around his back, pressed close against him, feeling his erection firm against her belly. Both of them were silent, intent, aroused. They kissed, the first time, tongues touching. Then he began very delicately to undo the little mother-of-pearl buttons on her sweater. He put his hands on the wings of her shoulderblades and she felt him steering her back towards the bed until the mattress was against the backs of her knees. Holding her steady, he bent his head. She felt his lips again, on the responsive skin of her breasts.

Desire was shimmering inside her. She thought, it doesn't have to be love. This will do, whatever it is, this will take me where I want to go.

So she was as astonished as he when she wrenched herself from his arms and whirled away from him. '*Don't!* I can't. I just . . . I can't.' She crammed a hand against her mouth, terrified she was going to throw up, unable to believe the violence of her emotions, the distaste – no, the revulsion – when only a moment ago she had been welcoming him.

In the darkness she could not see his expression, but for a moment he looked menacing, his body outlined against the light from the windows. She shook her head and gave a half-laugh, half-sob. 'I don't know what's the matter with me.' But she did. Then his shoulders relaxed and he shrugged.

'No big deal. I misread the signals.' His voice was hard, though.

'No, you didn't. It's me. I'm a mess.' She wondered if she could tell him about all of it. But telling would change nothing, and nice as he was, he would not wish to hear. 'I want to,' she whispered, 'I really do. But it just feels too soon. Sorry.'

Sorry for leading you on. Sorry for backing away. Sorry that my body and my heart react with such outrage when I try to override them.

He put a hand briefly on her shoulder. His voice was flat with disappointment and rejection. 'You're not the only one around here who's damaged goods.' So maybe he did understand. 'Get some sleep. I'll call you.' He turned and picked up his coat. In the gloom, the green message light was flashing on the base of the telephone. 'Did you know you've got a message?'

When he had gone, she slumped wearily onto the bed. She despised herself, apologizing for what she could not help, taking the blame, seeking to appease him because she seemed unable to function as a sexual being. As if that was all she was, all she had to offer.

It was eleven o'clock when she switched on the lamp. The cover was patterned, whirls and swirls of scarlet. The voice on the switchboard read the words totally without inflection. The swirls of scarlet moved in front of her eyes as she listened.

Urgent message. Gas explosion seriously damaged Little Barn. No one injured. Please telephone Derbyshire England 01332 . . .

Chapter Seventeen

Muffled up against the wind, she stood in the courtyard and surveyed her home. Len and Joan Smedley stood close, both short and burly in coats and scarves, one on either side of her. Whether this was for her support or their own was hard to say.

The smaller farm building that until two nights ago had stood against the Little Barn had collapsed into heaps of blackened stones and rubble. Burned spars from the roof lay among them and these, like the huge double wooden doors now on the ground, still smouldered and smoked. The courtyard was in chaos. Broken glass covered everything, a tractor lay on its side where the blast had thrown it. Broken roof tiles crunched under their feet. Even now, two days after the blast, there was a choking miasma in the air, a mixture of oil and dust, the smelling agent in the gas, the fire, and some chemicals the firemen must have used.

The Smedleys talked in turn. Tweedledum and Tweedledee.

'Them bally things been in there for yoinks.'

'Pre-war, they are.'

'And the rest. Me grandad put 'em in.'

Janie interrupted. 'What?'

'Calor gas tanks,' Len explained patiently. 'Bloomin' great things in there, you never seen 'em?' He gestured with his head at the remains of heavy metal cylinders, which had once stood fifteen foot high and eight foot wide, and were now twisted shapes lying in puddles of filthy water. She had a vague memory of them upright, held in metal braces Adam called sputniks: they used to watch the huge calor gas lorry filling them through bright yellow piping.

'Four of 'em, there was. Only one empty.' That was Joan.

'Down at Pilkington's they've twenty.'

'Big estate, that.'

Janie interrupted. 'But what *happened*?'

'Barn caught fire,' Len said. 'Would've taken hours for the tanks to heat up enough to ignite. Mebbe seven or eight hours of intense heat, the firemen said.'

'If they'd been modern tanks, it'd never've 'appened. Those old 'uns 'ad none of the safety valves and whatnot like nowadays.' Joan surveyed the remains of their building with deep gloom. 'It went up like a powder keg.'

The smaller barn had been built, like her own, of great chunks of Derbyshire stone which she would have believed could withstand anything. It was horrifying to imagine the force that could collapse walls that thick. At least, they had more or less contained it. Part of her kitchen wall lay in ruins, open to the elements and the gaping hole that had been the calor gas store.

Beside the damaged wall hung a pinboard, full of memos to herself, shopping lists, receipts. Among all the chaos this was untouched, the frail bits of paper still in place, although the old wooden kitchen table was scarred by debris.

Above it, the kitchen ceiling had a great hole and she could see up through the joists to the floor above where a portion of wall in the hallway had blown out. Apart from a few roof tiles, that seemed to be the extent of the structural damage. In her bedroom the dormer window, like most of those in the house, had been shattered by the force of the explosion. Shards of glass covered her desk and had even got into the printer of her pc, which would probably have to be replaced. The machine itself was covered with an oily film from the fire, but working. Her files and notes, in their drawers, were untouched.

She sat down heavily on the bed. Even that was filthy. The fire seemed as much a violation as a burglary was said to do. If Adam had been here, he might have been hurt. Both of them could have been killed. She wrapped her arms around herself, shivering suddenly. First she was pushed into the path of a speeding car, then weeks later her home was blown up. *Just because you're paranoid* . . .

What in God's name was going on? She could no longer ignore the possibility that it might have some connection with Mama and the book. She knew she must by now be worrying quite a lot of people. She was asking questions which went far beyond the brief set by the Krzysztof Foundation, she was turning up discrepancies, curious little slips, even obvious lies. Her trip to Poland had clearly annoyed Oliver Jodrell. And his reaction when she admitted she had seen old Major Lachowski had been disconcerting. But Jodrell, she was convinced, had no real power within the foundation. So who, then?

It might not be the foundation at all. With the Vatican, she had reached a level beyond her own expectations. Cardinal Uguccioni had insisted on talking off the record. Maybe the Vatican themselves did not wish to have these matters openly raised?

But she had left the cardinal only twenty minutes before the incident in the street. Don't be a fool, she chided herself. Those people do not involve themselves with such things. Then she thought of the press pictures of the body of the banker Calvi hanging beneath Blackfriars Bridge over the Thames. She put a hand over her eyes.

'. . . bang to rights in no time,' Joan was saying sympathetically, picking up scattered paperbacks as she spoke. It was an unfortunate choice of phrase. 'Insurance, see,' she went on. 'Thank the good Lord you wasn't inside, you nor the boy.'

When the two women went outside, Len was tidying up broken glass.

'Could of been a lot worse if the house'd caught fire. Doesn't bear thinking about, that.'

Janie finally asked the question that had been haunting her all the way back home. 'What started the fire in the first place?'

Len and Joan exchanged a glance. 'Fire investigation officer spent hours turnin' things over yesterday . . .'

'That's normal,' Joan interjected. 'They do that after every fire.'

'. . . wanted to know how old was the boiler, was there any petrol stored in there. 'E wrote down "insufficient maintenance".' Len's face reddened with indignation. 'Probable cause, 'e called it. But it were done only last March, I said, Drabbles came up same as always.' He bent and picked up more glass, coughing from dust. 'No need for further inquiries, any road up.'

Joan put a protective arm around Janie's shoulders.

'You all right, love? You look terrible.'

Chapter Eighteen

A couple of weeks later Janie made a phone call on impulse.

'Jim Harley? Janie Paxton here, I came to see you at Chalice House not long ago . . . Fine, thank you. I just wanted to thank you for your time that day. And I wondered about that woman, the one Mama was with in the ward?'

'You mean Mrs Desmond. Sadly, she died a day or two after you were here. It was . . .'

There, Janie thought, of course she didn't live, handclasping or no. Jim Harley was still talking.

'. . . remember David, the young man who couldn't speak?'

'Yes.'

'Well, he can now. Absolutely normally, if you call a strong Scouse accent normal. It's fantastic for him. If all goes well, we should be able to place him in some kind of training pretty soon. Unfortunately, we have no idea how it happened, so we can't patent it.' He sounded extremely cheerful.

'What did you do?'

'Nothing. We just carried on as we had been. He's spent two years with the Chalice, so maybe we finally got through. Or perhaps it was just his time to want to speak again. But it's kind of nice that he was sitting next to Mama that day she was here. A nice accident. He started talking at breakfast next morning, incidentally.'

Janie said slowly, 'It wasn't an accident. Mama made someone move so she could sit beside him. It wasn't just chance.'

There was a moment's silence. 'You're right,' Harley said. 'I'd forgotten old Patrick sitting at the head of the table.'

'And she touched David.'

'Did she? Are you sure? I didn't think there was any physical contact between them.' He paused. 'How did she touch him?'

Janie described Mama's hand on David's shoulder. But she didn't mention the sun behind the two of them, that image she had of a religious painting: it was too fanciful, and Harley was a practical man.

He listened carefully. Then he said, 'Well well well.'

'Had Mama met David before?'

'Sure. On her last visit she stayed two days and went all round . . .' She heard the sound of paper riffling. 'Hold it. David only got to us six months ago. So no, she hadn't. And no one had discussed his case with her, either.' Janie was embarrassed even to phrase the question, but she did.

'Have you seen Mama making one of her cures?'

'Negative. I've heard about them, of course, and some Chalice members claim to have been present at one or another of them. None of them ever said that anything extraordinary happened. No one ever gets up off a stretcher and walks, you know?'

'Do you think this is a cure then? A healing?'

251

He chose his words carefully. 'Mama does seem to be a natural healer. Like I said, I'm not a doctor. But we've all of us felt it. And I don't believe she does it consciously, either – she's like a force of nature. But did she cure David?' She could hear his breathing while he thought. 'There's two ways of looking at it. A cynic would insist that this man has responded finally to ongoing treatment: it was his time to recover. It was merely coincidence that Mama was there the day before he spoke for the first time. And a believer would claim David was healed because Mama put her hand upon him. What do they say? "Coincidence is a miracle where God chooses to remain anonymous."' He chuckled. '*I* certainly can't decide. You'll just have to pick your poison.'

'I'll do that,' said Janie.

Chapter Nineteen

The boy Patrice Akonda heard about Mama at Sunday school. Sister Ernestina told them this important lady was coming to Gabon to open a special house where people could go if they had big problems. She went all over the world helping people, said Sister Ernestina. She was an ordinary person, just like the children and the sisters themselves, but sometimes she performed miracles and wonderful things happened. The first miracle had occurred long ago, when she was a young woman. She had died, but she was found by angels and raised up from her bed, and made to live again.

Patrice listened, his round face intent and thoughtful. When he learned there would be a special bus to take the sisters to see the foreign lady they called Mama, he begged that he and his brother be allowed to go. Jean pleaded too, and because both children had always been favourites with the sisters, seats were found for them and their mother.

This did not surprise Patrice, for he had known how it would be. He had prayed, the way his mother said, and she had been right: he had his answer. This Mama had been dead, and a miracle had brought her back to life. If it could be done for a whole lady, then surely it would work for just one leg.

Chapter Twenty

Five weeks after Professor Portmain of the University of Urbana-Champagne had given her the name of the French priest who had been on the Pope's Commission of Inquiry, Janie flew to France. At Toulouse Airport, she hired a Renault 4. The simplicity of the initial procedure fooled her into thinking that driving the vehicle would be simple also. This proved to be very far from the case. Although she got the car hire girl to show her a large map, and despite having written out the name of each small town en route on a list which she stuck to the dashboard, the complexities of finding her way out of the city coupled with the unfamiliar gear system proved exhausting.

It took two hours' driving, including a stop at a Routiers restaurant for an omelette and crusty bread, so it was mid-afternoon before she reached Castres. She found it a place of twisting streets and narrow buildings, where tourists did not ruffle the bustling life around the food shops and the twice-weekly market. She booked into a *pension* and set off for the address she had been given by Professor Portmain.

Rue d'Horloge turned out to be an old, balconied street behind the church of St Raymond. A short flight of cracked marble steps led up to the house she sought. Unkempt creepers draped the stone walls, the windowsills were crumbling. The doorbell echoed as if through empty rooms.

She thought she glimpsed someone looking down at her from an upstairs window but another ring produced no reply. She walked up and down the road a couple of times. After half an hour it began to rain a little and she sheltered in a doorway opposite.

Professor Portmain had managed to interview the man she was seeking, and they had last corresponded a year ago. He had assured her that if he was alive, Père Sauvel would still be here. But after a further ten minutes she had just decided to leave and return later in the day when the front door opened.

The man who came out was tall and bent, skin sallow in the shadow of the umbrella he held with a narrow hand, the knuckles enlarged by arthritis. He wore a black coat over a black suit with a gold cross at his breast. Age had put a shine on the lapels. Bedraggled grey hair curled beneath the edge of his black hat, his white collar was a touch grubby. The toes of his heavy boots turned up from long wearing.

He started to make his way up the street, moving surprisingly fast. She ran after him, calling.

'Père Sauvel, excusez-moi – un moment, s'il vous plaît.' He stopped, glanced at her briefly and then looked away as if eager to be somewhere else. She went on, 'C'est très important. Je m'appelle Janie Paxton, je vous ai écrit trois lettres, mais pas de réponse.' She knew from Professor Portmain that the man spoke excellent English. But she also knew the French hated to be addressed in any language other than their own. The priest hunched his shoulders more emphatically. Whether against the rain or against her, she could not tell.

She added, '*Cardinal Uguccioni m'a dit . . .*'

He started visibly.

'*Le Cardinal Uguccioni? Vous avez parlé avec le cardinal?*'

'*Oui, certainement. Dans le Vatican.*'

He looked at her properly, gold wire spectacles enlarging the soft brown eyes, red-rimmed as if he read too much. Surprise had given way to concern. She held out the card she had lifted from the cardinal's desk.

Climbing the stairs ahead of her to show the way in the gloom he said, wearily, 'The Commission of Inquiry was convened forty years ago. I have forgotten all the details.'

Janie said, 'Is that why you didn't answer my letters?' The house smelled of cigarettes and damp.

'I cannot believe there is anything I can tell you that could be of interest.'

'But you are the only one left.'

He stopped, three stairs above her. 'And if you had been a year or two later, there would not even have been me.'

'I wanted to ask you about it,' Janie said.

He started walking upwards again. '*Évidemment.* As I . . .' she could hardly hear him now. '. . . little I can tell you.'

They reached what was clearly his study on the first floor. It was at the back of the house, and very dim, the light obscured by the roofed balcony which ran the full length of the window. After the narrow street outside, the view astonished her: it looked down a steep drop to a river, its waters brown and swift. Beyond, blurred by rain and mist, rose distant mountains. The room felt cold.

He took a matchbox from his pocket and bent effortfully to light a small gas fire. It caught with a dangerous pop, the flame flaring blue. Straightening with visible effort he said, 'I cannot imagine why you would be interested all these years later.'

She said, trying to hide her exasperation, 'Father, I wrote you a long letter explaining.'

In answer, he gestured helplessly towards his desk. It was piled high with papers and folders. Wire trays were full, more flowed onto the floor.

She told him about her book, the foundation. As she did so, she took in the rest of the room. The dingy cream walls were bare of any ornament save, between the windows, a large carved crucifix, the Christ figure painted in heavy dark colours, the sorrowing eyes almost black.

When she finished, the priest nodded. 'And you have spoken with Cardinal Uguccioni. Well then.' He smiled for the first time. 'I am in exalted company, no? Our . . .' he searched for the word, 'our task was to determine whether what happened to Magda Lachowska was arranged by her or was involuntary but occasioned by illness. And if we decided it was involuntary, we had to decide if what she experienced was a genuine religious revelation or of diabolic origin.' He shrugged out of his coat and let it drop to the floor. 'There is a difficulty in Rome: psychology and religion are very separate. Freud and Jung are atheists, and therefore little appreciated. We are nevertheless forced to acknowledge that sometimes a person can be sick, and this helps their religious development.' He moved some papers so that a chair was free and gestured to Janie with an old-fashioned courtesy. 'You probably will not know that psychological trauma and religious ecstasy have a similar appearance – a loss of bodily awareness and control, a lessening, and perhaps loss, of consciousness.'

'So what is the difference?'

'A true mystical experience may look the same but it enriches, it gives a deep perception of God.'

'And the commission was to decide whether this was what had really happened to Mama?'

'We were to go through all the evidence of parapsychological phenomena. There was to be an exhaustive series of tests and clinical studies.'

'What was the result?'

He was still holding the match. He snapped it between his fingers. 'There *was* no result. Cardinal Cesar Viani informed us that our services were no longer required. The commission was dissolved.'

She said, to give him time to catch his breath, 'Professor Portmain said such an action is unprecedented in the history of the Vatican.'

'Then he will surely be correct.'

She said, carefully, 'I understood that Pope John gave Mama's Chalice group the status of a religious order far sooner than his advisers in the Roman Curia wanted. That it was rushed through.'

'You appear most well informed, Miss Paxton.' His English was more elegant than her own.

'So maybe the commission was dismissed because it found things about Mama which would have prevented her from being accorded that status.'

'Certainly that might be one reading of the situation.' He gave her a quick, sideways glance. 'But then you are supposing that the cardinals and the Pope were united in their desire to prove Mama's case.' He added, half under his breath, 'Not every cardinal is a friend of every pope.' Just for a moment, in the gloomy room, he looked almost crafty. 'The cardinal was adamant that the visions were false,' the old priest went on, his voice quiet, unemphatic. 'He said the commission was certain to reach the same conclusion. He did not see how it could do otherwise.'

Janie regarded him thoughtfully, but Père Sauvel offered nothing further. By now she had absorbed enough of the atmosphere of the man and the room to scent disappointment here. The place was littered with papers and with books; on the floor, on chairs. Some were lying open, face down, others marked with strips of paper. Père Sauvel was no ordinary parish priest. He was a scholar, an academic. He had taught in theological colleges as a much younger man, had even served on a Commission of Inquiry. What was he doing here in Castres, in the depths of rural France among country people, this erudite man with his languages and books?

'Was it the commission which took you out to Brazil?'

'I was teaching theology at a seminary in the city at the time. This was nearly twenty years before the remarkable apparitions of the Virgin Mary appeared to a group of Yugoslav children in Medjugorje. Here was the chance to examine a visionary in a state of ecstasy, to attend the experience and talk to her afterwards. And of course, there were the claims of miraculous cures. It was just incredible, the whole thing.' His expression showed excitement and a kind of regret. 'And we – six representatives of the Church – reacted to it in a manner which now I can scarcely credit.'

'What do you mean?'

'On the one hand, we brought in the most up-to-date scientific equipment. The most sophisticated technical instruments.' He was silent for a moment, then added in a bleak voice, 'And on the other, we subjected her to practices more suited to torturers in the Dark Ages.' He stopped abruptly, as if he had said too much.

She sat up straighter at that, and her movement alerted him to the significance of the admission. She saw caution hardening his features and held herself in check: she found a question that would let him change direction.

'You do believe she had visions, then?'

Clearly relieved he said, 'We all assumed it was possible. There is a new rationalism in the Church now which dismisses such things as hallucinatory. But forty years ago we were less critical. Various tests were performed – medical, psychological, psychiatric.' He paused, lost in thought. The room was silent but for the rushing river below the window. Janie looked at the intelligent eyes burning through the gold-rimmed glasses, at the creased and folded mouth that must once have been passionate. Then he sighed and went on: 'One possibility is that she was schizophrenic. A schizophrenic may experience ecstatic states and mystical visions remarkably similar to those described by medieval saints. But our tests showed this was not the case with her. She was reassuringly normal.' He smiled faintly. 'Or at least she was in those days.' Suddenly he was all sharp edges. 'I argued then, and I do now – is normality a necessary proof of the validity of a vision? The great visionaries – Teresa of Avila, John of the Cross, Francis of Assisi – were highly neurotic, beset by deep psychological problems.' He leaned forward, caught up in his argument. 'If they were living now, they would be discounted as hysterics. St Francis was almost certainly manic-depressive. St Teresa apparently suffered from malignant malaria, and she was anorexic. She was probably an epileptic: it may be that her fits coincided with her description of being lifted into the air as God drew up her soul and her body.' He looked rapt. 'Lovely case. Lovely.'

Janie said, 'Hold on just a minute . . . didn't Mama have a very similar experience?'

He ignored this, leaning his elbows on his desk, and steepled his fingertips together ruminatively as he pursued his ideas. 'What does it matter how they came to their truths, so long as they arrived there? The work Mama does now, the good she has achieved – if these things have come about as a result of some weakness of her body or some unhappy emotional experience, I can't see that it matters.'

He stared up at the ceiling. 'Of course,

chemical means can produce those quasi-mystical experiences. LSD, for instance. Nitrous oxide. Cactus mescal. Mama uses words and descriptions that sound almost psychedelic. The saturation of colours, the dazzling light, the time-shifts. But if Mama took drugs, they evaded every test we could devise.'

Janie observed, quietly, 'It seems to me, Father Sauvel, that despite what you said, you have a perfect memory for all of this.'

'In my entire career, I have never come across a subject so fraught with controversy and intrigue.' He levered himself out of his chair, went across to a large grey filing cabinet and started searching through it, peering short-sightedly at the file names. He pulled out a file with a grunt of triumph and opened a tattered manila folder.

'You said a minute ago that Teresa of Avila was an epileptic. Could Mama be also?'

He nodded. 'We originally thought that might explain the first vision. A specialist made electro-encephalographic recordings of her brainwaves while she was experiencing an ecstasy. But the normal, alpha brainwaves occurred with a frequency of ten per second. No sign at all of the delta waves you get in the brains of epileptics.'

He took a series of black and white photographs from the file, spread them out on his desk. They were poor quality, obviously amateur, flash-lit. The subject was Mama, either alone or with the hand and arm of a man also in the picture. In one or two she was seated, wires attached to her head. In others, she was kneeling on the ground, apparently in prayer. Although they must be more than thirty years old, Janie thought Mama looked very little different: the same creamy robe, the coils of silver-gilt hair. The astonishing eyes dominated her face even more strongly than now.

Père Sauvel picked up one in which Mama was seated before a sort of periscope, her chin on a rest. A man was sitting opposite, looking into the other side of the periscope.

'The ophthalmologist,' said the priest, 'found no abnormalities. We used an estesiometer – a nylon thread, pressed to the cornea of her eye – to see if she blinked or flinched, to evaluate whether she was in a true trance. While an ecstasy was going on, the eyeballs didn't move at all, and she didn't even blink at bright lights. This suggests the normal visual pathways were not being used – in other words, she wasn't watching something, but experiencing it.' He was quiet for a moment, then he said, 'La Pucelle saw apparitions of angels from the age of thirteen. We are told she saw them with her bodily eyes.'

'La Pucelle?'

'Jeanne d'Arc.'

He found another picture and held it out. 'The same was true of hearing. Mama reacted normally to any loud unexpected noise – but while a vision was occurring, nothing we did made the slightest impression. The noise simply didn't register in her brain.'

Janie picked up another photograph. It showed Magda Lachowska on her knees facing what seemed to be a blank wall. A tall, very thin man stood just behind her, his right hand raised and drawn back as if he was about to strike her in the back with an object which glinted dangerously in his right hand. It looked like a slender knife. There was something deeply disturbing about it. Mama, lost in childlike absorption, looked totally vulnerable to the man poised like a murderer above her.

'Is that what you meant by tortures of the Dark Ages?' Janie asked in a low voice. The priest looked at her as if he wished his words back. Finally he nodded. Distaste was written on his face.

'Paulo Lopes was Professor of Dogma. Rio de Janeiro, I seem to . . .' Père Sauvel found another, similar picture, pointed with a finger that shook slightly, she couldn't tell whether from rage or age. 'See that huge . . .' he searched for the word, 'pin? No, no . . . needle.' She saw now that indeed it was, as long as the hollow ones the vet in Derbyshire used to take blood samples from the horses. In the second photograph, Paulo Lopes was pushing the needle into Mama's shoulder-blade. 'Unsterilized,' went on Père Sauvel. 'We said . . .' his voice rose, as it must have risen all those years ago, '*What in heaven's name are you doing, man?* He told us, I am prodding an ecstatic. Can you believe it?' He shook his head. 'This is a medieval test. *Medieval!* And brutal. Brutal,' he repeated, and his voice, too, was shaking. 'To do that to a young woman . . . Lopes should have been . . .' He made a dismissive noise and subsided into silence.

'Was she hurt?'

'She appeared to feel nothing at the time. But later we all saw the bloodstain on the back of her blouse. I do not believe any of us had the decency to inquire if it pained her.'

On the desk, there was a thick white cup without a saucer. He lifted it absent-mindedly to his lips and shuddered at the taste. She saw, as he put it down again, that it contained the dregs of what looked like Turkish coffee, dark and thick.

'We had a terrible row with Lopes after that. He had given us no indication of his intentions, you see. I told him . . .' the old man's voice rang with indignation, 'if you're going to do that, why not just tie her in a sack and throw her in a river? Then if she survived, we'd know she was a witch. It would have had as much basis in science as what he had just done.' He picked fretfully at a loose thread on his jacket. 'I suppose that was when it all started to go sour. There was something, some undertone that I found . . .' He shook his head. 'We subjected her to a barrage of tests. I don't mean she was unwilling, far from it. We were officials of the Church, we asked her permission – after Lopes and his needle, anyway.' He sucked in his breath as if it hurt him to remember the pain he had caused. 'We kept her on her knees for threequarters of an hour at a time with wires attached to her head. We applied heated silver discs to her skin to test her sensitivity to pain during her ecstasies. And she submitted to it all without complaint.'

Janie made a slight movement but he did not notice.

'While she was experiencing her vision, she was oblivious.' Behind the gleam of his glasses, one eyelid flickered with tension. 'And there were other things.' She could almost see him wrestling, then coming to a decision. He continued, quite loudly, as if making a statement long withheld, 'Magda Lachowska at that time was a young and beautiful woman. We were a group of clerics. I would be a liar if I did not admit there was a perverse excitement in what we were doing. A sexual excitement.' His eyes were on his hands now, his voice harsh and low. 'All these years later, it shames me even to speak of it.'

She took a deep breath. 'Did you say as much to anyone then?'

'I made my views clear.'

She said slowly, feeling her way, 'There must have been reports. Written statements.'

His voice was brusque. 'I understand they were . . . mislaid.'

That was the moment when Janie understood: Père Sauvel had been shunted off here, into this charming backwater, to keep him out of the way. To silence him.

As the recollection had silenced him again. When she cleared her throat, he started, remembered her, lifted a hand in wordless apology.

'There were other clinical studies, of course,' he went on. 'Electro-cardiograms showed her heartbeats during several ecstasies. Amazingly enough, she was absolutely relaxed. She seemed to be in a state of peaceful contemplation. The contractions of the heart were normal - in fact, they actually slowed at one point.'

They were both quiet. Finally Janie said, 'So you don't think she was faking.'

He looked at her sombrely. 'Psychologists specializing in apparitions believe that while a vision will apparently come from the outside – be external to the person, if you like – the reality is that that person is probably in touch with very deep levels of their own being. Yet when I observed Mama actually experiencing her vision, when I sensed the emotion, the pure wonder of it . . .' He hesitated, lost in his thoughts. His fingertips, pressed together, were white from pressure. Just when she was sure he had forgotten she was there, he went on, 'I believe she is touched by divinity.'

Janie leaned forward urgently. 'So you *do* believe in her?'

He drew a slow breath, and released his fingertips. He stared into the palms of his hands as if he expected to find an answer there. They were, she noticed, heavily calloused and wondered, what manual work did he do?

'Forty years ago I went into that commission full of cynicism and doubt.' He looked up into her face. 'I found something I had not anticipated.' He spoke simply. 'I believe God wrought a number of miracles through Mama.' She found that the words he used, which in anyone else's mouth would have seemed laughably trite, on his lips were powerful. 'She showed me the power of love.'

The quiet room was warm now, the gas jets burbled. Outside the rainy windows the river tumbled over invisible rocks.

Janie said softly, 'So on that commission, the one that was dissolved, you would have voted for Mama. You would have found her vision to have been divine. Perhaps the others would have voted the same way. And maybe that was just what the cardinal did not want to hear. So he stopped it all going forward.'

Listening, Père Sauvel seemed suddenly drained of energy. He heard her with closed eyes. Then he opened them again. His nod was imperceptible. 'But then Pope John prevailed, after all,' she added even more quietly. 'He just plunged ahead. He granted Mama her founder's status anyway.'

'It was one of the last things Papa John did. He declared her "a sign of the times".' Père Sauvel hoisted himself to his feet. Janie gathered up her notebook.

'Thank you so much for seeing me. I know I intruded, but I do appreciate your kindness. And thank you for the explanation you've given me. It makes everything clearer.'

'Does it?' Even his smile was tired. On the way to the door he paused, as if a thought had struck him. 'To explain,' he said, half to himself, 'is not the same as to explain away.'

Chapter Twenty-One

They had been airborne for more than twenty minutes before Janie noticed the woman in the window seat, and then she was only vaguely aware of a beautifully tailored tweed jacket, a sleek leather briefcase. A hostess leaned forward, solicitous: 'Can I get you a drink?' Janie ordered coffee. From behind a copy of the *Herald Tribune*, a low voice on her right said, '*Jus d'orange, s'il vous plaît.*' The hostess lowered their tables, placed the drinks on paper mats. Janie went back to making notes of her conversation with the priest.

They hit turbulence just as she was beginning to long for a drink. The pilot had scarcely begun his warning announcement when the plane lurched suddenly. A man passing in the aisle on his way from the lavatory stumbled as he reached her seat, and the paper cup of water he was carrying emptied itself neatly over her notebooks and tape recorder. As she struggled to extricate herself and push him back on his feet, her neighbour caught the small black machine before it fell to the floor. She put it on the seat between them and carefully wiped it with a silk chiffon scarf.

When order had been restored Janie said, 'Thank you – but your scarf must be ruined.'

The woman smiled and smoothed the fabric. 'Not at all. This is only water and it will soon dry.'

As she spoke Janie noticed her hands: rounded, French-polished nails, two baroque pearl rings that must be worth a small fortune. So it was disconcerting to see that the woman's knuckles were swollen as though from arthritis or hard manual work: odd, in someone so elegant and expensively dressed. Janie clicked the switch, heard the priest's intense voice in her headphones and turned it off with relief.

'It seems fine. I'm very grateful. This is work I couldn't have repeated.'

'I could see from your concentration it was important.' Her speech was formal, and although her accent was faint, Janie thought she must be German. She was a big woman, with large, even features and a way of carrying herself – head high, shoulders relaxed – which made her look younger than she probably was: her lined skin, those hands, put her in her late sixties at least. Her expression was enigmatic, Inca-esque, beneath hair pulled back into a French pleat.

The plane dipped suddenly and both women looked towards the porthole. It was almost dark but there were no lights below them. 'The Massif Central,' the woman said. 'You can just make out the mountains.' The crew were moving down the aisles, helping people with their seat belts. Craning, Janie glimpsed snowy peaks above the dark twisting spines of rock. The plane lurched again and in front of them, an English voice said, 'Oh God, are we going down?'

Janie only realized she must be looking concerned when the woman said gently, 'Even that would not be so bad, you know.'

'I'm contemplating getting into my lifejacket and checking the oxygen mask.'

As she spoke, the pilot's voice came over the intercom: '*Minor technical problem . . . Landing in Clermont-Ferrand . . . resume your journey tomorrow . . . apologize for any inconvenience.*'

The two women looked at each other. Janie shrugged. 'If it comes to it, I can work in a hotel room as well as anywhere else.'

'I have no one waiting in Paris, fortunately.'

Janie said wryly, 'No one meets me at airports these days. My time is more or less my own. Unfortunately.' She made a wry face, to take the edge from the words.

'When I travelled on business with my husband,' said the other woman, 'we used to enjoy such delays. They were somehow illicit . . .' She smiled at the thought. 'And after more than forty years of marriage, that is a rare sensation.' She paused for a moment. 'I miss him,' she added. Janie heard loneliness in the bleak little statement, recognized that it would only have been made to a stranger. She knew herself that loneliness is the best-kept secret.

'I'm sorry.' She hesitated, then added, 'I'm alone myself, now. Divorced.' She had long ago discovered one of the great rules of good interviews: tell people something intimate and preferably negative about yourself and it invariably produces confidences in return. It was not that she was particularly curious about her companion. Nor was she a woman who talked easily. It was, rather, a matter of professional habit: something in which she had schooled herself for so long, she did it almost without thinking.

'That is always sad to hear. It's far from easy, to have a good marriage. Viktor was very much older than me; I believe that helped us, in the early days. And he had a rich life. Not many people can truly say as much.' She held out her hand to Janie. 'By the way, my name is Alma Gysemans.'

Janie took it, and introduced herself. She looked at her companion thoughtfully. 'Can I ask . . . do you live in Brussels?'

Madame Gysemans was visibly taken aback. 'I don't believe I said anything about that.'

'About ten years ago I interviewed someone with the same name as your husband. Viktor Gysemans, the art dealer? For my newspaper. We talked in his London hotel – the Savoy, I think it was. He was charming. He told me a lot about himself and he used exactly the same phrase. "A rich life."' She reflected, with some relief, that it had been one of the very few interviews where she had liked the subject far too much to be critical.

Madame Gysemans's expression changed totally. Her smile of delight was open. 'That was my Viktor. It was in *The Times*, no? You used those words as the headline for the article.'

They shared a table that evening and lingered over their meal for a long time, finding each other easy company despite the disparity in their ages – or perhaps, Janie thought, because of it. That, and the fact that their worlds were so different, meant there was no competitiveness, none of the wary professional circling she often found herself engaged in with women her own age. They talked about work, though Janie said nothing about her present project. Like any journalist she was paranoid about work in progress, and though it was already obvious Madame Gysemans was a woman of discretion, such mistrust was too ingrained to ignore. Ideas were like colds: get too near someone and they caught yours. They discussed the pleasures and hazards of travelling alone.

'I still travel a good deal,' Alma Gysemans admitted. 'Partly in search of the sun, you understand, partly because I can't bear to stop working. The excitement of finding something good, something important . . . a drawing, a watercolour, that has maybe never been on the market before. I get a lot of pleasure from helping people form a collection.'

'Your husband told me, when you arrive in a capital city, museum directors rush to see you and the directors of the great auction houses compete to give you lunch.'

The older woman lit yet another cigarette and chuckled.

'He was a great publicist, Viktor. But that is true, I suppose. I sell things I like very much to people I like very, very much. It is a good way to live.'

'Do you still have the gallery?'

'Yes, in the heart of the city. I live over the shop.' She smiled at the phrase. 'That is the tradition, though now my son Piet does most of it. He still seeks my opinion, though of course he does not have to do so: he has all his father's flair and taste. And we hold no exhibitions. We are very private.' She gestured to the waiter for fresh coffee. 'And Brussels,' she added, 'is a fine city from which to do business. There is a lot of money there, many diplomats, many officials, many businessmen. And it is a good place to bring up a family.'

They moved on to the problems of children. Alma Gysemans assured Janie that no matter who claimed otherwise, nothing changed: combining the two had been a constant source of stress and anxiety when she was doing it many years ago. 'Not these days,' she said, with a sigh, 'now I don't see enough of them,' and brought out photographs of her three from a flat tortoiseshell case. 'Old ones,' she explained. Fernande, the eldest of the family, had her mother's calm expression as she stood among a clutch of children ranging from a toddler to a pretty teenager. 'Fernande and her husband met when they were in the same law chambers and far too young . . .' Alma smiled. 'But it has been a good marriage, thank God.' The younger son, Piet, who now ran the gallery, was shown as a slimmer, beardless version of the man Janie had interviewed. Beside him stood a woman and two small girls. 'And this is Karel.' She flipped to another picture, of a striking man leaning against a sailing boat. He had lean, sombre features under thick hair tousled by the wind. 'They say the middle child is the difficult one.' She smiled suddenly. 'When he was small, he used to complain he was the only member of the family with fair hair. So for years I used to bleach mine to his colour. See?' She showed Janie another picture: herself, much younger and blonde, her

274

hands on the shoulders of a thin little boy with an endearing gap between his teeth.

'What does Karel do?'

For a second, Alma's composure faltered. She looked bewildered, Janie thought. That was the only word. 'Uh . . . this and that. He has not found himself as yet. He is very shy, very uncertain of himself. There have been periods when I have worried a great deal about him.' Janie was curious: an odd way to speak of a man who must be fifty. She opened her mouth to ask but Alma added, with finality, 'He's away at the moment. In Indonesia, I think. He doesn't always tell me.' She slipped the photographs back into their case.

Janie found the older woman was herself a consummate listener: almost without being aware of it, Janie found their roles changed, found it was she talking about her marriage break-up and the resulting problems with Adam. Normally she was reticent by nature, and it was an unexpected relief to express thoughts that had been worrying her for so long.

'. . . perhaps if he wasn't an only child, it wouldn't be so bad,' she finished. 'Sometimes I think he's a lonely boy.'

Alma Gysemans stubbed out her cigarette. 'You're young enough to have more. And these days . . .' her expression was quizzical, 'one evidently need not be in the married state.'

Janie astonished herself by what she said next. 'I thought about it seriously, a couple of months ago. But then I got frightened.' She leaned forward and stubbed out her own cigarette with unnecessary force. 'I'd never had an abortion before. It seemed the best – the only . . . I didn't know how much I'd regret it, afterwards.'

She punished herself again with the words: it was something she had told no one else. She had not confided those regrets even to her sister. (Especially not her sister, plump contented Lou, comfortable in the Northamptonshire farmhouse with Harold and the children.)

She had assumed she would feel nothing but relief once it was done. When the time came to leave the clinic in Great Portland Street she had walked alone out of the building and climbed shakily into the taxi. Her body felt invaded, tampered with, sore. Her breasts hurt and the clumsy pad chafed between her legs. But she throbbed with an ache far more acute than mere physical discomfort. Everything around her had been the lifeless grey of her despair: buildings, pavement, sky, the faces and the clothes of passers-by. She had told herself, this will pass, soon it will be behind me. But it had not done so. If she let herself think of it, if she gave herself even a few minutes of empty time, it all came back.

She added, 'I read somewhere that the feeling of loss with an aborted child is as great as the loss of a full term baby. But it's something that has scarcely been recognized by the medical profession. So there's no allowance made for the need to mourn.'

There was a silence. Then Alma Gysemans said quietly, 'I think there must be many women who would understand very well what it is to lose a baby.'

Janie pressed the back of a clenched hand hard against her nose to counter the unexpected tears blurring her eyes. She thought she heard the older woman add, just beneath her breath, 'I do myself.' But she did not trust herself to ask.

Next morning Janie woke at six and knew at once she felt better. She had slept deeply, though she had not expected to do so. They said confession was good for the soul. Maybe her candour with the older woman had released something. She thought about it in the shower, and then realized she had been humming to herself.

They travelled together on the hotel bus back to the departure desk, to go once more through the familiar procedure of passports, luggage, seat allocation. Janie bought three newspapers and a pile of magazines. Waiting for their flight to be announced, she flipped through them, speed-reading as always, noting a piece to clip later: *Time* magazine carried a story about genocide atrocities in Rwanda. The reporter had concentrated on a visit made by Mama to widows and orphans in a refugee camp. There was a photograph of her looking down with infinite tenderness at the Hutu baby she nursed, his eyes dark and sunken by dehydration.

When the London flight was called, Janie bundled papers and magazines into the carrier bag. On board, she put the bag on the seat between herself and Alma Gysemans, indicating that she should help herself. A little later, when the plane was on course, the older woman did so. After a while, glancing up from her notes, something in the quality of her companion's stillness caught Janie's attention.

Alma Gysemans gazed unseeing out of the porthole at empty blue sky. She had taken off her tinted glasses. It was the first time Janie had seen her without them and she looked younger, less distinguished, with the defenceless, slightly stunned gaze of the myopic. She was deep in reverie. Her hands lay open and idle on her lap, palms up, in a passive attitude that was far from characteristic. On the pull-down table before her lay the copy of *Time*, folded back at the page she had evidently just been reading. *Tens of thousands slaughtered in Rwanda's bloodbath, say survivors . . .*

Despite her caution the previous evening, Janie found herself saying, 'I'm doing some research on Mama: that's why I was in France.'

She thought the Belgian woman would have been interested. But she merely nodded, closed the magazine and handed it back.

Chapter Twenty-Two

On the appointed day, Patrice Akonda was ready at 4 a.m. in his white T-shirt and shorts. Jean insisted on wearing long cotton trousers so no one could see he had a bad leg. In the cool of early morning the sisters scurried to complete their duties, to pack food and assemble in the court-yard. The bus was two hours late, the driver having had a fight with his woman the previous night, and by the time they set off – the remaining sisters and the patients waving from the verandahs – the sun was high. The bright blue bus bounced along the curving roads, the driver playing his transistor at full blast. After an hour or so he cheered up and added his considerable bass to the music. The sisters had to shout to each other in order to be heard. The seats were shiny leatherette and since Patrice's feet did not touch the floor he kept slipping off. There was a strong reek of goat. Jean, whose leg was hurting again, dozed against his mother's shoulder.

By the time they reached the long white colonial-style house, Mama was already inside and a dozen cars and jeeps showed how many import-ant people were there with her. An excited crowd was waiting for her to emerge again. A couple of elderly men wandered among them, wooden poles across their shoulders hung with used Fanta bottles of coloured drink. Young women carried baskets of liquid sealed in little plastic bags.

While his mother was settling Jean on the trolley, Patrice had already seen what he must do. Knotting the trolley rope securely round his waist, he pulled Jean round past the crowd as far as the house. Then he dropped to hands and knees, Jean lay down flat, and he steered the trolley along under the verandah. It worked better even than he hoped: they came out right at the front of the crowd, by the main door. Over this was painted the picture of a beautiful cup made out of hands the colour of the night sky and brimming with grapes. Jean read out to him what was written underneath, in the same colour. *Chalice of the Grapes of God.*

Patrice knew everything would be all right now: the words rang like a promise.

Chapter Twenty-Three

'Lady de Lisle.'

The waiter at the cocktail bar of the Savoy Hotel put Zazi de Lisle's gin and tonic before her with a flourish. Janie's drink – identical in appearance but minus the gin – received rather less attention.

'I think we need more olives, Salvatore,' the lady announced. 'And some of those lovely little biscuits?' She gave him a winsome look from beneath long false eyelashes and ran a hand through thick, jet-black hair. Her strong, arched brows were so dark she must dye them, also. With her impressive head on that narrow body, the bone-thin legs, she reminded Janie of that old-fashioned word, *mannequin*. When the olives arrived she proceeded to eat with a kind of ravenous absent-mindedness, her eyes on the activity below the window, where cars and taxis swung out of the Strand to deposit the occupants at the brightly lit foyer. She was like a child watching television with a bag of sweets. How much time must the woman spend here?

Janie said, 'It was kind of you to see me this evening.'

'I'm sorry you have had to wait so long.' The black eyes turned themselves on her, the smoky voice with its subtle inflections was charm itself. 'I have been in Bosnia. Magda wanted me there with her. She is very much alone, you know, despite the crowds who surround her.' Janie thought of her last glimpse of Mama leaving the cathedral, so upright, set apart.

'How is she?'

Zazi de Lisle considered her glass. 'Older. Tired.' She smiled, and in an involuntary gesture touched the soft, creased skin at the corner of her eye. 'Like the rest of us.'

'I wanted to ask about something you said once in an interview.'

The older woman sipped her drink. 'Which was?'

Janie did not need to consult her notes. She repeated, from memory, '*I met a young woman with her life before her, and I watched her struggle with demons.* What demons, Lady de Lisle?'

Zazi de Lisle crossed her legs and Janie tried to decide how old she was. Somewhere in her mid-fifties, from her looks. But Janie, who had been through the press cuttings, added another ten years, at least. When the woman smiled, her teeth were very sharp. 'A turn of phrase, merely. I did indeed meet Magda many years ago, when we and the world were different.'

'Where was that?' Janie interjected quickly.

With the deftness of the professional speaker, Lady de Lisle carried on as if she had not heard. 'She was beset by troubles in those days,' she continued, 'but I believe she vanquished them.'

'Troubles?'

The woman's shout of laughter was as raucous, as unexpected as a hooligan in a flower shop. 'My dear child, we all have troubles.' She leaned forward, tapped Janie on the knee. 'Magda is only flesh and blood. You must believe me . . .' she gave these words great weight, 'she is no saint. Though I can well understand why people wish her so.'

'Why do people want to believe she is? What *is* it about her?'

'Humanity has a need for saints, for living representatives of a God they seek, and the desperation of their need creates people prepared to fill the role. Magda is just such a person.'

Janie said drily, 'So you think she is just an ordinary woman pushed into doing an extraordinary job.'

'I imagine that is what most saints are, in truth. The rest is in the eye of the beholder. People want something to give meaning to their existence. Their belief in Mama has less to do with anything she has achieved than with their desperate desire for guidance. Especially if they belong to social groups who feel themselves rejected or marginalized by society.'

'What about the witnesses, the people who saw her die and live again?'

Zazi de Lisle lifted those oddly square shoulders. '*They* certainly come into the latter category. However, I believe if you go back and check very carefully, you will find quite ordinary explanations for many of the things they claim to have seen and heard.'

'What do you mean?'

'It was said that as she died, her room smelled of lilies. So maybe there were flowers – people take flowers to the sick, do they not? And the crystal tears. I can think of several things those could be. Perhaps she had some ornament which got

283

broken. Little beads might have fallen off a dress, or some embroidery, and then been found later. You take my drift? There was a white dove, apparently. Has it occurred to you that in the heat of the moment just about any bird might have been so described? Maybe she kept budgerigars. Perhaps a tame pigeon.'

Janie thought about it. She had found rational explanations for the ball of fire, the pillars of light, even a possible one for Mama's resuscitation, if that was what it was. But some things seemed to defy logic. 'What about the darkness, the wind? It was all so . . .' she searched for the word, 'so biblical.'

'Oh, please.' Zazi de Lisle spoke sharply. 'Do not make the medieval mistake of confusing unusual meteorological conditions with supernatural forces.'

Janie stared at her thoughtfully. Why was the woman so anxious to demystify Mama? What was going on here? 'And what do you make of the miracles, the cures ascribed to her?'

'Once this thing got under way, once people started believing in Mama's powers, they began to prepare themselves before they saw her. They would fast, taking only bread and water for forty-eight hours, in order that God should reveal himself to them. Even I can see how that would make one susceptible.' From her handbag she produced a tortoiseshell case and extracted a cigarette. She did not offer one to Janie. Salvatore was immediately at her side with a flaring lighter. She inhaled deeply and leaned back. 'I am not a religious person, Miss Paxton. Though there have been moments. But of one thing I am sure: there is no heaven so closed that prayer, fasting and penance cannot find a way into it.'

'She *has* performed some remarkable cures, though.'

Lady de Lisle shrugged. 'Some, I grant you, seem real enough. But others are open to doubt. Or at any rate to a healthy degree of scepticism.' She looked around for Salvatore, lifted her glass, arched her eyebrows. 'If you observe her with no more intelligence than does the rest of the world, you will be doing her a grave disservice.'

'Meaning?'

'Consider these facts. You will not have read of them in any newspaper. A baby died of a defective heart after the parents decided the doctors' diagnoses had been mistaken, and refused further medication. A young man believed himself healed and chose – wrongly as it turned out – not to have an operation for his cancer.' She lifted her head and blew a perfect smoke ring. It was a gesture redolent of the Thirties. 'These fatalities were not of course Mama's fault. The families believed they had been promised cures. But Mama only ever assured them that prayer and fasting were capable of accomplishing miracles. Any priest would have said the same.' She stopped as Salvatore arrived with a fresh drink.

'The sad truth is,' she went on, 'there are conditions which respond neither to medical nor divine intervention. No matter how ardently one may wish it otherwise. These stories are neglected by the media. I doubt they even make sad little newspaper paragraphs. Of course . . .' she picked up her glass, 'of course, not all are deaths. Take the paraplegic who felt a current run through his body as he prayed. He was able to get up, he even took a few steps. A blind man seemed to think he could see again. They were filled with elation, exalted almost. Yet if you followed up these cases, you would have found that months later the paraplegic was still confined to his wheelchair twenty-four hours a day unless he had two strong helpers, and the blind man had lost his recently acquired ability to discern blurred shapes.' She sighed. 'They are the poor deluded.'

Janie noticed her odd use of the phrase. She said, 'I also read about a little girl of five who was taken to Mama while in a coma. It was during those first days in Brazil. Mama apparently touched her, and the child woke up. She said, "I thirst." That's remarkable.'

'Apparently the phrase was, "I'm thirsty." It was in the translation that her simple words became invested with such powerful overtones.'

'If you're right, then how do these stories gain such credence?'

'Most people are desperate to find some meaning beyond science, which they see as unsatisfying and confining. They need little persuasion to believe in the supernatural.' She turned towards the bar, holding out the empty dish of olives. 'Salvatore!'

Janie was struggling to make sense of what she was hearing. She had regarded Lady de Lisle as one of Mama's strongest allies. They were so close that sometimes they even travelled together when Mama was on official business. And yet the woman seemed intent on destroying her myth. 'You're suggesting the whole thing is a farce, then. Are you telling me she's a phoney? That the whole thing – the Chalice, the way people worship her – is a con trick?'

Lady de Lisle put out an imperious hand. A great green stone glittered among diamonds.

'I said *no* such thing.' There was real fury in her voice. 'No one can look on her work and doubt her commitment or her achievements.'

'But you just told me, she is no saint.'

She sighed. 'I did. Don't you see, I want to save her from this doubtful accolade. I am not saying she is not a wonderful woman: she is truly astonishing. She is a source of light in many lives.' Zazi de Lisle leaned forward again, and that remarkable voice dropped to an even lower register. 'My only desire is to protect her.'

'Protect her? From me?'

'From herself. I see her struggle to fulfil the role people demand of her.' There was a suggestion of tears in those dark eyes. 'It is too much to ask of any human being. No one is strong enough.' She found a tiny white lace handkerchief from somewhere, dabbed beneath her eyes. 'My poor Magda.'

It was calculated, theatrical – and yet oddly moving. It was obvious this bony little woman truly cared for 'my poor Magda'. But if that was the case, there seemed no possible reason for her to cast doubts on Mama's powers.

With sudden insight Janie asked, 'You want to protect her because of something that happened when you first knew her. That's it, isn't it?'

Very gently, Lady de Lisle shook her head. 'If we can learn enough about the life of any individual then, with hindsight, we can demonstrate how they moved inexorably in one direction or another. But I have told you all I can. The rest is up to you.'

When Janie had paid for the drinks, Zazi de Lisle got to her feet.

'You must excuse me. I go to meet my baronet.' She was oblivious to Janie's startled expression at the possessive. 'I have my car and driver outside. He will take you anywhere you wish to go.' She seemed genuinely surprised when Janie declined. 'Well then, my dear, this is for you. Magda and I discussed it. I was less certain, but she insisted she wanted you to have it.' She gestured to a blue folder she had laid on the table before them. 'It is confidential. Read it when you are alone.'

The moment Zazi de Lisle had left, the waiter, Salvatore, came over, his tray borne discreetly before him, a linen napkin over his arm.

'Excuse me, madame. The gentleman wishes to know if you would join him for a drink.'

She did not even look in the direction he indicated but shook her head brusquely, her face cold and composed. A few months ago, it might have amused her. Even the slightly sleazy pick-up connotations would have spiced the encounter with the illicit: she would have left the bar with a swing in her walk.

As it was, the minute she thought about it, she found herself annoyed by her reaction. She had instinctively rejected an approach from a man –

she let herself glance briefly in his direction after a while – who was admittedly not her type. But he was the right sort of age – her age – well dressed, attractive. Accepting a drink would not have compromised her, after all.

She had refused because for months, since the embarrassing encounter – she amended that, since the fiasco – with David Chester in New York, she had been training herself to survive alone. Out of necessity, she had censored her eyes and her memory and her cunt: don't touch, don't need, don't want. She found she could live without a man, without sex, without even casual embraces. She could live without all these things. There was something oddly pleasurable about being by herself. She luxuriated in the freedom to work when she chose, go to bed whenever she felt like it, cook a meal or stick a frozen dinner in the microwave and read as she ate.

And then a sharp little inner voice asked, But can you live without them? Or are you becoming more dry and hard and closed with every day? It wasn't the act of sex itself she missed – though God knew she wouldn't mind that, would give almost anything for the feel of a man filling her up, quieting the clamour of her body. But what she really missed was the tenderness, the touching, being close to another human being. She could keep herself going solo, she supposed. But it wasn't simply the release of orgasm she craved. Just sleeping with another person beside you was a totally different experience, so you woke feeling more alive, renewed. Sleeping alone, she started each day exhausted, and it seemed never to lift.

She finished her drink and left the hotel. Cabs were easy to find at the Savoy. She did not need a man for that.

As the cab drove along the Strand, she opened the slim dark blue folder. It contained neatly typed pages of names and addresses. She stared at them. What were they? They seemed to be from all over the world. She flipped at random. *Cecilia Revilla.* An address and phone number in Panama. And then a date. 24.6.56. *Elio Mistretta.* The address was in Calabria. There was no phone number. The date was 18.3.59. *Colin McDowell.* Address and telephone number in Auckland, New Zealand. 19.2.93. *Letitia Woessner.* She lived in Greenwich Village, New York. 26.5.89.

There must have been twenty more names. Janie was astonished. She flipped the pages and saw that some of the names were followed by brief biographies. No. She looked again: they were *details of their health.* Some notes were of recognized medical conditions, others seemed to be descriptions of symptoms.

Janie read at random.

Stenfert Goedhuis. Age 4. Serious deafness following attack of measles at eighteen months. Learning and emotional development impaired as a result. Behavioural problems include tantrums, bedwetting . . . Healed.

Penny Caldwell. Age 8. Bright's Disease. Doctors' prognosis poor. Failing vision, headaches, shortness of breath . . . Healed.

Nita van Bloerk. Age 23. Functional paralysis. Left hand side only. Some facial paralysis, loss of speech. Possibly emotional in origin . . . Healed.

Friedrich Maas. Age 63. Tingling, pins and needles in the legs, stiffness. Formerly treated for pernicious anaemia . . . Healed.

These must have been the people Lady de Lisle had spoken of, those Mama had apparently cured. The dates after their names must be when they had seen her. But there were addresses and, for many, telephone numbers also: it would be only a couple of days' work to find out what had happened to them since then.

When Janie went through the blue file more carefully, in the train back to Derbyshire, she found half a dozen photostats of cuttings she had missed earlier. On one page a little girl's face, hair in ribboned bunches, smiled up from an article in the *Manchester Evening News* with a date in March 1965:

Little Penny – Home with Hope!

Eight-year-old Penny Caldwell from Sale was back home from hospital today, ready for the start of the new term at Doves Infants' School. She is one of a group of a dozen children and adults who attended a special service at the newly opened Chalice House in Leeds a month ago. The foundress of this worldwide religious community, Magda Lachowska – known universally as Mama – met the children afterwards. 'Mama didn't seem to do anything special,' said Penny's mother Karen, 32. 'She just held Penny, and you could tell she was moved by her plight because we could see her crying. Penny was really ill. She was constantly in and out of hospital, hardly able to look at her picture books for the last few months and she was always in pain. But now she's a different child. She hasn't had a headache since, and she's starting school again. Whatever the future holds, this time we all have together now is a miracle to us.'

Janie dropped the papers onto her lap and stared out into the grey light of early evening, the folded fields. What had Zazi de Lisle called them? *The poor deluded.*

Chapter Twenty-Four

Next day she made several international telephone calls. The first was to New York.

'My name is Janie Paxton. I'm ringing from England for Ms Woessner. Letitia Woessner. I believe she went to see Mama when she was ill . . . yes, that's right. Only I'm writing a book about Mama. So I just wanted to check how Ms Woessner was keeping now . . .' A long pause, then, 'Oh, I see. I'm so sorry. Was it . . . ? No, I realize that. Yes. Yes. Well look, thanks anyway for talking to me. And I do hope you don't mind my calling like this: I'm just so sorry . . .'

The second was to New Zealand.

'I'm calling from England, my name's Janie Paxton, I was hoping for a word with Colin McDowell. I understand he was cured by Mama and I wondered how he was getting on.' Her voice dropped in disapppointment. 'Oh dear, that's very sad. I really didn't know. Did he? Yes, I can imagine. So you must be his . . . Oh, right. Well look, I won't bother you any . . .'

Six more telephone calls followed. When Janie had made the last one, she sat with her head in her hands. She was baffled. Zazi de Lisle had insisted it was Mama's express wish that she be given these papers. She could not begin to understand the reason. All they proved was what Zazi de Lisle had said and she had been so reluctant to accept: that Mama's 'miracles' were indeed open to grave doubt.

Only one of the people she had telephoned was still alive.

At around the time Janie was making her third international call, Alma Gysemans finally abandoned any attempt to sleep in her suite at the Grand Hotel on the Boulevard des Capucines in Paris. She felt exhausted, empty, as though she had fought a long battle, and lost.

She drank her morning café au lait and ate a single roll. Afterwards she dressed carefully. Only then did she make a telephone call. It was local. To the next arrondissement, in fact. She gave her name, asked a single question, copied down another Paris number. She wrote it on a single piece of paper, so there would be no impression left on a pad.

A little later she went out. She did not move at her usual crisp pace but walked slowly, like someone very old. Or very reluctant. Opposite a lingerie shop, Madeleine, were two open telephone booths, both occupied. She waited, staring fixedly at the white, lace-topped stockings and diamond garters which were exhibited on shapely legs in the window, until a booth became free. It was a way of putting off the moment. When the number answered, she identified herself. She spoke briefly, very quietly, and with great intensity. During the conversation, she gave a name, *Jane Paxton*, and the Derbyshire telephone number. She did not say goodbye.

She replaced the receiver as though it weighed a great deal and glanced in the tiny mirror above the list of emergency numbers. She looked drained and white, a ghost of herself. Which, she thought with unaccustomed bitterness, in a way she was.

At eleven o'clock Janie tapped 'Save' on her machine and yawned and stretched and reached for her coffee. She picked up a cutting about Mama from *The Times* of June 1996. She read it, sighed impatiently and dropped it into her file box. It fell upside down. Idly, she stared at the other side of the cutting, at a photograph of palm trees bent almost double under a high wind. ULULONOH NI SEVIL SEKAT ODANROT, it said. She turned it round. And stared at it. Then she ran downstairs.

In the living room she went through her tapes, selecting one she had recorded two weeks ago but had not yet found the time to watch. She slipped it into the machine.

The documentary on miracles made for BBC-2 was fronted by a young Indian woman with long dark hair and enormous tortoiseshell glasses. This week the programme concentrated on the remarkable conditions prevailing at the time of Magda Lachowska's claimed resurrection. Speaking easily, she went back over the astonishing events of Mama's death and rebirth in São Paulo in 1946. She detailed the many inexplicable things reported that day: the green fog smelling strongly of sulphur, the pillars of fire seen only by the camera lens (here they showed the newspaper photograph Janie had already seen), the curious humming of invisible insects.

All these phenomena had been regarded at the time as part of a miraculous happening. But now, several decades later, scientific research was available which offered an alternative explanation. It was possible – more than possible, probable – that these things were caused by weather conditions prevailing at the time. The basic facts were still scarce and much of what was known was little more than guesswork.

The programme took in clips from the recent spate of films about tornadoes which had poured out of Hollywood in answer to the public's current fascination. Then the interviewer came on camera to explain that there were now several companies operating in the US which specialized in 'chasing' tornadoes. People paid large amounts of money in order to spend days at a time on a sort of guided tour, following the path of these terrifying occurrences across different states. There was footage of cars driving at top speed while a hand-held camera recorded incredible cloud formations, and the sight and sound of winds of terrifying violence. Then there were statements from people who had experienced whirlwinds from the relative safety of storm cellars.

The first one, a woman in Ohio, said, 'We almost suffocated. It was sort of a greenish gas? And there was this weird humming noise, only real loud. I never heard nuthin' like it.'

The second, from a teenage boy in Freeman, South Dakota, described the sulphurous smell which filled the room where he and his younger brothers were sheltering. 'It was like ozone, or that stuff we use in the chemistry lab – oxides of nitrogen. We'd been doing that just the other day. They're produced by electrical discharges.'

Another man from Toledo told reporters he and his teenage son suffered what looked like severe sunburn on his face and arms. The local hospital told them it must have been close exposure to ultraviolet rays from the electrical activity.

Janie sat on the floor in front of the television, arms round her knees, deep in thought.

For months now, she had been concentrating every effort on researching Mama's life. She had been hired to write a sympathetic biography, and that was what she had intended to do. At first it had seemed her only problem was handling the wealth of material. A large part of her mind did not want to look too hard: she had the book to write, she needed to get it finished fast, she did not want to make difficulties for herself.

For weeks now, she had sensed that something about Magda Lachowska continued to elude her. It had become like a sore spot she could not leave alone, though she would do better to cover it up. She had worried at it, probing and picking, uncertain what she was looking for.

Zazi de Lisle had made some strange remarks. She had offered a rational explanation of the extraordinary happenings in São Paulo: *she is no saint.* She had cast doubts on Mama's healing powers: *the poor deluded.* And yet clearly she and Mama were close. Lady de Lisle had just returned from spending a week with her in Bosnia. *Mama and I discussed . . .*

It seemed on the face of it a curious reversal of the way things had previously been conducted. Mama allowed – encouraged – the world to regard her as almost mystical. She could, after all, have totally denied the claims made on her behalf for the healings, the visions. Instead she had never, so far as Janie could tell, done anything other than foster this image.

It was understandable enough. She had been poverty-stricken, deserted and alone, in São Paulo at the time of her 'death'. She had to live and, as Mama, there seemed always to have been money available, activity around her, followers and supporters. The stories that had grown up concerning her in those early days had been powerful – and simple, for the people who repeated them were simple people, largely uneducated, in need of hope to light poor lives.

For these people, for so many others, the image was what they wanted. It was strong and memorable. Mama, in whose shadow lavender plants bloomed on stony ground and water ran again in dried-up brooks. Mama, for whom pale children smiled again. Mama, for whose eyes only, the veil between heaven and hell had been pulled back.

And yet, Janie thought, even as they gazed at the image, the real woman eluded them. She deliberately encouraged the impression because it was the easiest way to fade herself out. She left no trace of who she really was, of the emotions she truly felt.

Janie's experience in Poland had convinced her that Mama had been painstakingly built into a suitable myth in a massive public relations exercise. It was a sophisticated stratagem of evasion. What people saw was shadow play, and illusion. No one – not even sceptics like Janusz Pozomiek – chose to question, because of the good that was achieved, the lives that were saved.

And yet it seemed now as if Mama had made a different decision. The hints Zazi de Lisle had dropped, her desire to pour cold water on the more extreme beliefs, the file of case histories. *Mama wants you to have it.*

The case histories had, with one exception, confirmed Zazi de Lisle's scepticism. There had been remissions, possibly, but that was the most that could be claimed. And those, of course, could have been brought about by a burst of optimism and hope following Mama's intervention. Or they could have been spontaneous, in which case they would have happened anyway.

Whatever the truth was, she understood she now had to accept the overwhelming evidence that Mama was not the figure she and the Krzysztof Foundation presented. She was someone else, someone entirely different. Someone full of secrets.

And the greatest secret of all was her past.

Chapter Twenty-Five

The boy Patrice Akonda and his brother Jean held hands, so the pressure of the people behind would not force the child away from the trolley. They had long ago lost sight of their mother and the sisters. But they knew Mama was coming by the way the people fell silent, and then started shouting. From the uproar one word emerged, yelled over and over. The people turned it into a chant. '*Mama-mamamamama!*'

Patrice held his breath, waiting for someone in rich garments and a golden crown, a fringed canopy held above her head. He imagined her big and smiling, glistening and powerful. So when a thin person with a white face and white hair and a white robe appeared, followed by a shaven-headed man in dark blue, he stared past them, peering into the shady interior of the house, still waiting. More people came out – a couple of men in uniform, some ladies, one even wearing a hat. Still not the person he sought.

In the minute or two it took him to understand his mistake, Mama had come swiftly down the steps. She was already passing by the low trolley carrying his brother when Patrice realized who she was. Seeing his opportunity to attract her attention vanishing, he tried to catch hold of the hem of her robe. But he had not been quick enough, his arms were short, the creamy fabric slipped through his fingers. The blue man, joined now by several others, made a path for her through the clamouring, reaching crowd.

Dragging the trolley behind him, the boy struggled to force his way through the people. It was useless. From being right at the front they were now blocked by a sea of jumping, indifferent backs trying to catch a glimpse of the lady found by angels.

He looked down at Jean. He was sitting up on the trolley, holding his bad leg tightly, eyes glistening with unshed tears. He tried to smile at his little brother and shrugged to say, Never mind.

Patrice couldn't bear it. He put back his head and squeezed his eyes shut and clenched his fists. He was behaving like a baby, but he didn't care. His cry (*'Mama, Mama, aidez-nous!'*) was high and hopeless and lost in the tumult.

Chapter Twenty-Six

The fax had been spilling out over her desk when Janie walked into the office on Tuesday morning, a mug of tea in one hand, the *Guardian* under her arm. She read it while it was still printing, then ripped it out of the machine and read it again.

There was nothing on the page to register who had sent it or from where: no name on the top, no return fax or telephone number. It was neatly typed in a narrow, angular font which lent a curt authority to the summons, for that it most certainly was.

Re current project Vital you arrange to be in Bruxelles 12 October Dante will await you 20 Rue des Sables 22.00 heures.

Dante? Who the hell was Dante?

Janie telephoned Alma Gysemans at her art gallery in Brussels. They had talked at length several times, and agreed they would meet in London. Despite the short time they had spent together, Janie found the Belgian woman both sympathetic and stimulating company. She liked and trusted her. So it was easy to say now, 'I need your advice.' She explained the fax. 'Does the name Dante mean anything to you?'

The hush at the other end of the phone was tangible. Then Alma, her habitually calm voice urgent, said, 'I'll phone you back.' The line went dead.

Thirty minutes later, her telephone rang. Alma Gysemans sounded breathless.

'I must apologize for my rudeness. But that was my office telephone. I am in a public call box. Now we can talk.'

'I never meant to be such a nuisance. You had people in the gallery?'

'No. I was alone.'

Janie was puzzled. 'Is your line tapped?'

'Oh, I don't really think so. But the name you mentioned – one must be careful.'

Janie sat down. 'So you do know who I mean?'

'By reputation.'

'Is he dangerous?' She could think of no other explanation for Alma's exaggerated caution.

'No. No, of course not. But the people he deals with . . . he is involved in . . . difficult areas.'

'Criminal, you mean? Is he with the police, then?'

'No. Nothing like that. Look, I can't . . .' Alma faltered and fell silent.

'I shouldn't have asked you. I can tell this is disturbing for you. I'll just see if I can find out anything here—'

Again, Alma interrupted. '*No!* Better not ask too many questions. You don't want to alert . . . people.' Odd, Janie thought. What people? Another pause, then, 'If he's approached you, I think you should see what he wants.'

'I don't want to do anything stupid,' Janie said.

'Do you know if he is to be trusted?'

Alma's voice was serious. 'If you cannot trust this man, then believe me, there is no hope for truth or justice in this world.'

On 12 October Janie caught the four o'clock Eurostar from Waterloo, travelling first class. She read the newspapers arranged on the padded seats in the hallway as they sped through the lush Kent fields. The journey was almost silent and so steady that, at a hundred and eighty miles an hour, the champagne on the table beside the pink-shaded light barely swayed in its glass. They were slipping into the Channel Tunnel before she knew they'd reached it. She wondered what had happened to the British outcries about packs of rabid Euro-foxes infesting the sceptred isle, and decided any invaders would be mince long before they made it to the Kent coast.

As they reached Lille, Bryan the purser was bringing round breast of duck and spiced salad. Janie stared out at the darkening French fields. It was a long way to go to satisfy her curiosity. On the other hand, maybe it was more than curiosity. The last few weeks had been full of strange remarks, odd accidents, coincidences – and all of them had led her on, added another dimension, changed her perceptions about the woman she was investigating.

And Alma Gysemans's response had been very strange. The woman had impressed her on first meeting as being capable and calm. Yet she'd been flustered on the phone almost to the point of incoherence. And then at the end, she had insisted

Janie must stay with her, no matter how late her meeting went on.

Bryan was back again with coffee and Belgian chocolates in tiny gold boxes. Afterwards, Janie wondered whether the ordered, efficient calm of the travelling had been poor preparation for the bizarre meeting she was about to experience. Though what would have prepared her, she could not for the life of her have said.

The taxi turned onto a wide ring road, a hideous monument to the Sixties, lined with skyscraper office blocks of grey concrete designed like multi-storey garages, featureless and utilitarian. They branched off right, then through sideroads tracked back the way they had come. The Rue des Sables proved to be a dingy deserted street running lower than the ring road, and at right angles. The taxi passed a derelict bar, the words MORT SUBIT LAMBIC ANNO 1686 written across it in huge, faded letters of gilt and red. A printworks was boarded up, the once elegant Thirties façade pitted and decayed, windows broken. Nothing moved on the dark pavements. A fine rain fell as yellow haze under the few old-fashioned lights. She shivered even in the overheated vehicle.

The taxi driver stopped outside a high building. Number 20 was the *Centre belge de la bande dessinée,* according to the sign on the wall. In direct contrast to the dark street, all the windows here glowed brightly. One of the heavy double doors stood invitingly open and she stepped into the stream of light.

Before her, brightly lit from above, a great

hallway stretched into shadows. Wherever she turned there were ornate pillars, palm trees, screens of glass in the restored Art Nouveau building, though what its original purpose might have been, she could not imagine. A magnificent fin-de-siècle photographic portrait of a dark man in his late forties was blown up large, so his fiercely handsome presence dominated the place.

'Madame.' An attendant in navy suit and cap moved out of a doorway, gesturing for her to continue across the marble tiles towards the curving flight of stairs. The banisters were a massive swoop of wood, the struts wrought iron. Almost at the top there was a wide landing where the stairs turned, divided and continued up from either side.

Ascending the final flight, Janie was conscious of odd sounds. The hooves of galloping horses and footsteps, people laughing and the occasional distant rifle shot. Honky-tonk music made her think of old-fashioned Western saloons and she distinctly heard a train whistling shrilly.

At the top of the stairs she stopped in astonishment. In the vast space beneath an ornate glassed ceiling, in semi-darkness, dozens of cartoon images were showing on small bright screens. Some were frozen frames, others continuous film. What she could hear were the different soundtracks. On her left, it was all Western cartoons. On the far right she could see the familiar Tintin images; the wildly quiffed rushing boy, his fluffy dog Snowy.

Directly in front of her, like a stage set, was a mock-up of a cartoon Western town in vivid colours: saloon, store, and funeral parlour complete with lugubrious black-coated owner. In front of them all, twice life-size, a cowboy sat a bucking cartoon horse.

Suddenly, she felt exposed in the big, shadowy room beneath the glass ceiling. She walked over to the Tintin section. A series of thin cardboard walls had been erected to turn the area into a maze. Full of apprehension at what she might find, she stepped in. And found herself in a bizarre wonderland. Here were Thompson and Tompson, their identical black bowlers and walking sticks stuck on a wall with surreal humour. Here was Captain Haddock and the mad Professor Calculus. She found herself wishing Adam were with her, he'd love it. These were serious boys' toys.

She came out the other side of the Tintin section and there was another, steeper staircase in front of her leading up to a third level of the hall. She thought of calling out, but was too intimidated to do so. Instead, she climbed the stairs.

Up here it was even darker, so the individual lit screens were more vivid in contrast. She glanced at the one nearest her – and looked closer. It was a series of still pictures in which an arum lily grew to huge proportions, extended its long orange stamen and proceeded to penetrate the near-naked woman who was lying, legs wide apart, on a rumpled bed. Janie looked at the other screens. The stills were by different artists, set in different periods. Some were clearly Thirties. There were brilliantly coloured aliens in icy landscapes. Others were prehistoric, dinosaurs and huge flying lizards. All were exquisitely drawn. All were explicitly pornographic.

What on earth was all this about? For the first time, she experienced real fear. Maybe Alma Gysemans had got this Dante wrong. She'd been a fool to respond to a fax from nowhere telling her to meet a dead poet. She realized she had told no one else where she was going.

She went back to the top of the stairs and looked down into the upper hall. And now, finally, she saw someone. A tousle-haired boy in dark clothes was peering into one of the screens. He was utterly absorbed, his chin resting on his fists, his elbows on the wide shelf below the screen. There was a can of Diet Coke on the floor beside him. Again, she was reminded of Adam. That made her feel better. She went down towards him, walking quite noisily, but he seemed not to hear her.

'Hello?' She hoped her voice sounded more assured than she felt. In response, he waved casually in her direction without looking away from the screen. 'Dante?'

She had almost reached him. And he was no boy. The apparently artlessly tousled black hair was, she now saw, carefully cut and gelled to stay in place. The clothes were velvet, and expensive.

He did not move, not even to look at her. Janie stood beside him. On the screen a posse of cartoon cowboys whirling lariats chased after a steaming train.

'Was it you,' she inquired, 'who sent that fax?'

'Yup.'

His arrogance annoyed her: she had not travelled all day in order to be addressed in monosyllables. 'So why am I here? Who, exactly, are you?'

'It was imperative that I speak with you.' His English was perfect, fast, American-accented. He was still staring raptly at the screen. She found this intensely irritating.

'So speak,' she said, in the tone she used to Adam when she was cross. 'Where did you get my name? And my fax number?'

This time he straightened up – reluctantly, she thought – an incredibly lithe man in black jeans and matching shirt. It was impossible to tell how old he was. Twenty-six, maybe twenty-seven? Too old for cartoons.

He said, 'I heard about the book you're writing.'

'It's not exactly a secret.' She realized this disconcertingly self-confident young man was making her feel very defensive.

'There are things – circumstances – of which you should know. But I have learned you appear to be unaware of them. This worries me.'

She said stiffly, 'What things? I can't imagine how you learned anything at all about me. Anyway, why should it should matter to you what I find out? Do you know Mama yourself? No one has mentioned your name to me.' She voiced the notion that had struck her on the train. 'Are you a follower?' Or, she thought, he could be a publicist of some kind.

He seemed amused, but there was no hint of a smile. She had rarely come across anyone not an actor who was so striking, or so self-aware. 'A believer? Not me. What about you?'

'Of course not. I'm not writing hagiography.'

'That's the biography of a saint, right? You mean, you don't think Mama is all people claim?'

'If you want to see what I think, maybe you should wait and buy the book.'

He spread his hands in a gesture that seemed at odds with his appearance. 'You must forgive me. You have very kindly come all this way to see me, and I have not impressed you.'

She said drily, 'I'm afraid not.'

Now he did smile. 'It is very English, that, to say you are afraid when clearly that is the last emotion you feel.' He added abruptly, 'Coke?'

Taken aback she said, 'All right. Thanks.'

He produced another can like a conjuring trick, and handed it to her. It was ice cold.

'I still need to know who you are. Otherwise, I will have to treat anything you tell me as suspect.' She paused, waiting. When he said nothing she added, 'I should tell you I have a friend here who would not say your name over the phone. Why would that be?'

He rolled his own can between his hands. 'It might make problems for you later if you knew who I was. You will realize when you see what I have to show you. It came from someone who would be very angry if they thought I had made this use of it. But if you know nothing about me, then clearly you must have learned of it some other way.'

'Oh. Really?' She consciously drawled the words. What a poser. 'I think you're playing elaborate games.' She looked pointedly round the dark hall.

'I would ask you,' he said, 'to remember that I knew what you were doing, and I knew where to reach you. So I'm not without resources. And that's precisely why I wanted to talk to you. I have material which I believe should be in the public domain. It is not.'

'Material concerning my book?'

'You will have to decide when you see it.' He took another long swallow of his Coke. 'The Krzysztof Foundation is funding your work.' It was not a question. She looked at him sharply: how did he know that? Robert Dennison had kept it very quiet, only a trusted handful of people in the Odyssey offices had been told. And the foundation themselves had every reason for secrecy.

'What are you implying?'

His shrug was a masterpiece of contempt. 'Krzysztof Foundation. It sounds so respectable. It makes one think of Nobel prizes and fellowships and endowed chairs at universities. And then there are the fine offices. The letterheads. The fund-raising functions.'

Janie said impatiently, 'What are you suggesting?'

He looked at her from under dark eyebrows, and his eyes were impenetrable.

'How carefully have you interviewed the various members of the foundation board? Have you even met them?'

'Of course I have.' She answered quickly. Too quickly. She had, after all, scarcely talked to them at that initial meeting with Robert. She had requested interviews separately with board members. Oliver Jodrell had agreed, had set things in motion, he said. But somehow the meetings had never materialized. Apart from her encounter with

Lady de Lisle, no one had been available. Josef Karms had been preoccupied with urgent business. Edward Pellingham had been whisked into the Princess Grace Hospital in Baker Street for an operation and was subsequently too weak to talk to her. Monica Ziegler was in Florida. And to her discredit, she had not pursued them. As she should have done. But she wasn't about to tell Dante all this.

'I believe the foundation is little more than a brilliantly conceived marketing strategy. I think you will find several of the members are not what they seem.'

'You'll have to be more specific.'

'Karms worries me. That massive business empire of his has something nasty hidden away in the foundations . . .'

Janie recalled the disquiet Josef Karms had aroused in her, the brush of menace he had brought into that calm London room. 'Like what?'

He said simply, 'Right now, I couldn't tell you. I can't put my finger on it. But *something,* and early on. He claims to be Hungarian, but I don't believe that. For one thing, I've never come across a Hungarian who had any knowledge of him at all until around 1950. The man didn't spring into the world in his late twenties, after all. And Oliver Jodrell – your perfect Englishman, right?'

She thought of the Guards tie and said doubtfully, 'I suppose so.'

In the light of the screen, his teeth and eyes gleamed white. With his long dark hair, the dark clothes, he looked for a moment predatory. 'Not Jodrell. Janasz. Andrzej Janasz. Born in Poland.'

That gave her a jolt. Did she believe him? She remembered Jodrell holding her arm at that introductory meeting with Robert and the foundation board, the way he had stood too close. Most un-English. She said, 'Many people change their names.'

'I don't dispute it. But few people take such a step without a compelling reason. What was his?'

'I don't know,' she said grimly. 'But if it's true, I'd like to find out.'

The racing cowboys finally finished their chase and Dante moved across to another screen. 'It's black and white,' he said, as she followed him. 'German film, and fifty years old. Amateur, by the look of it. This is a copy, of course, the original is locked away. But I think you can see enough.'

They stood side by side. He clicked a button and the screen lightened, flickered and a film began. She had been half-expecting more cartoon cowboys but the first frame dispelled such frivolous thoughts.

The opening shots were taken from above, and in darkness. Wavering lines of lights crossed the screen. When Dante said, quietly, 'Torchlight procession. Soldiers,' she recognized she was watching footage of the Second World War: row after row of men carrying flares. They were in some kind of arena, and they filled it, more and more of them in endless ranks, the flames illuminating faces and hands, gleaming on leather, glinting on steel helmets, on the twin lightning-bolt icon of the SS.

On the soundtrack, in counterpoint to the triumphant marching, a woman sang in German, in a low key like Dietrich, but sadder and somehow harsh. Janie couldn't understand most of the words, but the emotion was overwhelming, the bitterness and despair of Europe ripped by years of war. In that strange, Art Nouveau building full of cartoons, it had a most profound and disturbing effect: it was as if the past moved up beside her.

'*Wo sind die Kinder . . .*'

Her schoolroom German was good enough: where are the children. The huge open space seemed suddenly very cold: the truth about Mama might be uglier than anything she had imagined.

The marching soldiers faded into darkness. The next frames were shot in daylight and the soldiers were in trucks, mouths opening and closing in unison, evidently singing. Now they held rifles, they must be going into battle. Their tough young faces were excited. Only one or two older men amongst them had grim lines of experience running from nose to mouth. The cameraman was obviously beside them. In the next shots he was still in the truck, filming from above while the soldiers moved onto the streets of a town. There were tall buildings, shops, pavements. People – civilians – were running in all directions. A group of soldiers had several men surrounded and were clubbing them to the ground with their rifle butts. On the right of the frame a woman was being dragged by a soldier who held her long hair wrapped like a leash round his hand: she stumbled behind him, half-falling. Other civilians were clutching each other, panic-stricken. Janie strained to read the name on a large shopfront: it looked like Wozniak. She said, half to herself, 'Poland?'

'Right. We've managed to date it approximately: 1943.'

'Where did you get this film? What is it?'

He pressed the controls and the frame froze. 'I told you. I am not without resources. People use me to make public . . .' he paused, searching for the word, 'items which they would be embarrassed to have traced back to them.'

'Why you?'

He said, simply, 'Because I am effective. I have been doing this for a long time.'

Janie considered this statement. Modesty did not appear to be one of Dante's more noticeable qualities.

He added, 'You will see in a minute what it is,' and clicked the 'forward' switch so the screen jerked into movement. The scene had changed. He added, 'Watch carefully. The camp is in Poland, too.'

She didn't want to watch, didn't want to look at the screen any more. She didn't need telling, either, she knew these camps, knew them from photographs, from television programmes, from old newsreels. They were part of twentieth-century consciousness. She could anticipate just what she would see: skeletal figures, beyond humanity, with eloquent sunken eyes. Eternal images of pure suffering.

As if he intuited her thoughts he said, 'It's not a concentration camp. This is a work camp.' His tone was sardonic. 'Subtle, the differentiation. But important, nonetheless. In the first, death was virtually inevitable. In the other, survival was a faint possibility. Though the inhabitants probably wouldn't have believed it at the time.' He turned back to the screen.

Janie was very tired, suddenly. 'Why are you showing me this? I really don't see the point of . . .' She'd seen enough, was indifferent to these people, whoever they were. It was all so long ago. There were other outrages these days to concern her. New wars. Fresh wounds.

Dante put a hand briefly on her arm and she fell silent.

The film continued. Once or twice part of the screen was obscured, as though something dark had been covering the lens. The figures she was watching walked with the jerky movements of early film. Wearing baggy trousers and shirts, with caps for the men and headscarves for the women, they stood, hundreds of them, in blocks of about twenty-five people. They were in some sort of open space, it seemed to be muddy underfoot. They did not look at each other. Their hands hung empty at their sides. Two soldiers stood with each group, rifles at the ready. Their mouths opened and shut, their shoulders moved as they shouted commands. But there was nothing on the sound-track to echo this. Only the woman's low voice, her subdued and melancholy song.

Now the camera was raised, and Janie saw what they were all facing: a long, wide bar supported at either end – a huge gallows. She saw the nooses hanging from it at intervals. Six, seven, eight. Eight threats. The camera returned to the pris-oners' faces. Blank and exhausted, they looked ahead but registered nothing.

When the camera focused again on the gallows,

316

it was much closer. It was obviously hand-held: sometimes it swooped and lost the subject, as if the cameraman had missed his footing. Or maybe he could no longer bear to focus.

Now figures were dangling from the nooses. Their heads hung at horrible, broken angles, their faces were distorted. She could make out swollen tongues and bulging eyes. Their feet pointed inwards. The last figure was far smaller than the rest. Janie thought at first it was a woman. The camera lingered on this figure and with a shock of horror she saw it was only a child, a boy of eight, nine at most. And he was alive, there at the end of his rope, twisting frantically, bucking and writhing with desperate strength. His eyes were open wide, his tongue stuck out of his mouth. There was a dark wet stain at his groin. Janie's hand went to her own mouth. The child was too light. His body weight was not great enough to kill him. She stared at an agony that was over fifty years old, and tears ached in her eyes.

Then someone, a guard, stepped forward to stand directly beneath the boy. He reached up and yanked sharply on the child's legs, adding his own body weight to the rope. One foot came off the ground as he pulled. The noose tightened, the boy's neck seemed to grow longer – and it was done. The guard stood back and left the child dangling there. He swung forward and back, forward and back. The camera did not leave him. Then, at last, his slender body was almost still.

'*Now!*' said Dante beside her. 'See?'

The guard moved away from the gallows and as he did so, turned towards the camera. Only then did Janie realize that she was looking at a woman. A woman in a skirt, a long dark coat and black boots, hair almost hidden under the military cap. Dante pressed a button and froze the frame. *'There!'* he said. A bar of light ran repeatedly down the screen, but still Janie could clearly see the woman's face. A young face, tired and drawn, the forehead shadowed by the long peak of the cap, but recognizable for all that. The transparent eyes were pale and direct, the tilt of the head, the proud clear lines of throat and jaw unmistakable.

Janie said, urgently, 'Again!' He rewound the film a little way, ran it again, more slowly. The second time, there was no possible room for doubt. The camera was too close, the face too clear, the resemblance too great. On the soundtrack, the woman's voice dropped even deeper.

> *'Wo sind die Kinder?*
> *Verlor – und vergess – . . .'*

Where are the children? Lost and forgotten.

'No.' It wasn't possible. 'No.' She didn't think she had spoken aloud. 'It can't be her. It simply is not possible.'

He nodded.

It suddenly seemed hot in the long room and Janie pushed the hair back from her face. It was more than she could take in. She walked away from the tilted screen, into darkness. The brutal act had pierced the cloak of her cool observer's interest, made something bitter rise in her throat so she wanted to vomit. She put her forehead against a glass panel. It felt cool and smooth and clean. Dear God. If only what she had just seen had been like all the other images in this place: products of the imagination, not of history.

If the evidence of the film was to be believed – and her every instinct told her it was genuine – then Mama was a war criminal. A murderess. A monster. With her own hands, she had taken that little boy's life.

That act alone made a mockery of everything else the woman had done. It put blood on every person she had healed, each hope she had raised, every life she had touched. For even if this photographed killing was the worst thing Mama had ever done, who knew how many other people she had treated with cruelty, how many she had inched towards tragedy?

And it made a mockery, too, of her own involvement with Mama. Janie prided herself on her gut reaction to her interviewees, on her instinct for the unpalatable truth people often wanted to hide, and sometimes did not even recognize themselves – until she unerringly pointed it out.

But with Mama, all that streetwise expertise seemed to have failed her. She had fallen under the woman's spell. Like some bloody amateur, without more than a token murmur, she had allowed herself to be won over. She had been right, all those months ago, when she feared she was finished. That dismissive overheard 'on the wane' had been spot on. She had lost it. Of that she was sure.

Janie turned back to Dante. 'So it looks as if Mama is a German. But what about Poland, they all remembered her there. Or at least,' she added, recalling the photograph of the plump child from Warsaw that had given rise to her first small doubts, 'they appeared to. I don't understand. What's going on?'

'Not German, no. There were many Polish nationals in the German Army. Soldiers were enlisted from all the neighbouring countries as the Germans overran them. So at the same time as millions of Poles were dying – soldiers and civilians both, in battle and in the camps – there was even a Polish SS.'

Janie said slowly, 'It *would* have been possible for Mama to have been at that camp in 1943. The claim is that she was in São Paulo by then, but there's no proof at all. I only know for sure she was there three years later, when the first miracles happened. Those are well documented.' She folded her arms across her body, defensive. 'It simply never occurred to me to question when she left Poland. I just accepted what I read. All the articles and biographies say she went to South America as a young girl to work as a maid with a Polish family there.' She shook her head. 'I'm slipping.'

Dante said quietly, 'Until you saw this, what reason would you have had to doubt those things?'

'Something's been worrying me all along.' Only when the words were out did she realize they were true. 'All the time I've been working on this book, it's been nagging away at me. I didn't know what, just something that didn't *feel* right But I thought maybe she'd somehow faked the visions, or got people to testify the way she wanted. I was looking for little things. For cheating, fibs, conjuring tricks. For witchcraft, even, like those ranting newspaper articles back in the Forties. And then I learned at the Vatican that she's all tied up with politics and money, and I thought, that's it, then, that's what felt wrong. But I could never have imagined *this*.' She gestured to the screen they had been watching.

He nodded. 'I couldn't believe it myself at first. Has anyone confirmed for you the date she left Poland?'

'No one seems really sure.' She chewed her nail as she thought. 'That film was taken fifty years ago. It could be someone else.'

'I admit Mama is not identified officially on this film. We've no name, no army or unit number, nothing. But several identification experts have examined the woman's features. We made prints, and then aged them – the same process they use when they want to identify someone who disappeared years before, you know? We finished with these.'

He opened a folder and laid out on the wide shelf colour prints, eight by ten, of a woman's face. She was clearly over sixty but still beautiful, with the challenging vitality of a much younger woman. There was a soft pouching beneath the chin, the hint of gathers along the upper lip, faint wrinkles spraying around the enormous eyes. The photographs had been coloured to look more lifelike. In one, the hair was dark. In the second, it was the astonishing pale moon-blonde of Mama's own hair. In both, the eyes had been rendered that extraordinary aquamarine. The third photograph, which he added last, was a colour picture of

Mama now, her hair partly hidden, as always, by the creamy hood of her robe. All three images were near identical. All three were undoubtedly the same woman.

Dante said, 'The face they made from the film matches the configuration of Mama's in every respect. Measurements, bone structure, mouth, hairline . . . though of course we can't see it all, under the cap. We did the hair two different colours. It doesn't make a lot of difference, as you see.'

'Her eyes looked the same in the film. That amazing pale look.' Janie pored over the photographs. 'Why didn't she have plastic surgery or something to disguise herself?'

He said slowly, 'Maybe at some point you should ask her. Perhaps she just didn't think it was necessary. She would not have been aware she was being photographed. It looks clandestine.'

'Don't they show film similar to this at some of the concentration camp museums? Auschwitz, for instance.'

'Those were put together much later, from various sources. They have voiceovers, and credits.' He pressed switches, slid the black carton of film out of the machine slot. 'This was in private hands and it's amateur quality. I'd guess it was all shot without permission by a soldier with a camera. Remember the way it swung around, as if maybe he was hiding it under his coat? He would probably have been an officer, to get away with it. The music could have been added much later.'

Janie said, 'You said private hands . . . ?'

'I really can't reveal whose. Let's just say

someone who knows what I do found it after his mother's death. He was emptying the apartment, and it was among her papers. The assumption must be that his father was the cameraman. This person never knew his father. Apparently there was a family silence about the man.'

'That's odd.'

Dante nodded. 'He himself suggested that his father might have been some kind of informant to the Allies. Perhaps that was even the purpose of the film.'

'Was the man German himself?'

Dante answered obliquely. 'An astonishing number of Germans opposed what was happening. Especially towards the end of the war, when they realized they had believed in something that was so corrupt, that had produced such acts.'

'I suppose so.' She sounded doubtful, and it was her doubts he answered.

'When the war was over, the Allies found camps where almost all the inmates were children. Well, those who hadn't died. All ages, all religions, many nationalities, though the majority were from Eastern Europe. Many of them were German. Their parents had protested in one way or another, and that was the price they paid.'

She was stunned. 'I never heard that.'

'No? It is true, just the same. Some were the children of officers, or diplomats. The great majority were never able to be reunited with their parents.'

Listening, it occurred to Janie that his face remained impassive when he discussed these things. It was partly that his features – the intense, heavy-lidded gaze, the high cheekbones, the set of the mouth – had a judgemental calm. But she thought also, he has absorbed these facts, heard and discussed them many times. They are a part of his life. It was a chilling thought. 'My father worked with the UN at the end of the war,' he went on, 'as a child welfare officer. One of the things he did was look after these child prisoners of the concentration camps. He told me that in Poland, when the war ended, unknown camps were discovered. No one outside had ever even heard their names.'

She gestured with her head towards the film he was still holding. 'What do you intend to do with that?'

'Nothing. This is all the evidence we have and, as you can see, it is nowhere near sufficient for a courtroom. We came across it by chance, during another investigation. In order to make any kind of case against Mama, we would need witnesses to corroborate the film, documentation, dates. These things all take many years.'

'I don't believe anyone could swear after fifty years that Mama and the soldier on the film are one and the same.'

As she spoke, he was putting the photographs neatly away in their plastic envelopes inside the folder. She watched his precise movements. He knew just what he was doing, but she did not. She found herself in the middle of something complex and devious, a network of people and information, of accusations and denial, that stretched back years, back to the war. It was territory where Dante moved sure-footed, but she could only stumble.

'Nevertheless, you might wish to ask Mama for her comments.'

'I can't imagine she would ever admit it was her. Why should she?' She gestured towards the folder. 'This is all third-hand evidence. Any lawyer would dispute these pictures, the film even, and win.'

'Almost certainly. But just suppose she did confess: she's a strange figure, after all. Unpredictable. And suppose you used the material in your book. I would hope people who remember might come forward. But more than that, I want her to know people are aware of her background.'

'You want to use me.'

'Your expertise, yes.'

'My potential publicity value, you mean.' He inclined his head in acknowledgement. 'I don't promise anything. I'm not even sure I'm going to go ahead with it after what I've learned tonight. I'm not sure I could bear to.'

'Just because the truth is dark does not mean it should not be held up in the light.' His tone carried a real rebuke. It occurred to her that this committed man would see a refusal on her part as weakness. Worse, as indifference. He added, 'And I did not ask for promises.' He handed her the folder.

'Shall I send them back to you?'

His look was quick, quizzical. 'Where would you send them back to?'

Janie nodded vaguely. She was still struggling to absorb the implications of what she had just seen. She said, 'Look, Dante, I really need to think about this. If I want to talk to you again, how do I reach you?'

He shrugged, moving with her towards the stairs. She understood she would learn no more.

She asked, 'How do you come to be interested in war crimes? You seem far too young.'

His expression lightened for the first time. It was almost a smile. 'Appearances can be deceptive, madame. I am thirty-six. As for my interest, I inherited it from my father. He is old now. And it's work I am proud to carry on.' She saw now why he protected his identity. If he moved in this strange, ugly world among old and terrible crimes, there must be many who would wish him harm. Descending the magnificent curving staircase beside him, she said, 'Dante isn't really your name?'

'Dante wrote of journeys through hell and purgatory. It seemed appropriate.' Another oblique answer.

She remembered their conversation earlier. 'That was *your* compelling reason?'

'Amongst others.'

At the door he shook her hand gravely under the gaze of the uniformed attendant, pointed towards a flight of steps a little way along the street. 'If you go up there, you will be able to pick up a taxi. Adieu, madame.'

She had climbed the long flight of steps to the main road and was looking for a cab when she remembered, with a lurch of annoyance, that she had left her notebook behind; she could picture it, lying open on the top of the display stand near where they had been standing. She had put it there while she examined the photographs. Damn,

damn. It held her notes of the meeting and tele-phone numbers, and while they had only initials against them – an old precautionary habit – she needed it. With a sigh she hurried back down the steps.

Less than four minutes had elapsed since she left the *Centre belge de la bande dessinée*. It had been an oasis of light and warmth in that dank street. But descending the steps, she could not make out which building she had been in. Everything was in darkness.

It seemed at first she must somehow have come down a different flight of steps. But no, there was the derelict bar, the printer's with its smashed and boarded façade. Just beyond, the windows of the museum were shuttered, the massive doors firmly closed.

She hurried along the pavement and pressed the brass buzzer. There was no response. She rang again, several times. Still no one answered, and the quality of the silence told her, no one would. As she waited, the misty rain netted her hair and surrounded the streetlights with a sullen aura. It was very quiet.

Suddenly apprehensive, she stood back and looked up at the building. The opening times were announced on the wall: 10.00–18.00. It had not occurred to her until this moment that no museum would normally be open at ten o'clock at night. But open it most certainly had been, and staffed – she remembered the attendant – and it was not possible that they could have turned out all the lights, locked and shuttered this vast building and left, in just four minutes.

She banged on the door with her clenched hands until it hurt, determined to make someone hear. She felt herself on the verge of panic. At her back, the Rue des Sables had become something out of a Simenon novel, the scene of undisclosed horrors and lost hopes.

Twenty-Seven

Janie talked. It was the only way to deal with the wrenching emotions of the last two hours. Alma Gysemans stood in the arch of her dormer window, arms folded tight against her body, and listened to her.

Galeries Gysemans, started by her husband's father in 1922, took up the ground floor of a Belgian Gothic house in the Rue d'Écuyer. Above that were the offices, and from her apartment, in the top two storeys, she looked out over the Grand-Place.

The astonishing skyline of the old square dominated the apartment. In deference to it, the only curtaining was loose-woven cream fabric, almost transparent, held back on brass hooks. In daytime she could see the tops of Gothic, Renaissance and baroque buildings, the statues of the old guilds – the drinking monks, the sleeping Moor and his harem, St Nicholas atop the House of Haberdashers, Le Renard. Number 5, the House of the Archers, had La Louve, the she-wolf, above its door and the figures of Truth, Falsehood, Peace and Discord standing on the High Renaissance façade. Above the House of the Brewers, L'Arbre d'Or, a huge golden horse pranced. High on the town hall, a gilded copper Michael heroically slew the devil.

Now, at night, it was if anything more breath-taking. Towers of pale stonework seemingly frail as lace were picked out by spotlights. Carved and columned façades glistened with pure gold leaf. On the front of Le Cygne a huge, long-necked swan reared up, shadows lying feather soft beneath the spread of its wings.

'Look,' Alma said to Janie, who stood beside her. 'Cocteau said it was the most beautiful square in the world.'

Janie's mind was full of the things Dante had told her, the horrors she had just seen, had just described in detail to Alma. But the revelation about the Polish guard who was surely Mama – that she had kept to herself. She said, absently, her mind still struggling with that conundrum, 'You are lucky.'

'Not always. Believe me, not always.' The unexpectedly sharp rejoinder puzzled Janie. The older woman moved towards a chair which stood opposite the window, half-groping for the high back, and sat down. Her movements for once were clumsy. 'Listening to all this is so very painful.'

Janie stretched out a hand. 'I never meant to upset you.' She's an old woman after all, she thought, with a rush of concern, and it's so late. It was just too much for her to take, at her age.

'No,' said Alma, 'you don't understand. It's not your fault. I had not told you, and you had no way of knowing.' She took Janie's offered hand. 'My dear, you should not be *telling* me about the camps. You should be *asking* me.'

*　*　*

Alma leaned back against the chair, so her face was half-hidden against the pale velvet. She started to speak, haltingly at first, then more fluently as she forgot herself in the telling. Janie saw she was living it through again. Sometimes her voice faded and there were long pauses. Sometimes she smoothed away the tears below her eyes with her fingers; a touching, childish gesture.

Janie had thought she knew about the atrocities of that war, about the transports and the camps and the dying.

She found she was wrong. To contemplate the suffering of millions, to read words on the page, to see photographs, documentaries, films – that was bad enough. But she was familiar with these stories, they were anyway half a century old.

To sit in a half-dark room and learn what happened to a woman, and a man, to the child who lived and the child who was lost, was a different matter entirely. Alma's quiet voice led Janie deep into a nightmare with no waking up.

In memory, the corridor was endless, longer than any corridor could possibly be. It stretched into the distance, light and dark by turns. There were many doors, all closed.

It was the first time she had left the apartment since the birth and she felt odd, unreal. It was very early in the morning, not yet seven o'clock. She carried the baby and held Fernande by the hand. The heels of her shoes clicked sharply on the wooden floor. The boots of the two grey-uniformed soldiers escorting her made a quite different noise, like blocks of wood clumping down. There were three of her footsteps for two of theirs: they were tall men. She didn't think of her fear, or who she was to see, or what might happen. She concentrated on the sounds of shoes.

A door opened ahead of them and a grey-haired man stepped into the corridor. He wore crumpled civilian clothes and looked as though he had not slept. He leaned against the wall, eyes on the ground, as if unable to decide what his next action should be. As they drew level, Alma distinctly heard someone inside the room say urgently in German, '. . . arrested Von Falkenhausen . . . last night . . . None at all . . . Reichenau, I think. You know how they never . . .' It sounded like a telephone conversation. 'No, I have no . . .' The door was slammed hard from inside.

Alma tried to breathe calmly. General Alexander von Falkenhausen had long been in charge of the German troops occupying Belgium. He was known to be anti-Nazi and sympathetic to the country he was running. If he had been arrested . . . she did not want to think of the implications.

The Gestapo official nodded to her. He was exceedingly polite, had risen when they brought her into his office.

He told her, please to sit down. Almost in the same breath he added that she was to make herself ready to accompany him immediately: there were questions she must answer regarding her husband.

My God, they had Viktor.

'Questions?'

'About his work. About the people who helped him propagate his political views.'

Alma thought of the times she had delivered

Viktor's sketches for publication in the clandestine news-sheet he helped edit. Nervous but determined, she had taken Fernande to see the fountains and slipped a rolled package beneath the arm of the bench where she sat. After ten minutes or so, the printer would saunter up. Once he had started to raise his hat as she stood to leave, then he had remembered. He had taken her place, studiously ignoring her.

She said, 'I was not involved in his work. I know nothing about it.' They had long ago planned how to handle just such a situation. She shrugged, indifferent. 'He earned little and expected me to manage on next to nothing. So we did not discuss what he was doing. Our marriage was . . .' She flicked her left hand in a dismissive gesture. *I'm sorry, Viktor, I'm sorry. It's for the children . . .*

'That is not my concern. I am instructed only that you are to be questioned.'

'Can't I answer them now? I can't tell you anything anyway so . . .'

'Unfortunately that will not be possible, Madame Gysemans.'

'Where then?'

He sucked in his cheeks thoughtfully. 'I have not yet received the orders. But you will be prepared to leave your apartment this evening at eight o'clock. You may bring one suitcase.'

A suitcase meant she would not be allowed home. Prison? A journey?

She took a deep breath to control herself. 'That is not possible.' She looked down at the baby's tiny face. Then she smiled up at the agent, confident, trusting. 'He is scarcely two weeks old.' She offered her excuse calmly, even regretfully. 'I'm sorry, but I could not take him out in the cold so late, you see.' She held her breath.

'Of course not.' The agent answered without hesitation and her heart leapt with relief. 'Of course not.' Then the hammer blow. 'Naturally the children will not accompany you. They will be well looked after. Just for a few days.'

If she had not been sitting down, she thought she would have fallen. She had never anticipated this. 'But – I *cannot* leave them behind. I'm feeding the baby myself.'

He shook his head sadly. 'Nonetheless, Madame Gysemans, he is to be taken to a home. He will be well fed, you can be sure of that. He and the girl will be well looked after. Just until you return.'

'No, you don't understand. I'm . . .' Embarrassed, she gestured towards her body. 'Without me, he *cannot* feed.' She hated the pleading note she heard in her voice.

'Come now, Madame Gysemans. You must have no fears. It is in the child's best interests. Our nurses are excellent, you know. They will be here in a few minutes.'

She felt her self-control slipping. '*Now?* They're to go *now?*'

She argued, protested. She need not have bothered. The agent was still polite. He still smiled when he spoke, so that his expression and what he was saying had no possible connection with each other.

Fernande leaned against her, very close, silent. The baby was warm in the crook of her arm, snuffling to himself, contented. Alma opened her mouth to ask if the children could be taken to her mother – and then stopped herself. Perhaps they did not know of her mother's whereabouts. If they knew, she too might be taken.

In a small voice she asked, 'How long? How long will I be away?'

Without looking up from his papers the agent replied absently, 'A few days. It's only a matter of a few days.'

'Where am I going? Not away from Brussels?'

No reply.

'Please. Can you be a little more specific?'

He shook his head. All the time, Fernande pressed tight against her thigh, thumb in her mouth. Alma forced herself to stay calm, for her sake. The child as yet said only a few words, but her comprehension was sharp. Her very stillness, now, showed she realized something momentous was happening.

There was a sharp rap on the door and a woman came in. She was starched and sturdy with a silver watch pinned to the breast of her grey-and-white nurse's uniform. Her body was motherly, but not her manner. Crisply, she asked Alma a series of practical questions: did Fernande eat well? Bowels? What was the baby taking? Conscious of Fernande huddling closer and closer against her, Alma tried to speak calmly, not to distress the child.

The nurse leaned forward as if to look at the baby. Then, before Alma fully realized what was happening, she simply plucked him from her arms. Alma stiffened. It was a huge effort, not to cry out, to grab back her baby, scream, panic . . .

She forced herself to stay still. The baby stared peaceably up at the woman. Her eyes had been blue too, Alma remembered now. Not a soft, milky blue like the baby's, which would soon turn brown, but a bright, cold colour.

The woman opened the office door and handed the baby over to another uniformed nurse waiting outside. There was no sound. Alma told herself, there now, he's so young, he won't know the difference, he'll be all right. But it was hard to breathe. Then the nurse turned back and held out a hand to Fernande.

'Come along, dear,' she said briskly. 'Off we go.'

Alma did her best. She buttoned up the child's coat to the throat and smoothed back the fine hair into its coloured slides, talking quietly. 'I'll come and get you very soon. This lady will look after you, so do what she says.' She cupped Fernande's face gently between her hands. 'You must be a good girl for Mummy.' She kissed the soft lips. 'Stay with the baby.'

The child watched her mother's face intently. She did not acknowledge that she understood. Only when Alma gently disengaged her, only when she felt the woman's hand on her wrist, did she start to whimper. The woman pulled Fernande towards her and then she screamed, her voice shrill with panic. She wrenched herself free and flung herself against Alma, wild with fear.

And Alma could do nothing. She stood frozen as the woman struggled with the child, clearly surprised by her strength. The nurse finally hoisted Fernande off her feet, grasped her firmly under one arm and marched out of the room. The child's high wordless cries receded as she was hurried along the corridor. The baby, disturbed, added his thin, piercing voice to the uproar. Alma started to shake.

The agent looked tired. He had seen all this before.

When finally she could speak, Alma said, 'What . . . what about their clothes?'

'You should pack a small suitcase for them and have it with you this evening. It will follow them to their destination.'

'What *is* their destination?' she asked faintly.

'They will be taken into the country. Somewhere safe. An institute perhaps.' He sounded bored.

'But *where*? Where do I go to get them back?'

'You will get them back.'

'When? When will I? *Please!*' She pleaded shamelessly, begged, tears streaming down her face.

That time, he did not even pretend to answer.

Twenty-Eight

The lorry lurched on the rough road, throwing Alma off balance against the metal side. She pressed her face to the narrow slit where two panels joined, reaching desperately for the clean scent of the rain outside, the water on her tongue. But the truck jolted her away again, she hurt her shoulder on the bare floor as she fell back into the stink of too many sweating bodies, of fear. The elderly woman in the beautiful fur jacket beside her had been retching weakly for hours, bringing up nothing. She would murmur an apology each time, dab her mouth with an embroidered handkerchief, smooth her hair back with a trembling hand.

Alma settled herself on her suitcase with her back to the wall, drawing up her knees. She tried again to make sense of what had happened in the last few days. It was difficult because the events were senseless, cruel. No one punished innocent children.

Everything had blurred into a single horror and only the most traumatic moments stood out: the way the Nazi agent had smiled, smiled as he made his false promises; the way the baby had lain so trustfully quiet in that woman's arms; Fernande's screams as she was carried away.

She thought about Fernande. She knew she

must be running a temperature because occasionally she found herself whispering, as if the child were with her. She murmured about Daddy, about what they would do when they got home. *First of all we'll have to go shopping, get something special for lunch.*

Her breasts, swollen with milk, were hard and painful after so many hours, and hot. *Oh, my God* . . . It wasn't true. It hadn't happened, not that, not that . . .

She felt her mind slipping out of control and tore her thoughts back to Fernande. *It rained like this when we were in the park. Remember how we took off our shoes and ran on the grass?*

The woman beside her had stopped retching at last. She sat slumped, her eyes dark and sunken from exhaustion. They leaned against each other from mutual need. From time to time Alma's head drooped so she felt the cloudy chinchilla of the woman's jacket soft and warm against her cheek. They did not speak.

Occasionally, the lorry halted and the prisoners were permitted to climb down but most people were too terrified to get out even for the water that was available, just a long swallow each. Some, braver than the others, had done so. A few, driven by hunger, had tried to eat grass. Now they suffered dysentery and lay in pools of their own watery waste.

Alma realized they had paused, she could hear the lorry engine idling. She struggled to kneel up, to find the gap again and peer out, but there seemed to be no break in the smooth sides of the lorry. Her fingertips were wet, the metal was running with moisture. She thought at first it was rain, then it dawned on her that it was the condensed breath of the packed cargo of human beings. She finally found another crack, low enough to let her see the rough road behind them, and crouched close to it. A woman's thick legs in knitted stockings and misshapen shoes moved into her line of vision. Then a child's grubby fingers poked between the metal panels and wiggled about. Alma called hoarsely, her voice cracking with urgency, 'Help us! Help us, please!'

After a moment, a bright eye was pressed against the gap and Alma caught her breath. 'Hello,' she said more quietly. The eye watched her. Then it disappeared and in its place, the small fingers came back. Alma grasped them in her own. 'Help us. Tell someone we're in here!' She called again. The fingers squeezed hers in response and a very young voice shouted something unintelligible. Even inside, Alma could sense the sudden silence. The child called again. This time, there was a flurry of activity outside, the sound of a sharp slap, a wail, and the little fingers were snatched away. The woman outside uttered a single word, harsh and dismissive. '*Dreck.*' A glaucous gob of spit appeared on the ground in front of the worn shoes. The truck revved. The woman's voice rose to a screech. '*Dreck!*' The driver slammed into gear and they were off again.

The rain became harder again, drumming on the roof. She must be losing her mind, because it was starting to sound like music. Her father's orchestra was playing Beethoven, the deep, irregular throb beneath the violins echoing her frightened heartbeat. Occasionally, when they slowed climbing a hill, a trickle of rain would drop onto her hair. The icy shock of it reminded her she was running a fever. On her left, the dignified woman shuddered uncontrollably.

Alma was sweating. Her breasts were full and aching and how could she forget, even for a moment. *Oh, dear God, my baby.* The thought triggered the tingling that heralded the involuntary flow of her milk. She pressed her palms hard against her nipples to stop it.

There was no time here, and her watch had stopped. Once she asked, *does anyone know what time it is?* But she couldn't be sure, perhaps she had only thought the words. In any event, no one answered. The interior of the lorry had darkened perceptibly.

Time didn't matter anyway. There was nothing to do to mark the hours. All the normal events of her day – making breakfast for Viktor, taking Fernande to her mother for the morning, going to the gallery, music practice, hurrying to shop before she went home – these ordinary activities seemed so remote, it was impossible to believe she had been living her life only days before.

She knew it was late because she was so desperately tired. She was worn out, there was no knowing when – or where – this endless journey would be over. Somebody was repeating wildly over and over again, 'I can't breathe I can't breathe I can't . . .' On her other side, a girl of about fourteen was scratching fiercely at her arms and legs, tearing determinedly until her flesh bled. Her face was closed and set, with the fierce concentration of mania. No one tried to stop her.

Alma closed her eyes and immediately dropped into what might have been sleep. Dreams that were no dreams ripped her mind, gouging wounds nothing would heal. *Oh my little love, where are you? How did I let it happen?* Time moved on because when she opened her eyes again, it was almost dark. She did not recognize the people huddled around her. The dignified woman was no longer there.

Despite the painful jolting of the lorry, Alma felt consciousness slipping away again. She wanted to resist, she knew she must resist. Only it was easier to let go. Warmer and softer and quieter.

She awoke to stillness, in their big bed at home in the Rue d'Écuyer. She could feel Viktor warm against her back, hear the bubbling of pigeons on the roof, the faint morning sounds of the café below where tables and chairs were being set out on the pavement. Then the familiar calls in the street of the old man selling coal from his horse-drawn cart grew louder, harsher, until he was yelling in a language she didn't recognize. They were making too much noise, putting up the metal café chairs in the bedroom . . .

Bolts were pulled with a harsh rattle, forcing Alma awake. The warmth against her back was urine and the sharp smell made her eyes water; the lorry reeked of it, of a hundred and fifty people shut in for so many days. The tail of the lorry dropped open with a crash. It was still dark, the storm coats of the men waiting for them gleamed

342

in the rain. Behind them, stretching up as high as she could see, a great web of barbed wire shone sharp and dangerous in the glare of searchlights. Amid shouted orders, the prisoners nearest the tailgate were pulled and shoved into the ruts and puddles of the gravelled area where they had stopped.

Alma tried to stand but she was trembling from exhaustion and her legs wouldn't support her. Nobody could walk: they had been too cramped, half-sitting, half-lying, for too many days. They crawled, like animals.

'Papa. Papa!'

A curly-haired boy, not more than three years old, was trying to scramble back up onto the truck. He was crying for his father, bumping blindly against the legs of the descending prisoners. Alma hesitated, leaned forward to take hold of him. How was this child in here, when her own had been taken from her? His parents must have hidden him somehow. Then one of the black-coated guards grabbed the boy and Alma was prodded from above with something hard, forcing her to move on. Looking back, afterwards, she marvelled that even then she was able to suffer for another woman's son.

'Szybko! Szybko!'

Polish! They were bawling in Polish. Was this Poland, then, in the rain and the dark? She dragged herself on hands and knees, pulling her suitcase along behind her. The remnants of her rayon stockings were hanging in shreds, her knees were sore where she had fallen. Now the little stones pressed painfully into her flesh. She must have bitten the inside of her cheek, she could taste salt blood in her mouth. She wiped her wrist across her open lips and when she looked, the skin was streaked with red.

Already, she had learned not to look at a face, to keep her head down, remain anonymous, instantly obey. So almost her first image of this place she had been brought to was at ground level: before the gates, outside the perimeter fences of wire, neat rows of stones enclosed rectangular flower beds. The earth was raked smooth and stuck neatly with wooden plant markers. The stones had been carefully whitewashed.

Because at that moment Alma had no idea what awaited her and her companions, she did not then appreciate the depth of callousness of this calculated deception, that their captors had taken the trouble to plant flowers here. She had no way of knowing she would be there to see those beds covered with snow, and then much later to see them flower red and white and pink. That rainy night, she did not know if she would ever leave. But afterwards, for a long time, those were the strongest images she had of that terrible place. Blood and flowers.

All their possessions were confiscated. Suitcases were opened, clothes and jewellery taken away. Alma was told to remove the pretty oblong emerald Viktor had so lovingly chosen for her engagement ring, her gold watch, her mother's pearls and the little drop earrings she never took off. An elderly man, too old for the harsh grey army uniform, carefully detailed everything and put all her pieces in a small brown bag. 'They will be quite safe,' he told her, and she could tell he had repeated the phrase many, many times.

'I will get them back soon?'

'You will get them back.' His voice was weary, flat. He had a country accent. She knew he lied but couldn't let herself admit it. Because the German agent had used the very same words to her in Brussels days before. *You will get them back*, he had said. At all costs she had to believe he had been speaking the truth, or she would go mad.

Finally, their coats and hats were heaped onto barrows. Everyone assumed this meant they were going inside, but they were kept out in the streaming rain for what felt like hours. As a barrow was trundled past her, Alma saw the distinctive chinchilla jacket from the lorry, but she looked in vain for the woman who had worn it. There was a lot of shouting going on, but none of them could make any sense of it. They were lined up five abreast and for the first time, they heard the refrain that was to punctuate their days: *Eins, zwei, drei, vier, fünf* . . .

When their part of the queue finally entered the long shed, it would have been bad enough if they had been ordered to take off their by now wet clothes. But without uttering a word, a woman guard caught her shoulder and simply slit her garments open with a pair of long shearing scissors – blouse, skirt, petticoat, camisole, panties – so they fell to her feet. She would have been horribly embarrassed by this at any time. Just now, her body still soft and vulnerable from the birth, her breasts swollen hard with milk, it was hateful, humiliating beyond anything she could ever have imagined.

The line of frightened, naked prisoners was pushed into an almost dark room. Alma couldn't breathe for fear, until she saw the X-ray machine. They were taking chest X-rays, there were even two white-coated technicians.

Just as she was beginning to feel hopeful – this concern for their health surely boded well – the worst thing of all began. She could see it happening to the women ahead of her: they were being shaved. The women behind, seeing what was to come, stirred restlessly and murmured. Alma looked around wildly to find someone to protest to, but then she saw the armed Polish SS guards beyond the open door. But their guns didn't frighten her as much as their caps, peaks pulled low so she couldn't see their eyes. And their shiny cruel boots. What protest could she make, in her state?

The women who did the shaving looked as if they might be prisoners themselves and they were careful, despite their speed, indifferent rather than unkind. Wordlessly, one cut off Alma's long hair with a few practised snips and dropped it into a large bag at her feet. She ran clippers over what remained. Then she gestured to Alma to lift her arms, swiftly shaved her armpits. Without warning, too quick for any resistance, the clippers took her pubic hair. Alma flinched, burning with anger and with shame.

She heard with relief the word 'baths' ripple back through the line of women. But she wasn't prepared for the unappetizing concrete troughs full of liquid that could not be water. One at a time, they were prodded forward, over the low edge. The trough was slippery, treacherous under her feet. The harsh solution smelt disgusting, of chemicals and vomit, like sheepdip at the farm on summer holidays. It was agonizing on her grazed knees, on the scraped shaven skin of armpits and crotch. She felt a hand on her head shove her under, instinctively closed eyes and mouth. Then she was out, gasping with shock and cold.

Among a group of other naked, freezing women she was ordered by the Polish guards to run (*Szybko, szybko!*) through a rough-walled tunnel. At the end of it, a vast echoing windowless room piled high with grey clothing. This was doled out to them without a word spoken.

That was only the beginning.

.

That first night in the camp, after the baths, Alma was ordered into a low, windowless hut along with the men and women from the lorry. There were perhaps a hundred and eighty of them. They found an empty space in total darkness. Part of the roof had not yet been completed, and rain poured in through an inadequate tarpaulin. There was nothing to sit on but the floorboards. A small stove stood in the centre of the hut but it was dead and they had nothing to burn in it, no way of lighting it. At first, they waited, assuming beds – blankets at least – would be given them. But the guards simply made pillow motions with their hands – sleep – slammed and locked the door. The floor was a mess of puddles. They had been given no food, and clearly none would be provided that

347

night. Everyone was cold, many were weeping. The more practical among them started to settle down on the dry area of floor, huddling together for warmth.

Alma made herself as comfortable as she could. She was shivering, as the fur-coated woman had shivered on the lorry. Alma supposed the woman had died, some time during that endless evening.

She thought of the crying curly-headed boy on the lorry. She had not seen him again. She thought of her lost baby, of the useless milk in her breasts.

She did not know how long it had been since she last saw her children. Four days? Five? She held her head in her hands, going through it for the thousandth time, trying to remember anything – anything she might have forgotten, any hint to where they were now.

And Viktor. What had they done with Viktor?

For the first time, Alma wept for what she had lost.

It was a work camp and the work was impossibly, brutally, hard. Crews of women and elderly men laboured sixteen hours a day breaking rocks by hand, wielding pickaxes. With the stones they built straight white roads under the eyes of the SS guards. The roads led into the dark Polish forests of fir and pine that stretched impenetrable around them on all sides. The forest was frightening in its blue-black silence. But not so frightening as the camp.

Sometimes Alma thought she saw people among the heavy trees. Once a boy of around seventeen watched them, another time a woman with wild black hair that hung to her waist beneath a headscarf. Both were unkempt, their skin encrusted with dirt. Alma almost smiled as she thought that: dirty as they were, they were not so filthy as she. The prisoners never attempted to speak to these silent watchers – the guards fired at the slightest alarm – but decided they must be Gypsies. Occasionally half a loaf of bread would be left where it was easily found. One memorable day Alma straightened up to see a far from clean woollen vest carefully folded on a stone near where she was working.

The prisoners wore always the same coarse greyish cotton clothes striped with blue, which had belonged to many other people first. They were too hot in summer and totally inadequate in winter. Many, like Alma, wore a coloured cloth triangle on the arm to identify their status: hers was red, since because of Viktor she was designated a political prisoner. The rough wooden clogs on their bare feet got sucked off by the mud.

The days were so long and the nights so short. These were spent in the windowless barracks packed now with tiered bunks to the ceiling. The bunks were scarcely more than two feet wide and squashed close together. Even so, two or three people crammed in each, so that when one shifted, all were forced to move. It was only possible because they were now all thin. But as there was never any fuel for the stove, they welcomed the body warmth of their companions. Even so, Alma scarcely slept, despite her tiredness.

At the end of the shed was a room where they could wash in a little cold water, and beyond that were rows of open, stinking, rudimentary lavatories. The filth, the sickly stench, wore away at them. It was worse even than the hunger, worse than the exhaustion. Unable to clean themselves or their clothes adequately they soon suffered from patches of rubbed, raw skin. Soon Alma had scabies like everyone else and itched badly at night as her body warmed a little.

But lice were the greatest threat. Transparent, yellowish, big enough to catch, they laid their invisible eggs along the seams of clothing and brought disease. Hours every evening were spent searching for them. It was disgusting to feel them crawling on her flesh, disgusting to crush them between her nails. But she had to find them if she was to live, for they carried typhus. None of them had it so far, but there were enough prisoners who had seen it in other camps to spread the warning: fever of 105° for a week and more. Delirium and hallucinations and then, for all but the strongest, a horrible death.

Before dawn every morning they were woken for roll-call on the dirt quadrangle where the gallows stood; they were counted, over and over again: *Eins, zwei, drei, vier, fünf.* Sometimes they were kept there for two hours, or ordered to 'rest' which meant standing for six hours. People died there in the ranks, eyes rolled back in their heads, to be stretchered away by the stronger prisoners. Sometimes they were brought to watch the hangings. Sometimes a public beating would be administered, twenty-five strokes for those caught stealing food. Only one or two survived this treatment. They were so weak, so thin.

Apart from the bowl of bitter liquid they called coffee at five in the morning, the single piece of heavy rye bread at night and a sole cupful of water, there was only one meal at midday after yet another roll-call (*Eins, zwei, drei, vier, fünf*), and this they ate standing. As time went on, experience taught Alma to find just the right place in the queue. First-comers got the thinnest stuff. Then the helpings became thicker, from the bottom of the great metal pot. But queue too far back and it might run out before she got any in her steel *Schüssel*.

After she had eaten, in the minutes of physical relief from hunger the meagre sustenance brought, she could shut out the noisy hut, the wild starved noises of her companions, their coughs and smells. For those few minutes, she closed her eyes and let herself believe the dreadful thing had never happened, and she still had her little family safe. Trying vainly to sleep, she would wonder if tomorrow would be the last day she would ever see.

It never was. Despite the hunger and the work and the utter misery, she survived. She found she carried the will to live in her blood.

Twenty-Nine

The two women sat in the warmth of the luxurious, softly-lit room. In the morning, Janie thought, life would move on all around the Rue d'Écuyer. People would run their lives, hurry about their business, make choices, decisions, mistakes, love. They would be oblivious to the chasm that had yawned beneath the feet of Alma Gysemans and so many like her. At best it would be the stuff of history books, at worst something about which they neither knew nor cared. But the woman beside her had lived through events which had cost millions upon millions of lives, and changed the course of many millions more.

As if she read her thoughts, Alma said, 'The oddest thing about it all, when I describe it like that, rationally, was the orderly way it all began. You see films and you read books, you imagine leather-coated sadists crazed with hatred bursting into your apartment, Sten gun in one hand and whip in the other. It wasn't like that. It wasn't like that at all.' She grimaced. 'But you can be sure I was sent to Poland by a bureaucrat in a government office who added my name to his lists before he went home one night, to make up the numbers, or because of my initials. Far from being a jackbooted Nazi, I expect my little bureaucrat wore glasses. He probably kept a budgie, and had two

352

children and was frightened of his wife and paid his taxes on time.'

Janie stared at her. 'God. D'you really think so?' She frowned. 'It makes it much worse, to think that an ordinary man could do something so dreadful.'

'But what he did – his bit of it – wasn't dreadful, was it?' Alma's voice was calm, reasonable. 'He was just putting a name on a list. And he was only following some edict, only pursuing policy designed to put the new order more swiftly into place. So was the official who interviewed me that day. And the SS agent who arranged the removal of my children was only carrying out commands he had been given. And the clerk who put in the order for the trucks that night had just been told where they should wait. And the drivers were simply doing what they were ordered to do. It wasn't their job to ask *why*.'

'But they must have suspected, they must have guessed.'

'A lot of people did guess, and a lot of people tried to do something. And many of them ended up dead for their trouble. You think there were no German politicians in the camps? No liberals, no journalists, no doctors? No priests? No artists? No thinking people whose friends vanished overnight and could not be found? You think they didn't go to police stations and ask questions? Of course they did. And they would have been taken themselves for their pains.'

Janie shivered. 'How did you manage to survive?'

Alma drew on her cigarette. The tip glowed as

she breathed in the smoke. Her voice was matter-of-fact.

'Many times I wished we had killed ourselves before we let it be done to us. But we simply couldn't believe anything really bad would happen. Not to people like us. Not to intelligent people with civilized lives.' She laughed, a bleak sound. 'We were so *innocent*. God.' The laugh turned to a sob. She took off her glasses and looked across at Janie. In the lamplight, her eyes were red and swollen. 'Such innocence. We went unprepared, and we went into hell. After that happened, how could there ever be innocence again?'

Chapter Thirty

Shepherded and protected by the men of the Chalice in their violet-blue robes, Mama touched the eager hands stretched out to her. She briefly cradled a baby held up for her blessing. She cupped the heads of children shoved forward as she passed, smiled down at a shrunken beggar woman. When she made a sign to him, the dark man who was always just one step behind her opened the door of the car. She bent and gathered up her robe to clamber in.

Then she paused, fingering the hem. Her head went up, listening, intent. She turned back, scanning the crowd. She was frowning. The dark man was immediately at her side, his black eyebrows raised, black eyes alert and questioning. He spoke, listened carefully to her reply, watching her face. Both of them looked back towards Chalice House, and Mama said something else, nodding her head vehemently, insistent. Then she got into the car. The people swarmed round the vehicle, pressing beseeching faces to the glass, so the other blue-robed men had to link arms to hold them back. The dark man began to forge his way through the crowd again, towards Chalice House, using his shoulders like a fighter.

★   ★   ★

The boy Patrice Akonda sat on the trolley beside his brother. His clean white T-shirt and shorts were stained with the red earth where he had crawled under the verandah. His wide-cheeked face was doleful and he was thirsty. In a minute he would pull the trolley and they would go and find their mother, and the sisters, and the bus. Just now, he was too miserable to move: he didn't even want to see the car which would take Mama away for ever.

Patrice was staring down at the tracks his tears had made in the dust on his feet and on his plastic flipflops, when two more feet appeared in his line of vision. These were large and masculine, shod in sandals with a broad band of leather round the big toe. They were planted wide apart, and pointing towards him.

Patrice's eyes travelled from the man's feet up the length of his body, taking in the heavily muscled legs, the rough-textured robe the colour of night, the smooth skin of the chest. And then the alert dark eyes under black brows, the shaven head.

The man bent, and said something to Jean. Then he picked him up in his arms while Patrice scrambled to his feet. Jean was slim-built but tall. Even so, the man straightened effortlessly. He carried the boy through the crowd, which obediently parted for him, and for Patrice trotting at his heels. When he reached the long motor car where Mama waited, the door swung open and he placed Jean carefully inside, on the heavily carpeted floor. He was about to shut the door when Mama looked up. Patrice could not see her eyes, behind

her sunglasses. She beckoned him to come forward.

The boy was by now terrified by the events he
had brought about. But he broke into a run: his
brother needed him.

Chapter Thirty-One

It was a brilliant day of clear outlines and crisp
edges. The turn for St Peter's Church was half a
mile along Brooklands Road in Cheshire, beyond
Sale station. The dubious delights of suburbia,
Janie had thought, driving past the clipped hedges
and two-car garages. But even she could appreciate the comfortable houses, the sense of order and
security. Nothing dreadful could ever happen
here.

She parked in front of the church. Her companion, a soft-faced woman with greying hair cut
in an elfin fringe, led the way through the arched
gate with its posters (*Jesus Sets Us Free*), details of
playgroups and outings for the elderly. The plot
lay in the second, newer half of the graveyard,
under the shadow cast by the spread wings of a
pink marble angel two graves on.

In remembrance of our dearest little Penny who fell
asleep on 12 February 1967 aged nine years and
eleven months.

From somewhere nearby there were playground
sounds; the happy shrieks of little girls, thud thud
of netballs hitting a wall, an adult voice lifted in
remonstration.

Karen Caldwell said reflectively, 'She'd have
been over forty now. Older than I was when she
died.' She looked down at the white-edged grave,

the pot of polyanthus bright against the pebbles. 'Makes my heart turn over, thinking that.' She bent and pulled off a faded leaf, rubbed a careful housewife's finger over the words etched on the headstone.

> *We had you for so short a time*
> *We'll miss you for so long.*

When Janie had driven Karen Caldwell home, she sat in the car for a long while, fitting together her thoughts.

That woman had lost her daughter, but still she had told Janie, as they left the cemetery, 'We held onto Penny that extra two years, you know. That was because of Mama.'

'Do you really think she kept Penny alive?'

Mrs Caldwell had not even hesitated.

'Yes. Mama touched her, and I swear I could actually see something happening.' She moved her hands apart to emphasize the wonder of it. 'She was at the end of the road, all the doctors said so. And I don't believe Mama said a word to her, you know, not anything. But it was like . . .' she struggled to explain herself, 'like watching someone fill up a glass with coloured liquid. Only it wasn't liquid. It was life.' She blew her nose vigorously. 'Sorry.'

Poor little Penny, who had missed her tenth birthday. Perhaps those two extra years had indeed been a miracle. But what about all the others, for whom there had been none? Even before Dante and his revelations, Janie had reached a point where despite her determined efforts to ignore her own instincts, it had become impossible for her to accept the seemingly universal belief in Mama.

Behind her she had a career based on a talent for scenting the flaws and weaknesses of successful people. The interviews on which she had built her reputation relied on her finding her subjects' most vulnerable points and attacking them there. And Mama was vulnerable now.

Yet if Dante was right – as she feared he was – did that change Mama's achievements? Would Karen Caldwell have refused those two years for her eight-year-old Penny, if she and not Janie had watched Dante's film?

There had been a phrase in an article in *The Times* which when she read it, she was almost embarrassed to recall, she had not found absurd. It had been simply a journalist's phrase, facile and apt, summoning up an instant image: *this superstar saint*.

It was an image, that was all. Only now she knew that behind the image lay something uniquely dreadful. Those things had been done, that past had been lived, by Mama. Yet even after that, she had still been able to bring hope and love to half the world. How could that be? How could both be true?

Janie saw that the image had not changed, but her perceptions had. Mama had always been the same, it was simply that now she herself had information which made her see the woman quite differently. Like the way the field of vision forms an inverted image on the retina of the eye which the mind, with all its experience, analyses so the inversion is not perceived. The image is still upside down. But it appears the right way up.

Now, she could see only the inversion.

Chapter Thirty-Two

The postcard showed an improbably blue sky over white slopes. *Aviemore, Scotland.* The single time she'd been near there, interviewing a Scottish poet memorable for the abundance of his whiskers, his whisky and his women, she had been shown the ski slopes by an enthusiastic PR man. She had an impression of dark rock sticking up through the thin snow and a damp wind howling in from the Cairngorms. Now she read Adam's card with a smile. Written two hours after his arrival, he declared everything – the centre, the bunks, the staff, the food – to be 'wicked'. Later in the week there would be an overnight trip. They'd be sleeping in caves and learning to abseil . . .

Adam had travelled by coach with the school for a week at an adventure centre. Janie, over-cautious since she and Paul separated, had worried he was too young. 'Scottish mountains are so high,' she had protested, 'and Scottish water is freezing.' But Paul had backed the boy's eager request. *He needs to stretch himself*, he had written, in one of the undirected, unsigned notes in which he now, reluctantly, communicated with her. *He will learn to take responsibility and grow up.* Janie did not see that the first was necessary or the second desirable, but could not argue with both of them. She outfitted Adam with a kagoul, two extra-thick sweaters, various thermal garments, boots and an ex-Swedish Army sleeping bag.

She stuck his card on the pine shelf in the kitchen. That was Wednesday.

On Saturday morning she got up early and did her exercises to music. She was about to get under the shower just after seven when she heard the doorbell. Running down in her bathrobe she could see, through the arc of glass over the front door, the postman's red van on the cobbles. She opened the door a slit as Johnny Cobb beamed his near-toothless grin and leaned in to prop the box against the wall. Her name was typed on a white label. It must be the stationery she'd ordered. She left it there while she made coffee and ate breakfast slowly, reading yesterday's paper; there was no newspaper delivery this far from the village. Nothing interesting in her post: credit card bill, cosmetic offer from Fenwicks, someone inviting her to a fashion show she would never attend.

She rinsed her cup and plate under the hot tap and was standing in the sunshine, stretching, when she remembered the box. Handling it for the first time, she decided it was too light to be the stationery. Now she came to think of it, they always plastered their boxes with self-advertising anyway. She put it on the old wooden draining board and found the kitchen scissors, running the blades down the wide strips of brown parcel tape.

For a couple of seconds she stared at the contents in puzzlement. A jumble of clothes tossed in all anyhow – denim, blue wool, something in white cotton, a single grey sock. Then it dawned on her that these were Adam's clothes. He must have sent them home for her to wash, though she couldn't imagine why. Confident now she had identified them, she picked up a badly stained white T-shirt. What had he been up to to get in this state? She held up a hand to shield her eyes from the sunlight and looked in the box again. Then she realized what she was looking at.

She turned away and immediately, neatly, threw up into the sink.

'Covered in blood. All over his clothes. Oh my God, Paul.'

His voice over the phone was deliberately, maddeningly slow. 'Any letter? A message?'

'Nothing. I can't make out the postmark. Old Johnny Cobb delivered it like always.'

'And you phoned the school?'

'Mr Candon wasn't there, but the deputy had no word of any accident or problem. He gave me the adventure place number so I could phone them myself, but I just got a woman who said there's no one there, they've all gone on the camping trip. She said if there'd been an accident, they would have been in touch. That was all she knew.'

'And the police?'

Her throat was hoarse. 'They asked, could I see any body parts?' She heard his intake of breath down the line. 'I mustn't touch the box. Someone'll be here soon, they've only two men on today. It could very well be a hoax. They'll check it's human blood. What does it mean? Oh Paul, if he . . .'

'I'll drive up now. Be there in about four hours, OK?'

She felt a huge rush of relief. She hadn't realized that was what she wanted. 'Oh yes. Please. Drive carefully.' She'd said it before she thought, the old loving warning. He put down the phone.

She had no idea how she got through the hours until he arrived. The day became disjointed, episodic. Things happened swiftly and then there were long suspended spaces.

A harrassed-looking police sergeant arrived, took a statement and carried the box of Adam's clothes away with him. In the vacuum created by his departure, she started tidying the living room. She could not concentrate and left in her wake leaves from the plants, dusters, old envelopes, pages torn from magazines.

Automatically, she went into the kitchen and set about making a *tian* for lunch. For ten minutes the therapy worked as she seared the aubergines in olive oil, interlaced them with sliced tomatoes, added breadcrumbs and fresh basil. Too late she realized her mistake: she had bought the deep earthenware dish during their last family holiday, in the villa not far from Palma. She stood in a daze, knife in one hand, bottle of olive oil in the other, seeing Adam crouched on the hot flagstones as he watched a lizard. *Look, Mum, a dragon.* His bare brown back, the vulnerable knobs of his spine. She shoved the *tian* in the oven, sat down and gave herself over to the painful luxury of memory. By the time she remembered it, the aubergines were burnt black at the edges.

Claudia phoned, answering the message Janie had left on her machine earlier. She was appalled, concerned, sympathetic.

'I don't know what to say.' Her voice was choked. 'It's too awful for words. Do you want me there? Can I do anything?'

'I guess not. Paul'll be here soon. Until we hear from the adventure holiday people there's nothing to be done anyway.'

'But who would do such a thing? Could it . . .' she hesitated, 'could it be some sort of joke?'

'Joke as in funny?' Janie sounded sharper than she meant. 'Who? Who could dream up such a thing? Certainly none of Adam's friends, they're all eleven years old, for God's sake.'

'You're right.' She paused. When she spoke again, it was hesitantly. 'You don't have – this sounds melodramatic – you don't have any enemies, do you? Those interviews of yours were sometimes very harsh. Maybe someone . . .' Even before finishing she stopped, contradicting herself. 'I'm being ridiculous. Forget I said that.'

Janie said, 'I haven't been nasty about anyone in print for nearly two years. And the sort of people I slagged off would be more likely to take out a writ than . . .' She let the end of the thought trail away.

'Yes.' Claudia thought for a minute. 'There's something else. I don't know how, but it's got to be connected to the explosion.'

Janie glanced out of the window. She had stayed away for weeks too traumatized by the shock of having her home blown up even to contemplate returning. There were piles of bricks in the cobbled yard, sacks of cement, slate tiles; it would be months before the effects of that night were absorbed.

'I think you're right.'

Claudia said hastily, 'I'm only saying it must have been deliberate. I'm not saying anyone wanted to kill you. Anyway, it would have been obvious the barn was empty. But if they wanted to frighten you . . . maybe this box of clothes is meant to do the same thing.'

'So you think this is all about her, too.'

'It's not impossible. She must have enormous power, a woman like that. And a lot to lose, if you're digging too deep. But it seems so out of character.' Claudia hesitated again. 'Only of course I don't know what new information you might have got recently. Is there anything to justify this?'

'Oh yes.' Janie felt hollow again. 'I'm very much afraid there is. I'll call you back later, OK?'

She put down the phone and brooded over what Claudia had said. There was no doubt, even before the meeting with Dante, that she had learned some disquieting facts about Mama. Involved in her research, she had not stopped to wonder what effect the information, released, might have on her subject.

If she told even what she had discovered before her visit to Brussels, it was more than enough to cast doubt on Mama's integrity. She believed that the Magda Lachowska venerated in a Polish port was a different person to the one born there. Her visit to the brother had only confirmed the suspicions raised by her trip to Swinoujście.

And then the business of the so-called resurrection from the dead. Even the Church appeared to accept the miraculous happenings in São Paulo in 1946 – and yet she had now put together an explanation of them that was rational, at the very least. If Mama's incredible revival was simply the result of random natural phenomena, it might make her a charlatan, or even a magician. But not a miracle-worker.

And if she were to reveal what Dante had shown her . . . Janie shut her eyes. Suppose Claudia was right, and someone involved with Mama was aware just how much Janie was uncovering. What did that make the box of bloodied clothes? A warning? A threat? The possibilities made her shudder.

Before Dante, she would never have believed Mama capable of harming anyone, least of all a child. She no longer harboured such illusions. And those strange people, the board of the Krzysztof Foundation – what of them? She thought of that first meeting, of her strong sense that the members of the board were suspect, shady. She remembered Josef Karms, the hint of menace and the brutal hands. And the unease that had seized her afterwards, her conviction that something, somewhere, was not what it seemed.

And that strange little cameo she had glimpsed through the half-open door in the Waldorf Astoria. Mama and Karms, talking with such intimacy, so easy together. Another pointer she had missed.

What a fool she had been, not to see the danger she was in while she continued to research Mama's life. She had behaved like an amateur, had allowed herself to enter a situation in which anything might happen. She should have understood long ago the need to be careful.

But she had not appreciated who she was deal-ing with. She had underestimated their power. And now they were demonstrating just how much they held.

The weather had changed with the astonishing speed of this hilly part of the world and now it was raining, beating against the windows, rattling a warning on the bedroom skylights when she went to put on some clothes. The room was filled with the watery light and reflected raindrops ran down the pale walls. She lay down for a few minutes and somehow almost an hour had passed. She was taken aback to find herself still naked beneath her robe. It seemed as if the cheerful woman who hur-ried down the stairs and answered the door to Johnny Cobb had been another person entirely. She stared at her clothes and found she could not face bright colours. She put on black trousers and a short black sweater.

When she went down, a bottle of whisky was out in full view. She had promised herself never to touch it again, but kept it as a kind of insurance, in case her need for it became unbearable. She had no recollection of fetching it from the back of the cupboard under the stairs. Had she put it on the hall table? She folded her arms across her chest though it wasn't cold. A couple of times lately, she had had brief but total blackouts of memory. Not long ago, after a lunch with Claudia, they had decided to take a much-needed afternoon off to go and see a film. She remembered leaving the cinema, but of the film itself she had not the slightest recollection. She had not told anyone, but she knew such episodes were common among alcoholics.

But she wasn't an alcoholic. Was she? She shivered again. It was dark here, with the window gone and the heavy tarpaulins over the beginnings of the new wall. Maybe the whisky belonged to one of the builders. It didn't, of course. They looked like beer drinkers to a man. What the hell. She reached for the dark bottle with relief. If ever she had needed a drink, it was now. She took it into the living room and had the top off before shame caught up with her. Adam might be in danger – could be injured, dead even – and look at her. At that moment she heard a car on the cobbles. She went round and opened the back door as Paul got out of his old Saab.

They regarded each other without speaking. She knew she looked awful, but he looked worse. She used to tease Paul for being an American's idea of an English schoolboy, clear eyed and wearing beautifully cut grey flannel suits. He was a keen tennis player who had given it up under the pressure of work and spent far too much time at a desk. As a result, his jawline was slightly blurred, his waist thickened, with the extra pudginess that comes to former athletes. It had appealed to her in those days, she used to make jokes about his love handles. All that was gone now. He was pale and – she saw this as he moved towards her – gaunt, as if he had not been eating enough, his jeans gathered under the belt and his sweater baggy. His unkempt hair, longer than she'd ever seen it, curled wildly all over his head, receding noticeably at the hairline. He had not stopped to shave. His eyes were red-rimmed with strain and the skin under his eyes was dark, emphasizing the narrow nose with the slight bump below the high bridge which made his face all profile. Unhappiness had made him almost wolfish.

She started to speak then and Paul said, 'Hold on, let me get in the house.' He seemed not to notice the rubble, the collapsed walls and builder's skips full of broken slates.

In the living room, she caught sight of herself in the old pine mirror over the fire. Before the police came, she had put on make-up without thinking. As if it mattered. Now her mascara had run, her lashes stuck in tearful clumps, her eyeliner smudged on swollen lids. Her nose was shiny and her hair tousled. He stood behind her and said, to the mirror, 'It'll be all right.' His voice sounded uncertain. It had often sounded like that, when they talked during the last eighteen months they were together. His lack of confidence had irritated her then beyond reason, had provided another justification as she dropped out of love. With a pang, she recognized it was something she herself had brought about.

'It's all my fault. Jesus, Paul, it's my fault. I'm to blame, I—'

He interrupted, his voice weary, 'I don't care about your feelings right now.' She saw his eyes on the whisky bottle and immediately felt herself bristle defensively. Nothing had changed. 'Just tell me.'

She went through it all again.

* * *

The police phoned just after Paul arrived. The school party could not be contacted but they were due back at base camp that evening. A police officer would be there to meet them.

'It'll be late tonight before we hear anything.' Janie held the phone, talked across it to Paul. 'Maybe longer.' She said into the receiver, 'Should we go ourselves?' She listened for a while. 'Oh, I see.' She listened again. Then she went quiet. She said, in a small voice, 'All right then. We'll be here,' and put the telephone back on its cradle with elaborate care.

'The police think it would be best if we stayed here. Weather conditions are poor up there. Dense fog. And they've got men on the spot.'

'Why don't those stupid climbing buggers have mobiles with them? A trip like that, with kids. They must be out of their minds.' He stared morosely out over the cobbled yard. 'What did you mean earlier, about it being your fault. How your fault?'

'I think this – whatever's happened – with Adam might be something to do with work. With the book. I've got hold of really shocking material on Mama. It could be that someone wants me to stop – that this is a warning not to continue digging. And something else. Claudia says she's sure the gas explosion was intentional.'

'You mean someone tried to blow you up?' He was horrified. His reaction comforted her.

'They'd have known I was away. Claudia thinks someone wanted to frighten me off.'

'*Frighten* you? Hell, the place looks like a bomb hit it. If anyone had been in the house they could have been killed.' He was really angry now. 'Some-one? Like who?'

'The Krzysztof Foundation.'

He made an irritated sound. 'You seriously think a large and rich organization like this – it's worldwide, for God's sake – is going to behave like the Mafia over something you've turned up in the files?' He sounded dismissive, insulting. 'You flatter yourself. The foundation's funding the book. They can pull the plug on it if they want and shut you up that way. They've no need for threats. And anyway, what on earth could justify some-thing like this? You've found out she fakes her miracles? She uses a Ouija board and tape-recorded voices, she conjures up spirits out of bits of net and smoke machines . . .'

She interrupted. His scorn angered her but she suppressed the impulse to quarrel. 'Nothing like that. I wish it were.'

She told him about Dante. As she went on with the story, he listened with increasing intensity. When she reached the part about the hanging child, he flinched and put a hand in front of his eyes. When she finished, he swallowed.

'Christ.'

She waited. Finally he said, his voice low, 'I can hardly believe it. But something tells me it's true. It's got that ring to it, you know? No one could have made that up.' He rubbed the stubble on his upper lip. 'And you say the footage looked genuine.'

'I'm convinced it was. They can do a lot with film, but I'd swear it hadn't been touched. And everything looked right. The clothes, the faces.'

'Do you know anything about your source?'

'I trust him, and so would you. He's serious. All this is incredibly important to him, it's an area he works in.'

'Works how?'

'He's a lawyer. He knows what he's doing.'

Paul swung round. 'I hope so. Because you can't use information like this without being absolutely sure of your ground.'

'You don't have to tell me. And I am sure. Quite by chance, I have at least one witness I can swear to. There'll be more.'

He shook his head in reluctant admiration. 'You always were bloody good. You still are.'

She flushed with pleasure. Whatever grudges he bore her, whatever bitterness there was between them, this hadn't changed. Their professional relationship had always been important to both of them, and his praise was genuine. She wanted to tell him how much it meant to her. But all she said was, 'Thanks.'

He seemed about to add something else, then changed his mind. You look different, he had wanted to say. She appeared to have grown taller, but perhaps that was just because she had lost weight. The rounded lines of her mouth had drawn out, become more resolute. She seemed older, stronger, full of tension. Things had not been easy for her either lately. But that haggard look around the eyes; that was the worry over Adam. He drummed his fingers against the glass, thinking. 'Tell me again just who's on the board of the foundation.'

Janie told him, ticking the names off on her

374

fingers. He listened intently, nodding recognition when she mentioned Josef Karms, interrupting after Monica Ziegler to say, 'Don't know about the widow. But her old man was a bag of bad news.'

'I thought he made millions selling pills made out of edelweiss and cowpats.'

Paul grunted. 'He was one of those men, you never heard where he made his *first* million. It was always said he got his hands on money secreted in Switzerland during the war. Gold from melted-down wedding rings and gold teeth. No one could ever prove it, but somehow the shit stuck. Who else?'

When she got to Zazi de Lisle, he said, half to himself, 'What do I know about her?'

'Used to be Zazi Castellòn, a very expensive lay. Got older than her plastic surgery, married de Lisle twenty-five years ago the way other people take out pensions.'

'There was something else.' He raked his fingers through his hair. 'No, I can't get it. Go on.'

'The rest are nobodies. David Preston, a Tory backbencher who never opens his mouth in the House. There was a scandal though,' she added. 'Years ago. An illegitimate child by his researcher, but since then he's been boring. And someone called Jarvis, from one of those City accountants where all the offices have wood panels and ancient secretaries built in. Vivian Arnold is a solicitor, looks as if he knows his way around.' She thought for a minute. 'I forgot Dennis Whitely. Professor at Surrey.'

'The historian? Came across his name in an autobiography I was reading. Apparently he tried to get into politics after the war – he was very young of course, twenty-four, twenty-five – anyway they showed him the door at top speed. Something to do with breaches of security. It's said his father got it hushed up somehow, but it stuck. After that he never really amounted to anything.'

'Yes.' She stifled her impatience: Paul was a pedant. Claudia had said it, after they'd split, and Janie had recognized a truth she had never cared to admit. 'Yes, but none of them are *dangerous*, are they? Not the sort of people to . . .' she hesitated, not wanting to put her fears into words, 'do anything heavy, and not to a child.'

'People are capable of anything, if they feel something they care about is threatened. And we already know what Mama has hidden in her closet. These people make me nervous. Most of them seem to have something to hide, one way or another. They're vulnerable themselves.' He frowned. 'And I have to say I was wrong. It looks as if, as things stand, you pose a very real threat to Mama *and* her foundation. I'd no idea you were digging up stuff like this. It's sure as hell not what they bought you for.'

'They knew who I was. What did they expect?'

'They expected a scissors-and-paste job, what else? You were chosen precisely because of who you were. And what you'd become.'

'Oh yes?' Her voice was dangerously low. 'And what had I become?'

'An old pro past her best. They'd comfortably anticipated you would be happy to pull together the cuttings for them, and effectively kill off any further attempts at unauthorized biography.' He looked at her furious face in amazement. 'Surely you realized that?' He sounded amused. 'And to think I thought you were a cynic.' Almost as an afterthought he added, 'I'd forgotten how green your eyes get when you're angry.'

She ignored that. 'Right now I don't give a shit,' she said fiercely. 'I'll shred the lot if it turns out to be the cause of all this.' Her gesture included the wrecked portion of the barn outside the window, themselves, their pain. He nodded.

'But shredded or not, you won't forget it.'

'Something's going on. I'm frightened, and I think you are, too. When Adam . . .' She heard the quaver of uncertainty in her voice and repeated herself, to will it to happen, 'I think when Adam gets back, we should take him away from school for a few weeks. Just until we know what's going on. He won't miss much work, and at his age it doesn't matter anyway.'

'I should have thought of that myself. But he can't come to either of us. If you're right, he'd be too easily traced. We don't want to have to put him under guard.' After a silence he said doubtfully, 'There's my mother.'

'There's mine. But poor Adam, with either of them for more than a weekend.' Despite everything, it was hard not to smile. She raked her fingers through her hair, thinking. 'What about Lou? No one would find him with her in Northamptonshire.'

'Brilliant. He'll love it there. Maybe he could even go to the village school with her lot. Will you tell Louise what's going on?'

Her voice was weary. 'I can't worry about all that now. Let's wait and see what happens this evening. I've made up the bed for you in . . .' She found she could not say, in Adam's room. But there was no need, he knew. He went to the door, looked back at her ruefully.

'You've got one hell of a story here. Only you may never be able to tell it.'

'I suppose it *would* ruin her, if it came out.'

He stared. 'You're kidding.'

'They say that every saint has a past and every sinner has a future. Maybe Mama has paid for her crimes by the way she's lived her life. Maybe people just won't care.'

He made a scornful sound. 'Tell that to the people who survived that work camp in Poland.'

The day still stretched endless before them. Now that they had talked it through a dozen times, they were reduced to monosyllables. All these months the impending divorce had been hanging between them, impossible to see around or beyond. Paul reacted by being remote and dignified. It was a form of self-protection which infuriated her. Paul sensed this and the knowledge reinforced the pattern. For a long time, Adam had been the only safe point of reasonable discussion between them. Everything else – selling the house in Putney, dividing the proceeds, the furniture and pictures, deciding on a school – was a confrontation. And now they could not even speak easily of Adam.

Their marriage had been wounded beyond the possibility of regeneration. When it became only too apparent that they could not bear to live together, before the lawyers moved in and restored a semblance of civility, they had said unforgivable things, given vent to vicious truths. They had come to expect the worst of each other. Now both of them were too drained for anger, or pretence. They were less than strangers.

There were other phone calls: the headmaster of Adam's school, alerted, wanted to know if anything had happened. Later on his deputy checked again. After they had eaten, Paul, sitting on the sofa, fell into an uneasy, exhausted doze, his head at an uncomfortable angle. She took the empty coffee mug out of his hand, stuck a cushion behind him, and pushed his head onto it. He mumbled and moved obediently, and in doing so reminded her painfully of his son. Unable to help herself, she got out photographs of Adam and stared till her eyes ached, as if that would somehow make him safe.

Paul woke quite soon, spoke into her reverie with a voice croaky from sleep. 'Anything?'

'No.' He saw the photographs and she watched him stifle the words. The phone rang and she caught it before the second ring. She identified herself, listened. Then she said, 'No, of course not. Yes. We'll wait here. Thank you.' She turned to Paul. 'It *is* human blood. They tried to put up a helicopter to find the school party, but it proved impossible, the weather's got worse. They'll call us the minute they hear anything.' She started to gather up the photographs and her voice was very low. 'The blood's Group A.'

'Adam's A.'

'They know.' She gestured with her head

379

towards the phone. 'Apparently that doesn't mean too much. Almost half the population's A.'

Paul made a heavy sound.

Before it got dark, they each walked the stony path round the top fields, quickly and alone, so the other was there for the telephone. The rain had stopped earlier, the clouds had cleared and left a deepening blue evening, long watery bars of yellow light in the west providing a dramatic backdrop for the black trees. When Janie halted, too caught up in her thoughts to move, the hedges dripped and rustled around her. Near the house, a great elm was laden with starlings bickering for houseroom.

When she got back in it was almost completely dark. She had forgotten to put on her boots and her shoes were wet through, the bottoms of her trousers soaked. She remembered she had never finished her interrupted shower: she'd have it now.

Afterwards she lay on the sofa while Paul walked. Just for a minute, just for a rest. She was desperate for sleep, for the brief respite from panic it would bring. But she could not let herself drop off, out of loyalty to Adam, to what might be happening to him. Might already have happened. No, don't even think that. If it had happened, there would have been alarms, messages from the Cairngorms. *Something*.

Chapter Thirty-Three

She half-woke several times, disturbed by the sound of her own ragged breathing. Then she burst out of nightmare, shards of terror dropping away as she opened her eyes. The room was nearly dark. Paul's voice said from the window behind her, 'What is it?'

'I want it not to be true. Oh God, Paul, I want it not to be true!' She put her hands to her head, the frenzy of her thoughts unbearable.

'Calm down,' he said, and she thought it was indifference that flattened his tone. 'Let's wait till we hear from the police before we go over the top.' He left the room abruptly, letting the door bang behind him.

Sitting bolt upright with a jerk she started to cry, the tears literally shooting out of her eyes. She went on and on, she simply could not stop, the burden of her guilt and despair too great. She was losing control, she could hear the raucous gasping sound she was making as if it came from someone else, a frenzied indrawn shriek uttered again and again on the same note. It was like a loud and violent mourning, mourning for Adam. Oh God, *Adam* . . .

Paul was there, face white, eyes hard. He said quietly, 'That's enough. You're hysterical.'

When she did not – could not – stop, he caught

hold of her shoulders and shook her violently so her teeth banged together. He hissed at her, 'Stop it, *stop it*!' She stared at him, her eyes wide with shock. That seemed to release something in her, a deep exhaustion. She drew a great shuddering breath and shut her face between her own hands. She stayed like that for a long time. She could hear Paul moving around.

Then he said, his voice deliberately calm, 'We'd be fools to get into a state at this point. It might all be nothing, you realize that.' He was speaking in that elaborately low tone she knew so well, that he had used in the past whenever she got excited. Whenever, she added to herself with a touch of the old honesty, she started to show the drink. Hearing it again infuriated her beyond bearing. She stared across at him, as if she could not believe this lack of emotion, this stoical calm. 'How can you be so . . . Adam could, he could be . . . and you don't even . . .' She was going to say, *dead*, but her lips refused to frame the word. She was going to say, *care*, but he interrupted her.

'Care? You think I don't care about my own son?'

'No! I don't! You're too bloody *English*, nothing gets through to you, does it? You don't have feelings, you tight-arsed, callous shit!'

'Let me tell you . . .' His voice was harder now, rough with emotion. She heard it with a kind of triumph – she could always make him angry, always slip under that relaxed façade he presented to everyone else. She could still reach him. '*I* was always the one he turned to, not you. When you were jetting off to your bloody interviews, d'you think nothing happened to us when you were gone? That we just froze until you chose to walk in the front door again and wind us up like toys? Damn you to hell, *I* was always the one who got phoned at the office when there was a crisis at home. *I* was the one who took him to hospital when they thought he'd broken his leg at school. I was always there for him while you were on the other side of the fucking world.'

She jerked upright. She could see his outlined shape against the window. 'Doing my job,' she yelled back. 'Earning a living.'

His voice was loud, desperate. 'And what was I doing, bringing home goddam peanuts? We'd have lived well if we'd just had my salary and you know it. What you did was never just about earning a living. You had to be the best, you had to prove yourself every fucking minute, you had to be seen to be successful. I don't understand why you're like that, but don't you tell me you neglected Adam and me to earn a *living*, you self-deceiving bitch.'

'It's you who's self-deceiving! You lost your ambition years ago, you're just time-serving, like all the other hacks. You were content to be a nobody and you wanted me to be the same.'

He lifted an arm as if to strike her, brought it down with a vicious thud on the chairback. '*Christ!* If that's how you see me, if that's really what you think . . .'

'What else? Listen to you, what else? You knew what I was like when you married me. If you wanted a simpering little fool in a kitchen why didn't you find one? Why didn't you just leave me alone to live my own life? What have you *done* to me?'

'What have I done to you? What have *you* done to *me*? You've taken my self-respect, you've made me like this . . . until you, I never felt such anger, not for anyone. I hate it, it's like poison inside me. *You* did that to me, you wanted me to know about the other men, you wanted to make me see you didn't need me for anything . . .' He was panting, she could see his face gleaming as though he was crying.

'And I didn't,' she screamed back at him. 'You're right, I didn't need you. Not then and not now. There's nothing you can do here, you're not getting Adam back, are you? You're useless, *useless* . . . I hate you . . . This is my fucking house so get out, get *out*!'

'And what about you?' He was screaming too. 'Living with you was like living with a bloody *man*. The last few months were horrible. You never said a tender word, you never touched me . . . I've picked you up at the airport after a frantic day and all you worried about was I'd parked on the wrong level . . . don't you know what that feels like, always being put down? Always being made to feel you don't matter, as if—'

'—your own fault, don't you dare blame me, I'm not responsible for your shitty self-esteem and don't you—'

'—never wanted to make a home for us, you don't even notice what Adam's doing half the time. You never think about anything but yourself and your fucking work. Christ, you've more testosterone than the whole fucking newsroom put together!'

'Then at least there's one man in the family, you bastard.' She was yelling into his face. 'Go on, go! Go now! I never ever want to see you again—'

All they wanted was to wound each other, and twelve years of marriage had taught them the tender places where a hurt went deepest. They said things that should never be said, that should not even be thought, and they would never get back from them. Some vestige of decency told her she should hold the words in but she could not obey it. All reticence had gone, they were like mad creatures, not caring what weapons they used, seeking only to drag each other down.

And then somehow the violence of the quarrel took them over the edge of words. He had rolled up his sleeves, so she raked her nails down his arm for emphasis, heard his indrawn breath as she hurt him. He caught her wrist, bent her arm hard behind her back, his greater strength almost matched by her wild anger. Then they were wrestling, fighting, she trying to claw his shoulders, his face, he pinioning both her wrists. Confined, she spat viciously in his face and he retaliated by wrenching her arms harder behind her. They were so caught up in their hating, they could not struggle apart. She kicked out but her feet were bare and he tripped her up so she fell heavily against the sofa, with him on top of her, let herself slide to the ground. She heard his groan, felt his mouth against her neck.

She was trembling. With anger, with fear, with bitter remorse and the terrible apprehension about Adam that had not left her for so many hours. Paul's irregular heartbeat told how pent up he was. They lay locked together, breathing heavily.

Janie could never have anticipated this: that the violence would become sexual. She had thought that was dead between them. He sighed, buried his face in the side of her neck and she felt him shudder. It was as bad for him, she knew that. Of course she knew.

He cradled her in the curve of his knees and belly and rocked her. She didn't think he was aware of it; it was something he always used to do with Adam as a baby, when he was teething or tearful and nothing else would work. She understood that now he was seeking comfort.

They shared the pain of that moment as they had so many things over the years, in the matrimonial past they would always own together. Youth and ambition. A decade and some disappointment. Love and anger. Adam.

She could not believe how, in these terrible circumstances, she was able to feel desire. In the midst of so many strong conflicting emotions – fear, despair, desperate hope, fury – where did she find the space for this great thud of longing? She craved his mouth, his touch on her flesh. There was no strength in her without him.

With a groan she turned in his arms and held him close, her hands pressed against his back, patting, smoothing. He felt different, harder, leaner. There was more grey in his hair than she remembered. He smelled just as he always had.

He gathered her to him as if he was saving her

from drowning and she was too exhausted, too emptied out to resist. She looked at him, and the sheen of tears in her eyes filled him with pity. He slipped a hand inside the white robe, to cup the soft sad weight of her breast.

She whispered, 'I think my heart is breaking.'

For answer, he bent his head to kiss the blind bud of her nipple. He murmured, 'It's all right. You're not alone any more.'

At first, she held back, hating the thought that they were using sex as an anaesthetic, blocking out their fears. But then she understood this was the only way to answer grief, the only positive act to assuage their loss. She ached for Paul, ached with love and anger. She gave a gasp and reached for him, thrust her tongue into his mouth.

They had been apart for so long, their bodies were no longer accustomed to each other. They blundered, searching, awkward as novices, as if this was the first time, as if they were without skills.

In the beginning, during those first hesitant caresses, other people lay in their embrace: the men she had slept with, the woman she felt sure had been with Paul that night when she telephoned. They existed in moves she made which she had never shared with him. They lingered when he stroked her hair – something she disliked, and which he had never done to her.

Then these other outlines became faint and faded altogether as they inhaled each other's scents, stroked each other's skin, touched and found again textures, tastes, sensations which once had been unbearably exciting and erotic to them both, in those first years together. Those years before marriage turned into imprisonment and she forgot how much she depended on Paul, and sought from others what once she had wanted only from him. It seemed incredible to her, that their bodies could assume those old easy patterns of tenderness and delight.

They made love without words, just broken murmurs, inarticulate sounds. They made love with their eyes and their hands and their mouths. And when at last they could stand no more waiting, when he slid his body into hers, he was no traveller in a strange country, but an exile returning home.

He said, 'You were the one thing that ever made sense. You've given me all the best parts of my life.' In the dark, his voice was rueful. 'And all the worst.'

She whispered, 'You never told me that. You should have told me.'

'Christ, you must have known how I felt about you. When we got married, I thought, now everything will be wonderful for ever.'

'Like a fairytale.' She smiled in the darkness at the thought, then added, 'But we both forgot the story.'

'Losing you was unbearable.' He rubbed his face against hers. She tasted his tears on her lips.

'Don't,' she murmured. 'Don't. I'm such a bitch.'

'Shit, it was me, too. Twelve years – of course there were resentments between us. Where we went wrong was denying them. We let anger harden until we couldn't move past it. I assumed you'd go on wanting me even if I didn't do anything to deserve it. I just expected to be loved.'

She said sadly, 'Isn't that what lovers do? They expect to be loved, and so they are.'

'Maybe I didn't work at it enough. Is that where I went wrong, d'you think? And then when I felt I wasn't, instead of trying harder, I just walked away.'

Often enough, she had cursed him for never conceding he might be less than perfect. Now, perversely, his doing so was painful. 'I don't think I ever didn't love you. It's just . . .' she frowned with the effort of candour, 'you were *there*. I thought I didn't have to worry, you wouldn't change or go away. I was such a fool, to imagine it was a part of my life quite separate from you and Adam.'

His name brought them to silence.

Just after ten o'clock, the telephone rang. She answered before the first ring had finished: it was Adam full of excitement. Relief made her so weak she had to sit on the floor.

'We've just got back this minute. I'm in Mr McLeish's office, he said I was to tell you we've had a brill time. I can come down a whole mountain in about thirty seconds . . .'

'It's so good to hear your voice. Oh, darling, I can't tell you.' Her own was shaky with emotion, but he didn't notice. 'Did it all go well, then? No problems?'

'Simon hurt his ankle and there weren't enough sausages.'

Paul appeared in the doorway and she turned to him, her face alight.

'Look, darling, Dad's here with me, he wants a word. When you get back, we're coming down together, straight away, to see you. And can he talk to Mr McLeish in a minute?'

'I'll be back at school tomorrow night. And I've got you a present. I won't tell you what it is.' There was a pause, then he added, unable to keep his secret, 'It's made of like pottery and it's got four legs and a lot of hair.'

Janie said, 'I can't wait. One thing – have you got all your clothes?' She swallowed painfully at the thought of the bloodstained garments. 'Someone seems to have sent some of your things here.'

He said, vaguely, 'I lost that blue sweater you just bought. And some other stuff. Sorry.'

'Don't worry, they're probably all here then. Darling, we'll see you soon.'

She handed the phone to Paul.

Janie woke in the early hours to find they had slept twined together in the old way, his head against her shoulder, his leg thrown over hers. He was still asleep. She lay for a long time, comfortable beneath his familiar weight.

Marriage was a mixture of sweet and bitter. Both were important, if the relationship was to grow. It had taken this shared fear for Adam to teach her she could not just turn her back on Paul and walk away, to understand that they were linked together, responsible for each other. Even if they could not always be lovers, they would always be what they had been first, before the sex and the marriage – friends, colleagues, collaborators. They admired each other, respected the other's work, their efforts, their honesty.

She thought about Adam. God knows what that had all been about, if they would ever know the full story. God knows how either of them would have coped if . . . She couldn't finish the thought.

'Don't leave me.' It seemed for a moment he was talking in his sleep, but when she turned her head, he was watching her. She had forgotten the warm golden-brown of his eyes. 'Don't leave me again.' His hand moved convulsively on the curve of her hip.

'Never.' She fitted her naked body to the length of his. Under her palms, she felt the steady drumming of his heart, against her thigh he stirred with a desire she thought she had foregone. When he entered her, she was complete. 'Never. Never, never, never.'

Chapter Thirty-Four

Next morning at dawn, Janie stood in the kitchen yawning as she waited for the kettle to boil. She could not remember all the murmured conversations during that long, strange, wakeful night, but she and Paul seemed to have reached many decisions.

They planned to drive to Adam's school later in the morning, and take him on to stay with Lou for at least a month, to give them time to plan the future. *Their* future. Paul was insistent that she move back to London immediately. His flat was too small for them both to share for long, but it would do for the moment. Whatever happened, he was determined she must not remain here alone.

She leaned her elbows on the deep stone windowsill, so recently rebuilt, and stared out at the cobbled yard, still filled with builder's skips and ladders. Maybe she and Paul would bring Adam back here in August, as they always had, but that depended on so many things. What, if anything, the police discovered about the box of blood-stained clothes. Whether she found any suggestion that Mama and the foundation had been involved in the fire.

Her head began to ache with anxiety and she ran her hands through her hair: take it one day at a time. She opened the window and breathed deeply. The day was growing paler by the minute, the humped vertebrae of the Pennines appearing between long bars of mist, monsters rising from a lost sea.

She reached up for the tin of biscuits with mixed emotions: Paul liked a biscuit in the mornings. She felt pleasure that she was doing this again after so long – and irritation that she was slipping so easily into the role of wife. Unnerving to think that perhaps after all she too wanted to retreat into domestic security, to become another Louise. She shut the cupboard with a slam. And why not? There was room for this, too. She would manage both the second time.

She had desired Paul's return, then, even if she had not consciously acknowledged it. She needed him. It had taken a long time for her to achieve this small amount of self-knowledge. She had wrenched it from the darkness of the last few hours. And if that misery was the source then somehow, though she could not work out how, it must be connected to Mama.

As she watched the early haze lifting from the hills, many things seemed to become clear to her. What people called fate was more than random external events. They were shaped by what was in her, by her expectation and her will. Their pattern followed one that existed already in her mind. She had somehow made them real by the intensity of her wanting.

She loved Paul. It was a revelation: she had forgotten what happiness was like, the fine simplicity of it. Even the air smelled wonderful, as it must to a prisoner shut away for years. She had not felt so good since that strange and lovely day in the valley, when she saw the creamy stag, that had looked to her like the white unicorn free at last of its confining tapestry.

That same dawn saw Alma Gysemans huddled into her sweater at her high window in Brussels as monotone grey became streaked with pink. She had been there all night, watching from her velvet chair. The city lights still flared below in the clustered shadows, but up here the gilded points and pinnacles of the medieval square glittered against the brightening sky as they had five hundred, a hundred, fifty years ago.

Fifty years. For fifty years and more, she and Viktor had locked what had been done to them away in a cupboard. After the first few months of reunion, they did not speak of it, even to each other. Even they had found that there are some things too deep for sharing. So they had lived for all that time with their backs pressed against the cupboard door.

Chance had seated her beside Janie Paxton on that plane from Toulouse. History had brought Dante to her. Under such pressure the locks of the cupboard had snapped and the door had burst open. Alma was discovering that the scars of fifty years ago hurt her still.

Chapter Thirty-Five

Alma Gysemans closed the dining-room door against the sound of heavy metal rock music.

'Enough,' she said firmly, pouring more coffee, 'is enough. Naturally I love to see Richard, but after a week here . . .'

They were in the town house off the Marylebone Road where Alma's daughter Fernande lived with her husband Justin Savory and their youngest son. Three storeyed, wrought-iron balconies hung with ivy, lacquered black front door. In the dark green room on the first floor, with its long windows facing over the elegant small square, the remains of Sunday lunch were still before them.

Janie had been introduced to Belgian hospitality with a traditional meal. *Mosselen* – mussels – had been served in individual casseroles, steamed in broth seasoned with garlic, eaten with the best French fries she had ever tasted. They had drunk Belgian beer tasting faintly of raspberries and finished with *manons*, which seemed to be pure Belgian chocolate filled with fresh cream. Janie promised herself she would eat nothing but fruit for a week.

Beside her, Alma's son said politely, 'Can I get you . . .' Karel stroked the air with his palm, as if half-formed thoughts resided there where he might happen upon them. 'Some cheese?'

She laughed and waved away his offer. 'I may never eat again.'

Opposite her Fernande said, gently reproving, 'It is important to eat. A good meal is more than just the consumption of food. It is a vital luxury, a shared pleasure . . .'

'. . . or a prelude to it,' her husband teased her. They had a habit of finishing each other's sentences. Justin picked up his wife's hand and kissed it: she gave him a tender look. Janie thought, they must have been married at least twenty-five years, and clearly they had kept the mystery and the sex alive. Watching them, she made Paul a promise.

'As I was saying,' Fernande went on, 'before I was so rudely interrupted. Sharing a meal is both necessity and ritual, and we forget that at our peril. It makes a time to speak at leisure, to replenish both body and spirit. It is no accident that every great religion has special food for different festivals.' Unlike Alma, she had no trace of an accent, though she spoke with the formality of someone for whom English is a second language. But mother and daughter were incredibly alike: their height and presence, their intelligence, their grooming, their solemnity.

Karel made his voice plaintive, 'I only asked your guest if she wanted cheese, my dear Fernande. Not a sermon.' Everyone laughed and he smiled at Janie. Even in this domestic setting, she could sense how desperately shy he was, how he screwed himself up to conversation and banter. She thought it an odd characteristic in someone so unusually attractive. Karel was tall, his unruly blond hair streaked with white, where all the rest of his family were dark - she remembered Alma's story about bleaching her hair to his colour when he was a child. His lean face was just saved from austerity by an endearing gap between his front teeth. Alma had said sailing was his passion, and he did possess that remote sailor's gaze, as if used to looking always to the horizon. And his eyes were steely-blue, the colour of a northern sea, with a faint hooding at the corners that somehow gave him a look of constant amusement. He must be fifty, but would pass anywhere as far younger.

Janie had met him only that day, and during the meal had once or twice caught Alma watching him with a curious expression. At first she had thought they might have had an argument, but then decided it was nothing like that. Rather, she looked concerned, almost anxious, as if he might at any moment do something unpredictable. He was seated opposite Alma and Janie noticed that when she spoke, he leaned his body attentively towards her; the bond of affection and respect between them was tangible.

Her thoughts were interrupted as the group round the table began to break up. Fernande and her husband were driving their son round to a friend's house to return the drum kit he had borrowed, a prospect which clearly pleased Alma. When they had gone Karel took his leave of Janie, bowing gracefully over her hand with an old-world courtliness that almost made her blush. When he took her hand, she sensed the tension in his own. She wondered briefly if he were homosexual: the youthful air, the closeness to his mother. But she decided, whatever the truth about Karel, it was more complex than that.

Alma followed him from the room and a little later Janie went upstairs to the bathroom. Coming out, she glanced over the banisters and saw the two of them below, by the front door. Karel was listening to something his mother was saying, his knuckles thrust into his mouth as if to stifle emotions. As she went back into the dining room, she caught the quiet voices. Perhaps because the family had been speaking English all afternoon, in deference to herself and Justin, mother and son still did so even between themselves.

'. . .will be all right? You have the medication?'

'Yes, yes, maman. I've still got Heffner's prescription. Don't go on, I'm quite . . .'

'Darling, I can't help it. What am I good for, if not to take care of you? When do you go back to the clinic?'

Janie, who had not meant to eavesdrop, closed the door. When Alma returned, she looked worn. Her arms were wrapped round her body as if she felt cold, hands tucked into the sleeves of her grey cashmere sweater. She sat opposite at the littered table, lit a cigarette, played with the lighter.

'I worry about him.' Usually so reticent, she clearly needed to unburden herself.

'Karel? Why?'

'He gets very depressed. So much so that he needs treatment. I don't mean tablets, he's a long way past that. Hospital treatment. He is always reluctant, he has to be persuaded.' She exhaled sharply. 'If only he had someone, I would not

398

worry so much. Of course there are women. A couple of times I thought for sure he would marry, but somehow it never lasts. I cannot go on for ever and then . . .' Alma was staring at the place where Karel had been sitting. The rest of the table was a jumble of used plates, coffee cups, crumbs, empty glasses, crumpled napkins: all the comfortable detritus of an enjoyable meal. Yet in Karel's place, everything was painfully neat. Unused cutlery was carefully aligned, his empty wine glass exactly in line with the water glass, the cheese knife straight on the plate. His napkin was meticulously folded, and if he had made crumbs, they had been brushed away.

Alma made a visible effort. 'I haven't seen you since you came to Brussels. How is the book coming along?'

'I think I'm going to drop the whole project. I honestly don't know whether I can go on with it now.' She fiddled with the stem of her water glass. 'Since that meeting with Dante, I see all the facts about Mama in a totally different light. And I can read them all two ways. What is she? I just can't see her straight any more, I'm totally confused. I can't set out to write a book feeling like this about the subject.'

The older woman said slowly, 'Perhaps not to write it would be taking the easy way out.'

'That's more or less what Dante said.'

Alma nodded. 'Of course, he has his own agenda.' She hesitated, then, 'I hope what I told you that night has not dissuaded you. That is the very last thing I would want.' She drew deeply on her cigarette. 'That was the first time for so many years I had let myself go back there. To that place. To the torment and the fear.'

Janie said, 'Alma, I'm sorry.' No need to say what for, the older woman understood.

'No, no, don't, there is no need. I have been thinking a lot lately. Meeting you has forced me to face something I have denied for too long.'

Janie gave her a troubled look. 'Maybe the past is best left alone.'

'But you see,' Alma said gently, 'it is not just the past. Not for me.'

Chapter Thirty-Six

It was a world of watchtowers. They stood two hundred yards apart inside the barbed boundaries of the camp: barbed-wire fence, then a trench filled with barbed wire, then another barbed-wire fence, then a flat space. The towers were solid, wooden, manned by guard units. Three sentries were in each tower at all times.

An area inside the wire fence was used for onions, radishes, potatoes. These were grown by the prisoners to be cooked for the SS in the kitchens attached to their own barracks. But sometimes the starving could not control their desperate hunger, and in darkness they would risk the run to grub up a cabbage leaf, anything, to put in their mouths. The guards almost always saw them. They had the right to shoot without warning any prisoner within this 'neutral' zone. For of course it was not neutral: it belonged to the oppressors.

Beyond the neutral zone, the electric fence looped thin and sinister from its many poles. Sometimes, she would catch someone staring towards it for long minutes. It was not freedom they were imagining: the world outside the perimeters of the camp had disappeared. Alina did not need to see their eyes to know the look that was in them: the hatred and the compulsion, the knowledge that it was waiting when they could go on no longer.

There were numerous ways of ending existence in that place.

Many prisoners were worked and harried until they dropped dead in their tracks. Many died violently – shot or stoned for a word uttered, or for silence kept. It was sport among the guards to order a prisoner on a work party to throw his cap into a field. He would then be ordered to fetch it. If he obeyed, he was shot in the back 'attempting to escape'. If he refused, he was killed for his disobedience.

All the inmates were assembled at least twice a day for roll-call, once at five in the morning, again at night. *Eins, zwei, drei, vier, fünf*. Sometimes they stood there for six hours at a time, in all weathers. On a platform at the front stood a huge gallows, with many thick hooks for the mass hangings. Alma was told that sometimes a rope would be too long, a prisoner too tall, so the hanging man's feet touched the ground when he dropped. Then a guard would use the heel of his boot to scrape a hole and let the twitching victim die at last.

Some chose their own end. One man picked up the body of his brother and kissed the dead face. Then he simply ran full-tilt towards a guard. He had not even reached him before the bullets cut him down.

Others could only find their path alone and in darkness. They summoned enough desperate courage to stand upon a box, throw a belt over a roof-beam, secure it firmly – and kick away the box. Every night brought three or four such suicides. Only it was not by hanging that they died, but suffocation: they choked to death, and slowly.

Some just gave up hope. But Alma learned it wasn't true that hope is the last thing to die. Even if they are starved enough, and sick enough, life does not easily leave the bodies of people before their time. Dead in all but name, their eyes vacant, blank-faced, they might wait many weeks for oblivion.

Alma knew of all these things, heard them as whispers, rumours. For some they represented a revolt, a cry of rage. By the time she had been in the camp for three months, she saw they could also be a kind of victory. It took the death of Violette Roussel to teach her that suicide was also a defeat, and that at all costs she must try to survive. If not for her own sake – and there were many times when she no longer cared what happened to her – then for her children. Wherever they were.

She was tormented by anxiety about her children. Losing them was like a wound: constant physical pain. She learned to cope by allowing herself two hours a day to think about them. To devote every minute to what might be happening to her babies was to court madness. On some powerful instinctive level, she understood that if she allowed the pain to gnaw too deeply, she would die. To get enough to eat, to try to limit the lice in her clothes, to keep warm enough at night so that she was still alive in the winter mornings, to stay away from the more erratic and undisciplined guards, to avoid the notice of the block warden – these things took all the energy she could summon.

But if she wasn't thinking of the children all the time, there was never a moment when she was free of the ache that was their absence. Fernande had been her constant companion for three years now, they were part of each other more surely than lovers. Alma knew every eyelash, every tooth, every inch of her daughter. In her dreams, she found her again. In her dreams, she was happy.

For the little one, the ache was different and not only of the heart. During the journey from Brussels she had been aware of the milk gathering in her breasts, but once they arrived in Poland, her physical need for her baby became desperate. By the end of the first week in the camp, she had been running a high temperature. Her breasts were swollen taut, she couldn't sleep, shivered constantly.

Her companions had tried to help. They were women who had children of their own and knew what should be done. They told her to express the milk herself, by hand, to relieve the pressure. But she could not: she was too engorged, it was impossible. They advised compresses of hot water, but they had no means of heating any. Even if they had, the water itself was so precious they needed it to drink. She heard them murmuring among themselves, she heard them whisper of milk fever. She understood death was a real possibility, a real risk. Fear rose in her, cold and black.

In a matter of hours she became delirious with pain and desperation: what was happening to the baby, was he able to feed, was he somewhere crying with hunger, dying of it, while she lay here feverishly awake? She started to whimper to herself.

In that place, too many people cried and there was no one to hear. But someone came to Alma. Nita was a Polish woman of maybe thirty with dark eloquent eyes, the shaven hair growing back on her fine-boned skull like little black feathers. The women in Alma's quarters had discussed her, decided she could not be a Gypsy because the Germans kept them in separate compounds. One of the ways they could have known was lost to them: the picturesque Gypsies in their scarves and beads and layers of bright clothing were invariably grimy, with a kind of voluptuous slovenliness. Only here, everyone was dressed alike in the coarse blue and grey cotton garments of the camp, and everyone was dirty.

Nita brought another woman over to translate and asked Alma, 'How long since you feed your baby?'

Alma struggled to remember. 'A week. Maybe longer. I don't know any more.'

'Do you want your milk to go away now?'

Alarmed, Alma said, 'No! I have to feed my baby when I . . . when he . . . oh, God!'

The woman stroked Alma's hot forehead. She spoke softly, and the second woman followed her words. 'They took me on the street. My children run away. They are not so little, now. I tell them, quick, go to my sister.' She paused, looking at Alma, both thinking the same thing. How long would they be kept here? Would they see their children ever again?

'So,' said the woman at last. 'Let me look.'

She examined Alma's swollen breasts with the efficiency of a nurse, touching the tense tissue with delicacy. Even that made Alma cry out, though she thought this woman possessed Gypsy skills. She was certain when Nita smiled briefly. Her teeth were beautiful, white and even. She said, 'I can help you. I do this two time, maybe three, and then you will bring the milk each day with your hand, you understand? Just a little, just enough.'

Alma whispered, 'Yes. I can do that.'

'Then you will permit?'

Alma did not know what the woman could do for her, but she trusted her.

'Yes.'

Nita sent the woman who had translated away. Then she lay down very close to Alma on the narrow bunk. She lay in such a way that her back shielded them a little from the room. Her body was warm and smelled of cloves and sweat. She said something in a low voice, then cupped Alma's breast with her long fingers and bent her head.

The sensation was so intense Alma gasped aloud and tried to pull away, but the arm around her waist held her tightly, and she was too weak to struggle against it. She thought she would faint: the woman's head pressing against her arm, the feel of her mouth urgent at the nipple as she sucked, keeping her lips over her teeth, not to hurt. Alma's breasts ached, her head throbbed. What the woman was doing felt almost unbearably erotic, even in that hideous place. Alma was seized by shame and embarrassment. She felt a stirring deep in her body, like the pull of the after-pains which had followed the birth. Only Viktor had ever done such things and Viktor . . . Viktor . . . She groaned at the thought.

Nita released her nipple and looked up into her face.

'Co to jest?' What is it?

Alma shook her head so the tears she did not know she had shed slid into the hair at her temples. She put her hand on the back of Nita's head, and the dark feathers of hair were fine as a child's. She smoothed them, pressed the woman's face closer.

'Please,' she said. 'Don't stop. Help me.'

It was the innocence of it she experienced now, the simple comfort of a supple body beside her own, the luxury and reassurance of letting some-one take care of her. Minutes went by as she lay there in a curious half-sleep. She could almost believe it was her baby's mouth tugging at her nipple, and all the rest only a terrible nightmare.

As the pressure in her breasts lessened, the pain began to subside. And with the relief came more understanding. Alma saw that it was another kind of loving that this strangely knowledgeable woman was giving to her. A gift only she could have made.

'Are you sure – don't you mind?'

The woman could not have understood, she spoke no German. But the meaning was clear enough. She stopped what she was doing and turned her head, her cheek smooth olive against Alma's white skin. Her smile was of such sweet-ness that Alma's eyes filled again and she felt her throat closing. She reached down for the woman's

407

free hand and lifted it to her lips. She opened the long fingers, and kissed the grubby palm, the way you kiss a child's hand.

'Thank you,' she whispered.

Violette Roussel was among the inmates brought from France. When the Gestapo took her, she had been on her way home from work. A waitress in a small café in Rheims, she never learned why she was sent first to prison, then to the camp. Perhaps it was a case of mistaken identity. When they picked her up, her five-year-old son had been waiting for her outside his school. She had not even been allowed to send a message.

For the eleven months she had been in Poland, she believed the boy was safe with his father. The thought of them together in France kept her going. And then she received a letter from her husband, who had finally learned where she was. He wrote that he was sending a parcel of food and clothing. And a warm coat for the boy. The parcels did not reach her. But of course that did not matter.

Alma was told this only afterwards. But that afternoon, as she crossed the open space where the inmates were assembled for roll-call, she saw a woman running towards her. Brown-eyed, a pretty woman despite everything, her features precise, her skin white. Her hands, her face, the front of her shirt were wet. It was so extraordinary to see anyone run in that place – they were too exhausted, too starved, even to hurry – that Alma paused.

By the time she realized that the woman was not

running towards her, but to the electric fence beyond, she had almost reached it. Arms outstretched, face eager, she rushed forward as if to a lover.

Alma could not bear to watch, and she could not look away. The woman neared the fence, the guards in the watchtower yelled – Alma never knew if their words were warning or encouragement. The woman did not hesitate. She flung herself against the wire and grasped it tightly with both her wet hands.

There was an ear-splitting *crack* and Alma distinctly heard the woman shout. Hundreds of volts pulsed through her body so that she jerked and juddered in violent spasm before she was hurled backwards.

Alma started forward but someone caught her arm. Even where she stood, the cruel smell of seared flesh, of singeing muscle tissue, seemed to fill her head.

The woman Violette Roussel lay on her back four or five feet from the electric fence. One leg was twisted beneath her, both arms were spread wide. The palms of her clawed hands were charred. A clog lay beside her head. Her hair, which had begun to grow again after its initial shaving, stood on end. Her eyes were wide as she stared up at the terrible blue of the sky.

They thought she was dead. Because she was in the neutral zone, no one could fetch her body without an order. She lay there for almost two hours. Eventually, one of the few women guards going off duty glanced casually across at the body. Something caught her attention, and she looked more carefully. She crouched down for a minute, then summoned a couple of prisoners. They went to get a stretcher and took the Frenchwoman to the long hut that served as the prisoners' infirmary.

Violette Roussel remained unconscious. She twitched occasionally, and trembled, but never spoke again. Sometimes her eyes were closed, sometimes open, but they never focused. Eventually, just before dawn, she died.

Alma knew this because during that time, she did her best to look after the Frenchwoman. The week before, she had been ordered to work in the infirmary. She was not a trained nurse, but there were only two in the camp.

There was little enough that could be done for the Frenchwoman. Alma asked the doctor if he could bandage the burned hands, she could see the bones of the fingers where the charred flesh dropped from them. The doctor, a Pole, a good man who was always so tired he sometimes fell asleep as he worked, shook his head. He had no medicines left, no morphine, no dressings. He explained there was nothing to be done, even the muscle was burned away. 'She is in shock,' he told Alma, 'and beyond pain.'

But she was not. Alma continued to stay with her where she lay on the floor, on straw covered with sacking. It was all she could offer. It did no good, but the woman's story was so close to her own.

Violette Roussel was still alive when the bell went for curfew. Or rather, she was not yet dead. Alma was moistening her lips with a damp cloth before she left, when the woman guard who had ordered the Frenchwoman to be sent to the hospital entered the room. The heels of her black leather boots were loud on the wooden floor. For a second Alma closed her eyes, remembering the sound of her own heels in the endless corridor the day she lost her children.

When she opened them again, the guard was at the bedside. Standing above them, she appeared huge, a great dark shadow in the dim light. Her name was Krolak, though no one ever addressed her by it. The inmates had another name for her. They called her Little Angel, but never when there was any chance she might hear. She was called Little because she was tall. And Angel because they knew what she was capable of.

Alma had been told how Little Angel had stepped forward at a mass hanging of those who had stolen food, and killed a young boy with her bare hands. So now Alma looked up at her fearfully: what could such a visit mean?

The guard did not speak. Her face was almost hidden by the peak of her grey cap as she stared down at the injured Frenchwoman, at the charred hands lying on the dingy sheet.

'Not dead?' She used a coarse country German dialect which Alma had trouble understanding. She made a deliberate effort to broaden her middle-class vowels, not to antagonize the woman.

'Not yet, Fräulein.'

Little Angel took off her cap to reveal the subtle modelling of jaw and cheekbone, the winged eyebrows. But she's only a girl! Alma thought. Seventeen, eighteen at most. The few other female guards were heavy-featured, arrogant, in their late twenties and thirties.

Little Angel asked abruptly, 'Are you sick?'

'No, Fräulein. I am working here.' She dare not add the words she longed to scream: Of course I am sick! We are all of us sick, all the time. There is not enough food to prevent it. Our skin erupts, our hair falls. Joints ache, eyes leak, teeth rot. We have dysentery repeatedly, infections, inflammations, ulcers. And these are minor complaints. Many inmates already have TB. Scarlet fever is rife. Typhoid is the greatest fear. We are defenceless against the violence of this disease, and it invariably kills. And most of us receive no care, nothing.

'You are trained as a nurse?'

'No, Fräulein.' She couldn't see the point of the questioning and the fact of it scared her: the guards rarely spoke except to issue orders. Now Krolak smoothed back tendrils of hair which had escaped from its pins. Even restrained, it gleamed in a dark red mass, draining all colour from her already pale skin.

Alma looked down at the woman she tended, squeezed another drop of water carefully onto the parched, dying lips.

The guard said, 'But you can look after children.' It was a statement this time. It seemed irrelevant in that place, but Alma did not stop to think.

'I have children of my own.' She had to seize even this slender opportunity. 'I must find out where they are. They were taken from me months ago in Brussels.' She was gabbling desperately.

'There has been no news of them. Can you, could you . . . ?'

The guard interrupted. 'I can do nothing to find your children.' Her tone was neutral. But there was something in her face that made Alma persist.

'If I could just be told if they're well? The baby is so tiny, only twelve weeks old. Fräulein, I am in despair.'

Little Angel had the air of a woman adding figures in her head. Calculating. She looked around the room, at the rows of huddled, sleeping forms. When she spoke again, her voice was very quiet, almost conspiratorial. 'Twelve weeks, you say?' Alma nodded eagerly. 'Did you suckle?'

Alma was taken aback. 'Yes.' She could not believe a guard was asking her these things. 'Why do you ask?' She added hastily, 'Fräulein.'

The Polish guard ignored the question. She chewed her lip, deep in thought, staring down at the Frenchwoman who lay so still between them on her pile of straw. Alma sensed an undercurrent she could not identify. What was going on?

'This is foolishness,' she said at last. 'Even if you were reunited with your child, you could not feed it after all this time. Here it would only die. It is better off where it is. The homes, the *Kinderheime*, they will take better care of it.'

Alma was on her feet, protesting. 'But I could, of course I could! I have my milk still! I would do anything. Anything, just to see my children again. There are other children in the camp, why not mine?' The last words came out as a wail.

Little Angel was tapping the toe of her glossy black leather boot impatiently on the wooden floor. Alma's brief burst of hope flickered to nothing. It was useless. She sank back onto the straw. She could not help moaning, more to herself than the guard, 'Please. Give me back my baby. *Please!'*

Abruptly, the guard swung round and walked away. At the doorway she paused and for a second Alma thought she was going to turn back, tell her something. But she went through the door and slammed it behind her.

Chapter Thirty-Seven

Little Angel stood in front of Alma. She held a wrapped bundle in her arms. Slowly, her eyes on the prisoner's face, she unwound the uniform skirt, pulled back the bit of blanket, the cloth beneath. They were out of the arc lights, standing in the shadows, but it was possible to see what she held. The baby's face was closed and perfect in the light of the cold moon.

Alma gasped.

Basia Krolak held it out, straight armed. 'Take it. It's for you.'

Alma looked from the baby to the guard. For just a fraction of a second, she hesitated. Then she shook her head.

'Take it!'

Alma looked down, her face shut tight.

Little Angel said, in a furious whisper, 'You wanted a baby, damn you. I have brought you one. Take it now.'

Alma raised her head and the two young women stared at each other.

Alma whispered, 'No. I want *my* baby. Not another woman's. My own baby!' She set her lips, mutinous.

'Your own baby may be dead.'

'No. He's not. He's not dead.' Alma was shaking.

The guard watched her intently. 'You do not know that. No one knows.' Her face was sly suddenly. 'He might be dead. Or you may never find him.' Alma's eyes filled with tears: her own fears, put so bluntly into words. The guard swiftly followed up her advantage. 'Take this one instead. It's a boy. Just like yours.'

Alma said nothing.

The guard's voice dropped to a harsh whisper. 'If you do not live to leave here, then for sure you will never find him.' She shifted the baby, held it briefly against her shoulder with her left hand. She pulled her fingers of her right flat and fast across her throat. It was a terrible gesture.

Alma whispered back, 'Will you kill me?'

'I can. You know I can.' She held out the baby again and the two women stared at each other.

Alma was too tired to fight any more. Enough. She closed her eyes and said wearily, not bothering to be quiet, 'Do it, then. Just *do it.*'

There was a silence. Alma opened her eyes. She had spoken with resignation. But Little Angel had heard it as defiance, and was hoist on her own threat: she needed Alma alive.

The Belgian woman felt a sudden surge of determination she had not expected in herself. To both of them came the dawning realization that their roles had somehow, subtly, reversed. Now the guard was weak, Alma could be strong.

So it was the prisoner who said, 'I don't want it. It's not mine.'

In the poor light, Little Angel peered at the figure in front of her. Alma Gysemans's clothes were soiled, her face streaked with grime under the headscarf she wore to hide her cropped hair. She smelled sweaty, there was dirt under her nails. But she stood planted solid on the ground like a tree that would not be uprooted. There was wisdom in her face, a depth of endurance. The Polish woman could feel the force of her will.

She tried again. 'It's a healthy boy.'

'It's madness. How can I look after a baby in this place? I am a slave, not a nursemaid.' She wiped her eyes with the back of her hand. 'Give it back to its mother, for God's sake. I know what she must be going through. Give it back.'

Little Angel frowned. 'I cannot,' she said. 'I will not. You must take it.'

'She's dead, isn't she, the mother? And you want the child to die too.'

'You do not understand.' The guard was impatient. Alma feared her anger. 'I want it to *live*. I will get you sent to the kitchens. Tomorrow. You can keep the baby with you.'

'You must be mad.' Alma was forgetting herself, raising her voice. 'No worker's child here has even a chance of survival. Babies are dying all the time – my God, don't you *see*?' Little Angel lifted a warning hand. Alma dropped her voice. 'The baby might get sick.'

'Maybe. Maybe not. But it will not be long now, maybe only days, till—' The guard broke off abruptly. Then she said, as if denying an admission, 'I do not know what is going to happen.' She looked down at the bundled baby.

Alma lifted her head, straining to catch the nuances here. The whole camp had heard the rumours. Something was happening. In the last few days speculation had intensified: the Allies were in Eastern Europe, in the Ukraine. They had reached deep into Poland . . . Perhaps it was true. Perhaps the Thousand Year Reich was on the brink of collapse after all. If Little Angel was speaking to her like this, something must be changing beyond the wires and the watchtowers. She was so tired, her mind so sluggish. If only she could understand. She struggled to make sense of it all.

The Polish guard took her long silence for obduracy. It was impossible for her to beg from a prisoner, she did not know how to start. For the first time in her life, she had someone weaker than herself to protect. When she spoke again, her hoarse whisper made her words more vehement.

'It needs milk. It's had nothing. It will die without milk. You have milk, you told me so. *You are the only one.*'

In answer, Alma folded her arms defensively across her breasts, hugging her elbows.

Little Angel felt very hot suddenly, and her legs quivered so she could hardly stand. There was blackness spreading at the edges of her vision. Only Alma's face was in focus. Only the frail weight of the tiny body in her arms felt real.

She reached deep into herself for all the passion of which she was capable. She found desperation and urgency and an overwhelming need. But still she could not utter the single word she must. So she put everything into her gaze.

Alma looked into the eyes of the Polish guard and could not understand why she had never noticed them before. Even in the gloom they were extraordinary, unearthly, pale and yet deep at the same time. The depth of colour was matched by the intensity of expression. They were vehement with meaning, more compelling, more insistent than mere words. They were powerful as a prayer. Alma could no more deny the naked pain in them than she could let this helpless baby die.

She gave a groan of protest. But slowly, slowly, she reached out and took the bundle from the guard. She held it stiffly in swollen, grimy, outstretched hands.

The child gave a faint whimper. As if the sound was a trigger, she bent over it, smelled the top of its head as an animal will, feeling against her cheek the quick pulsing of the fontanelle. With hands suddenly grown greedy she pulled back the sheet and looked at it more closely, peering at the crumpled creature, mewling a little with the cold. She hastily covered it again, murmured to herself, in wonder, 'A newborn!'

It was like a miracle – a birth, in this place where so many died. But where had Little Angel got the child?

With sudden comprehension, she looked up at Basia Krolak. Wits grown sharp at last, she took in the misbuttoned jacket, the way the woman clutched the uniform skirt she held, in which the baby had been hidden. Hidden. Of course. She lifted her eyes and noted the wild straggles of hair escaping from beneath the cap. She registered the skin drained of colour, the swollen eyelids. Even in the dark, she could see the cracked, parched lips. It was the face of a woman pushed beyond her strength, at the very end of her resources.

For a moment – no longer – she started to say,

I cannot. And even as she shaped the thought, she felt the little bundled creature stir in her arms. Already, its warmth had begun to still the ache she had carried for so long. Exhausted as she was, hungry and worn, Alma's own eyes blazed with compassion, and anger.

'God pity you,' she said.

Chapter Thirty-Eight

'How could I refuse?' Alma asked Janie the question, spread those capable hands in a helpless gesture that made a nonsense of any answer she could find. 'The child, at least, was innocent. I could not let a tiny baby die when I had the power to make it live. Perhaps if I saved this baby, someone would save mine. I thought, if I look after it, if I do what I can, surely that would not be too much to ask.' Alma put her hands over her face. 'Oh, God.'

Janie asked at last, 'Why did she give the baby to you? Why did she care what happened to it?'

'It is hard to understand another human being.' There was a passion in her voice which Janie registered only much later. 'The soul is an abyss.'

'What happened to the baby?'

This time Alma rose and walked to the window. The lights in a house opposite had come on, people passed to and fro before the bright windows as if on a stage. 'You've just been sitting next to him for two hours.'

Janie stammered, 'Are you saying . . . *Karel*? Karel is not your own son?'

Alma shook her head. She was pressing her hands against the skin of her cheeks, her jaw, her temples, as though she was holding herself together by force of will. Her eyes were distant, her voice bleak. When she spoke again, it was at a tangent, as if the subject was too painful to approach directly.

'Little Angel was right. By the time she gave me the child, Germany was on its knees. Our camp was taken over by the Russians three weeks later. Too late for Violette Roussel.' She paused, then added with unaccustomed bitterness, 'And in some ways too late for me also. I hadn't even seen my husband, just heard that he was alive. My mother wanted to come immediately from Belgium to see me. But it was impossible to get a travel pass, one had to beg officials for everything. There was no transport. Only the Americans had power, but they knew nothing. The SS had taken my children, but there seemed to be no records, nor anyone to ask. Eventually the United Nations appointed special officers to find lost children. And then my mother and I spent – oh, weeks, months, I can't tell any more – looking for my babies. There were so many, so many . . .' Her voice trailed away.

Then she said, more firmly, 'You would not believe what we saw. In the camps, children of all ages, all races. Ukrainians, Russians, Poles. Some were German, the children of men accused of treason against Hitler. You cannot imagine what they all went through. Taken from their families by force, living together like little animals. There was one German girl, six or seven, someone had given her a piece of bread. She came up to me and held it out, and I thought she wanted to give it me. But she asked me, What is this?

'People tried to help them. They told them what

they told me: You will forget, it will all be like a bad dream. They wanted to keep us quiet, you see, they thought then it would all go away. But it never does. Never.'

Janie said, quietly, 'Were your children . . .'

Alma smoothed the velvet of the curtains. 'Not there. Everything so disorganized, such panic, you can have no idea. And I did not know where to begin to look. The children were taken from me in Belgium – but I had been sent to Poland, maybe they had also? My worst fear was that they had been taken to Germany. Later in the war, the bombing devastated the country, they could have been killed . . . So much of Europe was at a stand-still when the war ended. For those months, I can't tell you what it was like. Telephone lines were down, trains did not run, roads were blocked. There was no way to send a letter, a telegram. It was total chaos. And everywhere, the endless columns of refugees, everywhere the homeless and the hungry. How was I to find two small children in all that? Two tiny children whose names might have been changed?' She was silent, staring back down the years. 'Children whose parents were arrested by the Gestapo were often sent to orphanages. Institutions.' She said the word with hatred. 'My mother and I found Fernande in such a place, in Austria. It took a long time; the war had been over half a year before we got her back. They had changed her name to Geisner and she had never said her real name. Perhaps she had forgotten it. Perhaps she was afraid. No one there had any idea who her parents were, or what they were supposed to have done. But when the Germans changed a child's name, they always chose one quite similar. They are a methodical people. So Geisner was near enough for us to suspect when we read the lists, and of course when we saw each other, it was Fernande.'

'And your baby?'

'No.' Alma's fingers tightened on the velvet. 'Not then.' Almost whispering. 'Not ever.'

There was nothing to say.

'There were organizations to help,' Alma went on. 'The Displaced Persons Bureau – they eventually brought me and Viktor together. And special offices were opened, to try to trace children who had been taken. But wherever I went, I always needed another office, a different permit.' She put her head in her hands. 'My God. What that was like.

'A few weeks after we found Fernande again, the Allies closed the children's homes. The *Kinderheime*. Any children who had not been claimed were given to local people.'

Janie thought she must have misheard. 'What do you mean?'

'Given away like little parcels. Some were adopted, some were just kept as part of the family. Some were used as unpaid servants – slaves, practically, God help them.' She turned to look at the younger woman and shook her head. 'You have no idea how many children were lost. Thousands. Thousands. If my baby had been in Germany or Austria, in Poland perhaps, I had no way to find him. And if he were not . . .' Then she added, in a new, harder tone, 'And so help me, if I had seen him, I could not have recognized him anyway. The last time I saw him he was two weeks old.'

'What did your husband say?'

Alma turned her face to the window again, and her voice was muffled. 'It was months more before Viktor and I found each other, longer before he could leave hospital. Fernande was already with me and of course she had accepted the baby as her brother. I never told Viktor they had taken Karel from me. The baby he knew was barely two weeks old. By the time we were reunited, the child was getting on for a year. There was no question of recognition.' She drew a deep breath. 'If our own son had been found, even months, even years, later, then of course that would have been another matter.' The set of her shoulders was eloquent of despair. 'The need did not arise.'

Janie said in disbelief, 'So your husband never knew the baby was not his?'

Alma said very simply, 'I could not bear to tell him. I honestly don't believe he could have faced up to the truth if the child were not his own. It would have meant his son was lost somewhere, perhaps dead. Perhaps worse.' Her voice shook. 'Viktor had been through so much, far more terrible than me. He was ill for many, many months.' She was speaking almost in a whisper. 'His face when he saw us again . . . I could not ask him to endure any more.'

'You endured it.'

Alma shook her head. 'I deserved it. It was my fault. I let them take the baby from me.'

'That's not true!'

'No? But there's some truth in it, all the same. If I'd fought for him, screamed and shouted . . .

who knows?' After a moment she went on, 'But I tell myself, I have my eldest boy . . .' She looked back at Janie and for a moment her face was radiant. 'I have this lovely person in my life, I could not bear to lose him.' She paused, her eyes fixed somewhere she had been many years ago. 'Even after all these long years, I dream of walking again down that long corridor and opening the door of the room where they took my baby from me, and going in, and there he is, safely returned. But then I wake – and where is my baby boy?' It was a soft screech of pain.

Janie got up and went over to stand beside her. Alma pressed her hand over her eyes, eyes that saw again what she could not bear to look at.

Finally Janie asked, 'Does Karel know he is not your own?'

Alma made a visible effort at control. 'I could not tell him when he was young. Partly, yes, because of Viktor. And then he was such a sombre little boy, old before his time. I did not wish to take anything further from him: a child without a childhood is tragic. Then later, there were other reasons not to speak of it.' The glance she gave Janie was full of meaning, of confidences. 'He has problems enough already. I saw you watching him. You can see. If I thought he could gain anything – understanding, self-knowledge – I would do it. I realize his troubles may well be inherited. But to burden him with parents who did not want him? God knows what fresh terrors I would unleash for him.' She added, without self-pity, 'At least this way they are mine only.'

She started to draw the curtains, shutting out

the houses opposite, shutting out the darkness. The windows ran the full length of the room. She had moved away from Janie and now she stood still. 'I am full of guilt already for my duplicity. I go over it and over it, because everyone surely has a right to be told who they are. Should I have taken him as a baby? Should I have told him I had done so? Is the key to his despair locked in what happened fifty years ago in another country? One day I decide, yes, I'll tell him, I'll do it tomorrow. And then I panic. We are a close family, we all love each other.' She looked at Janie, who nodded affirmation. 'If he is already so insecure, so uncertain,' Alma went on, 'despite our love, what if he feels I am pushing him away? What if, in my rush to tell the truth, I destroy the only foundations he has?'

She went on mechanically drawing the curtains. She did it very slowly. Finished, she seemed calmer. 'It was an extraordinary time,' she said, reflectively. 'To succour another's child in the midst of a world war is not so strange, after all. My own son was probably dead, but even if he lived, he was lost to me as surely as if he had been. And the way it was, at least I had a baby in my arms again.' She patted the velvet folds with elaborate care. 'For me, it seemed a small miracle.'

Chapter Thirty-Nine

The boy Patrice hunkered down on the floor of
the car, arms round his knees. He had never
dreamed of such luxury. The carpet was softer
than fur. They were travelling fast, but there was
only a soft rumbling no louder than a cat's.
Wide-eyed, he watched Mama and Jean.

The woman was on the very edge of her seat
so she seemed to hover over his brother. Jean,
tranquil despite the extraordinary events, lay
facing her, head and shoulders supported by the
partition which separated them from the driver
and the shaven-headed man. She had not spoken
a single word; no one had. Slowly, almost reluctantly, Mama reached forward. She laid a narrow
hand on Jean's leg – the bad leg, the left leg –
on the long bone of his shin beneath the thin
material of his trousers, the bone the doctors had
murmured about, the bone Patrice knew was
dead.

Mesmerized, Patrice stared at her face. He
thought she was the oldest person he had ever
seen and the most beautiful: he could not imagine
why he had not known her the moment she
stepped outside the big white house of the
Chalice. Her eyes were wise and pale and yet
drenched with colour, but it was no colour he
could name, as he could not describe the pure

colour of water, or rain. He was sure that was how the angels had found her, because her eyes held peace.

Jean stared at her too, with a look on his face that Patrice had not seen for a long time but recognized: hope. And fear. The woman returned his gaze steadily. Neither moved. But Patrice felt something pass between them, between that part of themselves that was not governed by intelligence or reason, but only the heart. He did not understand this at the time, or for many years. But the day came when he remembered it for what it was.

Finally Mama sighed and shivered and took her hand from Jean's leg, and passed the other over her face as if she was holding herself together, as if she might collapse. With great effort she spoke, her voice rough with exhaustion. There were long gaps between the words.

'Walk with God.'

She sank back, tears gleaming beneath her eyes. She did not attempt to wipe them away, but from somewhere took out a pair of silver sunglasses, and covered up her eyes. Neither boy made a sound. Mama seemed to fall into a little sleep.

The car travelled on for many minutes. Then it stopped, and the shaven-headed man helped Mama out and they were in front of a building taller and brighter than anything either boy had ever seen in all their lives. Lights flashed and sparkled, windows shone. There were trees *inside* the building. Men wore suits with fine gold buttons. Everyone had shoes.

Mama did not speak to the boys: she was there and then gone. The shaven-headed man gave an order to the driver. The car swung round and twenty minutes later the boys were back at Chalice House.

They related what had happened. The sisters were clearly excited that Jean had been singled out, but their training made them cautious. Their mother was bewildered and kept saying, Patrice, what am I going to do with you.

But: 'How did she know it was my leg that was bad?' Jean was mystified. 'How did she know? She never asked.'

Chapter Forty

Hunched atop carved columns, two huge stone eagles marked the driveway. They belonged to another era, and beneath their cold stare grass and weeds rampaged where once a smooth raked ride must have led invitingly towards a grove of trees. Janie turned the car in and followed the driveway to the top. At the crest of the hill, she braked.

Below her, beyond the trees, an ancient house lay sheltered from the weather in a dip in the misty Lincolnshire countryside. It had absorbed the styles of different generations – a round turret here, a mullioned window there, a square tower, a Victorian folly – but nothing softened its solid uncompromising bulk. At one side of the house was a stone terrace with steps down to a lawn. Beyond, she glimpsed a narrow gleam of water shadowed by trees.

As she parked, the front door opened and an elderly woman, her hair bound in a scarf, peered out.

'Thought I 'eard a motor. Come along, do, I 'aven't got all day, no matter what some people think.' She held the door wider and her squat, shapeless body was revealed, in an old-fashioned flowered overall. Many of the flowers were, on close inspection, stains. Her face was heavily seamed, her mouth pinched by vertical lines. She slammed the door behind Janie and led the way through the sudden darkness.

In a beamed hallway a vast wooden table pocked by years carried a pewter bowl of dried hydrangea heads. Against the staircase stood two coats of armour, the empty mailed fists holding halberds. There was a pungent smell of cats, damp wallpaper, fusty books. The woman hurried on, her backless shoes slapping on the stone floors. At one point she kicked a wellington boot out of her path. She opened a door, said unceremoniously into the room, ''Ere she is, madam,' and waved Janie forward.

Zazi de Lisle was kneeling on the floor in front of a magnificent carved marble fireplace in which burned a few meagre logs. She was surrounded by newspapers and clippings, scissors and paste and engaged, Janie saw as she walked towards her, in sticking photographs of herself into a large album. She sat back on her heels and waved gaily. She looked just the same as she had in London, formal and dressy, as if she was about to open a garden party or host a luncheon. Today she was wearing wine-red, a suit with a matching satin shirt bowed at the throat. The clothes were too elaborate for the country, but in them she was dramatic.

'I am happy to see you,' Zazi de Lisle said. Purred. The voice, too, just as Janie recalled it, caressing and strident at the same time. Then she snapped her fingers sharply. 'Tea, please, Nanny. And sandwiches. *Little* ones,' she added warningly. The old woman gave her a venomous look, muttered something and the door slammed shut. 'Sit down, Miss Paxton, do. Nanny,' she went on, as if Janie had asked, 'looked after Crispin.' Janie blinked. That slovenly woman – *Nanny*? Crispin de Lisle, occasionally shown on television speaking in the House of Lords on esoteric rural matters ('mainly mangel-wurzels,' as one Parliamentary sketchwriter had unkindly but acutely remarked), had seemed ancient as long as anyone could remember, despite his hairpieces. How old, then, must Nanny be?

'I appreciate your finding time to see me.' Janie took a small upholstered chair beneath a portrait so hideous it had to be ancestral. The velvet she sat on was frayed, the Persian rug beneath her shoes faded: all quintessentially English. To her right, French windows showed the terrace and the garden beyond, where a stooped workman in a cap pushed a laden barrow.

'Not at all. You are quite right, Magda should talk. Woman to woman,' she added meaningfully. Meaning what? Janie wondered. 'You have had only one real conversation with her, is that so?'

'Yes, in New York. I have another appointment but it's not for a month. I was hoping you could perhaps intervene for me.'

Lady de Lisle made a balletic gesture so expansive it seemed almost to be mime. 'Of course. Of course you need more time with her. I shall tell Jodrell immediately that he is to facilitate this. What areas are there still to be covered? What subjects are on your agenda for discussion next time you meet with her?'

Oh no you don't. 'I'm afraid I can't tell you.' She was deliberately sharp.

'So, there are no difficult areas for you, no problems with Magda's history, her background, nothing you do not understand?' For a fraction of a second she paused. 'Nothing in particular I can help you with? Magda and I go back a long way . . .'

'I remember you said that to me before,' Janie interjected. 'I'd be very interested to know just when you did actually meet?'

It was a repeat of their last encounter. Zazi de Lisle simply ignored any questions she did not wish to answer. She said now, as if Janie had not spoken, 'The Krzysztof Foundation is anxious that you have the right perspective on her.' Hurr. She purred the word, Eartha Kitt again.

'And you're worried I'm not getting it.' Janie made her tone dry.

Zazi eyed her, as if she knew the younger woman was up to something.

Janie said, very quietly, 'If the foundation merely wanted a mouthpiece for Mama, why did you choose me?'

'No no no,' the older woman said quickly, 'you misunderstand. But we are a little concerned about the *quality* of your information. You have a *lot* of opinions. For instance, you have spoken to many people who knew her.'

'That's right.'

'And what did you learn?'

'Oh, this and that. I'm convinced a lot of the information available about Mama is . . . incorrect. That it's hagiography, if you like – something everyone would like to be true because it's easily acceptable, it's suitable. It's safe.'

Zazi de Lisle's arched eyebrows rose. 'Whatever can you mean?'

'Just that I find a lot of it unbelievable.'

'Or you have decided not to believe it.'

Janie shrugged. 'It's not a question of deciding. It's instinct. Either a thing feels right or it doesn't. And I have to say, a lot of what I have learned about Mama disturbs me.'

Zazi de Lisle pounced on that. 'Disturbs you? How?'

'I have been told things about her which are hard to accept. Terrible things.'

Lady de Lisle's stare was baleful. 'Terrible? Explain yourself.'

'I can't discuss this with anyone but her. It's too serious a matter.'

'What are you *talking* about? I don't understand you.'

Janie thought, she is not surprised. This is something she has been expecting.

'I imagine you are keen to dramatize your story,' Lady de Lisle added.

Patronizing bitch, Janie thought. But aloud she said, 'Then your imagination is in overdrive. It's scarcely a story that needs extra drama.' She kept her voice cool. 'Until I get a chance to talk to Mama, until she either corroborates them or disproves them, I can only have my view of the facts. And I should tell you that either way, I am not at all sure I can continue with the book.'

'You will upset the foundation. They will not like that.'

'I couldn't care less what they like.' Annoyance made Janie reckless, and she forgot caution. 'They have deliberately and systematically turned Mama into a figure people will find sympathetic. A figure the world is eager to support. And I think that through this created person, the foundation makes a great deal of money. I do very much hope it is all spent as they claim because . . .'

The door opened abruptly, propelled unceremoniously by Nanny's blue-flowered bottom as she appeared carrying a large tray. Janie stopped talking as the woman began to assemble the cups and saucers.

'Thank you, Nanny, I can manage now,' her employer said.

Openly disappointed, Nanny made another noisy exit. The two women clearly disliked each other intensely.

Lady de Lisle bent over the ornate teapot. It was silver, tarnished to a dull yellow. Janie took the proffered cup from the narrow hand with carmine nails. At the base of the thumb the skin was puckered and gathered in an old scar.

'Tell me,' her hostess went on. To Janie's astonishment – and rather to her admiration – she was now conducting an entirely new conversation. 'How is your little boy? I understand he is at boarding school near Chester? I am always puzzled by this English convention.' She spoke casually, her eyes on what she was doing, the remark apparently no more meaningful than the plate of sandwiches she now offered, and Janie refused. (Normal-sized sandwiches, after all the fuss.) Taken aback by this abrupt change of direction – it had not even occurred to her the woman knew she had a child – she answered in neutral phrases: Yes, he was fine. He was very happy there.

Even as she spoke, her thoughts were going off like firecrackers. She had never discussed Adam with anyone at the foundation, and she was certain Robert Dennison would not have spoken about her private life. But the woman knew where Adam was at school. So did whoever had arranged for the box of bloodstained clothing to be sent to her.

There was no hint, thank God, that anyone had learned he was now with Lou and her family.

She must never stay alone at the Little Barn again.

She was scarcely interested in the woman's next, abrupt question.

'So,' Lady de Lisle wanted to know, 'apart from me, which of the foundation members have you spoken with?'

'I'm afraid I cannot remember.'

Zazi de Lisle's head came up fast. Her eyes were very dark, very bright. 'Can you not?'

Janie said nothing.

'You're telling me it's none of my business how you do your work.' Zazi laughed again, the same unexpected, full-throated sound. 'Of course. I deserved that.' She was suddenly, unpredictably, charming. 'But you would remember if you had talked to Josef Karms. He is not a man one forgets.'

Outside in the gardens, widening circles on the still water revealed the presence of fish. Zazi de Lisle had dropped Karms's name to her like a lure. As bait. Trying to discover how much she knew. Janie kept quiet, wondering again about the woman's background, and found she could well believe the scandalous stories. She was chic, worldly – and then that laugh dropped her straight into the gutter.

'What do you know about him? Beyond the obvious, the companies and so forth. I mean the personal. Do you know, for example, his nationality?'

'He's Hungarian.' Janie shrugged. 'He makes no secret of it.'

'Rather the reverse. One should ask oneself why a man habitually so discreet makes that fact so very public.' The older woman put her head on one side. 'Would it surprise you to learn Josef Karms is a Pole?'

Janie shrugged. It seemed unimportant. 'He's probably just avoiding taxes. Or alimony.'

Zazi de Lisle's voice was very soft. 'He is a Pole,' she repeated, 'like Magda.' Her intent gaze was on Janie's face, waiting for a reaction.

'There's some connection between them. That's what you're telling me?'

The older woman moved her head very slightly in assent. 'Mama wanted you to know.'

Janie was taken aback.

'*Mama* wanted me to . . . Why?' And why did she choose to tell me through you? she added silently. There were nuances here she could not catch.

'I am to tell you . . .' Zazi de Lisle was not looking at her now, but at the window, the gardens beyond, 'I am to say, she intends you to know everything. It is cowardice on her part to withhold the facts. Magda will submit herself to judgement.'

'Judgement about what?' But Janie thought she understood very well what Mama meant. It could only be that Dante's facts were after all the true ones. Was Lady de Lisle aware of them – and that any admission from Mama would put the future of the Chalice of the Grapes of God in jeopardy? It seemed unlikely: she appeared remarkably unmoved.

Before Zazi de Lisle could answer, the telephone rang. The older woman got to her feet with the supple grace of someone half her age.

'Hello? Yes. Yes, I will.' She covered the receiver with her hand. 'It's Magda's office. It won't take long.' Then she said to the instrument, 'Yes, this is she.'

Janie flipped through a copy of *Country Life*. After a moment, aware of the silence, she twisted round in her chair.

Zazi de Lisle was standing beside the ornate table which held the phone, the instrument still pressed to her ear. Her other hand was clutching her throat, crumpling the satin shirt. Tears were streaming down her face. As Janie watched, she dropped the phone so it fell almost to the floor, dangling from its cord. The sound she made was a hiss of pain. '*Aaaaaaaiiiiiieeeeee!*' Then she stumbled with uncharacteristic clumsiness from the room.

Janie waited, debating whether to follow. She wandered over to the window and found it looked onto the terrace. A door banged and Zazi de Lisle came into view, groping her way down the steps to the lawn. She moved awkwardly, the heels of her shoes catching and sinking in the rough grass. It did not seem to bother her, she was ploughing on in the direction of the water.

Janie tried to open the French windows but they were locked and there was no key. Before she could decide what to do, she saw that behind Zazi de Lisle was Nanny, hurrying in her wake. The old woman was surprisingly fast and her shoes did not hinder her. Halfway across the grass she caught hold of her mistress's arm and, as Janie watched, pulled her round. The two women strained in different directions, Zazi de Lisle struggling like a mad thing, clearly intent on getting to the water. But against Nanny's stolid bulk she was a stick figure, without substance or strength. Thwarted, she threw back her head and even through the glass the sound she made reached Janie. Wild and desolate, a cry of mourning.

'*Tomas! Madre de Deus . . . Tomas!*'

Then her knees buckled and she collapsed into Nanny's arms. The old woman staggered a little, held her close, stroking her back, soothing, pacifying. Eventually Zazi straightened up, still in Nanny's embrace.

They stood like that for a long time. Then, Nanny's arm protectively round Zazi's thin shoulders, the two ill-assorted figures trudged back across the grass towards the terrace.

Janie waited. Ten minutes went by. Another five. What the hell was going on here? She put away her tape recorder, took her bag and went out into the hallway. All the doors were closed and blank. She called, 'Lady de Lisle? Hello?' No answer.

She retraced her steps to the entrance hall

where the suits of armour stood alone. There was a smell of cooking from the other direction and a murmur of voices. She followed the food smells, reminiscent of school dinners, of potatoes and sprouts, and at the end of another long corridor found a half-open door. She could just see a flag-stoned floor, dingy cream walls. An old-fashioned stone sink was set beneath a high window, and she made out the corner of a vast black kitchen-range. The voices, which she now realized came from a radio, resolved themselves into the familiar sounds of *The Archers*.

The two women sat at a wooden table piled with dishes and glasses. In the cleared space at one end Zazi de Lisle slumped unmoving, her face buried in her arms. Nanny was stroking her hair and talking, talking, in a low voice.

Janie said, 'Is there anything I can do?'

Neither woman moved and Janie repeated herself, slightly louder. This time Nanny heard and looked up, as if astonished to find anyone there: they had clearly forgotten all about her.

Janie said, 'Can you tell me what's happened?'

Lady de Lisle sobbed softly in reply. Nanny gave Janie a look in which anxiety, scorn and impatience were mingled. At that moment Janie was aware of the gardener at her side, in his stained work trousers and faded corduroy shirt. He had removed his cap so his white hair stood up round a bald crown. He was pulling off a pair of heavy-duty gloves as he passed her. Then, as he saw the two women at the kitchen table and summed up the scene, he took a step back and held the door wide for Janie.

'Please,' he said, 'I must ask you to leave. At once.' It was a cultured voice, too authoritative for a gardener.

Janie glanced back at the kitchen as she reached the corridor. It was only when she saw Zazi de Lisle turn from the table and bury her face against the workman's shirt that she realized who he was.

That night at nine o'clock, she and Claudia were sharing a Marks and Spencer cold roast chicken and watching the BBC news. The fourth item was about Mama. The previous day, she had been holding a prayer meeting in a hall on Bukit Timah Road in Singapore. Enthusiastic crowds had pressed to see and touch her as she left afterwards, and a section of the crowd control barrier had collapsed. The cameras showed the joyful chanting turn to screams of panic as people at the front fell beneath the throng. As always, the violet-blue robes of the men of the Chalice surrounded Mama, and Janie and Claudia could see them straining, arms linked, to hold the people back and give her time to get to her car.

The images on the screen were heart-rending – a mother sitting on the ground, the body of her adolescent son limp in her arms; a sobbing man clutching a child's shoe.

'Seven deaths have been recorded so far,' said the voice of the woman reporter, 'and more are expected when those taken to hospital are accounted for. Among the dead, it has been confirmed, are two members of Mama's Chalice order. One of them, known only as Tomas, was her chief co-worker. He had been with Mama since he was a young boy when, it is believed, Mama cured him of epilepsy . . . '

Tomas was on the screen now, just as she remembered him from that first meeting at Chalice House in the East End. On footage that was obviously part of an earlier news item, he was shown standing as always a little behind Mama on her right: the golden skin, the smooth-shaven head and intense, dark eyes beneath black brows. 'It seems Tomas was crushed as he struggled to protect Mama from the pressure of the crowd. Mama is in a state of shock: Tomas was considered the favoured candidate to take over the running of the order when Mama finally decides to retire. In an unprecedented move, all her appointments for the next few days have been cancelled.'

Janie lay awake that night after Paul had fallen asleep, her mind rerunning the events of the day like the reprise of a film. The meeting in Northamptonshire had been full of undercurrents, of assurances that could be heard as threats. In retrospect, they seemed ominous.

Zazi de Lisle had as good as told her she – and therefore the Krzysztof Foundation – had sent that box of bloodstained clothes. The lady who clearly was no lady was reminding her what could happen if she did not do what was wanted.

And yet almost in the same breath, she had seemed about to make some further revelation.

Mama intends you to know everything . . . will submit herself to judgement.

Why would Mama do that? And why choose so

unlikely a person as Lady de Lisle to be her mouthpiece?

There were important facts here. She could sense them, but their shape was hidden from her.

She remembered Zazi de Lisle taking the phone call from Mama's office, telling of the deaths in Singapore. Why did Tomas matter so much to her?

Janie thought of many things. Of the images of the crowds in Singapore. Tomas's intelligent eyes and golden skin. The scar on Lady de Lisle's thumb and her scream of distress that echoed in Janie's head. She thought of the way Nanny had held the thin foreign woman, cradling her like a child. A child . . .

And then she had it, and had to force herself to lie still, not to wake Paul, so great was the surprise. And yet, now she understood, it was of course no surprise at all. She knew why Mama had chosen Zazi de Lisle: she saw how their lives were intertwined through the years.

Mama's first witness in São Paulo, that fateful day of her death and rebirth, had been Cuci Santos. The seamstress whose hand had been trapped beneath her sewing machine but healed, she said, almost instantaneously at the touch of Magda Lachowska. Cuci Santos, who had followed Mama to her mountain retreat and then, a few years later, vanished without trace, taking her illegitimate young son. Tomas.

Chapter Forty-One

Over the next two weeks, Janie and Paul planned what they would do if Janie wrote the book about Mama as she now saw it: she wanted to tell the truth – or a good part of it – and there would undoubtedly be repercussions from the Krzysztof Foundation. They must be prepared to drop out of sight until interest in the whole matter waned.

The money from the book would be considerable. Enough to enable Paul to leave his job for the moment. They would be able to live for at least two years in seclusion. Paul was excited by the idea of finding a remote Tuscan farmhouse and writing the play he had long wanted to try. Adam, he declared, could learn Italian and have a tutor. Janie, slightly more realistic, thought perhaps a change of name and maybe a village in Dorset.

A few days later, Janie sent a new outline to Robert Dennison at Odyssey. She wrote of the remarkable Polish woman who died in a slum in São Paulo, where she experienced a miracle and survived to tell of it. She wrote of the lives Magda Lachowska had saved, of those she had transformed. She recorded the influential meetings with world leaders, the miracles with which she was credited. She described the punishing timetable, in which there was nevertheless all the time in the world simply to hold the hand of a dying person.

Janie also detailed what she knew of the Polish camp where Mama had served, and her involvement in the death of the small boy. This material, she pointed out in her draft, had yet to be discussed with Mama. But her source was impeccable. And she wrote her proposed ending:

It may be that the Polish woman who was the cruel tool of a vicious regime, should by any laws of justice have paid with her life for her involvement in the camps. What she did was morally evil, acts she must answer for. This she did not do: she escaped justice. But in another sense, she has been her own judge, for she has spent a lifetime atoning for what she did. Many people have had their lives, and often their deaths, transformed because of her presence and her care. She has become a symbol of hope in a world grown cynical. Once evil, she turned herself into a force for good. Perhaps she shows us that the shadow has the same stature as the light.

This is one woman's story, and it is a strange and terrible and wonderful one. I have seen Mama at work. I was present when she put her hand upon a man who soon afterwards regained the power of speech, lost for many years. If it was some kind of quack chicanery, that man does not care. And it just might have been a small miracle. She is already widely considered to be a saint, and perhaps she is. She is certainly an ascetic who has abandoned most of the world's comforts and almost all its pleasures.

Whether Rome chooses to canonize Magda Lachowska at some distant time or not, she has long been a saint in the eyes of people of all faiths and beliefs. A saint for our time.

Magda Lachowska learned slowly that she possessed a power she could not begin to comprehend. People sensed it in her and responded with adoration. They understood, if she did not, that her touch would heal, her word would cure, her thoughts sustain them. A million beseeching whispers reached her, coalesced into a single cry for help. She heard, and discovered compassion. She listened, and came to love.

She did not know – for who can know – if there is a God. There had been a time when she had no faith. And even when she thought she had discovered it, there were long periods when her belief faded to nothing and she heard only God's silence.

Despite all this, her life – that long battle with herself – has become triumphant as a hymn. Mama has made her existence into a paean to God.

Robert Dennison read the manuscript and the additional material, and telephoned her immediately.

'You realize this will be completely unacceptable to the foundation? They wanted the feel-good story of a modern saint. You're planning to write an exposé to shock the world.'

'I know.' She added, lamely, 'Sorry.'

'Sorry? *Sorry?* What are you talking about?' She could almost see the satyr's smile. 'When's your next interview with the old girl?'

'In two weeks.'

'Great. You go in hard, confront her with this, see what she says. And make absolutely sure you tape. I'll talk to the lawyers, see where we stand on using your war material whether she says yea or nay. Hopefully, the fact that the foundation concealed so much will invalidate the contract. If so, we can return the foundation's advance to them and publish ourselves. I don't need to tell you to keep *shtumm* about this. It's explosive stuff.'

As Janie had feared, Robert Dennison's optimism proved unfounded: the contract the foundation had drawn up was watertight. Odyssey had no grounds for cancelling. But now, Janie found she could no longer contemplate writing the book the foundation wanted.

Nor could she confirm the details Dante had given her. Despite the fact that no one else knew of the draft or the conversation with Dennison, Janie's next interview, already confirmed by letter through the foundation, was cancelled without explanation. Repeated requests were all refused. Mama, she was told, was still in retreat after the death of Tomas. Then she was too busy, was giving counsel. She was unwell, involved in important talks – always some indisputable reason.

One night, Paul came home with some news.

'Your publisher's parent company has been

bought by De Groots. It'll be on the news tonight.'

'The Dutch conglomerate? I only know the name.'

He drizzled olive oil on his bread. 'They're huge and secretive. All their money's in massive ventures – oil, gold.'

She stared at him. 'It's bound to affect Odyssey. I bet they put someone from their head office into the building to oversee everything that goes on. Poor old Bob.'

'And guess what – apparently Joseph Karms is a member of the De Groots board. Owns a very large number of shares.'

Janie's eyes widened. She counted out the facts on her fingers. 'Karms is on the board of the Krzysztof Foundation, who are anxious to keep the material I've got well out of the way. And now a company where he has influence buys up the publisher.' She added, doubtfully, 'I suppose it *could* be coincidence. But I think it will have repercussions on me.'

Three weeks later, the Dutch conglomerate acted. Janie received a lawyer's letter offering her the entire sum due on completion of her book, including those amounts due to have been paid on hardback and paperback publication. It was made clear that Mama retained her rights over the material that was her life. In exchange, Janie was to hand over the half-finished manuscript together with all her notes and files. The book, she realized, would never now see the light of day. And the foundation had protected its own.

Janie accepted.

To her amazement, this did not bother her. She

was simply too happy to care: she and Paul had rediscovered each other and this time both were determined to make it work. The experience of writing about Mama had changed her. It was as if everything she had learned, the stories she had uncovered, had put her own life into perspective. It had not altered her ambitions for herself, but she was no longer prepared to let her emotional life come second. She did not want a successful career and an empty heart.

Paul put his apartment on the market. The day they accepted an offer on it, he was appointed managing editor of the *Daily Mail*. They bought a narrow, three-storey house in Maida Vale and Adam came home.

As a result of that long-ago interview with Bacall (the writing of which had been interrupted by Adam's early birth), Janie landed a contract to write a biography of Humphrey Bogart for an Anglo-American publishing house.

The half-written book about Mama continued to languish in a curious limbo. Rumours circulated about its contents, and there was speculation on the reasons for the non-publication. The general feeling seemed to be that ugly facts about Mama's past were being suppressed. In the broadsheets, columnists commented. Various international newspapers – the *Herald Tribune*, the *New York Times* and *Allgemeine Zeitung* – reported briefly. It was a small item on television news programmes. The UK tabloids covered it and *Private Eye* ran a scurrilous article. No one ever got their hands on the story Dante had told to Janie, although two journalists uncovered what seemed to be a scandal involving Mama and a dying woman in one of her European hospices who had begged to be helped on her way. The Krzysztof Foundation swiftly issued a couple of writs, which were settled out of court.

A curious thing happened. The feedback they received convinced the media generally that people did not welcome such material concerning Magda Lachowska. Following even mildly anti-Mama stories, newspapers found that sales actually dropped, while the switchboards of television companies were jammed with protest calls. Eager though the public usually was to see idols brought down, when it came to Mama it seemed they did not want their faith destroyed. And so the stories grew less frequent, and then stopped entirely.

Janie understood what was happening. Mama's reputation would ensure that the whole structure continued as before: the shrine at Swinoujście, the homes and the hospitals, the caring and the love. The Chalice of the Grapes of God would go on, with all its false faces, and all its real virtues.

Mama had done it again.

Chapter Forty-Two

Radio Three was on, a piece she did not know, elusive veils of music. The early morning sun was warm on her bare legs and she had just poured a second mug of tea when the phone rang.

Claudia was almost incoherent with joy. 'I'm trying not to go over the top,' she blurted out, 'it mightn't mean a thing. She watches television, maybe she's just copying . . . But Jesus, Janie, she hugged me! Lucy ran up to me and *looked into my face* and hugged me tight! Just now. Round the waist, so hard I couldn't breathe. I can't believe it, she's never, not *ever*, done that before.'

Janie was equally excited. She made Claudia go through it all again, slowly.

'OK, then what did she do? Where is she now?'

'She didn't say anything – well, she often doesn't. Just wandered upstairs. She's listening to music. Shostakovich, I think, she likes the dramatic stuff.' Janie had forgotten how carefree Claudia's laugh used to be. 'I realize it might be a one-off. Maybe it'll never happen again. But oh God, to feel her do that, to see her *look* at me, as if she actually saw me. Do you think it means – could it have been something else, all along? Not autism, maybe something she's growing out of?' Janie could not remember the last time she had heard her friend's voice lift like that with hope.

452

'Have you told Lewis? What does he think?'

'He's here.' Claudia said something away from the phone, then her voice was loud again. 'He was sitting at the table eating . . . what're you eating, darling? . . . scrambled eggs when it happened. He says, if he hadn't seen, he'd never have believed me. Janie . . .' Her deep voice broke, 'I tell you, it's such a tiny thing. A *hug*. Just a hug. But maybe – *maybe* – it's a start. We feel we've just been given something wonderful.'

When Janie put down the phone, she finished her tea and thought about her talk with Mama in St Patrick's Cathedral in New York. Mama had explained how long the process of healing could take. Months could pass, she had said, before there was even a slight improvement. That day, she had looked at Lucy's photograph and divined the girl's problems, though there had been no sign to tell her of them. She had smoothed her finger over the child's face. It was invariably reported that she shed tears, when a miracle was granted her – and she had hidden her eyes immediately behind her dark glasses.

Janie caught herself up. That had been too long ago. And anyway such things did not happen. Not in real life.

It was because Claudia wanted to lunch in Fenwicks that, a week later, she found another link in the chain that somehow bound her to Mama. Though she did not recognize it at the time.

At the table behind theirs, two chic, thin blonde women with minuscule handbags, clearly mother

and daughter, were engaged in one of those endless feminine wrangles over clothes. The
daughter's, naturally. The item she wished to buy
– it seemed to be a cream suede suit – was,
according to her mother, too short, tight, imprac-
tical, unsuitable and expensive.

Claudia and Janie had eavesdropped unashamedly while they ate their chicken and
ciabatta and then forgotten the couple until, leaving, they found themselves behind them on the
escalator. The daughter had turned to look behind
her and her gaze swept unseeing over Janie. Who
had drawn a quick, astonished breath.

For the young woman, pale blonde hair drawn
tightly back into a sleek chignon, could have been
Mama. Not Mama as she was now, but the way
she must have looked as a girl, the resemblance so
strong it was eerie. The same broad, calm brow
and tender-lipped mouth. The same long eyes,
though the girl's were a pale, pretty blue where
Mama's were that mysterious cool colour apparently unique to her. Then the older woman turned
and Janie saw the girl also had a look of her
mother. You're mad, she told herself. It must have
been a trick of the lighting. And sure enough,
when she looked back to the girl, that first
impression had paled.

But for days, something niggled in the corner of
her mind. It bothered her, irritating as a hangnail,
she couldn't leave it alone. She worried at it,
teased it around. Nothing.

The following Thursday, another link. At dinner,
Paul reached for another chunk of French bread

and said, 'There's going to be a piece in the paper tomorrow that'll interest you. The business pages have had a long-running research project going on Josef Karms. We had a look at their stuff today, in view of the takeover. First interesting thing is, there's nothing but a passport to prove he's Hungarian. We sent a man to Kelebia, where he is supposed to have been born. The name appears on church records there, but that's it – no trace of family or anyone who knew him. And it's only a two-street place with a railway running through it, which makes that very strange.

'That's the bad news. The good news is, it seems he lived in São Paulo at one point: his first chemical business was established there with a partner by the time the war ended. To do that, he must have arrived there before or during the war. The researchers came up with a couple of newspaper articles that referred to him as being Polish. But of course that doesn't mean much. Still, the de Lisle woman sounded very positive.'

'She was.' Janie did a quick calculation. 'Karms would have been somewhere in his late twenties when the war ended. So whether he was Polish or Hungarian, why hadn't he been fighting?' She thought for a minute. 'Maybe there's something wrong with him.'

'He was playing squash until a few years ago. You have to be bloody fit to do that in your fifties and sixties. No, I think we can take it he left Europe to avoid conscription. Or maybe he just absconded.'

'Mama worked for a Polish family in São Paulo. A businessman. I never could find out his name. I got really suspicious that she was with some old Nazi . . .' She stared at Paul. 'Was she with Karms, d'you think?'

'How many Poles could have been living in the city at that time? Not too many, I'd say. Incidentally, there's a picture of his daughter in the *Standard* tonight.' He folded it back to the 'Londoner's Diary' and passed it across the table. She saw a photograph of the young woman from Fenwicks: the astonishing face, so familiar, so unknown. The name Karms leapt up from the piece below:

Nuala Karms, eighteen-year-old daughter of the chemical magnate and his third wife Susanne, will shimmy down the catwalk tonight for London's biggest charity evening . . .

'The Fenwicks' girl!' she exclaimed. The young beauty on the escalator, the face that might have been the youthful Mama, so alike were they. Nuala Karms.

Karms. The night of Mama's enormous charity evening in New York. That brief glimpse she'd had of Josef Karms and Mama in the small room at the Waldorf-Astoria, the curious impression of intimacy she had received from the two of them, the feeling that she was intruding on something very private. Her certainty that an important and long-standing relationship existed between them.

She said thoughtfully, working through it, 'D'you remember I told you that after New York, I was sure Mama and Karms had known each other for a very long time? Well, look at the picture of his daughter again – she's the image of Mama. Could be her when she was a girl.' She handed the paper back to him. He looked at it, bewildered.

'You're saying Karms and Mama – but the girl's far too young to be Mama's daughter.'

'No. Not her daughter.' The past was unfolding for her like a Japanese paper crane. So complicated. So simple. 'Mama worked for a Polish family in São Paulo, remember, she lived with them. She told me she was sent out there after Poland was taken by the Allies.' She was almost jumping out of her chair. 'What Mama did, she just went to her own family.'

Paul spread open hands. 'You've lost me.'

'Mama had two brothers, a bit older than her. Both of them joined the Polish Army and one was killed when the Germans invaded Poland. At least, that's what everyone thought.'

'I still don't get it.' Paul's face was creased and puzzled. She smiled at him, relaxed in her certainty.

'Josef Karms and Mama – they're brother and sister.'

Chapter Forty-Three

The photographs dominating all the papers the following Tuesday were of a small child, perhaps seven or eight, her blonde hair tousled, her right hand held up in a bloodied makeshift sling. A man in the white coat of a hospital worker and the round skullcap of a Jew steadied her shoulder. Her face was fearful, wary. The caption said she, her sister and her father were being treated at Jerusalem's Hadassah Hospital for gunshot wounds.

Many papers carried the second picture on the inside pages. This showed a group of young Arab women, their faces contorted with anger beneath their chadars. Beside them, boys were hurling stones at Israeli soldiers. That was in Hebron, one of the oldest cities of the world, part of ancient Judea.

The two incidents were part of the same story. Hebron was the last of seven West Bank towns to be handed over to the Palestinian authority by the Israelis, in accordance with the Oslo agreement. A hundred thousand Palestinians lived there, and among them around three hundred and fifty Jews inhabited six scattered settlements. They were there partly for religious and historical reasons, and partly because of the subsidies and tax breaks which had been offered by the Government to encourage Jews to move to the settlements and expand them before the Palestinians took over. It was known that these settlers walked the streets armed. They referred to their Palestinian neighbours as terrorists. They considered they had been betrayed by Israel when Israeli troops handed over much of the area to the Palestinian authority, and made dire predictions of a massacre of Jews.

Fifteen of these Jewish families lived in a settlement in the heart of the town. Directly opposite them was a school for Palestinian girls. One morning, the children arrived to find the slogan 'Daughters of Dogs' daubed in scarlet letters across the white front wall. That afternoon, as they left school, they were met by a hail of marbles fired from slings by Jewish children. The glass marbles made ferocious weapons. One twelve-year-old, struck in the face, lost an eye.

When the schoolgirls retaliated and threw stones in self-defence, adult settlers started beating them up. Arab women and boys tried to defend the girls as Israeli soldiers arrived, and several arrests were made.

That night, many miles away, the Avigdor family – the young parents and three children between three and nine – were driving home to the Israeli settlement of Beit El on the West Bank, near the Palestinian village of Surda. Coming towards them on the dark road from Ramallah was a car with blue West Bank licence plates. As the two vehicles drew level, gunmen fired on the Avigdor car with automatic weapons, spraying bullets everywhere. Rebecca Avigdor was killed outright.

Her three-year-old son died later in an ambulance. The two little girls were both grazed by bullets. Joseph Avigdor took another in the shoulder and the car careened off the road into a herd of goats.

Throughout the following day, television cameras around the world showed the Arab school in Hebron, dwelt on the harsh graffiti and the schoolgirls cowering under the assault from Jewish settlers, while women in chadars and Arab youths threw stones. In a second sequence, lights picked out the wrecked car near Surda; the tiny body on a stretcher, the dazed, bandaged faces of the two little girls, the haggard young father clutching his wife's bloodstained sweater.

In the afternoon, it was announced from the Chalice's mother house in Rome that Mama was flying out to the Middle East to take part in urgent talks with the Palestinian leader and the new Israeli Prime Minister. It was felt that her involvement would cut the risks of further Palestinian suicide missions into Israel; her pleas that these should cease had been heeded on two previous occasions.

A week later, Janie Paxton received a telephone call from Mama. Almost without preamble she said, 'Will you do something for me? I am on my way to Israel. I should like you to be there.'

Startled, Janie said, 'But you wouldn't even talk to me. Why do you want to see me now?'

There was a pause. 'I don't understand. I have never refused an interview with you.'

'Well, that was the message I kept getting from the foundation.'

Mama's sigh was audible. 'Oh. Yes. I see.' Her voice became brisk. 'They acted without my knowledge. But let us not be concerned with that. I want to see you for a different reason.'

'You do know the book will never be finished? Never published?'

'Certainly I know.' She dismissed this as if it were of no importance. 'Well? What do you say?'

Janie chewed her thumbnail as she thought. 'Can I have my interview? Will you see me alone?' She hardly knew why she asked. Perhaps it was for herself, and for all the people like Alma Gysemans, that she wanted answers.

'Yes. Yes, I will arrange it. So you will come? There will be a ticket to Jerusalem at the El Al desk at Heathrow. You must check in at four o'clock this afternoon.'

'I'll be there.'

Chapter Forty-Four

Her Israeli guide, a squat man in an open-necked, short-sleeved shirt, ostentatiously armed, shepherded Janie through the West Bank city of Hebron to her meeting with Mama. They passed a couple of middle-aged men in Arab dress, who considered the guide first, and only later looked at Janie. On the other side of the road, three youths in jeans and very white T-shirts, with different priorities, assessed Janie before turning their gaze to the Israeli and the Mauser in the crook of his arm.

Mama had been given the use of an Arab house. Separate from the others, on a patch of land but still within the confines of the city, it was easily guarded. The Israeli and Arab security officials, overriding Mama's protests, had insisted on a twelve-strong guard. All were Christian Arabs: it was felt their loyalty to Mama would be total.

Before they reached the door, two of the Arab policemen came forward, young, tough men with hard faces in the drab olive uniform and crested beret. The first shifted his rifle to his left shoulder, held out his hand. The driver produced a pass and turned back the lapel of his shirt to show a badge. They let him keep the gun. Janie showed her own permit which was carefully examined. The second guard pointed at her shoulderbag. 'Leave that at the door.' She had expected as much. 'I need these,' she said, taking out her notebook and tiny tape recorder. The second guard opened the machine, took out the tape, checked that. Then the first guard gestured with his thumb for her to enter.

The door to the white house was opened by a heavy-set man in the familiar violet-blue robe of the Chalice. For a moment, until he spoke and she remembered, she thought it was Tomas. The man said, 'You are welcome,' and stood aside for her. The room was stone-floored, the windows shuttered, the sole piece of furniture a long, low table on which stood the remains of a meal; dates and nuts, tiny white cups of thick Turkish coffee. Three more men of the order were seated cross-legged on rugs. There were two lamps on the floor. In one corner, a huge television set was turned on but without the sound. An episode of Dynasty: she caught a glimpse of Krystle in shoulder-pads and diamanté.

'Please? Janie?' A violet-robed woman was standing in the shadows at the top of the steep stairs. Janie followed her. The woman led her through a bedroom of the utmost simplicity – a single bed covered in a cotton spread, a book on the floor beside it, a cupboard, a lamp – and up yet more stairs.

They came out onto the flat roof. It was cooler up here, where a faint wind from the hills reached them. Low walls guarded against the drop, lemon and bay trees flourished in great tubs. In the centre of the roof a large rug was covered with cushions and a tray bearing bread, a piece of pale goat's cheese, a dish containing the pits of a half-dozen olives, some fresh dates: Mama had dined frugally as ever. Above it, a black and brown striped awning was folded back. Across the space, a couple of lights were strung from poles. The darkness was syrupy with cooking smells, with coriander and olive oil and the waft of roasting meat. Several radios were playing different stations loudly: a woman was singing in Arabic, the ululating sound shiveringly seductive.

Mama was standing with her back to them, looking across the roofs. The dichotomy struck Janie afresh: that this woman could request, and get, meetings with heads of state, religious leaders. Yet the feeling that emanated from her was a deep loneliness. An impenetrable isolation. Following her gaze, Janie saw more guards standing sentinel on adjacent roofs. A bird called, twice, a soft warbling cry that sounded like no bird she had ever heard. The disquiet she felt was intense and instinctive, and she struggled to push it aside.

At her approach, Mama turned. She did not smile. Her face held that shining, meditative look Janie had seen before, in St Patrick's Cathedral. She seemed to have lost weight and every line of her body and face was taut, in defiance of her age. The darkness deepened her eyesockets into little pools of shadow. In the dim light, in her creamy robe, she looked more than ever like the saint so many believed her to be. Janie saw her with something like despair: how could there be any question of confrontation with a woman such as this?

'I am happy to see you once more. I have an hour, and then I must rest. I do not sleep well these days, but even to lie quietly is a blessing.'

They talked for a few minutes, about the town, about the local mayor whose house this was, about the meetings Mama had attended that afternoon. The woman attendant brought a second tray, bearing two tall glasses of pale liquid, a long-stemmed spoon standing in each, and a bowl of sugar. She placed the tray carefully on the parapet beside them.

'Camomile tea,' Mama said. 'Will you . . .?'

Janie chose her moment carefully. As Mama reached for her glass she forced herself to say, very softly, 'I'm afraid I am a spectre at the feast. I have to tell you, I know about Poland. I know about the camp.'

It seemed as if her own words brought a silence to the world. The air ceased to stir. The sounds of cars and horns, carried on the warm night from distant streets, faded to nothing. Voices from adjacent houses no longer reached them. A kid, which had been bleating tremulously where it was tethered somewhere below, stopped at last.

The silence built like a tower. Even the dark notes of the singing woman were hushed. Even the occasional cough from the guards below them, the tinny noise of the competing radios, the occasional burst of laughter from an invisible television, all had vanished. A plane flew low overhead, lights winking red and white, and though Janie strained her ears, she could not catch so much as a hum from the engine.

For a moment – no more – something fierce flared in Magda Lachowska. It peered from behind her eyes, it changed her face. It was in her movements as she straightened her back, in the way her hands shook slightly as she spread them before her, as if to fend something off. Even as Janie wondered, is it anger? it was gone.

But it sent a bolt of alarm through her. Below them in the lower room were men of the Chalice. Outside stood armed guards. More watched with rifles at the ready on the roofs beyond. Mama had only to cry out, issue an order, and she would be finished. She remembered the explosion at the Little Barn, the box of Adam's bloodied clothes. And that had happened at home. It would not be difficult to arrange a disappearance in this dangerously volatile place.

She cursed herself for a fool. No one even knew where she was. Presumably the Krzysztof Foundation were aware of her presence – although on second thoughts, maybe not. Mama had arranged this meeting herself, which she did not normally do. The airline ticket had been given to her at the airport by a woman, a member of the Chalice, who had approached her as she reached the El Al desk.

There had been no time to phone Claudia. She had left a hurried message on Lou's answerphone for her and Adam, giving no details. Paul had been at a lunch meeting when she rang the office so she had talked briefly to his secretary, saying she was rushing to Israel and would be back in forty-eight hours. She had not wanted to leave Mama's name in a message to a newspaper. She had planned to

466

telephone him from the hotel, but in her haste she had forgotten.

If anything happened to her, she would not be the first journalist lost here. Even as she hesitated, trying to calculate the risk, Mama picked up her glass, and now her hands were so steady the liquid scarcely quivered. Very slowly, she turned away from the parapet and walked across to the rug beneath the awning.

Janie became aware that as Mama moved, so the sounds came back. As if, after a pause, a film had begun to run again, life moved on normally once more. The woman continued her harsh, wavering song. The kid made its piteous bleat. The echo of the plane's passage reached her ears. Janie uncurled her clenched fingers.

Mama seated herself on the rug. She lifted her eyes to Janie's and even in the fitful light of the lamps they were luminous as ever. There was candour in them, and clarity. An extraordinary mixture of supreme confidence and supreme humility. 'What do you want me to tell you?'

Janie could only look at her, stupefied. Whatever response she had anticipated, it had not been this. Despite the hints Zazi de Lisle had dropped about Mama submitting herself to judgement, the cancelled and refused interviews could only be seen as a change of heart. So she had expected vehement denial, fury even. She had been prepared for that. Perhaps explanation. Maybe justification. Or even frozen silence. What she had not for one moment imagined was this simple, open acquiescence.

She remembered the things Dante had shown her, the things Alma had said. She wanted the pieces fitted in completely. She dreaded what she would hear. But a stronger fear – that if she did not learn it now, she never would – made her say:

'Tell me who you are.'

At first Mama was hesitant, as if the facts were beyond the reach of memory. She struggled visibly, wrestling her thoughts from somewhere very deep where they had been hidden for a long time.

Then, after the first few sentences, it began to come more easily, as though she had always accepted that one day, it must all be said. Janie listened so intently she felt herself becoming almost invisible. As though there was nothing in her but the woman's words.

Mama spoke in a quiet voice. Her story was occasionally disjointed. Mostly, it was surprisingly frank, the words she used simple and direct. They gave her a terrible force of conviction. But sometimes her phrases, her pauses, seemed designed to conceal another, different truth. Even now, Janie thought, it was as if Mama was playing a game of hide-and-seek with herself.

Basia Krolak was born in an insignificant little Polish town which lay near the Odra River as it ran to Stettin Bay. Metno, north of Cedynia, was a place of one-storeyed houses, paraffin lamps and dank cobbled alleyways. So close to the German border, the people spoke both languages, though their German was *plattdeutsch*, an almost unintelligible dialect.

It is not good to live near a border in wartime.

First the Russians invaded Poland, peasant

soldiers with no boots, their bare feet bound with rags. Everyone had stories of atrocity, of murder and rape. It was a time of fear and children were forced into adulthood overnight. Her older brother joined the Polish Army.

A year later, the Germans crossed the border. *Their* border. The troops arrived packed in open lorries from which they leapt to club protesters, drag children from their parents, haul women through the streets by their hair. Her brother disappeared, lost in the fighting. They never heard where he died.

He had been her only real friend. Her mother was a tired, taciturn woman, despair ran deep in her nature. Her hands were hard and her life harsh, she veered between ignoring her children and beating them. The three of them had occupied rented musty rooms and her mother took what work was available: selling galoshes, washing other people's clothes.

The mother had long ago begun to retreat from reality. She stayed indoors a good deal and made the girl stay with her: her own mother had been mentally disturbed towards the end of her life, and she believed she had inherited this illness. Perhaps it was a self-fulfilling prophecy: there were days when the mother heard voices, when she raved and screamed out all sorts of biblical words, about retribution, about hellfire and damnation, until she fell into a stertorous sleep.

Basia Krolak was ten years old when she finally grasped the meaning of the gossip that had always skittered around her: that she was illegitimate and her mother had wished her dead in the womb. Her

469

inner turmoil was evidenced by the fact that she began to wet her bed and for this, too, she was beaten. She dared not ask questions but she fantasized about her father: that he was a wealthy young man who had loved her mother until his cruel family forced him to give her up. Or a farmer who was going to leave his land to them one day. In time, she began to wonder aloud. Has he red hair like mine? Does he own a house? Her mother either pretended not to hear or flew into a rage about something else. There came a day when she turned to her daughter and said in a neutral voice, 'He didn't stop long enough to tell me his name.'

The words opened a chasm at the child's feet. They smashed the fantasy that one day he would come for her, and take her to a house that was warm, and buy her things.

The words made her see that she mattered to no one. Much later, after her brother's death, she found there was nothing to keep her in Metno, nothing she loved, no one who loved her. Still, it took her another five years to summon up the courage to run away. She left without a word, empty handed. By then Poland was under German occupation.

In a world where so many were dispossessed, she was only one of hundreds, thousands. Even if anyone had tried to find her, it would have been impossible. There were ways she could have survived. Many young women sold themselves for no more than a little food, a brown bag of coffee, a few cigarettes. But the very idea of sex terrified her. And there were the stories of young blonde Polish girls snatched from the streets and taken to

Germany to be impregnated by German soldiers and bear Aryan children for the Third Reich. So she dyed her hair dark brown to make herself plainer still, lied about her age – not difficult, she was tall and awkward – and claimed to be an orphan, her papers lost when she fled the Russian soldiers who killed her mother and burned their home. And she joined the German Army.

She was sent to Danzig and then by truck to a re-education camp for soldiers conscripted from subdued countries bordering Germany. Matzkau, set on top of a steep hill, was designed to give 'ideological correction' to such people, to imbue them with the true Nazi spirit. It was a brutal place. It denied the gentleness, the innocence of her nature. And denying, it destroyed them.

She arrived in Matzkau a nervous girl. She returned to Poland as a serving soldier in her grey uniform and black leather boots. She was very proud of the boots: she had never possessed anything so beautiful. She was not quite sixteen years old.

As she talked, Janie understood that Mama would always be shackled to her past. Whenever the two women had met, Mama had been completely in control, of herself and of others. Now, in the lamplight, her face had an ashen pallor, her lips seemed hardly to move. She had become a conscience-stricken figure, tormented and tormenting.

She described the death of the eight-year-old boy which Janie had seen on the old film among the cartoons, that night in Brussels. Janie had no sense that the woman was unburdening herself and so laying something aside. Rather, she understood it was like self-flagellation: an endlessly repeated process of pain and guilt.

'There was no way to save him, no appeal in that place. That is what I tell myself, now.' Her voice was ragged, husky. 'I helped a child die because I had not the courage to help him live. And I have lived every day since then with an overwhelming sense of shame for those things I did. Can you understand that? Can you? People sit at my feet, they call my name and touch my clothes.' Her fingers plucked at the hem of her creamy robe. She looked up at Janie, and her eyes now were sunken, lustreless. 'And all the time, all the time, *that* . . .' she gave the word a curious emphasis, of disgust and revulsion, 'gnaws away at me. The people don't understand. I hear what they say, that I am a saint for these times. They have created a person who does not exist. The truth is I am like an animal. Less than an animal.' She put her hands in front of her heart with a curious churning movement. As if trying to exorcize herself almost literally, trying to scoop out of herself the shameful person who held her hostage. 'I killed my own kind in order to survive.'

There was a silence. Out of it, Janie observed, 'Your shame didn't exactly hold you back.' She heard the hardness in her own voice.

'Why do you think I stayed alone all those years in the mountains?' Mama demanded. 'Seven long years. I meant never to leave. But they found me.'

'They?'

'The first were two who had witnessed my death: Cuci Santos and her boy. They believed I had cured the child's epilepsy, and refused to go even when we were all on the brink of starvation. And soon the local women made their way to me. They convinced themselves that I could grant easy childbirth.' She paused. 'Then it was the people of the *favelas*. I told them who I was.' She added, more fiercely, '*What* I was. I refused to do as they wanted. I would not even try to help them, to change their lives or heal their children. But they would not take my refusal, they said they did not care what I had done.' Her voice dropped. 'They said, I had died already for my sins.'

'And so, in the end, you did as they wished.'

'In the end,' Mama agreed. 'I feared to do what they wanted, I feared the world and what it would do to me. But I also coveted it.' There was something heartbreaking in her voice, a reluctance made palpable and moving. It was clear she did this against her own wishes; she saw it as her destiny and her atonement. 'So I tried to be the servant of the people, not their master. I came to see that if God had wished me to die, I would not have lived through the storm. He brought me back. He gave me a vision wonderful beyond anything I could have imagined for myself. I learned that sometimes, for some people, I can bring about what they choose to call miracles.' She sighed. 'I do not know if that is what they are. When we talked in the cathedral, I told you, I cannot understand what happens. But the Bible says, no man can do miracles except God be with him. So that is what I tell myself. That it is God's hand I hold.'

'Is everything linked, then?' Janie was struggling

with the idea. 'They say, every saint has a past. Perhaps all these things were somehow brought about because of what you did, what you were. Perhaps one would not exist without the other.'

Mama's expression was more vulnerable than Janie had ever seen her, full of yearning. 'We all carry our crimes within us. I am no more than the sum of my past – and the past makes the present.' She bent her head. 'There was a man . . . someone I loved.' Her voice cracked with emotion. 'He told me, the camps made beasts of some people and saints of others.' She shook her head, unable to go on.

Janie finished for her:

'And made you into both.'

The sounds of an Eastern night gradually reasserted themselves. The kid bleated, the radios still played from invisible windows, the woman sang her shivering song. Janie shivered herself. These things Mama had done were incomprehensible to her, beyond the range of her experience. They were inhuman. She had killed a child.

Recollection came suddenly, cold and unforgiving: and so have I. But that was totally different. Wasn't it? Another time, another place. A different reason.

How ironic to realize only now, too late, that she was in no position to judge Mama, because of the hesitant morality by which she lived herself.

She asked, 'Then who was Magda Lachowska? The girl who lived in Swinoujście, the one the people there remember and praise?'

'Just a girl. A girl I met when I left home. On the

road somewhere. Soldiers had given her a lift and Swinoujście is not so far from Metno. We were about the same age. We travelled together for a little time, but she was foolish. She told me she had left home because she was pregnant and her mother would kill her. We were hungry, there were men everywhere. She went with them, for coffee, for money. She was never frightened, not like me.' Mama's normally erect posture drooped in recollection. 'Poor, silly child. I can hardly remember anything except her name. And what happened to her.' She paused. 'I think she had a squint.'

After a moment Janie asked, 'What did happen to her?'

'At night we stayed in barns when we could. One morning I found her outside, on the ground. Her skirts were up over her head and her throat . . .' Mama put her hand to her own throat, 'cut.'

Janie drew in her breath sharply. 'Magda's brother – the old man, Romuald?'

'He does not know. I have never even met him. How could I? He would have seen immediately I was not his sister.' Her voice dropped. 'I should have told him. No one mourned that girl's death.'

'You've left it a bit late, haven't you?' She was angry at the deceit which had been practised on so many. 'This means that everything in Swinoujście is just lies. Did you plan that?'

Mama looked at her intently. 'I have never been there. I did not arrange anything.'

'The house is a shrine. Endless pictures of you now, masses of stuff about your childhood. Only of course it isn't yours. Pictures of a little girl who is supposed to be you, but who certainly was never even the real Magda.' She shook her head, irritated. 'I suppose the Krzysztof Foundation did that too. I suppose it isn't any worse than the stuff they put out about any public figure.' And then her anger grew. 'Except that you're not an actress, are you, or a singer? You're meant to be about truth and integrity.'

Mama said quietly, 'Forgive me. I let those things be done in my name and I did not stop them. But it was I who asked the foundation to pay Magda's brother an allowance each month. I suppose in exchange they schooled him in what to say about her.'

'And fair exchange is no robbery.' Janie meant the words to sound hard.

'I took nothing from Magda Lachowska which she had not already lost. I did no evil under her name. When I escaped from Poland, when I needed to be a different person – that was when I became Magda.'

'Tell me how you got to São Paulo.'

Her expression now was opaque, unreadable. Every sentence was followed by a pause.

'I was taken to another camp. Imprisoned. Someone . . . arranged for me to leave. I never learned who it was. I was given a Red Cross passport.'

'No one just gets *given* a Red Cross passport,' Janie interrupted. 'What did you tell them?'

'I had received identity documents. False, of course.'

'From?'

'A priest.' Her tone acknowledged the irony. 'A Catholic priest. I didn't ask questions, I just took them. I travelled by sea. It took a long time. When I reached Brazil someone met me. There was a job waiting with a family of Polish immigrants.' She stopped, fingers plucking at a stray thread on the skirt of her robe and she kept her eyes on it. 'My brother's family,' she added. 'You have met him.'

'Josef Karms.'

'I stayed there for a long time, until I became sick, then they made me leave the house. I had a disease of the skin, they were afraid for the children . . . I didn't mind. They made sure I had money. And I wished to be by myself.' The pause this time stretched out. When she spoke again, her voice was deep, vehement. 'I didn't understand,' she said. 'I thought then I was free.'

Those words were important, they meant something, but Janie couldn't think what: tiredness swept over her. She had not eaten since the plane, not slept for almost twenty hours. And it was all too much to take in, she felt dizzy. She said, 'Sorry,' in a muffled voice and put her head down.

Mama reached over and for the first and only time, put her hand on Janie's bare arm, holding it just below the elbow in a clasp that was light but somehow caring.

'So you are to have a child.' It was not a question but a statement.

'No,' Janie protested. 'Nothing like that. It's just been a long day.' She couldn't be pregnant anyway, not now. And then her mind jumped. Her period had been due last week. She forced herself to remember the date. The twenty-first. That meant she was ten – no, twelve – days late. *Twelve days*. What had she been thinking, not to notice?

477

Since moving back together, she and Paul had not discussed the possibility of another baby. That had been an area fraught with such anxiety and pain in the past, when they had tried so hard and still failed to conceive, that they had by unspoken consent avoided it. But she could imagine very well what he would say, the joy he would feel. Her heart leapt at the thought.

And then she wondered, how did Mama know, when she did not know herself? She moved her free arm. In the crease of her elbow, she inhaled her own scent. Sure enough, her skin smelled subtly different. Sweeter, somehow, milky. Then she knew it was true. Mama was right. This was the perfume of pregnancy she remembered from when she was carrying Adam, the faint message from her body, wiser than any doctor, any test.

Mama poured a glass of water, put it into Janie's hand and watched her drink. She nodded to herself, ignoring the denial. 'I think so,' she said, and added, 'This time, it will be different.'

Janie licked her lips. All her senses were vibrating at the implications. Only Lou and Claudia had known of the abortion. She had not even told Paul. Yet the inflections of Mama's voice made her meaning, her understanding of the situation, absolutely clear.

Mama put her hand back on Janie's arm. It felt soft and dry. It occurred to the younger woman that there was an incongruity here: she would have expected to flinch away from the woman's touch. But instead it had the strangest effect on her. It was intimate, exclusive.

Mama seemed to read her mind, for she said

sadly, as if offering both apology and repentance, 'Both right and wrong are the work of our hands, Janie.'

Those hands had pulled the body of an eight-year-old child against the rope that strangled him. They had gentled a dying derelict. Evil and good, separated by an angel's hair. It is as full an explanation as I will find, Janie thought. And perhaps the only one that she can give.

After the fears she had harboured half an hour before for her own safety, it surprised her to find how comforted she was by Mama's warm grip in the dark. She had not planned to ask it now, but out of the reciprocity of the moment she said, urgently, 'Tell me. The baby you gave to the Belgian woman Alma Gysemans. In the camp. The baby whose life you saved. Whose was it?'

Mama's hand dropped to her side. She got slowly to her feet and moved across to the parapet beyond which lay dry distant hills. She did not answer for so long, Janie thought she could not have heard. But then she let out a deep breath. She came slowly back to the carpet and her movements, usually so graceful, were tense and jerky, as if she were walking in her sleep. Her face was drawn, the narrow nose suddenly hawklike. She had aged five years. The look she gave the younger woman was stark. Her eyes were wise, compelling, luminous as ever. Only now, they held also a haunting loneliness.

Janie looked up at her. The stress and emotion of the moment and the place sharpened her senses. It struck Janie forcibly that there must be terrible damage. It was just that she could not see it.

As she came to this thought, something changed. She sensed a fusing between her and this mysterious woman, a sharing, an understanding. Out of that understanding, she said, slowly, 'In New York, when we talked in the cathedral, you told me you once held a newborn baby. It was born dead. But then it lived.'

Mama still did not speak. She gazed at Janie with those intense light eyes as though she could see into her soul. As though she would show her own, her own soul stripped bare. She held nothing back. The overwhelming conviction came to Janie that she could see right through Mama's skin to the emotions, the thoughts, the fears beneath. There was complete insight between them, total comprehension. And there, at last, was the truth.

Chapter Forty-Five

Mama told Janie many things, but it seemed to her afterwards, she did not hear them with her conscious ear. It was almost as if they came to her without speech, like the communication of a dream.

In Room 224 of an army barrack, a woman lay on a bed, naked under her white cotton slip. Her extraordinary hair was tied in two heavy plaits, emphasizing her extreme youth, sharpening the cheekbones. Hers was a complicated, angular beauty, gauche and without polish, self-distrustful. Now, agitated and clumsy, she was plain. Her skin was white with strain, her eyelids swollen by fatigue, her lips crinkled and parched.

The barrack was one of many recently built in Poland, hidden deep in forests of fir, isolated, unknown. It was an oblong building separated from the main part of the camp. This one was used solely by the Polish troops of the German Army and, like the three or four identical buildings on either side, it appeared to be three storeys high. But in reality, there were five storeys. For below the barracks were detention cells. In the roof were the smallest, attic rooms, each little wider than the dormer window which gave it air. The most junior of the guards occupied these. In Room 224 was Basia Krolak.

The late afternoon sunlight slanted long rays onto the bed, making the room unbearably hot. But Basia Krolak dared not open the window, for she was afraid she might make sounds, and that they would be noticed. Too many people lived here. Not only the camp guards, but members of reserve units of the Waffen-SS stationed in the zone. No high-ranking officers, though – their houses were separate, set in gardens, where their wives and children lived with them. Several of the guards rooming on this floor were women. They were older than she, and had been in the camp longer.

Noise carried oddly in these buildings, something to do with the way they were constructed. She knew this very well because, even up here, she caught the voices of the special prisoners who spent their last weeks in the detention cells. It was never officially stated who these prisoners were, but she suspected some at least must be priests. She guessed that from the singing.

Other sounds carried, also. Very early in the mornings, she would occasionally hear the unmistakable, drawn-out sounds of someone's pleasure, someone who either didn't care about being heard – or more likely, relished it. From the ribald remarks at breakfast, many others heard also.

But no one – *no one* – must be allowed to hear the sounds she knew she might make during the next few hours. For one thing, she'd been mentioning violent headaches for a few weeks now, and had been several times to the hospital for aspirin which she had not used. Last night, when she felt the first delicate questings of pain, she had gone to the office and put in a request for the day off she'd been saving for weeks. So if she closed her window and kept very quiet, the occupants of the attic rooms near hers might assume she was out somewhere. She had locked the door from the inside, but of course there was a key downstairs if anyone wanted to enter. She thought that was unlikely.

She had planned carefully. She had clean cloths ready, a pair of nail scissors to cut them up. She had a little food: biscuits, a couple of apples, even – incredible luxury – a bar of chocolate. There was a basin in here, so she would have water to drink, and to wash. She had no idea how long it would all last. She seemed to remember a first baby could take a long time, maybe days. Only she must be quick or someone would discover her . . . she wouldn't think about that.

She'd had the foresight to bring up a short piece of rope. She would be able to bite on it when things got bad. Her grandmother had told her once, that's what all women did, when their time came. She hid it under the bed.

The first pains had been hours ago and very faint, little more than twinges. Then they seemed to go away completely. She had no idea what to expect next. She'd been alternately dozing and worrying. A fly buzzed monotonously against the window as she fell into a heavy sleep in the airless room. As her muscles relaxed, her hand opened and the narrow necklace she had been clutching dropped onto the white sheet. It was made of glass beads, iridescent in the last of the light.

When she awoke, it was into a world of hurt she had never imagined. She was being torn all ways, forced open from within. Her bones were being pushed apart. Sweat was pouring from her, she could smell herself. She clenched her jaws till her teeth ached, dug her nails hard into the palms of her hands to make another, sharper hurt that might draw her mind away.

It seemed to work. Gradually, the spasm passed and she let her muscles relax. Briefly released, she opened her eyes and saw from the shadows she must have slept for hours. She sat up, propped against her pillow, pulled up her slip. In all the months of her pregnancy she had never dared look at herself. She'd feared that if she acknowledged what was happening to her body, then that knowledge would be in her eyes, and people would see and know. She had anyway remained so small throughout the pregnancy that for days at a time she'd almost been able to forget about it.

Only this last week had been different. Despite herself, the baby had become real to her, a presence, a personality. She had determinedly ignored earlier movements but now they were strong, so insistent they woke her in the night. And the child's shape was recognizable within her own: she knew when it flexed its back, turned. Often she felt a foot kicking.

Here in this attic room, when it would soon be all over, she stroked the tense mound of her belly. Tremors rippled the taut surface of her skin. She envisaged the baby curled and still in there, waiting, resting, readying itself, a swimmer before the race.

There were almost imperceptible pale blue lines traversing her belly, running forward from her hipbones. From her flattened navel the faintest smudge of dark red fur had grown with the pregnancy, running down to the hair between her legs.

She looked down at her breasts. Always small and firm (he had sucked them, called them his little lemons), they had become rounder, fuller. Deep blue veins marbled them, making them appear very white. The pale skin around her nipples had grown more noticeable, deepened to a soft brown.

After a while, she slipped a hand between her legs to try to feel what was happening. The familiar sleek sheath of muscle seemed to have vanished. Her genitals felt swollen and distended, slippery and dangerous to her own fingers. When she brought them away they were wet: her waters must have broken. The old midwives' phrase had sounded faintly biblical, made her think of Babylon and hanging gardens. Now it had a perilous ring to it.

As she thought that, she felt the next pain coming. It began faintly, somewhere deep down, a quiet plucking. She breathed softly, listening to it, trying to keep calm, not wanting to admit the fear she felt. It got stronger, fiercer. Very quickly it was huge, bigger than her, overwhelming, unbearable . . .

She heard a deep, harsh groan close by. With a shock she recognized her own voice. It was an almost impossible effort to feel around under the little bed for the rope, but she found it and hauled herself back up onto the mattress.

Only just in time, she clamped her lips around the rope, bit down hard. When she couldn't help herself, when she had to make a noise, it came out muffled.

When the pain ebbed, she was desperate for water: the dusty taste of rope made her mouth so dry she couldn't swallow. She must have water. She had never needed anything so badly in her life. But the water was in the taps, across the room.

She heaved herself to the edge of the bed. Slowly, one arm laced around her belly, she inched her cautious way to the basin, holding onto the walls for support. The tiny room felt enormous to her then. When she finally reached the basin she had to rest, bent almost double, clinging to the taps. It was just as well she was there, because she threw up, violently and unexpectedly.

The next contraction was on her before she finished retching, sudden and so intense she let go the edge of the basin and dropped to her knees, supporting her weight on outstretched arms. She couldn't reach the piece of rope this time, and she couldn't keep quiet, but the sounds she uttered were low and hoarse; exhalations rather than cries.

When it passed, she found her thighs were trembling so she knew she had to lie down fast before she fell. She let herself slide right to the floor, rolled over until she rested on her left side, knees drawn up. She could move no further. The narrow bed under the dormer window might as well have been on the moon.

The linoleum was hard to lie on. But she understood that like the birthpangs, it was something she deserved. The huge and powerful force that had her in its grip was indifferent to her needs. This child would be born, no matter what. Without warning, not knowing she was going to, she started to cry, gasping and sobbing, the tears streaming down her face. She wiped them from time to time with the back of her hand, then she didn't bother any more. She, who never cried, did so now with a kind of luxurious abandon. She was little more than a child herself, despite everything. She forgot the urgent necessity of silence, she forgot about caution.

There were always people in their barrack rooms, sleeping, coming off duty, or due on in a couple of hours. But by some fluke on this late afternoon the top floor was deserted and there was no one to hear.

She couldn't help herself, she sobbed aloud. This had been coming to her for a long time now, she had always known that.

She had spread her legs for him shameless as a whore, and instead of retribution she had been given love.

At first, he had been apparently indifferent to her clumsy approaches. The German troops considered themselves the elite and were contemptuous of anyone conscripted from occupied countries. Such people had not absorbed the true Nazi spirit. She assumed he felt the same. But she found in this she was wrong. It was not contempt which made him aloof, but an extreme and painful shyness. It had always been bad, right from childhood, but now it had become pathological.

Until the war he had been a physics teacher in Hamburg, where he was born. He had set off to fight for his country with Rommel's Afrika Korps. Eighteen months later, wounded, he found himself working in the prison camps. Gradually the reality of what he was doing came home to him. Perhaps because he was older, a mature and educated man, he knew truth was never simple. Some individuals did despicable things, certainly, maybe some races more than others. But he did not believe any human beings were intrinsically evil and worthless. He was a scientist. Biology did not work like that. Even as he moved among these people he was told were the dregs of humanity, he understood that what he was being called upon to do was the evil. He came to despise himself and his masters.

Although he was in his early thirties he had an almost adolescent gawkiness, the slight stoop of someone above average height. His hair, which always needed brushing, was receding at the temples but a dark blond lock always fell untidily over his forehead. There was a gap between his front teeth. Before the desert, that had only emphasized his bony good looks. Now, he could not even bear to look in the mirror when he shaved. He had two profiles: the acceptable, normal left – and the hideously disfigured right, the discoloured skin stretched taut and shiny over the shattered jaw. And the scarring on his neck, the ugly healing burns visible above the high black-and-silver collar of his uniform.

She was virgin when they met, and believed he

was the most wonderful man in the world. He had been surprised that she noticed him when he was many years her senior, and married. He did not see that it was precisely those things which made her feel safe. Like many shy people, he found the company of the young preferable to that of contemporaries: he was more at ease, he listened when she talked. She had been the ardent one, the writer of notes, the pursuer. His wounds lay far deeper than his skin. He was hideous to himself, and all his sexual confidence had gone. He loathed what he had become, both physically and morally. It was months before he let himself accept it was not pity which drew her. It was almost impossibly difficult for them ever to be alone together, and this added to their desire.

But his relationship with the Polish girl swiftly altered balance. For one thing, he learned how very young she was: barely seventeen. She had lied on her papers. His wife and children were far away, she was isolated from her family, and both were lonely. He saw her change during the months of their loving. Around the camp, at work, she looked pinched and drawn, her vivid hair scraped up beneath her cap, her extraordinary pale eyes wary. She was competent and hard. But with him, she softened, unfolded.

She had absorbed her training and indoctrination in a way he had never done. He could not blame her for this: when they sent her to Matzkau, she had been only fifteen years old.

All the young recruits had lived in filthy barracks, under the surveillance of SS guards. It was at the top of a steep hill and freezing in winter. The recruits were ruthlessly exercised by the guards for hours each morning from five o'clock: even the women had to drag themselves along the ground on their elbows. Although the senior SS in charge of the camp ate well – fresh vegetables, meat – these inmates were half-starved. She had told him all this, but much of it he had known anyway: the place was infamous.

How could she be blamed if, after months of such treatment, she came back from Germany to Poland and meted it out to others? Nonetheless it disturbed him. One day, when the guards had assembled all the prisoners to witness a mass hanging, he watched her throughout. He watched her eyes, and her mouth. Even as the dangling figures twitched and spasmed and soiled themselves, he saw no expression written there. She could have been watching marionettes, not men broken on the ropes.

Another time, he saw her strike an exhausted, elderly woman across the face with the back of her gloved hand. The woman crumpled to the ground. He had witnessed far worse a hundred times that very day: but this girl's casual callousness hurt him more than if he had seen his own daughter do such a thing.

He tried to tell her that. When they were alone, he would talk to her like the teacher he was, explain the politics of hate in which they were caught up. He taught her, there is a natural justice, we defy it at our peril. He told her that the destinies of individuals were important, that men and women were neither the property of others nor their slaves. He said, with all the intensity of which he was capable, these are human beings who came from the same seed as you and I, live beneath the same sky, breathe as we breathe, die as we must die.

His convictions were hard to reconcile with what she had been taught. They clashed with everything she thought she believed: that these people were in the camp because they were criminal, or worse, without morals; they defiled everything they touched. That her own actions against them were therefore honourable and necessary. That she must be pure to enforce the new ideology, pure and fierce and strong as a blade. Worthy of the million flares that glowed for the Führer.

But she knew he was taking a risk in telling her these things, just as she was in listening to them. Because she loved and admired him, she struggled to grasp that what he said was right.

Now she lay beached and ungainly on the floor of her room, and thought of other times when she had willingly made her bruised body into a cushion for him on the hard ground. All around them the Polish forest had stretched secretive and silent. They said wolves roamed here still.

The fir trees had ensured their privacy, his gun on the ground by his hand secured their safety. With avid tenderness they removed from each other the hard shell of their uniform and revealed the soft and vulnerable bodies of the people they were. He was shamed by his ugliness and it was a long time before he was able to accept her touch on his scars. But gradually, he let her caress the shiny purpled patches on thigh and calf, soothe with her tongue the bitter puckered wounds which seamed the flesh of his chest and abdomen. 'Let me,' she said. 'I'll make you better.' Her tears dropped hot on his flesh as she kissed, desperate to absorb his suffering. 'I'll take it all away.' He almost let himself believe she could, so certain was she of her new power over him.

She finally learned something of what had happened to him in the desert. He whispered of the convoy of burning tanks, the agony, the ruined men who continued to scream long after they had ceased to look like men. She was the only one he could tell.

They laced their arms and legs together, tasted each other, stared deep into each other's eyes. They murmured words that made sense only to them, shared private smothered laughter.

His weight had crushed her and she had welcomed it, welcomed the intent silence of the act. He told her once, every other woman he'd known had cried aloud. But not her: she arched under his body, and when she arrived at the place she needed, she did so with her eyes squeezed shut to keep tight hold on her pleasure.

She flowered in his arms. Her skin warmed and glowed, her eyes shone. She became beautiful, and what had started casually for him grew into a passion. He became obsessed by her moods, her silences, her sudden enchanting smiles. The innocence she had, and the passion. The strong lean white body on the pine needles, the startling mass of hair that smelled of her, the way her eyes opened, after. Those eyes, the luminous intensity of them. He told her, your eyes change all the time, they're never the same.

He said once, ruefully, that it was her history which decided the course of their affair. She thought later, maybe it was as he said. She supposed her history would determine her entire life. In so far, she added bitterly to herself, as she had a history.

Chapter Forty-Six

For a long time, she had no idea she was pregnant. Working in the camp was stressful and her cycle had always been irregular. Her mother had told her, it was because she was such a scrawny creature. This time, it ceased for three months, then she had a brief bleed and stopped worrying. Anyway, he always withdrew before he came, so she was safe.

By the time she realized her uniform skirts could no longer be fastened at the waist, she must have been at least four months gone. Too late, she knew, to do anything about it, though she tried. Hot baths, liquor – she stole a bottle of schnapps but succeeded only in making herself giddy and sick. There were potions she had heard about, made from plants, but she had no idea what they were or how to get them. And she secretly felt relief that the decision was taken from her, that she could not do what her mother had sought to do to her.

She told him about the child one afternoon. It was so cold, they had left on most of their clothes and pulled out the seat of the jeep to keep them from the freezing ground. When they had finished, he lifted her skirt back and kissed her there and laid his cheek against the faint swell of her belly above the pale red-gold spring of pubic hair:

you're turning into a fat old lady, I'll have to find someone younger. She told him quickly. Her words hung in the blue fir forest silence, unanswered, for what seemed a very long time.

He was a weak man. Not cruel, or uncaring. Just weak. It had simply never occurred to her. He was older, cleverer, his rank was high. And he looked so strong, he looked invincible, the left profile so taut and hard above the tight officer's collar. But it was all a trick of the eye. He was timid, she saw that now. Frightened. That was why he spoke with such conviction of individual rights and freedoms – and yet continued by his actions to deprive thousands of innocent people of them. He was a moral coward. He would be no use to her now.

He did not want even to hear about any baby, why did she think he'd been so careful? He had three children already. Around then, he recalled he had a wife also, so he told her that too, although she had not forgotten. A man in his position . . .

She didn't hear his reasons, only the panic in his voice, the anger that came from fear. She straightened her clothing while he talked and told her to be sensible, to be grown-up about this. He struggled, cursing, to stuff in the tail of his shirt, button his trousers. *Gott in Himmel*, she'd have to get rid of it.

'No.' She shook her head, looking away from him, into the forest. 'Too late. I'm too far gone.' She thought she saw something move among the trees, but it was only the blur of tears. She blinked and turned towards him, and her eyes were huge and filled with light and fear. 'I might die.'

For a moment she saw him waver, saw a trace of

the old tenderness. He visibly pulled himself upright. But at least he did not say that again. 'Then you must go back to your mother.'

She said, contemptuously, 'If I could leave the army. If she is even alive. If she would have me. If I wanted to.'

While he hauled the seat back to the jeep, she stood gazing into the forest. The sturdy pines and slender firs, the white saplings, stretched away before her. A sliver of moon was icily transparent in the deepening sky. When they had first lain here, many months before, the air had been aromatic and full of mists. Now it smelled new and green.

He drove her back to the camp. His knuckles were white with tension on the driving wheel and she remembered how strained he had been when she first met him. Just before the watchtowers came in sight he spoke. 'It's goodbye, then.' She could not answer: he was speaking of more than this moment. As always, she got out before they reached the gates, to walk back in unaccompanied after he had gone ahead. He sat staring silently at the long straight white road. The prisoners they both guarded had been forced to lay it with their bare hands. For those people, that road had only one destination.

Ten days later, he drove along the white road and left the camp behind him. She did not try to find out where he was posted.

That had been over four months ago. Since then she had just carried on as if nothing was happening to her. She had refused to think about it, about him, until this began. Was that only yesterday?

It seemed hours before the pain faded, then it continued to echo faintly through all her veins and arteries. It had been so bad, it would surely never completely leave her again. Impossible that after such hurting she could ever be the way she was before.

It was around that time, though she understood this only in a hazy, uncertain way, that things started to go badly wrong. It had been going on too long. She was dry now, down there, any movement was harsh and grating. She was being torn internally, she ached in every muscle, every tendon. The light was fading and her eyes found in the shadows a denser darkness.

The giants of birth and near-death crowded the tiny room.

She knew at some point she was supposed to push the baby out, but that was the last thing she wanted to do. She had kept her secret for so long, now her every instinct was to hold it in, keep it back. She clenched all her strong muscles to do just that. But it was no good, she knew it was no good. The child was coming anyway. She was losing control, panting harshly, an animal in a trap. There was a heavy pressing pain. It grew more and more powerful. She was *hurting*. Oh, God, God—

Oh, God, the baby was *here*!

It was escaping from her, bursting out of her, a wild surge of liquid and life she could no longer contain. She uttered a cry, loud and strange and long drawn out, a cry so wild it shocked her. She lifted herself on her elbows. It was there, between her spread thighs. As she watched, first the head and then, on the next pain, the shoulders, started to emerge.

Something was terribly wrong. A thick purplish cord, broader than a man's finger, was wrapped tight as a garotte around its neck. She stared at it, unable to think. God in heaven, what was it? What? The baby's eyes were closed, the heavy lids mauve, its head tilted back. It made no sound. It looked like a dead baby bird.

(For a long, dreadful moment, she saw another face, saw the young boy's agonized eyes as he battled for life against the rope, heard the wheezing suck of his breath. There had been no time then, either, no alternative.)

Somewhere a voice was muttering, '*Mamusia! Mamusia!*' She had done this. It had happened because she had squeezed and forced her growing belly to fit into her skirts, denied the pregnancy, refused to admit this tiny life. She had thought she wished her child dead. But now she was desperate for its survival.

She fumbled frantically to pull the cord from its throat. It was warm and slippery, hard to grasp and so strong. She needed the scissors, couldn't reach them. She didn't know how she managed it, but she got her fingers between cord and baby and loosened it, pulling it away from the stalk of the throat. She struggled to kneel up – the baby still only half-expelled, dangling from her body – to the ledge beside the washbasin where she had placed the scissors. It was a long reach, but she seemed to have a superhuman strength. Grasping them, she sank back.

Now the baby was out as far as its waist. When she stopped trembling, she used the scissors to make an opening, then ripped the lace strip off the end of her petticoat. This she tied tightly round the cord as close to the navel as she could. She positioned the scissors just above the knot and struggled to cut the cord. It was hard to do, the scissors were too small. She had to saw at it before it would part. There was more blood than she expected, the cord was still pulsing.

Hissing with effort, she finally managed to uncoil it from the baby's neck. She wanted to check if it was alive or dead, but then another pain came, and with a final burst the hips came through, and it was out.

When she could move again, she reached down. The child lay on the linoleum in a puddle of creamy stuff. It was quite limp when she touched it, like a rubber toy, and an ominous bluish colour. She picked it up but she was too frightened to do much, terrified by how tiny it was, how fragile: far smaller than the doll she had had as a child, its frail limbs slippery, the cap of hair plastered flat to its round skull.

She propped her back against the wall and held the baby, half-lying against her breasts, its head somewhere under her chin. She put one hand flat against its back, the other supporting the tiny buttocks. There was no movement, not the faintest flutter: it must surely be dead.

She could not bear it. Here in the dark, stripped of everything, raw and naked to truth, self-knowledge came to her. She had no right to ask but, most desperately, she wanted her child to live.

She did not pray – she did not know how – all she could do was continue to hold the child close. By now pain and panic had emptied her mind. Her heart was in her hands.

And then something very strange occurred. A great warmth flooded through her and all pain disappeared. It was as though every cell in her body was charged with a savage energy, a fierce exultant power. Never had she experienced a sensation like it. She did not see anything, there was no revelation, no burst of comprehension. It was not of the mind. Whatever was happening, it lay deeper than that, in some dark inner primitive place where she had never dared venture. She lost all awareness of who she was: it was like a slipping of the soul. Terrified and exhilarated, the enormity of what was upon her emptied out breath. She thought, I am dying.

She had no way of knowing that this was to happen again, and many times, during the course of her life. It would always come like this, unheralded and overwhelming. It would never be at her behest, but only in circumstances she could neither predict nor precipitate.

Just then the child on her breast made a quick, convulsive movement. Hardly daring to breathe she looked down, touched the minuscule fingers – and they tightened round her own. Then the mouth opened and incredibly, the baby yawned. Alive! She tipped her head back against the wall. Tears – of gratitude, of thankfulness, of weakness – slid down her cheeks.

It was not over yet. For ten endless minutes, she feared another baby was coming out of her: she could feel its progress along the birth canal. But what emerged was a slippery, livid mass the colour and size of a dark liver. The end of the cord that had encircled the baby's neck was implanted in the smooth centre. The other side was rough, veinous. She hated the thought of it inside her and at the same time feared it was a part of herself she had lost.

She allowed herself to rest a little. When her watch showed nine o'clock, she hauled herself up from the floor, clenching her jaw with the effort to move. The muscles quivered in her thighs and calves. Her back and shoulders were stiff with strain, the tendons in her neck corded from effort. But she had to do it now. Time was running out. She put the baby on the bed. She used a soft cloth to clean it as best she could and the cold water – all she had – made it cry for the first time. Her breasts tingled in response to the paper-thin wail. She put it in a shapeless garment she had sewn from a flannel nightdress. She wrapped it in a square of blanket, dampened a bit of sheet in water and used it as a dummy. Its suck was a surprisingly strong sound.

It made her remember her own need: she got to the washbasin and drank two glasses of water quickly. Too quickly: she brought it back immediately, like a reflex, all over the floor.

She filled the basin and washed the blood from between her thighs. The place of pleasure, he called it. She could never lie with anyone again. Not if it brought this. She let the water trickle down her body, soothing, cold. She stuffed a napkin between her legs, pulled on her under-pants to hold it in place. Her belly was as big as if the child were still inside her. She cleaned the bloodied scissors. Very slowly, holding the cloth, she got down on her knees and carefully went over the floor where she had lain, wiping blood and mucus.

In the towel she had used, she wrapped the cloth and the purple fleshy thing that had followed the child. It was too big to flush down a lavatory, she was afraid it wouldn't disappear. Then she pulled the stained sheet from her bed and wound it tightly round the towel, stuffed the whole lot in her suitcase. She had this ready under her bed. With a groan of effort, she pushed it under the narrow wardrobe. When she had an opportunity she would put the sheet and its contents in the great outside boiler.

Thick grey stockings, garters. Heavy grey uniform skirt. It was a struggle to pull on the leather boots. She opened the wardrobe and took her shirt and jacket from their hanger. Her fingers were trembling so she could hardly coerce the buttons into their stiff fabric holes.

Then she went over to the mirror. A madwoman confronted her, face pale with red hectic patches on either cheek, eyes huge and strained. Her hair was tangled and sweaty, and she lacked the strength to hold her arms up. Two pins, and she pushed the rest under her peaked cap.

Finally, she picked up the bundle from the foot of the bed, wrapped her spare uniform skirt tightly around it like a parcel and put it under her arm. She straightened up, breathing quickly. She unlocked the door. And stood there for a long moment.

Very quietly, she locked it again. She knelt on the floor beside the bed and placed the bundled uniform skirt on it. Then she undid it all. The baby – *her* baby – lay on the piece of grey blanket. She looked at it for a long time, knowing that she would never see it again. Its clenched fists brought something back: *we come into this life with closed hands. With open hands we leave it.* The naked little body was pinker now, the skin creased and puckered as if immersed too long in water. There seemed to be no flesh on the tiny bones. Straggles of damp hair showed dark on the skull. It hated to be uncovered, she could tell by the way it squirmed.

She still thought *it*, but the child was undoubtedly, astonishingly, male. The soft pouch of the testicles, the thin, pure curve of the penis, seemed out of all proportion to the rest, as if his sex were the most important thing about him.

She covered it – him – up again, wrapping the makeshift shawl tightly round him, over his head. The crinkled face, the funny little pursed-up old man's mouth, reminded her of no one she had ever known. She put a tentative forefinger to his cheek. Perhaps it was her touch that made him open his eyes.

And then she knew who he was. His father's eyes looked up at her. Not only the colour – didn't all newborns have blue eyes? – but the shape, that characteristic faint amused droop of the lids, made her catch her breath as if the man were in the room with them. She looked harder.

He was only minutes old. Could he even see? And yet, as he gazed up into her face, his eyes held the bright dust of intelligence.

Just after eleven o'clock, Basia Krolak went down the stairs. Each step cost her dear. As she passed the door of the mess hall, it opened on a blast of noise and cigarette smoke. A sergeant came out, not even glancing in her direction, and hurried out to the urinal, unbuttoning as he went. He had not noticed her; he was farting freely.

She left the barrack without signing herself out and went towards the upper camp. The bundle was beneath her right arm. She forced herself to move purposefully, as if it was her shift. The sandy paths, yellow in daylight, were pale under the arc lamps. As she brought her heels down sharply, she felt every fibre in her body shudder in protest. She stopped at the many gates in the barbed-wire fences, identified herself to the guards on duty, passed through. One of the other Polish guards greeted her. '*Czy jest spokoj?*' Everything all right? She answered briefly, '*Tak.*'

When he had gone about his business, she unlocked the door of one of the long sheds housing prisoners. The stench from the rudimentary latrines hit her, the damp fetid smell of too many unwashed people, of their sour hungry night-time breath. She put a hand on the wall to steady herself and it was running with moisture.

In a harsh, peremptory voice, she called out Alma Gysemans's number.

Chapter Forty-Seven

Back in her hotel room that night, Janie made a telephone call to Brussels.

'You always knew the baby was Mama's, didn't you? But you would never have told me she was Karel's mother.'

The pause at Alma's end of the line was emphasized by distance. 'No. I don't think so. You must forgive my lapse of candour.'

Janie almost smiled at the exquisite courtesy of the phrase. But she could imagine what unhappiness lay behind it. Even so, she puzzled aloud, 'But you worry so much about Karel. Mama could tell you everything. The father . . .'

'No!' Anger hardened Alma's voice. 'I want nothing more from that woman. Nothing, do you understand?' She was almost shouting, and even over the wire the loss of control was shocking in a voice normally so calm and measured. 'What if there is something terrible? What if she tells my Karel something he cannot bear? What then?'

Janie was silenced, remembering what Mama had said about her mother back in Metno, terrified always of her own mother's insanity, raving and screaming out biblical curses. Mama had hinted that the father of her child was someone from the camp. But was he oppressor or victim? What was his history?

Janie realized Alma Gysemans's instincts, as always, were sure. These were things she wanted never to learn. Such knowledge would only implant further fears of an inherited taint, drive a wedge between her and the man who was, in all but blood, her son.

Janie thought of Alma at their last meeting, speaking to her of the day they took her baby. She remembered the erect figure, the hand covering the eyes. And it suddenly came to her, with absolute certainty, that it was Alma who had engineered that night meeting with Dante in Brussels. There was no other explanation, no other way it could have happened.

The Alma Gysemans she had met, the civilized elderly widow, with the loved son given to her in a Polish camp fifty years before, would not want Mama's guilt made public, for there was a chance that Karel's parentage would be discovered.

But there was another Alma Gysemans, the one she had glimpsed that afternoon in London. The young married woman whose baby was snatched from her arms, who had endured alone in the camp where so many died, whose husband came back to her broken in spirit and in health. That woman could not sit passively by and watch a journalist eulogize Mama.

Janie felt an immense relief. If she had still been writing the book, she would have faced a huge problem. She would have been impelled to tell the whole truth, to expose Mama's crimes.

But the truth, Janie saw now, was not all that mattered. She could tell it – and shatter the hopes and maybe the lives of all the people who depended, in one way or another, on Mama and her Chalice of the Grapes of God. If she had told the truth six months ago, that homeless woman Mama cradled in the East End house might have died alone on the streets. And a young man might have continued to live without speech.

And there were many things she could not risk revealing. She could not have identified Mama as Basia Krolak, the Polish camp guard from Metno. Too many people, in the camp and before it, would remember the young woman who came to be known as Little Angel. She would have had to remain silent about the birth of Basia's son, for fear others would be able eventually to trace that child, as she herself had accidentally done.

She would not have been able to so much as hint that the woman whom the world honoured with the title that meant parenthood and protectress, was a mother in body as in name. Not to save Mama – a woman of over seventy, she reasoned, was a long way from that frightened seventeen-year-old, was by now a different person – but to protect two innocent people. A Belgian man in his early fifties for whom sanity was already a precarious balancing act. And the woman he loved as his mother.

Chapter Forty-Eight

There had been a faint, pearly mist at first, but by ten o'clock it had dispersed. Janie found the light was already brilliant enough for sunglasses, despite the covering cloud. Rows of seating had been erected not far from the summit of a slight hill outside the city of Hebron. Just below the summit itself, on a piece of flat ground, stood two imposing wooden desks each with a swivel chair. Behind each chair, a great flag hung in the still air. The formal arrangement had an absurd quality here in the open, like a film set for a bizarre medieval joust.

The choice of site was symbolic: this ground had been designated neutral territory. Here, in a few minutes, Israeli and Palestinian leaders would publicly and finally shake hands and sign the long-awaited accord between their peoples. It had been hammered out by several teams of negotiators, and had in fact been completed only three hours earlier. There would of course be countless further signings and countersignings, but these would take place in quiet rooms, away from the glare of publicity.

Throughout the negotiations, both sides had been advised by teams from other countries. Apart from the Jordanians, well represented and led by King Hussein, there were also diplomats from

Egypt and Syria. American mediators had been involved through countless earlier negotiations, and there were small contingents from France, Britain and Sweden.

But it was understood by all involved that the accord, finally achieved after years of broken promises on both sides, would not have been secured this time without Mama's intervention.

Janie found a seat amongst the hundred and fifty or so ministers and political aides, international observers and accredited journalists. There was a buzz of excitement, of high anticipation. Dozens of camera teams were sited with a good view of the signing desks. Camera lights were already flashing, and television reporters of all nationalities were in position doing pieces to camera.

Below the blocks of seats, a little further down the incline, were groups of Jews and Arabs. These stood apart from each other, even now. Some were obviously school groups with teachers, here for the historic event. There were students, one or two carrying banners. Among the Jewish watchers, Janie noticed a number of pale-skinned youths in the long black silk coats, round black hats and curling earlocks of the ultra-Orthodox.

Among the Arab watchers was a talkative, curious, unruly group of local women and children, many under school age. A Palestinian policeman in the olive uniform and beret had moved them on twice, but they had returned. In the last few days, there had been more trouble in Hebron: Israel still had not handed back promised chunks of land to the Palestinians, the Israelis were continuing to control the centre of the city. But this morning the mood was hopeful, positive, and the policeman seemed disinclined to press the matter.

Janie noticed that two of the children, a tiny girl and a boy, maybe five years old, had wandered apart from the others. The boy was pushing a toy tank in the dust, moving it in wide sweeps and making engine noises, while the girl stood beside him sucking her fingers. They were playing in the open corridor created by the human barriers of Arab police on one side, Israeli soldiers on the other.

There was a burst of clapping from among the Jewish watchers and Janie looked across to see the Israeli Prime Minister had reached the desks. He was a native-born *sabra*, short and youthful looking for his forty-two years, in constant movement, his pale curly hair, now noticeably thinning, rendering him highly visible among the four sharp-eyed, wide-shouldered guards surrounding him. Immediately behind was the President, a dark husk of a man winnowed by a life that had brought him from Eastern Europe to the kibbutz. In honour of the occasion both men had abandoned the Israeli politician's uniform of open-necked short-sleeved shirt for formal suits.

The Arab leader, a squat, powerful figure, wore the familiar chequered *shmag* around his head. As a symbol of goodwill, he had followed Mama's suggestion and he also wore – for the first time ever in public – a dark business suit and tie. His relinquishing the battledress and dark glasses in which he was always seen was a statement of intent that would mean more to his followers than

510

any signature. Beside him, a hand on the Arab leader's forearm in a carefully calculated brotherly gesture, walked the impressive figure of the recently appointed American Middle East envoy. He was bigger than any of them, a milk-fed man glowing with health and self-confidence.

King Hussein of Jordan, now visibly ageing, walked with his customary dignity. And there beside him, and noticeably taller, was Mama. She seemed more slender than ever, her tired pallor emphasized by the creamy robe. She too had several bodyguards nearby.

Janie, like the others, kept her eyes on the figures assembled at the top of the slight rise. From a distance, unable to hear what was said but observing the body language, the deference with which Mama was heard – and, tellingly, the even greater deference with which she *listened* – Janie was aware more strongly than ever of the power this woman wielded: she was midwife to the new trust. The announcement would soon be made: she could see an almost celebratory look on Mama's face.

Watching the dignitaries and the public intently, weapons held loosely at the ready, were soldiers. Palestinians guarded one side of the hill, Israelis the other. Everyone knew that somewhere, discreetly positioned out of sight, were Israeli tanks and armoured personnel carriers bearing snipers. Attack helicopters were primed and ready. All these reinforcements had been poured into the West Bank days earlier, against the possibility of terrorist attacks from the fundamentalist group Hamas, or shows of strength from them against the Palestinian leader's faction Fatah, which supported the peace process.

The Palestinian leader had now moved to his desk, and he gave the Israeli Prime Minister an informal salute for the cameras, which was returned. Every eye now was on the two men. The Palestinian leader stepped forward to one of the microphones to begin his speech.

A man's voice yelled a warning, '*Dir ballak!*' and suddenly everything changed. The group of Arab women erupted into sound, moved apart, pushing wildly in panic – and there were older boys there with them, teenagers, in T-shirts and combat trousers or denims.

At the man's cry, one of the boys had moved, his whole body eloquent with rage as he drew back his arm and with astonishing power hurled a stone towards the Israeli soldiers. Beside him another youth materialized and flung his stone. The Israeli soldiers assumed firing positions. A barked order prevented them from shooting: the Arab women and children were masking the older boys, and even rubber bullets inflict terrible damage.

The Palestinian police closed ranks and moved in to act as buffers and block the stone-throwing youths, but the Arab women deliberately hindered them. The police were always reluctant to use crushing force against such boys because that would turn the entire Arab population against them – a position the youths exploited. Today, with cameras present, they were more wary than ever. 'Collaborators!' one of the boys screamed in Arabic as a policeman cuffed him.

Then, above the yells of alarm and anger, a

woman's voice rose in a frantic screech: the two children Janie had noticed straying from the group were still absorbed in their game and had wandered within range of the spinning stones. The Palestinian youths, standing among the women, looking over their heads towards the Israeli soldiers who were their targets, could not see them.

Everyone seemed frozen by the sudden surge of violence, and every eye now had shifted from the signing to the boys and the soldiers. Only Mama ignored them all. She had begun moving before the danger had become apparent to the others, had started down the hill towards the Arab children even before the mother's anguished cries reached her.

A Palestinian policeman called to her, put out a hand to catch her arm. A couple of Israeli soldiers moved forward to block her path. But Mama pushed back the hood of her robe so her distinctive silver-gilt hair was visible. She made a dismissive gesture and the men, recognizing her, hesitated to impede her – and she was past them, almost running now, with those quick, supple movements so unexpected in a woman her age.

Oblivious to it all, the two tiny children continued their game on the rough strip of no-man's-land separating the two groups. The boy was pushing his tank over a heap of stones.

As Mama neared them Janie saw, from the corner of her eye, the television crews hauling their cameras in a ninety-degree turn to focus on her. As if conscious of their scrutiny – though how could she be, Janie thought, with the cameras at her back? – Mama turned towards the watchers just as she reached the children. She spread both arms wide, in the generous, protective gesture so movingly and memorably captured in the Hungarian photographs. She had stood so in front of armed men before, and come through unharmed.

Mama bent, scooping up the little girl in a single movement. The child was small, accustomed to being lifted and carried, and accepted it placidly. Mama caught the boy by the hand, whirling him around with all her strength, so his feet briefly left the ground. In the silence, they heard his yelp of protest as he was dragged away from his toy. Tugging him along, she started back the way she had come.

She concentrated on the treacherously stony ground, moving fast. Like every other human being, she did not want to die. This was the most dangerous thing she had ever done. She prayed, let me not be afraid at the moment of extinction.

They were almost halfway back. The girl clung to her neck, but the boy dragged his feet, wailing: he wanted his tank, he wanted to go back to his game of pretend death.

To those who saw, it looked as if someone had punched Mama unexpectedly on the back of the neck, had struck her a blow that came without warning. Her shoulders came up defensively, she paused uncertainly, then went on. A huge round stone rolled away behind her feet. Then another stone, even bigger, a small rock, hurtled against her chest and this time everyone saw it. The blow was to one side, hard on her ribs. Hard enough, surely, to smash them, driving the breath out of her with a grunting exhalation they all heard.

Her eyes – those amazing, light-filled eyes – opened wide. She grew pale in a moment, and an expression of pure wonder dawned. Janie watched knowledge expand upon her face. It was as though she had at last seen something, understood something, *found* something for which she had been searching all her life, and which had always eluded her. Until now.

She stumbled on the stones, almost lost her footing, apparently recovered. Still she held the little girl in her arms, still she gripped the boy tightly. She took a few more steps, holding her left hand out in an attempt to shield the boy's head and another stone struck her sharply on the wrist, smashing two small bones.

(Later, doctors were to say they could not understand how she managed even to stay upright, let alone move. The first stone had caused a fracture at the base of her skull: clear drops of cerebrospinal fluid the colour of pale wine already leaked from her right ear. The blow to her chest had fractured two upper ribs in two places, so they floated free, compressing a lung. She was, to all intents and purposes, already dead.)

The boy, obedient now it was too late, cowered at her side. At last, as if released from the spell of their horror, people were reaching out, coming forward to help her.

Mama stood still, swaying slightly, waiting for them. The luminous look was still in her eyes although her pupils had become huge and black, her face grey. The boy tugged his hand free of her weakened grasp and had the sense to run as fast as he could to his mother.

Mama's hands, open now, empty, hung by her side. *With closed hands we come into this life. With open hands we leave it.* A Palestinian police sergeant, the first person to reach her, caught hold of the little girl who was still clinging frantically round her neck.

In a tone of great urgency, Mama uttered a single word. They did not understand in what language she spoke: later, it was thought to have been her native Polish.

She dropped to her knees and toppled slowly sideways to the stony ground.

The singing was neither male nor female, nor the sweet unbroken heartless voices of choristers. These voices knew anguish and pain, they were full of humanity and yet not human at all. They were low and soft, they came from a far deeper level than any she had ever heard. The singing poured over her until she was immersed in a pool of sound. It flooded her, sucked at her legs, her thighs, held her captive. The music that was no music she had ever known before engulfed her, she felt herself disappearing into it. She no longer heard it, she *was* it. It drew her gradually down, so she sank trembling to the earth as the tide of sound rose and flooded and closed over her head.

And then the sound coalesced into a great white silence, became a pale peaceful sea on which she lay. Nothing mattered any more. Nothing could touch her now, she was gone, out of it.

The silence was not an emptiness but a presence. It grew to meet the silence in her, until it was all-pervasive, all-consuming. And at its centre there was a stillness. A waiting.

The distraught Arab woman squatted on the ground, the little girl in her arms. The boy crouched by her side, puzzled and silent, conscious that he was for some reason the centre of this loud fuss, unaware of what he had done to provoke it.

Dazed, Janie watched the woman and her children. And thought of Cardinal Norberto Uguccioni, cardinal-prefect to the Sacred Congregation for the Causes of Saints, who had spoken of early martyrs stoned to death. Cardinal Uguccioni, who had written the article which said: *The concept of martyrdom has been widened. It is possible to be a martyr of charity. To give their life so that others might live, to die for peace and for justice is martyrdom for the sake of the kingdom.*

The woman rocked backward and forward. She held the edge of her black veil so they could not see her face. But they could hear her voice.

'*Rab al-alamin . . .*' She repeated the words, an incantation.

'What is she saying?' Janie demanded of the Arab journalist beside her.

'Lord of the worlds,' the woman chanted. 'It is a miracle for my babies. Mama has given us a miracle.'

Chapter Forty-Nine

Magda Lachowska remembered the darkness from all those long years ago as she lay in the rooming house on the Rua Santa Rita. And in the darkness, the vision she had been granted.

The darkness had returned. She opened her eyes wide but the benediction of the sky had been taken from her. She could see nothing. Her eyes looked inward.

And then she saw him. The ancient dream. He was there, as clear as all those years before. Clear and glorious to her sight. He glowed still with an inner fire that in her mind's eye had never faded. This time his face was towards her, and he did not turn away.

He seemed hewn out of the air itself, insubstantial and yet with great weight. Unborn and eternal. He was massive, with the translucent magnificence of ice, of crystal. She believed, as she had that first time, his was the body of a man. But that was only because she possessed no vocabulary, no language, visual or verbal, with which to define this celestial being. She thought she saw arms open to her in the compassionate gesture for which she had longed. As before, she could not be sure. She was certain only of his divinity.

She could not stare enough at the face she had held in her heart. The features of indescribable power, etched with lines of sorrow and acceptance, the beak of the nose both harsh and gentle, the mouth at once innocent and sensual. The smooth eyelids were heavy, weighted with the curved lustre of golden lashes.

And there, behind his shoulders, the great pale mist lifted and shimmered, flexed and rustled with supple, muscular strength. She had guarded the texture, the opaline colours of this tender pearled plumage – oyster, azure, amethyst – had carried it all these years in her mind's eye.

The strength, the power, were as she remembered. But there was something different, something pared down, stripped back. She was aware that though the colours of the wings were still wonderful, they were less flamboyant than before, more subtle. It was as if everything superfluous had gone.

The vision had come to her first when she was on the cusp of youth and maturity. It had been all-consuming, overwhelming. This time it was pure, concentrated, burned down to the essence: the vision of an old woman who had seen much.

The great wings folded about her and she cried out in joy. His whisper thrummed against her heart. She felt the deep reverberations of his words surge through her body. She knew again the thrill of trumpets, even though she heard no sound louder than the susurration of silk.

They achieved a pure and empty space where the sky gave translucent promise of endless dawns, where distant mountains thrust through coils of cloud and silence sang in her ears. She had taken it as a sign, had lived seven slow years in the foothills of the Andes, in isolation, for the expiation of her sins.

Still, remorse and sorrow were hers. No matter what good she had done, what efforts she had made, what kindness she had enacted, she had once been a part of cruelty beyond bearing. She had longed for forgiveness. She had struggled for grace. She had sought out her soul. And now the moment of reckoning had come. This was her passion, this her dying. Nothing could be hidden: the Angel of Death has many eyes.

Now the mystical mountains faded, and mist rolled in, covering everything.

In the end as at the beginning.

Chapter Fifty

Three months after Mama was killed, the brothers Patrice and Jean Akonda were able to play football together again.

The medical staff at the convent hospital examined the leg many times. X-rays were taken. A specialist was consulted. There was no mistake: the bone was healthy, the leg sound. The sisters and the doctors said it was a cure they could not explain. They said, 'Regeneration of dead bone is not possible.'

Chapter Fifty-One

Exactly a year and one day after Mama, as Magda Lachowska was always known, was killed, a twenty-two-year-old Polish man named Leszek Sikora was working on his motorcycle in the street outside his home in Metno. It was early evening when there came a flash of lightning from a clear sky and the house opposite lit up as though on fire. It was a small, shabby building, long uninhabited, with the wood and plaster finish common in that part of the world before the beginning of the century.

Straightening up, Leszek Sikora saw a cloud over the house, violet and dark red as a brilliant sunset, and heard a noise like a great gust of wind. The cloud seemed to sink slowly into the earth, and from it emerged the luminous but indistinct figure of a woman, apparently dressed in a pale garment.

The dozen or so watchers granted that first apparition claimed to recognize her instantly. It was Mama. She was dressed in the same clothes Mama had always worn, and she was shedding tears for all the unbelief in the world.

The following night, around fifty people gathered to see the radiant pinkish glow again suffuse the house. One of them, a local woman doctor who had always been openly cynical about the cult of Mama, reached out and touched the place where the others told her the luminous figure had stood. Immediately she felt a fierce tremor run the full length of her arm. It was, she said, like a severe electric shock. She let it be known she could no longer be considered an unbeliever.

The number of visitors to the little house each night increased: they left bunches of flowers and coins strewn across the pavement. The cloud and the figure of Mama appeared only on rare occasions, but the house glowed as before, always for about one hour. At times it was impossible for the locals to cross the street against the press of people carrying children, pushing wheelchairs, flourishing Day-Glo posters of Mama. Penitents arrived on bleeding knees and young girls wore their white first-communion dresses.

All empty rooms in the town were taken and two campsites opened in fields on the outskirts, where people huddled in tents and campervans and behind windbreaks. Services were held in the open air with loudspeakers, since there was no single building in the town large enough to accommodate the multitude.

Telephone lines were so blocked they became virtually unusable. People flocked from all over Poland, many walking and bringing food and sleeping bags with them. Then they began to come from the rest of Europe. Several hundred AIDS victims booked to fly in.

Members of the Chalice arrived in Metno to organize the crowds. The police erected crash barriers and established a one-way system for traffic. They brought in uniformed men on horseback.

There was a brisk trade in plaster statues, post-cards of Mama with different world leaders, pieces of her robe and even keyrings bearing her likeness. Everyone was elated and enthusiastic, as if they were attending a huge party.

Not surprisingly, these circumstances induced a measure of hysteria: it was said that when the apparition appeared there was a heavenly fragrance so strong, so sweet, that watchers were overcome and several fainted. At one of the campsites, a man who fell and broke his leg found it healed immediately.

Mama's followers claimed the manifestations were part of the endless mystery. Proof that she was once more found by angels and caught up into paradise.

No one could ever explain why Magda Lachowska, who so far as the world knew had never been there, should choose to appear in the remote and insignificant little town of Metno.

Each night, the people held candles as they made their way to wait patiently outside the glowing house, the little lights gleaming, a necklace of pearls in the darkness. They stood before an illuminated hoarding which bore the famous Bown picture of Mama: the compassionate face with its tender mouth and haunting, light-filled eyes. And behind her head, the rays of the dying sun glowed solid as the aureole around a medieval icon.

THE END

SACRED & PROFANE
by Marcelle Bernstein

'Mesmerizing, brilliant . . . A riveting read'
Manchester Evening News

On Christmas Eve, in the stifling heat of a Latin American country, a nun collapses at prayer. In agony, she feverishly cries out words no one can understand.

At the same moment, thousands of miles away in London, a young woman wakes panic-stricken in her prison cell. Words of a strange language are screaming in her head: something dreadful is coming, and she's a child again, tense with fear.

What links these two women in a way that is inexplicable, threatening – and, ultimately, deadly? As the nun nears death, a Jesuit priest tries to find out, uncovering the hidden past. In doing so he is forced to face his own demons, releasing emotions long repressed and denied . . . and learns no one ever keeps a secret as well as a child.

A Bantam Paperback
0 553 40803 8

GRAND AFFAIR
by Charlotte Bingham

Unaware of the misery that surrounded her birth, for the first four years of her life all Ottilie Cartaret knows is love. And when her mother, Ma O'Flaherty, moves her family to what she believes will be rural bliss in St Elcombe in Cornwall, their fortunes seem set fair.

Tragedy strikes when Ma dies and young Ottilie soon finds herself in unfamiliar surroundings. Adopted by the Cartarets, the wealthy couple who run the Grand Hotel, she grows up pampered and spoilt, not only by her adoptive parents but by all the visitors -- with the exception of their mysterious annual guest, nicknamed 'Blue Lady', with whom Ottilie is unknowingly and inextricably linked.

But as times change, and the regulars to the now-decaying hotel die off, the Cartarets find they are unable to adapt to modern ways. Only Ottilie has the means to save the Grand, even though she may sacrifice too much of herself before learning once again the power of love.

A Bantam Paperback
0 553 50500 9

SEXTET
by Sally Beauman

'This is a peach of a novel . . . *Sextet* is a hugely
entertaining read, seriously romantic and with a
terrific sense of atmosphere'
Kate Saunders, *Daily Express*

Journalist Lindsay Drummond is about to re-make her
life: she plans to move out of London, change her job,
and above all cure herself of her hopeless love for her
unfairly handsome colleague, Rowland McGuire – but
then a chance encounter teaches her that the best-laid
plans can go delightfully awry . . .

In New York, actress Natasha Lawrence is also trying to
rebuild her life. Pursued by a stalker for the past five
years, still bound to her ex-husband, the celebrated film
director Tomas Court, she retreats with her son to the
precincts of the exclusive – and haunted – Conrad
apartment building. But will it provide her with the
security she so desperately seeks, and will she and her
husband be able to lay to rest the ghosts of their past?

Lindsay's and Natasha's lives become inextricably
entangled; when the cast of characters gathers for
Thanksgiving at the sinister Conrad building, anything
can happen, for romance and retribution, marriage and
murder are in the air.

'A complex cracker of a plot with vivid characters
and atmospheric locations'
Daily Mail

A Bantam Paperback
0 553 50326 X

A SELECTION OF FINE NOVELS
AVAILABLE FROM BANTAM BOOKS

THE PRICES SHOWN BELOW WERE CORRECT AT THE TIME OF GOING TO PRESS. HOWEVER TRANSWORLD PUBLISHERS RESERVE THE RIGHT TO SHOW NEW RETAIL PRICES ON COVERS WHICH MAY DIFFER FROM THOSE PREVIOUSLY ADVERTISED IN THE TEXT OR ELSEWHERE.

50631 5	**DESTINY**	Sally Beauman	£6.99
40727 9	**LOVERS AND LIARS**	Sally Beauman	£5.99
50326 X	**SEXTET**	Sally Beauman	£5.99
40803 8	**SACRED AND PROFANE**	Marcelle Bernstein	£5.99
40497 0	**CHANGE OF HEART**	Charlotte Bingham	£5.99
40890 9	**DEBUTANTES**	Charlotte Bingham	£5.99
50500 9	**GRAND AFFAIR**	Charlotte Bingham	£5.99
40895 X	**THE NIGHTINGALE SINGS**	Charlotte Bingham	£5.99
17635 8	**TO HEAR A NIGHTINGALE**	Charlotte Bingham	£5.99
40973 5	**A CRACK IN FOREVER**	Jeannie Brewer	£5.99
50556 4	**TRYIN' TO SLEEP IN THE BED YOU MADE**	DeBerry Grant	£5.99
40996 4	**GOING HOME TO LIVERPOOL**	June Francis	£4.99
50429 0	**KITTY AND HER BOYS**	June Francis	£5.99
40820 8	**LILY'S WAR**	June Francis	£4.99
50475 4	**THE MONKEY HOUSE**	John Fullerton	£5.99
40846 1	**IN THE PRESENCE OF THE ENEMY**	Elizabeth George	£5.99
40238 2	**MISSING JOSEPH**	Elizabeth George	£5.99
40845 3	**PLAYING FOR THE ASHES**	Elizabeth George	£5.99
50385 5	**A DRINK BEFORE THE WAR**	Dennis Lehane	£5.99
50584 X	**DARKNESS, TAKE MY HAND**	Dennis Lehane	£5.99
40884 4	**FAST FORWARD**	Judy Mercer	£5.99
50586 6	**FAREWELL TO THE FLESH**	Gemma O'Connor	£5.99
40944 1	**APARTMENT 3B**	Patricia Scanlan	£5.99
40945 X	**FINISHING TOUCHES**	Patricia Scanlan	£5.99
40947 6	**FOREIGN AFFAIRS**	Patricia Scanlan	£4.99
40942 5	**PROMISES, PROMISES**	Patricia Scanlan	£5.99

All Transworld titles are available by post from:

Book Service By Post, P.O. Box 29, Douglas, Isle of Man IM99 1BQ.

Credit cards accepted. Please telephone 01624 675137, fax 01624 670923 or Internet http://www.bookpost.co.uk. or e-mail: bookshop@enterprise.net for details.

Free postage and packing in the UK. Overseas customers: allow £1 per book (paperbacks) and £3 per book (hardbacks).